Ain't Nobody

WHEN WE LOVE

Book 3

By

Tracey Gerrard

Copyright © Tracey Gerrard 2020
This book is sold subject to the condition that it shall not, by way of trade or otherwise, be lent, resold, hired out, or otherwise circulated without the publisher's prior consent in any form of binding or cover other than that in which it is published and without a similar condition including this condition being imposed on the subsequent publisher.
The moral right of Tracey Gerrard has been asserted.
ISBN-13: 9798652806729

This is a work of fiction. Names, characters, businesses, organizations, places, events and incidents either are the product of the author's imagination or are used fictitiously. Any resemblance to actual persons, living or dead, events, or locales is entirely coincidental.

CONTENTS

Chapter 1 .... *1*
Chapter 2 .... *22*
Chapter 3 .... *27*
Chapter 4 .... *35*
Chapter 5 .... *51*
Chapter 6 .... *56*
Chapter 7 .... *68*
Chapter 8 .... *78*
Chapter 9 .... *92*
Chapter 10 .... *100*
Chapter 11 .... *112*
Chapter 12 .... *122*
Chapter 13 .... *130*
Chapter 14 .... *136*
Chapter 15 .... *143*
Chapter 16 .... *153*
Chapter 17 .... *162*
Chapter 18 .... *168*
Chapter 19 .... *175*
Chapter 20 .... *183*
Chapter 21 .... *196*
Chapter 22 .... *212*
Chapter 23 .... *221*
Chapter 24 .... *232*
Chapter 25 .... *245*
Chapter 26 .... *259*
Chapter 27 .... *268*
Epilogue *276*
About the Author *290*

ACKNOWLEDGMENTS

Once again, I need to give a huge thanks to my family and friends for their continued support. I'm always blown away with your kind words and encouragement.

A special thank you to Charlie, Lisa, Millie, Little Charlie, Sharon, Sarah, Margaret, Catherine, Angela, Serena and Vicky. You have all played an enormous part, no matter how big or small, and I couldn't have done it without you all.

I would also like to thank my publishing team at Kindle Book Publishing for taking my manuscript and turning them into such beautiful books.

And lastly, but at no means least, to YOU the reader. Thank you, I hope you enjoyed reading this series as much as I enjoyed writing it. Please leave a review before you go and look out for my next book.

Thank you xxx.

Chapter 1
Vlad

Running my hand down the front of my charcoal-grey suit jacket, I tug at the knot on my royal-blue tie then look down at my black leather shoes, my reflection gleams back at me. My hands are twitchy, so I shove them in my trouser pockets and blow out a long drawn out breath. I'm a mess. I shouldn't be, I've been willing this day to come for what seems like forever and can't wait until Holly is standing here beside me.

"Nervous?" Sebastian teases, knocking his shoulder against mine. Without taking my eyes away from the end of the aisle where I know the most beautiful woman I have ever laid eyes on will appear soon, I nod my head.

"A little," I tell him and I'm not lying. I am a little nervous but, if anything, impatient would be what I am. I haven't seen Holly since yesterday morning and I miss her. Yes, I spoke to her on the phone last night but it's not enough, I need her here with me and I need to hear her say those two little words. Fuck, I'm a lost cause. I listen to his chuckle just as Mrs White approaches us. She stands in front of me and fiddles with my tie then pats my chest.

"Vlad, eyes down here love," she says while shaking her head. She's only five foot two so she's not blocking my view but she's hell bent on getting my attention when she reaches up and tweaks my ear.

"Ouch… What are you doing?" I look down at my housekeeper who has her arms folded across her chest, her lips are tight, but I can see a twinkle in her eyes. She's amused that I've gotten myself all worked up and in a turmoil.

"You're going to set the flowers up in flames if you stare any harder. Holly's not due for fifteen minutes. Nicholas and Lucas will tell us when the car arrives. You need to relax. Holly doesn't need to see a bag of nerves when she arrives," she scolds me, rambling on. "Will you tell him, Sebastian?" she asks my son.

"It's no use, he's been like this all morning. I've told him to have a drink and chill out, but he won't listen." Nicholas comes and stands alongside me, that mischievous smirk on his face.

"Here," he tries to shove a glass in my hand. "Drink," he orders, "it will calm your nerves."

"I'm fine… " I don't get to finish what I was going to say when my other two sons descend on me.

"Paps take the brandy, we can see how on edge you are from the other end of the garden," Daniel moans at me while Mary takes the glass from Nicholas and thrusts it into my hand. I'd been adamant that I wasn't going to drink while Holly was pregnant but the night I proposed, my boys knew I needed a little Dutch courage and they know I need it now. Taking it from Mary, who has been a godsend along with her husband Tom, my sons and Izzy, all of them wanting to plan and arrange our wedding, leaving nothing for Holly and I to do except choose our wedding outfits, I move the glass to my mouth and let the liquid slide down my throat, burning and soothing away my anxiety.

When I asked Holly to marry me, I wasn't planning on a long engagement. We're both adults, we know what we want so there was no reason for us to wait. But she wanted to wait until after the baby was born, I didn't. When I asked Holly where she wanted to get married, I expected her to say the church that she had attended while she was growing up. She could have chosen anywhere she had wanted. Five-star hotel, some secluded beach or the registrar office. She didn't choose any of them. Holly took my hand in hers and led me out into our front garden which also runs along the side of the house and told me this is where she wanted to get married, amongst the evergreen trees and shrubs. It is a beautiful spot, even in the winter with the deep green pine trees and burnt orange, yellows and red plants and bushes. Tom maintains the garden all year round, it's one of his hobbies, that's why it blooms throughout the four seasons and is a haven for the local wildlife.

My sons jumped in straight away to organise our big day along with Izzy and Mary. They told us to leave it to them and we couldn't refuse them, not with how eager and excited they were.

Therefore, with Holly getting what she wanted and the boys getting their's, it was only fair that I got mine which is why we are getting married three months after Holly agreed to marry me. Between them they've done a fantastic job with minimal fuss.

The enormous white marquee stands tall, covering a vast area of the garden and is set out with enough tables and chairs arranged to seat our guests for the wedding reception. They've hired chefs who are using portable chrome electric and gas cookers and hobs to prepare our meal and waiting staff are busy serving glasses of champagne and orange juice as people arrive. Daniel's band have already set up for later in the day and, even though it's a warm winter's day, numerous heaters have been situated around the garden and inside the marquee ready for when the sun goes down and the temperature drops.

The area for the wedding ceremony looks beautiful with a small aisle for Holly to walk down. At either side of it are rows of white chairs, each one with its own silky royal-blue bow tied around the back. Our family and friends have been asked to just sit anywhere, we didn't want a bride or groom side. And the alter where we will be married will blow Holly away. The archway has been decorated with countless tiny white daisies and twinkle lights and even though it's daytime you can still see the lights shimmering. It would be safe to say that a wedding planner couldn't have done a better job in such a short time.

"Feeling better?" Seb asks, as I watch the guests taking their seats. I can see Daniel has moved and is now in his place, sat at the back of the aisle with his guitar in his hand ready to play our song; a slowed down, acoustic style version of "Ain't Nobody." Nicholas and Joseph are standing ready to give him his cue and Lucas is stood with his big brother by my side. It's time and my heart races.

"Do you have the rings?" I turn to look at them both. Panicked. They both produce them from their waistcoat pockets, each sporting a wide grin. I rub at my chin and nod at them, knowing they wouldn't let me down. I watch Nicholas nod to Daniel then he gives me a mega smile, walking to his seat with Joe, sitting at the front with Izzy and Ben. Daniel strums the first cord of his guitar, lifting his head so his eyes meet mine and they smile with joy. My heart swells twice its size for my sons, who are my world. Then there's these two. The tornado two. Rebecca and Megan, who have made an appearance in their frilly white bridesmaid dresses decorated with royal blue flowers. Each have ringlets in their hair and a tiara on their heads. With wide grins they skip down towards me, scattering white and blue petals from a small basket that they both are carrying. Olivia, Holly's chief bridesmaid, follows closely behind them, keeping them in check. Crouching down, I tap both my cheeks, my granddaughter and Holly's goddaughter place a sloppy kiss on each side then set off giggling to their seats at Olivia's side.

When I stand my breath is stolen from my lungs and my racing heart quickly changes to a staccato rhythm. Breath-taking. Holly appears like a vision. Her hand is tucked into Jack's arm and as she floats down the aisle, as if she's walking on air, a lump forms in my throat. My angel. She's a picture of beauty. Her golden hair has been pinned up with a few loose curls and as usual she's wearing minimal make-up. The royal-blue wedding dress with its empire waistline holds her small pregnancy bump and the V-line neck with spaghetti straps show off her bare shoulders and the swell of her breasts. My first thought is of how stunning she looks. My second is that she must be cold, and I get ready to take my jacket off. Then as she comes closer, I shake my head because I'm thinking I should cover up her boobs that look fucking fabulous so that no fucker can see them but go against it, knowing she'd kill me.

Her smile captures my stare as she steps in front of me, Jack gives her a quick kiss on the cheek then shakes my hand. He takes his seat and I take both of Holly's hands in mine. We stand facing each other and I can't help but lean down, placing my lips near her ear.

"Don't ever leave me overnight again." There's humour in my voice but I mean every word, I've tossed and turned all night without being able to hold and snuggle up with her.

"Miss me?" she teases, rolling her eyes.

"Yes." I don't mind admitting it. I've missed her lips too, so leaning down I steal a soft kiss. She doesn't stop me, just runs her tongue across her bottom lip as I straighten up, she gazes at me, that cheeky smirk in place.

"Brandy?" She knows I wouldn't have drunk it if I hadn't needed to. I nod my head at her. I also notice having her here now, our hands held together, my heart rate has now returned to its normal pace.

There are a few chuckles from our guests which gets our attention and a small cough. We both turn to see the grey-haired registrar waiting patiently for us.

"Shall we begin?" he asks, raising one of his eyebrows.

I take a glance at Holly. "Ready?" I ask, a contented look on my face when she nods her head. "Let's get this show on the road then." I grin as we both take a step forward, so we're standing under the arch.

As we both stand there, hand in hand, Holly engrossed in the registrar's speech about how we are here to celebrate our union and commitment to each other, I thank god that we are finally here.

Once he gets to the part where he asks, "If there's anyone who knows of any lawful impediment why Holly Spencer should not be joined in holy matrimony to Vladimir Petrov then speak now or forever hold your peace?" I almost tell him to move the fuck on because nobody here, not that's been invited anyway, would step in to spoil our day. Luckily, nobody does but there is a bout of raucous laughter that comes from our family and friends. Holly places her hand on my chest, grinning at me as she shakes her head and when I glance at Mr Hamilton, the registrar, his eyebrows are raised and eyes wide. Yeah, I growled. Must have been louder than usual to get a reaction like that. I don't apologise for my slip up; I just shrug my shoulders, not caring and smirk at my angel. "Moving on," he says when everyone calms themselves down, including Holly who is now chuckling so hard her boobs have threatened to pop out of her dress, she's even leant into me, trying to hide the snort of laughter. Once she gathers herself together and moves her head from my chest, I nod at the registrar to carry on.

He continues with his script, explaining that marriage joins two people in the circle of love and is a commitment for life. It is both a physical and emotional joining that is promised for a lifetime. While I agree with what he is saying, I just wish he'd hurry the fuck along so we can get to the part where we exchange rings. Glancing at Holly, I study her carefully, taking in every word the old man is saying. Mesmerized by how her sapphire-blue eyes flicker, then sparkle. How her mouth twitches then rises at one side and when she glances my way, squeezing my hand, I realise that this is one of those moments which needs to be treasured and remembered.

So, I listen carefully when he tells us, the purpose of marriage is that we will always love, care and support each other through both the joys and sorrows of life. And I know that we will.

It's our turn to solemnly declare that we know not of any lawful impediment that we may not be joined in marriage which Holly says, speaking slowly with a smirk on her beautiful face, I run through it knowing it's a waste of time, we both know there's nothing to stop us.

"Vlad and Holly your friends and family are here today to encourage, support and celebrate with you at this special time. So, I ask you now.

"Holly, do you take Vladimir to be your lawful wedded husband, to be loving, faithful and loyal to him for the rest of your lives?" We're both standing side by side now, facing the registrar but Holly turns her head to face me and I swear my heart skips a beat when she says the words, "I do."

Her smile overwhelms me, and I swallow hard to rid the lump that's formed in my throat. He directs the same question at me and, of course, I turn to my angel, taking her gentle hands in mine when I say with so much love in my heart, "I do."

Our guests are asked to stand as we move to the more formal and final part of the ceremony. With our fingers threaded together and our bodies so close I'm sure Holly can feel my heartbeat, she gazes up at me, our eyes meeting. So pure and beautiful, I just want to lean in and kiss her soft lips. I don't. I can wait a few more minutes. A smile graces her lips when she speaks.

"I call upon these persons here present to witness that I, Holly Spencer, do take you, Vladimir Petrov, to be my lawful wedded husband to love and to cherish from this day forward." I repeat the same, then it's time to exchange our rings. Lucas steps forward and

Holly takes the ring from him. She places it on my finger, her hands a little shaky.

"I give you this ring as a visible symbol of our love. I promise to love you, care for you and to always be faithful and loyal through good times and bad, in sickness and in health. I also promise to always encourage Nicholas to wind you up, so I get to see that loving smile on your face every day." The little minx, she's done that on purpose! I can hear our friends and family chuckling away and Nicholas cheering at her promise. I chuckle too, shaking my head because between the two of them they'll drive me insane. "And I promise this for as long as we both shall live and beyond." We didn't want till death do us part. I would like to think that our love will last for eternity.

Sebastian steps forward and hands me the ring and I place it on my angel's finger. "Holly I give you this ring as a visible symbol of our love. I promise to love, care for you and to always be faithful and loyal through good times and bad, in sickness and in health. I also promise to flirt with you and work harder than ever to keep our love alive." I give her a wink; she knows what I mean and so does our family. "So, I get to see that cheeky, sexy smile on your face every day," I tell her. Her shocked face changes and she lets out a giggle and our family laugh along too, knowing our sex life is off the scale and I've just raised the stakes.

"Congratulations. I now pronounce you husband and wife." I don't wait to hear him say you may kiss the bride, I just sweep in, claiming those lips I love so much, and Holly is only too willing to oblige. I do hear friends and family cheering, clapping and whistling. When we break apart Mr Hamilton announces, "I give you Mr and Mrs Petrov."

*

Sebastian and Nicholas stand, tapping their glasses to get everyone's attention. The waiting staff have just finished clearing our desert dishes and everyone's glasses are filled with champagne and wine.

"Thank you," my eldest says once our guests have quietened down. "Wow! What can I say?" he turns to look at both Holly and me. "What a beautiful couple you make." Everyone cheers in agreement and I nod my head with a satisfied look on my face because yes, we do. "I was told to keep my speech short and sweet which I will... " His brothers applaud, hoping he keeps to his word and not ramble on too much, I'm sure they'll all want to have their say. "But," he says, shaking his head at them. "I do have a few words to say to our father... You tell us every day how proud you are of us all and you've shown us every day of our lives how much you love us, but I don't think we've ever told you how proud we are of you, and we are." My sons all clink their glasses, agreeing, and so does Izzy. Even Joseph and Rebecca copy them, and I choke up a little. Holly squeezes my hand as she sits there listening attentively to Sebastian.

"Dad, some people might think that you're unapproachable" There's a few sniggers and tapping of tables and I just laugh it off because it's nothing I didn't already know. However, I have mellowed over the last few months. My angel turns to me with her bottom lip out and strokes my face, she knows I'm a big softy, well I am with her. "A little bit scary and broody," he continues, "but they don't know you. You have one of the biggest, kindest selfless hearts going and we are lucky and proud to have you as our father. And we," he points at my family. "love you very much." The women all coo at him, his brothers stand up with him then everyone applauds him. Holly puts her hand on her heart and sighs while trying hard not to shed a tear at his words.

"Holly," he says once everyone settles down. "You are such a caring, loving and, just like our father, selfless person. A beautiful woman inside and out. One that saw beneath his hard exterior and took a chance showing nothing but love and devotion for the old man. We've been privileged to have you in our lives where you have shown unconditional love to all four of us. My children and my wife and I can safely say from the bottom of my heart that we all love you and are delighted that you chose to marry our father." There are tears building in Holly's eyes, overwhelmed by Sebastian's speech and I watch her bite her bottom lip as she fights to stop them from pouring out. She rests her head on my shoulder and I kiss the top it, trying to fight back my own emotions. "So, could you please stand and raise your glasses to congratulate Holly and Vlad." There are cheers, whistles, clinking of glasses, everyone standing as the celebration continues. Sebastian takes Holly in his arms and kisses her cheek then shakes my hand. I pull him into me, hugging him as I tell him how much I love him.

Nicholas wants his say and gets everyone sat back down. "Well, I'm not going to keep you long, I just have one thing to say. Something I've been dying to say all day." There's a smirk on his face as he picks up his glass and raises it in the air. "Mum, Dad congratulations." Holly burst out laughing while our guests applaud him. He walks over to Holly, giving her a hug, kissing her on the cheek then he hugs me. Daniel and Lucas join him, hugging their step-mum and me.

Jack gives his speech, agreeing with what a beautiful couple we make and how he knows that I will always take care of Holly, who has been just like a younger sister to him, his wife Olivia, his brother Nick and his wife Sarah. He tells everyone he's never seen a couple looking so happy and in love then wishes us all the best for the future. He then toasts our little one, telling us that when he or she arrives it will never be short of love.

I keep my speech short. Thanking everyone for coming and the kind words from my sons and Jack. I thank my angel for becoming my beautiful bride, telling her how she's made me the happiest man alive and how lucky I am to have her and a new baby on the way. I tell everyone to enjoy the rest of the afternoon and evening then I take my wife in my arms and kiss her in the way that she is accustomed to, leaving her knees week and wanting more.

Leaving my jacket on the back of my chair, I lead my beautiful, sexy wife onto the dark wooden dance floor for our first dance as husband and wife. She really is stunning and I'm going to struggle to keep my hands off her until the end of the day.

"Come on, old man, get that sexy mama up here," Daniel calls out over the microphone as he strums his guitar. Holly shakes her head and smiles at him, and I ignore him. Too engrossed in the feel of my wife as I take her in my arms.

Holly asked me if I would like to choose the song for our first dance and while we have a few favourite songs that we love to dance to, one in particular, I wanted something different. Something that sums up how I felt when I first saw her. So, after speaking with Daniel because he's the one who will be singing it, we came up with a favourite at weddings.

Holly hears the strumming of the guitar chords and the gentle tinkling of the piano keys as they play the introduction and a smile graces her lips, her eyes sparkling; she's happy with my choice.

"The first time ever I saw your face I thought the sun rose in your eyes and the moon and the stars were the gifts you gave..." Daniel's deep voice hums, giving me goose bumps as Holly lays her head on my chest. We sway in time with the music, just happy holding each other, and when he sings the next verse Holly's head lifts, our eyes holding each other's stare. *"The first time ever I kissed your mouth I felt the earth move in my hand like the heart of a captive bird that was there at my command..."* Holly's lips are warm and soft as I gently place mine on hers, feeling the love we share through our touch and I know that it will last forever. Throughout the dance I hold her close to me with just the occasional twirl, turning her so her back nestles into my chest then I kiss her slender neck.

As the song ends, everyone claps and cheers and I can see a few tears of happiness from some of the women, including my wife. Wiping the tears from under her eyes, I kiss her again as the dance floor fills, the band playing a more upbeat song.

"I can't wait to whisk you away tomorrow," I say just loud enough for Holly to hear over the music as we hold each other while everyone dances around us. "Just you and me for five whole days, sweetheart." My teeth graze her ear, taking a little nibble.

"Hmmm, I can't wait either," she murmurs, dazed, loving the feeling of my mouth on her skin. "Can you speak French?" she asks, lifting her head, gazing into my eyes.

"Oui."

"Seriously," she stops our dance, keeping her hands on my chest, her head tilting to one side waiting for my answer. I nod my head then take her hands from my chest, joining our fingers together. Holly takes in my answer, her eyes widening then she drags me from the dance floor over to the bar. "I mean fluently not just the odd word," she says as I order two glasses of sparkling water then take my angel in my arms.

"Assez pour s'en sortir," *Enough to get by.* I say, then nip her bottom lip when her mouth falls open.

"Wow, your accent is good and very sexy. Nobody would

understand a bloody word I said if I tried to speak a foreign language." She pulls that cute face at me and I bend down and nip her bottom lip again.

"I'm sure you'd do just fine if you gave it a go."

"No. I have trouble speaking the Queen's English. Your grammar is better than mine and you're bloody Russian," she laughs loudly, and I laugh along with her. Yes, I can speak a few different languages but only because I had no other choice. Even though my mother was English, my father made sure that I had extra English lessons. He also had me learning French and Italian from a very young age. Italian was not for me; I can only remember the odd word. "It's a bloody good job one of us can speak the lingo, I'd go to order a cup of coffee and end up with a pork chop," she chuckles as the tip of her tongue licks her bottom lip.

"What else can you say?" she asks, putting her hands on my chest, her sapphire eyes twinkling.

"Tu es si belle, et tu as fait de moi l'homme le plus heureux vivant. Et je t'aime de tout mon cœur." *You are so beautiful, and you've made me the happiest man alive. And I love you with all my heart.* I say, my mouth close to hers, our eyes gazing into each other's.

"Hmmm, that sounded beautiful," Holly reaches up and kisses me softly. "I can't believe I didn't know you could speak French," she chuckles, shaking her head. "Tell me what you said." I move my mouth to her ear and whisper the words in English and she melts into my arms.

"Can you keep the dirty talk until you get home, you've got a whole five days to yourselves?" Nicholas says as he slides up to the side of us closely followed by Sebastian and Daniel, a wide grin on his face. I didn't even realise Daniel had finished singing and the disco had started.

"Ignore him," Daniel says, stealing my wife from me and dragging her onto the dance floor. "He needs to get laid," he chuckles over his shoulder and I see my wife yank on his ponytail then they join the guests who are now all dancing in a line to some eighties shit.

"Cheeky bastard," Nicholas moans. Sebastian slaps him on the back, loosening his tie then orders a round of drinks.

"Here," he passes one to my son, smirking at him. "Having trouble with the ladies?" he jokes, lifting an eyebrow at him as he takes a drink from the bottle.

"Not at all," Nicholas answers as he takes a drink, his eyes seeking out Lucy over the neck of the bottle. "I'm just very particular ... Waiting for the right one."

"Yeah," Seb says, following his line of sight. "You hang in there, bro," he tells him, passing me a bottle of beer. I lift my glass of water to him letting him know I'm fine with what I've got, and he just shakes his head at me.

"Come on, paps, have a proper drink with us, you've got a free pass. It's your wedding day. You could get shit faced and nobody would care." The barman places four shot glasses alongside another four bottles of beer which disappear in no time at all, my sons making short work of them.

I decide to join my boys, having a couple of drinks to celebrate my wedding. I'm not planning on getting drunk, not that Holly would mind, it's my decision to give up drinking and I've done pretty well so far, so I take the bottle from him and enjoy watching my wife grinning as she's twirled around the dance floor.

Just as I'm on my second Jay, Jack and Nick join us along with Dave and his wife.

"Never seen that lass looking so happy," Jay says as he proudly smiles at my wife who he looks at like a daughter. We both laugh as she's passed about like a prize in pass the parcel. She throws her head back laughing at something Olivia is saying then Sarah takes her hand, twirling her around. Lucy and Izzy grab hold of her, raising their arms in the air and shaking their hips. Holly's eyes meet mine over the crowd and she blows me a kiss, laughing.

"We're both happy," I tell him, a wide grin on my face, not able to take my eyes off her.

"Yeah, I can see that." He slaps me on the back, turning to retrieve his drink, passing me one when he does. "She'll make a fantastic mum," he says as we continue to watch my wife with her friends, my son Daniel in his element with all the women. When Holly spots Lucas and drags him to join them, him happy to be fussed over by her, I know she already is.

"She already is," I tell him what I am thinking, knowing that Holly treats him as if he is her own and Lucas looks upon her as his mum. He watches their interaction and nods his head agreeing.

"You've given her the family she's always wanted. One of her own." Yeah, I have but she's given me so much more, her love. And that is all I will ever need from her and hopefully a daughter. Daniel leaves the ladies and joins us at the bar, taking a large drink from the bottle that Nicholas passes to him.

"Bloody hell, your women can move," he laughs, speaking to all of us. "They couldn't keep their hands off me," he says with a cocky grin on his face. He takes off his tie that they probably loosened then tucks in his shirt that I did see Olivia tugging on. It's all harmless fun, they love winding him up because he is a big flirt with the opposite sex no matter how old they are.

Holly makes her way through the dancers, closely followed by Olivia, they're both fanning themselves, clearly all the dancing has got them hot and bothered. Before I have time to take her in my arms Zach and Frank make an appearance and intercept her, placing their arms around her shoulders and kissing the top of her head. She snakes her arms around their waist and chuckles at them both when they whisper in her ear, then, as the two bastards lift their heads, they smirk at me. Where not so long ago this would have wound me up, bringing out another side, now I see it for the humour in which it's intended. These are our friends and I know how much they both love Holly.

"Looks like she's traded you in already," Dave says, getting a laugh from my sons and our friends. "And for two younger models," he smirks knowing there's not much difference in age between me and Frank. I put my hand out and Holly takes it, still laughing at Dave's comment.

"They don't have the stamina to keep my woman satisfied," I joke, winking at Holly who slaps my arm playfully and hides her face in my chest, trying hard not to chuckle. When she lifts her head, she's giving me a tight smile but amusement dances in her wide eyes. "What?" I question, amused that she is a little embarrassed. I love that flush on her cheeks and can't help myself when I swoop down and take her mouth with mine. Our friends and family cheer at the groom kissing the bride and once I've had my fill, I turn her in my arms, so her back is snuggled into my chest.

"Why are you all stood propping the bar up?" Mary my housekeeper asks, a slight slur in her voice and appearing a little wobbly. She's joined by her husband, Tom, who clearly is trying to keep an eye on her but doing a shit job. Mary isn't a drinker but there's been an enormous amount of champagne and wine served today which I'm sure she's had her fair share' of. Pushing past my sons, a huge smile on her face, her glacier eyes take in Holly and me, she's on a mission. Tom gets my attention and mimics lifting a glass to his mouth then points to his wife, shaking his head. Once she's stood in front of us, she reaches up and grabs my cheeks, causing me to chuckle. "I bloody love this handsome bugger. He's the son I never had." My sons chuckle at her display of affection and the women sigh. I pull her into me, giving her a hug and kiss her cheek. Mary is a sweet woman and has always taken care of us since we came here to England, I don't think I could have managed without her. "Take care of him, Holly, he's not as tough as he looks," she sniffles, and this time Holly joins in on our hug. My housekeeper knows I have a big heart when it comes to my family, she's also aware that they are the ones who can break it.

"I know," Holy whispers, glancing up at me, her eyes watery.

"And you," Mary looks up at me, tapping my cheek affectionately. "Take care of this one, she's special. Never let her down, Vlad, and always keep her happy." I can't help but smirk when I think of all the ways I keep my wife happy and how thankful she is afterwards. Where I keep my thoughts to myself, my son doesn't.

"Oh, he does often," Nicholas chuckles, pointing the neck of his beer bottle at me, his eyes swimming with humour. "And she keeps him happy too. It's like the call of the wild when they're at it. A bit of sound proofing wouldn't go amiss or a sock in the mouth to drown out the noise. Mainly him," he nods his head towards me. I bite my lip to suppress my laughter, amused at his comment. I can't help it; he is funny sometimes even if it is personal. Nobody is shocked at his reference to our sex life, they all find it quite funny, even my little minx gives a little chuckle but then she laughs at anything he says and is the one that is usually egging him on. Although Mary does have a smirk on her face she does move pretty swiftly for an old lass and bats him around the neck, causing everyone to laugh harder. Nicholas finds her hilarious when she tells him off for his cheek and twirls her around, dragging her onto the dance floor.

Once everyone calms down, Holly tells me she needs the ladies' room. Instead of venturing into the house she decides to use the portable ones that my sons have hired. Even though I wouldn't have minded our family and friends using the toilets in our home, it would have been a little awkward. With only having one downstairs the rest upstairs, it would have meant everyone tripping through the bedrooms to the en suits. So, Sebastian hired a cubicle of four for the ladies which are situated to one side of the marque and have a gazebo with sides covering them along with a floor-standing mirror where they can check out their appearance and touch up their make-up. The men have had to make do with a couple of single loos at the other side of the marque.

"You don't need to come in with me," Holly says as we make our way under the blue covering. I can see the toilets are all vacant, so I follow her in, holding the door of the cubicle open for her.

"There's no one in here," I say, shrugging my shoulders. If someone comes in, I'll leave. "Just do what you need to do before someone comes in. I don't know why you couldn't use the bathroom in the house?"

"I was desperate," she says, pulling up her dress as she crouches to pee. "You don't want me wetting myself..."

"Paps, what are you doing in here?" Izzy, my daughter-in-law asks as her and Lucy join us, giggling like two schoolgirls. It's good to see the two of them getting along, Izzy has never really had any girlfriends since I've known her. She has no family, her parents are dead and she has no siblings, so she's just hung around with my sons for the last six years.

"Waiting for my wife," I say, watching them both as they give Holly a little wave through the small toilet doorway.

"Hi," Holly says, waving back, not one bit bothered about them seeing her sat on the toilet.

"Hurry up," Lucy says to Izzy ,pointing at the toilet next door. "Go pee while I top up my lippy." She moves to the mirror, rummaging through her bag.

"I'm not using the loo while Vlad's here," Izzy says, shaking her head, her voice a little higher than normal. I chuckle at her and so does Holly.

"Izzy love," I say, turning to her. "I've rescued you many times from my rose bushes with your knickers around your ankles."

"Oh my god, Vlad," she smacks my arm, her eyes wide and her face heating up. Holly stands from the toilet, her head bent down as she pulls her wedding dress into place. Her shoulders shake and when she lifts her head she wipes at her eyes and tries to suppress her laughter by covering her mouth.

"What the hell were you doing in the rose bushes with your knickers round your ankles?" Holly asks once she's contained herself.

"Having a wee," she casually answers as if it's the most natural thing to do, pissing in my flowers. She crosses her legs, desperate for the loo. "Sebastian had forgotten his keys, it was a few years ago when we lived here, and I couldn't wait so I went behind the bush only I fell into it. Vlad came to the door to let us in and there I was tangled up in the bloody thorns of a rose bush." Izzy runs into the cubicle no longer able to wait then shouts over the door. "So, there I was knickers round my knees and my father-in-law," she shouts mockingly, "just laughed." And I'm laughing now because I still find it hilarious, she wasn't hurt but she did go back for more. At least another three times she's fallen into that bush not able to wait until she got into the house. I'm not the only one laughing, Lucy's chuckling away while she applies her lip gloss and Holly has just sat back down on the toilet needing to pee again, her bladder unable to hold it in.

"Come on, big guy, out of the way, lady needing the loo." Olivia knocks my shoulder, rushing past me like her arse is on fire. She chooses the end cubicle, closing the door behind her. She sighs with relief and I shake my head, wondering how I got myself into this situation. "Vlad, why are you in the ladies?" she questions as I hear the toilet flush.

"Just listening to you ladies pee," I say as she opens the door, smirking.

"Kinky," she chuckles at me, raising an eyebrow.

"Olivia," Holly says as she steps out of her cubicle.

"What? I actually thought that I'd walked in while you two were getting it on." Fucking hell, we'd flatten this plastic box if we were.

"Mother!" Lucy says, shaking her head while Izzy laughs as she opens the door of the toilet she was in.

"Takes the heat off of me," she taps my shoulder, giving me a wide smile then kisses my cheek.

"Does Tom know you watered his roses?" Holly asks, still amused at her.

"Oh, god no. Please don't tell him," she covers her mouth, "I'd die of embarrassment." She chuckles.

Olivia washes her hands in the tiny aluminium sink with a confused look on her face, her head tilted.

"I'll tell you later," Holly says, shaking her head as she rinses her hands, still tickled with what she's just learnt about Izzy. I take her hand once she's dried them and move us to the door. How the fuck I ended up in the ladies with a bunch of cackling women, I'll never know.

"Come on, woman, I need a drink," I say, placing my hand on the small of her back as I move us both outside and back to the celebration.

*

"Ready to leave, sweetheart?" I ask, turning Holly in my arms so my chest presses up against her back then I kiss her neck, inhaling her sweet smell. We've been wrapped around each other for the last half hour, happy just listening to the band as we sway to the music. Holly must be shattered. It's been a long day and since our first dance as man and wife, she hasn't sat down except to use the ladies. She's been spun around the dance floor by all my sons, Jack and Nick, even Jay, led her into a slow dance with a pot on his foot. He was originally going to give her away but about a month ago he broke a bone in his foot, and he's been wearing a boot ever since. He knew it would be on for a while, so Jack jumped in only too happy to walk Holly down the aisle.

"Hmmm, think so," she says as she turns in my arms and gently pecks at my lips, her eyes closing. "I'm exhausted, hubby," she chuckles while placing her hands on my chest.

"No chance of consummating our marriage tonight then," I joke, winking at my wife then I pull her hips into mine as we carry on swaying to the music.

"Oh, I don't know, it depends on how quick you can get me out of this dress." Her eyes hold mine, sparkling sapphire eyes, seducing me. The one thing I've come to learn about my wife is that her sex drive is as high as mine. Holly complains it's my fault that she was never as brazen until she met me. I tell her she probably was, but she needed me to let her inner self loose.

"Oh, I don't know, Mrs Petrov," I run my hands up her outer thighs, feeling the garter she's wearing and giving it a little twang. "We could always leave the dress on." I would love nothing more than to make love to her while she's still in her wedding dress and the way she's turned, taking my hand, hurrying off the dance floor, I think she's up for it too.

As Daniel gives out over the microphone that we are leaving, we give a quick round of goodbyes. We haven't got far to go since we're already in our garden and we don't need to worry about the wedding party or clearing up, my sons will sort everything out, part of their duties as grooms' men. And they'll lock up, taking Lucas with them when everyone has gone.

Holly and I don't need to be up early in the morning as we're not leaving for our five-day honeymoon to Paris until late tomorrow afternoon and Nicholas is dropping us off at the airport.

Approaching the front door, I stop us when we're a couple of feet away. "What are you doing?" Holly squeals when I scoop her up into my arms.

"Carrying you over the threshold." I make quick work of opening the door and striding up the staircase to our room. Once inside I place Holly on her feet, tucking one of her loose curls behind her ear. God she's beautiful.

"You won't be able to do that for much longer," she laughs, placing her hands on her swollen belly. My hands lay over the top of hers as my lips graze hers.

"Yeah, I will," I murmur into them because whether she's six months pregnant or nine months it won't stop me from carrying her in my arms. "Have I told you how beautiful you are?" I ask as I pull away from her mouth, keeping tight hold of her hips.

"Only a thousand times," she chuckles. "Have I told you how handsome you look, especially with this waistcoat on? It highlights your broad shoulders making them look even more powerful than they are." I sweep her up again in my arms and sit her on the dressing table, my manhood straining for release when her eyes rake over me seductively and her teeth nibble at my chin.

I nestle myself between her thighs, pushing up the lacey material of her dress, then my mouth kisses the swell of her breasts.

"Your boobs look fucking magnificent in this dress," I kiss them again while my fingers slowly stroke up her inner thighs.

"They need releasing from this dress, it's been cutting into me all bloody day," she groans. When her hands come up to cup her boobs, she gives them a little jiggle. "They're getting too big," she moans. Oh, I don't know, I think they're fucking fantastic, but I do help her out, unfastening a few of the hooks from the back of her dress then tug on it so her boobs spring free.

"Better?" I ask, loving the relieved look on her face.

"So, much," she says, blowing out a breath, then her eyes close and she hums when my thumbs stroke over the heat between her legs and my lips latch on to her left nipple. I listen to her moans as I move up, nibbling at her neck, then kiss her hard enough to make us both dizzy while my hand finds the edge of her knickers, ready to rip them from her. Usually, she'd be lifting her bottom by now, knowing what was about to happen, but when her hand grabs my arm and she pulls away from my mouth. I raise my eyebrow, questioning what the problem is.

"Don't tear my knickers," she commands, breathless.

"Why?" I chuckle, confused.

"They're my wedding knickers, I was going to wash them and save them in a box with a few other things from our special day." What can I say? If Holly wants to save things to remind us of today, then who am I to argue with her.

I move back to her lips, kissing her passionately and continue to rub my fingers over her heat, swallowing her moans and leaving her knickers intact. "I love you," I tell her as I trail kisses down her neck and onto her collarbone while her hands roam under my waistcoat and start to unfasten my shirt buttons. Her hands are warm on my skin and when her nails score at my chest, I let out a moan of my own, my hardness twitching with approval.

"You drive me fucking crazy," I say against her sweet-smelling skin.

My body is overheating, and I know I'll need to get rid of my shirt and waistcoat soon. Normally, Holly would have rid me of them by now and had my trousers undone but at the moment she's happy with me fully clothed. Her mouth is on my neck, muffling her moans that are coming faster and louder as I hold her on the brink. I move my fingers faster, wanting to get her there before I burst into flames. Needing to hear her tip over the edge, I stroke my thumb over her sensitive nerve endings and move my mouth to her ear. "Holly, come for me, sweetheart." That has the desired effect as her teeth latch on to me while she spirals out of control, her face lighting up like a thousand-watt lightbulb. I give her a few minutes to recover then I attempt to strip out of my clothes only to be stopped when I try shrugging off my waistcoat.

"Leave them on," Holly instructs, her voice croaky, eyes dark and full of lust.

"Why?" I ask as she tugs at my belt and unfastens the button on my trousers, lowering the zip slowly; her grin mischievous and seductive as she tries not to catch my very hard bulge.

"Because you look so bloody sexy... With your shirt sleeves rolled up and this still on." She tugs at my waistcoat. "I want to remember you looking like this, all manly and sexed up, in years to come when I think of our wedding night." She kisses my chest, then leans back on her arms, lifting her hips. "Rip them off, Vlad... it doesn't matter if they're torn it will just remind us of how passionate we are together." With a chuckle, I do as my wife asks, pushing her dress up over her hips, I rip her sexy fucking knickers clean off her and drop them on the floor. Leaving her blue and white garter where it is; halfway up her thigh, I sink into her, losing myself in her warm heat.

Within minutes we're both dropping to the floor, Holly giggling as my legs give way, white lights dancing before my eyes as my chest heaves heavily. "You ok?" She smiles at me then plasters herself across my chest, her fingers playing with the short hairs on my stomach.

"Hmmm," I mumble as I try to sit up, my breath levelling out. "What did you mean, I look all manly with my sleeves rolled up and my waistcoat on? Don't I always look manly?" I raise an eyebrow, smirking at my little minx, amused when she bites her top lip and her eyes widen.

"Yes. But you looked so sexy in that moment fully clothed, I couldn't resist... And yes, you are all man," she kisses my sweaty chest.

"Good to know." I slap her arse then ease her off me so I can stand up. I help Holy up then slowly strip her of her wedding dress. She takes pleasure in ridding me of my waistcoat and shirt then pushes my trousers and boxes down my legs. Both naked we tumble onto our bed that's been decorated with petals, Holly marvelling at how pretty it looks. I just roll my eyes and pick up the alcohol-free champagne and glasses that's been left on the bedside table in a bucket of ice. Once we've shared a glass of the fizzy stuff, we indulge in another round of love making, both of us deliriously happy in wedded bliss then we slip into a peaceful night's sleep, looking forward to our honeymoon.

Chapter 2

Holly

There's nothing nicer than being woken by a pair of soft lips caressing the most sensitive parts of my skin while feather-light touches run circles over my tummy. "Hmmm," I murmur, snuggling further into my pillow. Vlad chuckles then rolls me over on to my back. As I open my eyes, he smiles wide at me then leans down to steal a kiss. I take him in as he sits on the edge of the bed freshly showered, his hair still damp, wearing a pair of tight-fitting black boxers. Good enough to eat.

We arrived at our hotel yesterday evening around seven o'clock which is situated about two hundred meters from the Champs-Elysees. It has a classic and elegant feel to it and our honeymoon suite is luxuriously furnished with a separate lounge and private patio. Not wanting to go back out once we were shown to our room, we settled to order room service from the Michelin star menu, had a soak in the hot tub then made excellent use of the four-poster bed. This morning we decided to eat out and went on a walk, hand in hand down the main street of the Champs-Elysees. Stopping at a small patisserie just off one of the side streets, the smell of the fresh bakery products were too enticing for me just to pass by, so we ordered one of their breakfast specials. Various types of golden glazed croissants, jams, fresh strawberries, butter and cheeses as well as a steaming cup of hot chocolate. Of course, I ate too much and needed half an hour before we could go explore all the famous shops.

Although I wasn't really interested in buying any new clothes, I had brought enough with me including plenty of sexy underwear, I did have a browse in Louis Vuitton and some other overly priced stores. We continued to explore the shops and walked until we had reached the end of the avenue where we were able to take a good look at the Arc de Triumph.

We returned to the hotel at three so I could have an afternoon sleep then get ready for tonight, although I haven't got a clue as to where we are going. Vlad is keeping it a surprise, I'm sure it will be romantic whatever it is.

I know we have plans tomorrow evening to go on a Paris night tour where we will get to see the Eiffel Tour lit up which I'm sure will be breathtaking. Then the day after we have tickets to visit the Louvre Art and History Museum, we've been told to expect to be there the whole day and probably still not get to see everything.

"Sweetheart if you don't get moving, we'll be late. The car is picking us up in an hour." Vlad taps his watch and I pull the sheets back to get out of bed, realising I've slept nearly two hours.

"You should have woken me earlier; I can't believe that I've slept so long."

"It's all that walking this morning, you must have needed it." I walk into the bathroom to shower, Vlad following me.

"Where are we going?" I ask, yawning as I switch on the twin head power spray, I'm soon woken up. Vlad taps his nose then walks back into the bedroom to dress.

Forty-five minutes later I'm dressed and have fifteen minutes to spare.

"How do I look?" I ask, placing my hands on my hips and giving a little twirl as I step into the living room area of our suite. Vlad is fully dressed in a charcoal suit and white shirt with the top button undone, no tie tonight. He looks yummy.

He steps towards me, taking in the sleeveless black cocktail dress with its V-line neck which shows off my cleavage and makes my body look longer and a little slimmer. I'm wearing a pair of diamond cluster earrings with matching necklace that Vlad bought me as a wedding present and with my engagement ring and wedding ring, I'm terrified of losing one of them knowing they cost a fortune. I'm a simple girl, not bothered about expensive jewellery. Never had it bought for me and I certainly wouldn't buy it for myself, but my man loves to spoil me and he's hard to say no to when he wants to give me gifts.

"Superb," *stunning,* he whispers into my ear as he puts his arm around my waist, bringing us closer together. The low sexy rumble of his voice causes a shiver to run down my spine and has me wanting to undress him while he undresses me, whispering words in any bloody language he chooses.

"Thank you for the necklace and earrings," I say, kissing his warm lips as I twiddle with the sparkling pendant.

"You are very welcome," he pecks at my lips. "You can thank me later," he winks then gives me that sexy smirk as he moves to get my coat. He holds it out for me to put on. Once I've put it on, he asks if I am ready, I turn to him and mastering up as much courage as possible, I speak to him in his native tongue.

"Всегда для тебя, мой сексуальный мужчина." *Always for you my sexy man.* I say slowly, pecking at his lips. I've been practicing a few words in Russian for a while now. I seem to understand it better than I can say it, certain words anyway, so when he says nothing my face heats up, embarrassed that I've said it wrong and made a fool of myself. A moment passes and his lip rises. He smiles the smile that makes my heart race then I think maybe I didn't sound too bad. He takes hold of my hands and places them on his chest, and wraps his arms around me, his hands on my bottom. His lips touch mine softly then he speaks.

"You did good," he says as our foreheads touch. "But it is you who is *sexy,* and I am *always* ready for you." He bites my lip and as he pulls away, "Я тебя люблю," *I love you,* he says, and I swoon again.

We make our way out of the hotel and into the sleek black car that awaits us. The driver holds the door open as Vlad helps me in then rounds the car and climbs in the other side. I'm excited to know where we are going and don't need to wait long before the car pulls up close to the docks. Vlad takes my hand and as he leads us towards a beautiful boat with floor to ceiling windows, anxiety grips me. I've never been on a boat and I'm not that good a swimmer.

Stopping Vlad when I pull on his arm, he turns to me. "Vlad, I'm not good with boats," I tell him, biting my lip. His eyes widen and he takes both my hands in his. I feel bad because it's obviously something he thought I'd enjoy. That we would enjoy together.

"What do you mean, Holly?" he asks softly, confusion in his eyes. These are little things that we don't know about each other but I'm sure most newly married couples aren't privy to everything about their partner.

"I don't like boats," I murmur. Looking up, I watch disappointment pass over his beautiful face as he glances towards the boat. The boat really is grand with its glass roof and I can see many couples boarding.

"Okay, sweetheart, don't worry we don't have to go." He gives my hand a gentle squeeze, reassuring me. "Have you had a bad experience on a boat?" His tone is caring. I shake my head at him, feeling like a fool for not wanting to get on it. It's not that big and I'm sure it will cruise along the River Seine at ease and if it's as beautiful on the inside as it looks on the outside, I can only imagine how romantic it will be. "I've never been on one."

"What?" he questions, tilting his head a smirk appearing on his face. "How do you know you're not good with them then?" He repeats my words back to me and I shrug my shoulders at him because I can't give him an explanation as to why.

"Holly, it's an experience that I'm sure once you're aboard you will love." He smiles then brushes his lips against mine. "If we don't try new things we would miss out on so much." His thumb strokes over my cheekbone, "Plus I'm with you and I will always keep you safe." I know that he means what he says and he's probably right, I need to try things instead of putting them off.

"Okay," I say, taking his hand and leading the way, trying to be brave.

"Are you sure?"

"Yes. Come on before I change my mind," I tug a little harder on his hand, causing him to chuckle. "You know I'm not a good swimmer," I say dramatically. He looks down at me, biting at his lip, trying hard not to laugh at how pathetic I am.

"We better hope the boat doesn't sink then." He laughs loudly then bites his lip again when I throw him a dirty look.

"Not helping, Vlad," I shake my head at him and elbow him in his side.

"Sorry, couldn't help myself." He rubs at his side, still laughing at me, and places his arm around my shoulder. "You're going to love it, Holly," he says as we step onto the boat.

And I did. From the live music to the unobstructed view of Paris and its famous monuments illuminated as the sun set. The French cuisine was delicious, but I did pass on the cooked snails. The staff were pleasant, and Vlad was a charmer. He kept me entertained throughout our two- and half-hour romantic cruise with his playfulness. My husband knows how to flirt and get me all hot and bothered and he did a fine job of it. So much so that when the cruise was over and our car drove us back to the hotel, I couldn't keep my hands off him in the back of the car and practically jumped him in the lift on the way up to our room.

The rest of our honeymoon went by so quickly with all the sightseeing and Vlad making me feel like the most beautiful woman in the world that we promised ourselves that we would come back again in a few years.

Chapter 3
Vlad

Holly stirs when I shift my leg, cramp setting in from being stuck in the same position too long. She's been fast asleep for the last hour, me tilted to one side so her head rests snugly into my lap. Her legs are stretched out along the settee and I don't want to disturb her. It's late and if she wakes up now, she'll probably be awake for the rest of the night.

Since coming back from our honeymoon five days ago we've stayed in our loved-up bubble and have been inseparable. I should have been back in work Monday but decided to have a few more days off, not wanting to be separated from my wife and our little bump just yet. My hands stroke over Holly's stomach and she stirs again, bringing one hand up and resting it on mine. I promised her I would go in for a few hours tomorrow while Olivia and Sarah are visiting, knowing we need to get back to some routine.

After our engagement, Holly was still helping out Sebastian and Izzy with the club but then took on some hours at Dimitri's when Maureen the manageress needed some time off to recover from her knee operation. She only went in a few days a week where she would cover the bar, seat the customers and attend to the rotas. Holly had already met a lot of the staff before then and developed a good relationship with them. She's due to cover on Friday lunch time but

I'd rather she didn't.

For the last few days, she's suffered really badly with heartburn and even though it's normal for a pregnant woman, I still make a fuss. That's why she's asleep on my knee and not in bed because usually she can't sleep until she's polished off half a bottle of heartburn mixture and a couple of cups of peppermint tea. So, knowing this, I put a late film on for Holly, Lucas and me to watch, only Lucas took himself off to bed before Holly fell asleep then my angel dozed off not long after, not having the chance to take the pink liquid.

Just as I'm thinking about carrying her up to bed, she stretches out, letting out a soft moan then her eyes flicker open. "Hmmm, you're so comfortable," she says, sitting up, throwing her legs off the settee.

"Thanks, glad I could be of service," I chuckle. "How are you feeling? Still have heartburn?" I ask, stroking her back.

"No, all good," she answers, rubbing her belly.

"Good. Let's go to bed before it comes back. I need to be up early in the morning, seeing as I'm being kicked out to go to work," I complain as I stand us both up, moving to check the patio doors are locked while Holly wanders into the kitchen.

"Ow, you poor thing," she chuckles, opening the fridge and grabbing a bottle of water. "You've had almost two weeks off and I'm back covering for Maureen on Friday while she attends a hospital appointment." She takes a drink of the water then offers me a drink. "We need to get back into some routine over the next few months because when the baby comes... " A loud thud at the front door stops Holly from finishing what she was going to say and has us both turning our heads towards the noise.

"What was that?" Holly asks, startled.

"Don't know," I answer as I make my way out of the kitchen and into the hallway. There's another loud thud then a knocking and before I have time to open the door the knocking gets louder. I throw open the door, annoyed that someone is knocking so late, Nicholas comes tumbling in.

Staggering into the coat stand, he grabs hold of one of the hooks to steady himself, then his back slams against the wall where he proceeds to slide down it until his arse hits the floor with a bump.

"Whoops, that's gunna hurt in the morning," he groans.

"Nicholas what the fuck… Look at the state of you… " He's absolutely shit faced which is unusual for him. Yeah, he gets merry, but I've never seen him staggering around not, when he's come home here anyway.

"Shushhhh… " He puts his finger to his lips. "You'll wake Holly." My son's eyes close then open as he tries to get himself up from the floor. Pushing hard, he makes it to standing position only to fall back into the wall again.

"Come on, let's get you to bed, you can explain yourself in the morning." I'm too tired to get into it now, so I grab hold of him and lead him towards Sebastian's room; not a good idea to take him up to his own room.

"Thanks," he says as he puts his arm around my neck. "You're the best. Oh, hi Holly. Thought you'd be in bed," he greets when he sees her standing by the entrance to the kitchen.

"Had one too many, Nicholas?" she says, giving him a concerned smile.

"You could say that," he slurs, wobbling into me.

We make it to the downstairs bedroom, bouncing off every wall we pass on the way then I drop my son on the bed, he's a dead weight and bounces a couple of times when he lands. "Wooh, the room's spinning," he hiccups, and I know I won't be sleeping in my own bed tonight. I can't leave him in this state just in case he throws up. I take one of his shoes off while he lays there with his hands behind his head, mumbling away to himself, and Holly takes off the other one. We both take a sock each and are subjected to a fit of laughter. I try to help him out of his jeans once he's stopped laughing but it's a struggle.

"Hey, leave my dignity intact, paps, don't want mum seeing the goods," he chuckles as he lifts his arse, holding onto his boxers. I shake my head, wondering what's made him get in this state. I don't think he's been out to a party; he didn't mention anything when he was here earlier in the evening. Rolling him on his side, I cover him up with a sheet, taking him in. Something's bothering him.

"I love her, you know," he says, pain in his voice. I look at Holly and she shakes her head at me.

"Who, Holly?"

"Nooo. Well yeah, I love Holly... But she's not who I meant." His eyes close and he pulls at the sheet. "Lucy, I love Lucy..."

Aw fuck, I rub my hand through my hair, putting my arm around Holly when she comes and stands at the side of me, leaning her head on my shoulder. It's not a bad thing that he's fallen for a beautiful woman, but Lucy is Holly's goddaughter and she's very protective of her. We've known from the day they met at Olivia and Jack's barbecue that they have got along famously. However, I think we were all under the same assumption that they were just friends. Good friends who could go out drinking and have a laugh, obviously we were wrong, and my son has fallen hard.

"Nicholas," Holly sits on the side of the bed next to him, placing her hand on his head, she strokes his hair, "I'm sure she loves you too."

"Yeah, she does but she doesn't trust me..." he fades off, quickly drifting off to sleep. I take Holly's hand and help her up, wrapping my arms around her, my chest to her back.

"Let him sleep, I'll speak with him the morning." I rest my chin on her shoulder as she looks down at my son. She thinks the world of Nicholas, but she loves Lucy like her own. I'm not sure how she will deal with his revelation, even if it is a drunken ramble. She's witnessed how well they get along and I'm sure that I'm not the only one who's noticed how they look at each other.

Holly turns in my arms, a look of concern on her face. "I know she cares for him but it's not just about Nicholas and Lucy, she has a daughter to put first and then there's her career. She's worked so hard..." I put my finger on her lip to stop her from beating herself up about it.

"Holly, I know, she needs to put them first. He's a grown man he'll get over it," I tell her but I'm not sure he will. If he's anything like me and Sebastian, then she's the one, he wouldn't have declared his love for her if she wasn't.

"I'll sleep in the chair tonight," I nod my head towards it. "Just in case he's sick." Holly agrees, nodding her head, he's had a lot to drink and shouldn't be left alone.

"Let me get you some pillows and a blanket." I follow Holly out of the room and towards the stairs, no point her coming back down plus I'd rather her not carry them down the stairs. Once I have what I need, I kiss her goodnight then make my way back downstairs to take care of my son.

*

"Arrrrrrrrrrrg," Nicholas groans as he saunters into the kitchen, stretching out and yawning. "My fucking back is sore," he moans as I sit there, Holly massaging out the knots in my shoulders from sleeping in a fucking chair all night while listening out for the little shit in front of me. "Looks like it's catching old man," he chuckles as he pulls out a chair and sits down. He's too fucking chirpy for someone who was off his head last night and seemed a little upset about a certain young lady.

"Yeah, well if I'd have been able to sleep in my own bed last night instead of being curled up in a fucking chair listening to you snore all night then I would be just fine."

"Oops. Sorry," he says, rubbing his hands up and down his face then bites his lip, tilting his head to one side. "I did have one too many last night and I was going to go stop at my apartment but when I got in the taxi, I couldn't remember my address so had him drop me here." He shakes his head, chuckling.

Holly stops massaging my shoulders and pours him a cup of coffee then gives him two painkillers for his back.

"Get back here, woman, with those magic hands." I reach for her, bringing her back to me, tapping the sore spot. "He's big and ugly enough to get his own coffee." She slaps my arm and he pulls a face at me.

Holly continues to work her magic, soothing away the tightness in my muscles while she chastises my son. "You need to be careful getting in those states, Nicholas, anything could have happened to you on your way home," she says, sounding like an old mother hen. I can't help but laugh when she stands there with one hand on her hip. It also warms my heart that she cares enough to reprimand him. He sees the funny side too and gives her a lopsided grin then gets up out of his seat and kisses her on the side of her head.

"Won't happen again, mum," he teases then steps out of the way when she tries to slap him on the back of the neck. "I'm going for a shower then I'll get a lift into work," he shouts over his shoulder.

"And you can stop laughing," she chastises, rolling her eyes at me.

"Ouch," I moan, rubbing the back of my neck where she's just slapped, it didn't hurt but it gets me a gentle kiss from those lips of hers. I pull her gently round to my front, settling my angel between my legs then cover her mouth with mine. Need to get my fill before I go into work.

"Morning," Lucas greets, dropping his school planner on the worktop then pours himself a bowl of cereal.

"Morning," we both say in unison as we watch him sit down then shovel his breakfast down him like he's never been fed. Lucas has had a growth spurt over the last month and there's no filling him at the moment. Looks like he's going to follow in his brother's footsteps.

"Will you sign my planner, Holly?" he asks between his mouthfuls of cereal.

"Of course," she smiles at him, passing him a cup of tea.

"Err will you sign my planner, Holly," I mimic, screwing my face up at him. "Not good enough for you now, am I?" He doesn't ask me to sign it anymore, I think he prefers Holly's cursive writing especially when she writes notes to his teachers asking how he's getting on and if there's anything he needs help with. They always write back letting her know he's working hard and loves to learn. I knew that anyway but it's heart-warming to watch Holly taking an interest.

"It's better than your chicken scratch," he smiles wide at me, getting off his seat to wash his breakfast bowl. "Can you drop me at school, dad? The bus was late yesterday, and I missed my mark."

"Oh, I'm not good enough to sign your planner but you'll use me as a taxi service," I joke, getting up from my seat to rinse out my cup. Holly takes it from me then slaps my arm playfully, rolling her eyes at me. She then opens the planner, reading it carefully before she sets about signing her name, I gaze over her shoulder just to check she's writing Mrs Petrov. My little minx turns her head, narrowing her eyes at me. "Just checking, he's not been in any bother," I lie but she's seen straight through me just as I have seen that she's just got the devil in her, so I quickly whip the pen from her hand.

"Don't you dare," I warn, holding the pen away from her when she tries to take it back.

"What?" she grins at me, looking all innocent. "I was just going to sign my name," she takes a pen out of the drawer and returns to the planner.

"I know what you were going to do," I tap her on her bottom. "It better say Mrs Petrov otherwise I'll be divorcing you." She rolls her eyes, smirking, knowing I don't mean it.

"Who's divorcing who?" Nicholas questions, an eyebrow raised and that fucking smirk on his face as he strolls into the kitchen.

"Me. I'm divorcing you and her." I try to slap Holly's arse as she moves past me but miss when she steps out of the way, chuckling. She thinks she's fucking funny.

"Ah, who are you trying to kid? You'd rather chop off your left testicle than be without Holly and me." He wraps his arm around Holly as she throws them squinty eyes at me. My little minx moves out of Nicholas' hold, coming to stand by my side with the planner.

"You call him a drama queen," she points the pen at my son, "but you're just as bad." She taps my chin with the end of the pen then turns, placing the planner on the worktop. She signs it then holds it up to show me. She didn't need to, I knew she'd write *Mrs H Petrov*, she's been practicing her new signature even before we got married. I wink at her and kiss her cheek.

"When are the gates getting fixed?" Nicholas asks, sitting down and taking a drink of his coffee. The electric gates are stuck on open and have been since yesterday. When I telephoned the company that fitted them, I was told it would be tomorrow morning.

"Tomorrow," I tell him, placing my arm around Holly's waist. I rest my hand on our bump, stroking my thumb up and down. "What time are Olivia and Sarah coming over?" I ask Holly.

"About an hour," she smiles, "and Sebastian is dropping Izzy and

Ben here once they've taken Rebecca and Joseph to school."

"Make sure you lock the door when they leave, you never know who's hanging around." I don't like that the gates are stuck on open and Holly will be here on her own.

"Dad, we live in one of the nicest areas with less crime rate than anywhere in the city, you worry too much," Nicholas states, shaking his head.

"I don't care. You can't be too careful." Holly understands that I'm a worrier when it come to my family, she'll lock it.

"Don't worry," she says, wrapping her arms around me, a reassuring smile on her face "I'll even put the chain on." Bending down, I softly kiss her, thanking her for always putting my mind at ease. "Anyway," she says when I pull away, "I was going to suggest a family tea so Izzy might stay all day if everyone agrees."

"Count me in," Nicholas jumps in quickly. "Sebastian will be a definite and so will Izzy and I'll ring Daniel later. He was practicing with the band last night, they were all staying at the drummer's house, so he might not be up yet."

"Great," she says, happy to have the family all together.

"I'll be home at two so I can give you a hand," I tell her as my sons make their way out of the door waiting for me to give them a lift.

"Will you speak with Nicholas today?"

"I will." I know she's concerned about what he said last night and to be truthful so am I.

Chapter 4

Holly

"Where's the wedding and honeymoon pictures?" Olivia asks, taking a sip of her coffee. Izzy has just settled Benjamin down for a sleep after feeding and changing him. He's adorable and she's had such an easy time with him. No sooner is he fed and changed then he's content and he either lays there gurgling, taking in everything around him or he drifts off to sleep, pacified.

"I have the honeymoon photos on my phone, but the photographer said that the wedding photos won't be ready until next week."

"Let's have a look then," Sarah says as she opens up the bag of Danish pastries she has brought with her. With my senses on high alert, my stomach rumbles on cue; they smell absolutely delicious.

"Get the pastries out while I get my phone," I tell her eagerly, getting up from my seat, practically drooling. They all laugh when I inhale them again, my appetite out of control, no wonder I'm struggling with heartburn every evening. Sarah gets up and searches the cupboards for side plates, and I retrieve my phone from the living room table.

Picking up a cinnamon swirl, I scroll through the photos until I get to the start of our honeymoon in Paris. What a wonderful time we had. I know it was only five days but with being six months pregnant and having Lucas at home, we didn't want to stay away too long.

Izzy grabs her laptop and the lead of my charger and connects it to my phone; she sets it up so we can watch them on a roll.

"What a beautiful hotel," Sarah comments as she continues to watch the screen.

"Yeah, it looks glorious. I bet the wedding photos are fantastic too, I can't wait to see them," Olivia says, lifting her head from the screen. "This place looked picturesque and you and Vlad looked stunning together."

"Thanks," I tell her. "It was a spectacular day; I don't think we could have wished for a better day with all our friends and family together."

"You're dress looked absolutely out of this world; Jen did a fantastic job with the design in such a short time. You looked beautiful, Holly," Sarah states, picking up her coffee and taking a drink.

"She did. There was a time that we both thought it wouldn't be ready on time, but she did it."

Jen works as a waitress at Dimitris. She's a lovely young woman who works hard to provide for herself and her younger brother Joshua. We get along really well, and I felt extremely lucky when Vlad and I offered her a lift home one-night afterwork. Well we didn't exactly offer but had to practically force her to except.

We'd been working together until ten o'clock that night, me behind the bar and Jen waitressing. Vlad had come to take me home and when we were passing the bus stop not too far from the restaurant, we saw Jen waiting. Pulling over, we told her to jump in and we would take her home. She declined our offer, telling us she was fine, that the bus wouldn't be long, but my husband wouldn't take no for answer and neither would I. It was cold and wet, and we weren't going to see her hanging around for public transport. She's not just an employee but someone who I've come to care about, and I certainly didn't want her walking through the streets alone when she had gotten off the bus. With a bit of persuasion, she excepted and when we pulled up outside her house, I needed to pee. Jen offered the use of her toilet and while we were there, I noticed the manakin in her living room with an ivory wedding dress. It wasn't finished but I could tell that when it was it would be undeniably beautiful and one that I would love. So, after a long discussion on whether she would be able to design mine on time for the wedding and the choice of colour and material, she said yes. Jen was paid well for her time and the dress which came in handy as she has a fifteen-year-old brother to take care of as well as all the household bills to pay. She was also well compensated for the overtime shifts that she had to decline as well as any tips she may have lost due to her not working. It was only fair. Jen is a well-liked and sought after waitress by some of the regulars and is tipped well for being efficient, polite and someone they can chat to if they choose to.

"She's very talented, let's hope with word of mouth she can get a few more."

"I hope so."

We continue to look at the honeymoon photos as we chat about the wedding.

"I need to see the wedding pictures as well as any videos people had taken because I don't remember much of about the evening," she chuckles, shaking her head.

We all laugh with her because I do remember Jack holding her up before Vlad and I left the reception. "Jack told me he had to carry me into the house when we got home, undress me and put me to bed."

"Funny that," I laugh loudly. "I was carried into the house, undressed and put to bed too."

"I bet you were," Sarah says, chuckling. "I hope that's not all that happened when you were put to bed," she raises an eyebrow at me.

"Oh, that happened before I was undressed and then again afterwards," I smirk at my friends and ignore Izzy's high-pitched squeal of embarrassment. She's been around my friends long enough now to know that they always bring up my sex life. They still find it a novelty that I got involved with a man that on many levels is so different to me it's unreal, however that didn't stop me from falling madly in love with him or marrying him. Through my eyes, I don't see the hard-faced bastard that a lot of people see. A man whose dark intense stare would send the devil running back to hell. No. I see the love that oozes from him. An all-consuming affection for his family that I am now a part of, and my friends see it too and that is why they have grown to love him so much.

As we get to the end of the photos, I look at my watch. It's took well over an hour to get through them as they wanted a well detailed account of our romantic time away.

"Holly I can't believe how much your life has changed within the last year," Olivia states once I've shut down the laptop. "In fact, it's less than a year."

"I know," I smile, agreeing with her and I wouldn't change a thing.

"This time…" she thinks for a minute, tilting her head. "nine months ago, you were moping about over Rob not wanting to go out, happy just sat in your little apartment. Well not happy but you know what I mean. Now look at you," her smile is wide and reaches her eyes. "Married and pregnant. Truly happy and in love."

"You're going to be a fantastic mum," Sarah says, placing her hand on mine. They're both aware how much I wanted a child when I was married to Rob but I'm glad now that it never happened. Now I know what it is truly like to love someone and to have that love retuned in a way that makes my heart flutter and takes my breath away every day, I know I never really loved Rob like I thought I did.

"Thank you," I tell them both. I am grateful to have them in my life because if it wasn't for them persuading me to go out that night then I wouldn't have met Vlad.

"When are you giving up work? Are you still helping out at the restaurant?" Olivia asks as she gets up, gathering the plates then switches on the coffee machine.

"Well I'm covering for Maureen on Friday while she's at the hospital. She's still not back fulltime yet so on Monday I'll be returning to cover the shifts I was doing before the wedding and then I will help my little friend here whenever she needs me," I say, smiling at Izzy. We've both not done much at Aphrodite since Izzy had Benjamin and I found out I was pregnant, but we do work well together.

She smiles back then speaks. "Don't say anything to Vlad yet, I think Sebastian wants to speak to him about selling the club and ploughing the money into property."

"He does?" My eyes widen at her. "And do you want that?" I'm shocked.

"Yeah," she nods her head. "We both do. There's a lot of late nights which was fine before but now we want to be at home with the children." We all nod at her, understanding; they have three children now one of them being a baby. "I know we have staff to cover but I think we would both enjoy taking on projects where we could work with you and Vlad. Sebastian loves working with his father and... Well I've loved working with you. It will be cool choosing bathrooms and kitchens, designing the layout and..." she stops, shrugging her shoulders when she notices we're all staring at her.

"Aw Izzy," I say, getting out of my seat. "I've loved working with you too and love that idea as I'm sure Vlad will." My arms wrap around her shoulders as I give her a hug.

"Don't say anything to him, I think Sebastian wants to speak to him tonight about it."

"My lips are sealed." I look up at Olivia and Sarah, I don't want them going home telling Jack and Nick just yet, they're likely to be on the phone to Vlad to discuss putting in a bid for their company to do the work as soon as they buy somewhere else.

"Our lips are sealed," they both say in unison, mimicking zipping up their lips.

"You do realise though that when I'm eight months, I'm giving up work until she starts nursery."

"She?" Olivia questions, raising her eyebrows at me, smirking. "Is there something you haven't told us."

"Oh, no." I laugh, shaking my head and place my hands on my stomach. "Vlad's so obsessed with having a girl, he's got me believing it too."

"Are you wanting a girl or not bothered?" Sarah asks.

"I'm not bothered really but it would be nice to have a girl. I think Vlad will die if he has another boy." They all laugh, knowing Vlad is praying for a daughter.

"You can still work from home though," Izzy says, "I mean we could even go for a walk in the park with the babies then to a café and discuss any plans or whatever," she shrugs her shoulders and smiles.

"Yeah, that would be great and if I know Vlad, he will have a playpen/travel cot in the office not wanting to leave us both at home," I smile. "Maybe we could leave them for an hour to go to the gym. Get rid of some of the baby weight."

"I think it's a brilliant idea, we both worked from home when the babies were born," Sarah, states, pointing between Olivia and herself.

"Yeah, I remember. I don't mind working from home or even at the office as long as this little one is with me," I rub my little bump. "But like Izzy, I don't want long hours and late nights," I tell them.

Olivia and Sarah stay for another hour, arranging to meet up at the weekend at Olivia's for Sunday dinner.

*

Arriving home just after two, Vlad lounged around entertaining his grandson who was happy just kicking away laid out on the rug while Izzy and I decided what we were having for tea. She told me earlier that she had invited Lucy and Megan to join us when she saw them at school this morning which will be interesting as I'm not sure what has gone on with her and Nicholas but I'm not going to let that stop them from coming. Both of them are my goddaughters. Lucy is getting along really well with Izzy and of course Megan and Rebecca are inseparable, spending everyday together at school and over the last few months their mothers have taken them out together.

We decide to make lasagne with jacket potatoes, salad and garlic bread, knowing that everybody enjoys it. Daniel arrives first and helps Vlad bring extra chairs from the garage so there's enough to seat everyone when they get here. Sebastian collects Rebecca and Joe from school and brings Lucy and Megan with him. Not long after Nicholas and Lucas stroll in, bringing with them a new game for the boys to play on.

By five o'clock we're all sat around the table enjoying our meal, laughing and joking. Vlad's sons are taking great pleasure in commenting on how much my appetite has increased since the wedding and keep dropping hints about me having a large baby.

"Ignore them, sweetheart," Vlad says, putting his arm around my shoulder and kissing the side of my head. Which I do. I take it all as a bit of fun and place my hands on my swollen stomach. I'm not that big really, it's my boobs that have gained the most weight.

"Give it a couple of weeks," Sebastian says, nodding his head towards his dad, his grin wide and his eyes shining. "You won't know what's hit you because it won't be just her appetite for food that will be enhanced," he chuckles, wiggling his eyebrows. Izzy gives him a slap on his arm while Nicholas and Daniel laugh along with him, knowing exactly what he means. The girls haven't got a clue what he is talking about. Lucas continues to explain the new game he's got to Joe, not one bit interested and Lucy smirks at his comment. When I turn to look at Vlad, his lips are twitching, and that devilish smirk appears.

"Can't wait," he whispers when his mouth moves to my ear then he leaves a kiss on my cheek. I shake my head at him because I've heard how a woman's sex drive multiplies towards the end of their pregnancy. In fact, I know Olivia used to be ripping at Jack's clothing as soon as he walked in from work and Sarah was the same. I'm sure Vlad knows what to expect, even if not from Natalia then I'm sure Sebastian would have shared a few titbits with him from when Izzy was pregnant. And from the satisfied look on his face I can only assume he can't wait for when I'm pawing at him.

Nicholas, Daniel and Sebastian are finishing tidying up in the kitchen while Izzy and Lucy are sat at the dining room table glancing through the baby magazines that I'd put there after we had eaten. Both Nicholas and Lucy have gotten along fine which tells me whatever the problem was between them has now been sorted out. The girls are colouring at the table and Lucas and Joe have gone upstairs to play on their new game. Vlad has Ben sprawled across his chest with me leant against him, my hand stroking Ben's back. Chewing on his fist, he lifts his head and his face reddens just as there's a rumble in his nappy. "Oh," I chuckle, sitting up.

"Bloody hell, what's he been eating? He stinks." Normally, if it had been one of his sons that had left a smell behind them he would have been cursing the F word but he's trying to rein in his language in front of his grandchildren and with the baby on its way, I have told him that Benjamin's and our baby's first words will be F***ing hell. Vlad sits up from his comfy position of lounging on the settee and lifts his grandson in the air, his face scrunching up when Ben turns beetroot red again and another rumble as well as a squelching sound erupts from his nappy.

"Do you want to tackle this one?" My man asks, his nose twitching as he holds Benjamin under his arms, Vlad's arms are outstretched. Ben now cooing and babbling away, happy even if his nappy is full.

"I think this is a two-man job," I laugh. We've both had enough experience in changing baby's shitty nappies, but it's been a few years; until this little fella came along.

"Here, I'll take him," Izzy smiles then scrunches up her nose when she smells him. "I want to put him in the bath and get his PJs on, he's bound to fall asleep on the way home so I might as well get him ready now," she states. "Pooh, you do smell, little man," she chuckles while kissing his head. Vlad plonks himself down on the settee, taking me with him, so I'm sat on his knee, a welcome relief on his face.

"We need to get used to changing stinky nappies," I chuckle as he nuzzles my neck.

"Huh, I think you're forgetting we're having a girl and our little princess will smell like roses." He leans down so he has access to my tummy then blows a raspberry on it and my tummy flutters.

"Wooh!" he jumps up quickly, his eyes wide with amusement. "She's just kicked me…" It's not the first time he's felt our little one kick about, but it surprises him every time.

"Vlad," I choke out in a fit of giggles. His face is a picture of happiness, I wish I'd had my phone with me so I could have taken a photo. "You know *she* could be an *he*," I say once I've contained myself. He's not listening, too engrossed with our little one. With both hands on my stomach and his mouth as close as it can be without touching it, he chunters on chatting to the baby. My heart skips a beat as I listen, my hands stroking through his soft hair. I'm so in love with him, I've never been as happy as I am now, and I know the feeling is mutual.

He leaves a gentle kiss when he finishes and lifts his head, loving eyes glisten as they gaze into mine. God, I hope we have a girl.

"Dad," Daniel calls out, bringing us both back from our little moment.

"Yeah," Vlad says, planting a soft kiss on my lips before he sits up straight, his hands still gently placed over my stomach.

"You have a couple of visitors," his tone sounds bothered. We both stand up, turning towards the kitchen where Vlad's two eldest are stood tilting their heads, regarding their brother through the open entrance to the hallway and whoever it is at the door. Confused, Vlad looks at me and shrugs his shoulders not knowing who it is. As a rule, nobody ever calls around to the house to see him without contacting him first, anyone who isn't family would ring or call on him at work.

With determination in his stride, Vlad enters the kitchen. "I hope this is important," he grunts, displeased with been interrupted during family time, he continues passing by Sebastian and Nicholas and out into the hallway, his brow furrowed.

Unable to hear or see who it is, I make my way into the kitchen and stand at the side of Seb. "Who is it?" I ask just as Lucy joins us and the two little ones fly up the stairs taking with them their colouring. We all know it's not anyone we know because Daniel would have let them in. We're not waiting long to find out when we see Vlad open the door wider and gesture with his hand for whoever it is to come in.

Vlad's dark blue eyes catch mine and I can see he's concerned and confused as to why a policewoman is stood in his doorway. He's not the only one as we all look at one another puzzled. Everyone who Vlad cares about are here in the house apart from Mr and Mrs White and straight away my heart pounds in my chest and I start to shake, thinking the worst. Grabbing hold of Sebastian's arm to steady myself, he looks down at me. His arm comes around my shoulders when he sees the distressed look on my face.

A middle-aged man, wearing a dark grey suit follows her in and Daniel closes the door behind them. His slim frame stands tall and upright as his light brown eyes study the family pictures that line the walls in the entrance.

"Is there somewhere we can talk in private, Mr Petrov?" the policewoman asks when she notices all of us stood in the kitchen. Although she's not wearing the full police uniform it's easy to tell she works for them; the badge that's attached to her black trousers being a big give away.

"Whatever you have to say you can say in front of my family," his voice is firm as he stands there with his arms folded across his broad chest. Dressed in a pair of faded jeans and a tatty T-shirt with nothing on his feet, Vlad looks nothing like he does when he's at work where he wears designer suits and has that intense authoritative way about him, but right in this moment he's taken on his work persona. Not happy that he's been disturbed at home. He has nothing against the police, he interacts regularly with the local police force when they visit the clubs. Some of them call into Dimitri's frequently. He genuinely doesn't like being bothered at home.

I'm not sure if he has realised that they have probably come to give him some bad news so stepping forward I approach my awkward husband. Placing my hand on his arm, I greet the policewoman. "Hi," I say, putting my hand out. "I'm Holly, please come in." She gives me a tight smile and shakes my hand. Then I put my hand out to the man who's yet to say anything. He steps forward and shakes my hand too, that's when I notice the identification badge he is wearing around his neck and my childhood years come flooding back like a bad dream.

"We're sorry to interrupt your evening…" He stops and takes everyone in. "We can see you're busy, but we really do need to speak with you on a matter of urgency." His soft eyes turn to Vlad.

Any worry I had about Mary and Tom is now gone and images of a man and woman taking me from the squalor I lived in with my biological mum flood my mind and has me wondering what does someone from social services want with Vlad?

Gathering myself together, I lead them into the living room and narrow my eyes at my husband who really does need to get off that high horse he's on because these people don't call at your home at seven o'clock in the evening for nothing. He heeds my warning and drops the pretentious act and asks them to take a seat.

"Right, how can I help you?" His tone is still bordering on

condescending but at least he wants to get on with why they are here.

"Mr Petrov, why we are here is of a very delicate nature which would be easier if we could speak with you alone," the policewoman speaks calmly as she looks around at the amount of people in the house. Although Vlad's sons and Lucy are sat at the dining room table, they are still in ear shot of the conversation. Turning to look at them, Sebastian raises his eyebrows at me, standing quickly, "We'll get out of the way." With that the four of them stand and make their way upstairs.

"I'm sorry," I say as I sit down. "I didn't get your names." The policewoman sits up straight, her long light brown hair that's tied up loosely swishes across her shoulder as she unclips her badge from her waistband.

"Sorry, we did show our identification to your husband... " She stops as if she's waiting for my confirmation that we are married. I nod my head at her just to verify. The man who's sat by her side produces his badge, a tight smile edges on his face. Probably not happy that Vlad is being a little rude.

"Nile Stanton, I work for the child services and this is PC Joanne Grimes, she's a police liaison officer." He picks up his briefcase and takes out a small file then pops the case back on the floor.

"Mr Petrov what we have to say is of a very serious nature so your cooperation would be most helpful." Although Joanne's tone is professional, she still has a caring approach about her when she speaks to Vlad.

"Okay," he says, taking hold of my hand, giving it a gentle squeeze. "You have my full attention."

As Mr Stanton fiddles with the file in his hand, Joanne speaks, "Mr Petrov have you ever visited the Tall Trees Nightclub?" Her pale blue eyes study him while she waits for his answer.

"Yes," he answers, nodding his head, not keeping her waiting long.

"Can you remember the last time you were there?"

"It must have been... " His head tilts to one side, his hand covers his mouth as he thinks. "About three or four years ago," he says.

"Thank you," she smiles gently, happy with his answers. Mr

Stanton takes a photo from the file and passes it to her, and she places it on the table. "Do you know this woman, Mr Petrov?" Both Joanne and Nile's eyes flick between Vlad and me then onto the photograph. Vlad glances at it while I take a good look. The woman has delicate features, her face soft with hazel eyes. Mousy brown hair layered into her face, she looks around the same age as me and although she has a beautiful smile, her golden-brown eyes with a greenish tint hold sadness.

"No," he says, not even picking it up to have a proper look.

"Please take a good look," Mr Stanton says, pushing it forward so the picture is nearer to Vlad. This time he takes hold of it and observes it carefully. Once he's finished, he places it on the table, lifting his head he turns to me, his eyes apologetic as he acknowledges that he does know her. I don't know why he feels he needs to look sorry, maybe it's because something from his past has reared its ugly head again.

"Maybe... Yes... I think I remember her." His voice is low.

"And do you remember if you slept together... "

"Excuse me. What the hell has that got to do with you?" he almost bites off Mr Stanton's head as he growls out his question. Joanne gives her colleague a sideways glance, not happy he has jumped right in with such a personal question.

"Sorry Mr Petrov," she says, sighing. Then looks at me, giving me a reassuring smile, obviously she feels bad bringing up my husband's sex life up in front of me.

"It is relevant to our enquiries whether you slept with this woman or not and we do need you to answer the question," she says calmly.

But my man is irritated now, and they'll be lucky to get any information out of him, in fact I'm surprised he hasn't asked them to leave. Luckily, I am one of the people that can calm him, so I turn to face him. My hand in his, our knees touching, my eyes search his face.

"Vlad answer the question so we can get to the bottom of why they are here." He nods his head, inhaling deeply through is nose. I want him to answer them truthfully and quickly because I too want to know what relevance their questioning has to his sex life.

"Yes," he admits, blowing out a breath. "Now can you tell me why me having a one-night stand with this woman three or four years ago has brought you here? Because this conversation is a little one sided. I answered your questions now answer mine."

"Of course, Mr Petrov. I can understand that we have been vague in why we are here, but we had to make sure we had the right person before we divulge any information." Joanne points to the photograph on the table, her face unreadable. "Miss Rogers died six months ago," as she says it her eyes fill with sadness and I grip Vlad's hand a bit tighter. "She left two sons, the eldest being fifteen years of age… "

"I'm sorry to hear that but what as this got to do with me?" Vlad cuts in, and I know he will sincerely feel for them because he does have a big heart. However, he doesn't like being pissed about, he prefers people not to waste his time and get straight to the point.

My breath catches in my throat and my heart aches for this family. Two boys left without their mum… That's when one by one pieces start fitting into place. Social services, police liaison officer, and although they have said the eldest is fifteen, they haven't said how old the youngest is or mentioned their father. Where Vlad is clueless at the moment as to what they are about to reveal to him, I have an inkling. Taking in a deep breath and covering my mouth with my hand, so Vlad doesn't see my lip trembling because I know if I am right it will tip him over the edge.

"Mr Petrov, after Miss Rogers died, her eldest son was searching through her things when he came across his birth certificate stating who his father was. He also found his three-year-old brother's which states father unknown. But attached to the back of it was a piece of paper with your name written on it. Which leads us to believe that you are the father of the youngest boy."

Emotions run high. What I'm feeling at the moment I can't describe; they're so mixed up it's hard to detach one from the other. Sadness for the two boys. Shock that Vlad may have another son. I've always had a maternal quality about me and at this moment I have an overwhelming urge to want to wrap them in my arms and tell them everything will be ok. Love for the man sat at the side of me and what he will be feeling right now. He's a fantastic father and I'm sure he will be hurting that he has missed out on three years of his son's life. I dial down what I am going through because the unfamiliar noise that's just erupted from Vlad is something I've never heard before.

"You're joking, right," he says with an intense sarcastic snigger. When they both just shake their heads, I feel his body tense and shake. Abruptly he stands, dropping my hand and storms to the back of the settee, running his hand through his hair. He levels them with a look that I've never seen before then he grips the back of the settee. I didn't expect this from him.

"Mr Petrov... "

"No!" he barks out, stopping the policewoman from speaking. "You will listen to me now. I am nobody's meal ticket. I have four sons who I have protected, provided for and loved since the day they were born and I have a baby on the way," his gaze catches mine and I know he is struggling with how he is feeling but he needs to remember he did sleep around for years and this happens all the time. "Do you know how many times some woman has said she's carrying my child... ?" He shakes his head in annoyance. "Too many and if I'd have excepted their lies, I would have needed a house twice the size of the one I have now."

"Vlad... " I try to reason with him, but he just holds his hand up, stopping and dismissing me like I'm someone insignificant in his life.

"I'm sorry the two boys have been left without their mother but it's not my problem. So, you can leave now and go find the poor excuse of a man that's abandoned his children." With that he marches off into the kitchen and opens the fridge, taking out a bottle of water. The arrogant arse. I'm so shocked at his outburst that I just sit there not knowing what to say to the two people that are sat on our couch not preparing to move.

"I'm sorry about my husband," I say, feeling guilty that he has just dismissed them like he did me. Joanne nods her head and smiles at me while Mr Stanton takes out a card from his pocket.

"It's ok, Mrs Petrov, we see this reaction all the time, but I must say that the little boy in question does look a lot like your husband and the men who were here when we first got here," her smile is genuine. "At this point we understand that your husband needs time to process this, so we'll leave, but even though I'm ninety percent sure he is the father we do need to do a paternity test. And the sooner the better. I'm sure once he's calmed down, he'll come around," she says, standing as Mr Stanton passes me his card.

"You can contact either of us on this number when he is ready and we'll set up the paternity test," he tells me, ready to leave. But I'm not ready for them to go yet and I'm not putting up with my husband's cantankerous ways. This needs to be sorted now. There are children involved who probably have no one to care or love them and that I can't let go.

"Please sit down, I need to ask you a few questions." They both sit back down, waiting for me to speak. I glance over to the kitchen to see if Vlad has calmed down, but he is not there, so I just go ahead without him. He's not interested but I am and I'm also bloody annoyed at him for disappearing.

"Where are the boys now? Are they with family, someone they know?" I ask, knowing that I have a man from child services in my living room which means these children could have been placed in foster care or a children's home. My heart bleeds.

"We're sorry, Holly," his sympathetic tone tells me he's not going to answer my questions. "We can't divulge any information about them until we know for sure that your husband is the father and although we think he is, by law we need the test to come back verifying it."

I nod at him understanding that their hands are tied with legal tape. "Are they safe?"

"Yes," he answers just as Vlad stalks back into the room, his lips tight and jaw set.

"You two still here." It's not a question it's him being arrogant and dam right rude and I've had enough of his attitude.

"Vlad stop this," I don't shout but my tone is firm as I stand to face him. "You need to get that stick out of your arse and face the fact that you could be the boy's father." I jab him in the chest with my finger and glare at him. "These people are doing their job and you've been nothing but disrespectful and uncooperative." I shake my head at him, and he knows I'm on my soap box. "This is about a child who has lost his mother and is probably stuck in foster care and you act as if you couldn't care less. I'm disappointed in you. Now there's a paternity test that you need to take, Vlad, get it organised and stop being pig-headed." I jab his chest again and he tries to take hold of my hand.

"Holly..."

"No Vlad," I cut in with, stopping his pleading tone for me to listen to him. It's not happening. I don't understand how he can be so dismissive of this whole situation when it involves the welfare of a child and his attitude stinks. So yeah, I'm pissed at him now. Turning towards Joanne and Mr Stanton, "I'm sorry about this," I tell them sincerely then I turn to my husband who has a worried look on his face. "Organise the paternity test, Vlad. Condoms aren't always safe." I state then storm off, so angry with him I can't even look at him at the moment.

As I'm passing through the kitchen Sebastian lands at the bottom of the stairs. "Everything okay, Holly?" I can't answer him. My emotions are spiralling out of control and I'm so bloody tired, I fear if I speak, I'll break down, so I don't. Shaking my head, I make my way up the stairs leaving him to knock some sense into his father's head.

Chapter 5
Vlad

Resting my back heavily against the front door, I slam the back of my head, hitting the solid oak wood hard. "Fuck," I curse, frustrated and angry with myself for being such an unreasonable jerk. I've upset the woman I love, annoyed my sons and probably put a black mark against my name with the authorities, leaving them thinking that I'm some unreasoning egotistic bastard. And sometimes I can be all three when I feel I need to be. When dealing with jumped up council officials that are dragging their feet with planning permission or when someone in the business world needs putting in their place but tonight, I'm sorry to say, wasn't one of those times and I should have dealt with it differently.

When I let Mr Stanton and PC Grimes in, I didn't realise one was from social services. I thought they were both from the police and they were here because of something to do with one of my clubs. Normally, I know who is visiting me at home but with the electric gates broke they were able to gain access without being buzzed in. Already annoyed at being interrupted while relaxing with my family, I dismissed them straight away, not wanting to listen to what they had to say. As they relayed the reason why they were at my home, I knew that what they were saying could be true, but I wasn't letting anyone knock me off the cloud that I'd been floating on since Holly moved in with me, told me she was pregnant then agreed to marry me.

We've been married for less than two weeks and having my past brought up, knowing it would bring us both back down to earth with a bump, was shattering our little bubble. Well, I wasn't going to let that happen. My boys tell me I have a big heart. That I'm caring and selfless but tonight I was none of those things. Selfish would be one word and heartless would be another.

So now after locking the door, my boys have just left, leaving Lucas upstairs still playing on his game. Holly hasn't come back down since she put me in my place, and I'm left wondering how the hell I'm going to explain myself to her.

Anxiously, I make my way up the stairs hoping Holly has calmed down because seeing her so upset and disappointed with the way I behaved broke my heart and made me see sense. So, when she disappeared, I gave Nile and Joanne my undivided attention and planned to have a paternity test first thing in the morning. I was also told off by my sons for upsetting Holly and I don't blame them for putting me in my place.

Opening the bedroom door, Holly is sat up against the headboard reading. Wearing one of my T shirts that she's claimed as her sleeping attire. She doesn't look up or acknowledge that I've entered the room which tells me she's still vexed with me.

"Holly," I say, my voice low and apprehensive; she can be a little spitfire when she's annoyed and I don't want her upsetting any more than she is. Gingerly, I sit on the bed placing my hand on her leg. "I'm sorry." Her blue eyes flick up from the book she's been reading, and I move closer hoping she can see how sorry I really am. I love this woman too much to hurt her, we've had enough of that in our relationship. Now we're all about showing how much we mean to each other and I know I will do anything to keep my angel happy.

"I could have dealt with that differently," I explain, keeping my gaze locked with hers. "Should have dealt with it differently and I'm truly sorry I didn't."

"Yes, you should have, and you should have thought about those poor boys who have lost their mother. God only knows if there's been a man in their life... A father figure because if the child services and police liaison officers are involved then I'm afraid they probably have no one to care for them," she sniffles and swiftly I have her in my arms, comforting her.

"I know, I'm sorry, Holly, for being heartless," I breathe into her hair.

"I know you are, but I don't understand why you would behave in such a way. Knowing how much you love your sons, I thought you would have been distraught and in a hurry to find out if that little boy is yours." Like a sledgehammer to my chest her words hit me, and I hold onto my pregnant wife as images of a three-year-old boy, the double of my sons when they were that age, lost and alone fills my head. What a thoughtless bastard I am.

"Vlad," she soothes when she feels me shaking and I struggle to form words. "Are you ok?"

"No," I manage to say as Holly holds me tightly, her hand lightly stroking my hair as I burry my face into her neck, ashamed of myself for acting the way I did. We stay like that for a few moments and when we pull apart both our eyes are wet.

"I'm sorry Holly, you know that, right?" She nods her head at me, and I take both her hands in mine while I try and explain my behaviour to her. "These past few months, Holly, have been the best months of my life. I've never been happier. You, our baby," I place one of my hands on her stomach, loving that I get to do that. To feel it growing inside her overwhelms me. She places her small hand on top of mine and listens attentively, "My sons, Izzy and my grandchildren, I have so much love for you all it scares me. And since we've been married, I've created this bubble and nobody else is allowed in. I just didn't want anyone or anything bursting it. How you look at me… Your eyes, your touch tells me you feel the same, so I guess I didn't want something from my past ruining that like it did before. I love you too much to let that happen again." I place my hand on her cheek and slowly move my mouth to hers, gently letting our lips touch.

"Vlad, nothing will come between us. Whatever happens we're in this together, so don't ever think that I will stop loving you for things that are out of our control," she says and I see on her face that she loves me just as much as I love her and that she's sincere when she says we're in this together.

"Did you organise the test?" She raises an eyebrow at me.

"Yes, and I gave my apologies for being an arse."

"Good. When do you go?"

"Tomorrow morning at the police station, I need to be there for nine o'clock." She nods her head at me, chewing on her lip.

"Did they tell you anything about the boys? Their names or where they are?"

"No. What do you mean where they are?" I tilt my head to look at her confused.

"Their mum died six months ago," she blows out a breath. "Haven't you wondered who's been taking care of them since then? Or why the authorities are involved?"

"Well no I hadn't but now… "

"Don't," she cuts in with. "You'll worry yourself sick. Let's wait. Have the test then they'll tell us everything," and I'm blown away with how she says us.

"Okay," I need to listen to her because I'll go fucking crazy with all the different scenarios that could circle around my head.

"Shower with me." I stand, not letting go of her hand, I need my angel close to keep me from going crazy. "Or come and talk to me while I shower." She climbs off the bed with my help and we make our way into the bathroom. Stripping Holly of my T shirt, she helps me off with my jeans and shirt then we step into the shower together. Even though my mind is on other things my body reacts to being so close to her. She's so beautiful, how could it not? Taking the body wash from her, I turn her around, so her back is to my front and give myself a pep talk, trying to cool my body heat and the electricity that has surged straight to my manhood. My angel is tired and the last thing she needs is me worshiping her body although I'm sure it's one thing that would take our minds off tonight's shock. I know she feels my hardness digging into her back because she lets out a little chuckle but instead of chancing my luck, I continue to concentrate on letting my hands and fingers massage the tense muscles in her shoulders. Once I've finished soaping up her back, I let it rinse then move to our little bump gently giving the same loving touch. When she's all done, I quickly shampoo her hair then let my angel take over and as she tenderly runs her hands over my rigid frame, I relax into her touch.

Holly's touch bewitches me. Like magic she has the ability to bring out the savage beast in me. Where we tear at each other's clothes. Bite and scrape at each other's skin. Lust running wild, electricity flowing like wildfire through our veins. Our bodies moulded together until you can't tell where one of us begins and the other one ends. A feeling so intense our love making can be heard like animals in the wild. Or my angel can and does calm the beast in me. When I'm stressed and highly strung her warming touch relaxes me. When I'm irritated the feel of her soothes me like nothing else can and as, she continues to work her magic, massaging the shampoo into my hair, I groan loudly and thank God for this woman that I cannot live without.

Stepping out of the shower, I retrieve a towel and wrap it around my waist then take another one and lovingly pat Holly dry. I grab one of my T shirts for Holly and a pair of boxers for myself while she dries her hair. Once she's finished, we slip into bed. Wrapped in each other's arms; needing a good night's sleep. I know whatever the outcome, Holly will be with me every step of the way.

Chapter 6
Vlad

Having time to digest the news that I may be the father of a three-year-old boy that I knew nothing about up until seventy-two hours ago has left me feeling so many emotions that I'm struggling to know which way is up and which way is down.

The morning after I found out about him, I took the paternity test and I've been like a cat on hot bricks since; this morning being no exception. Two days seem to drag on forever when you're waiting on news that may change your life. I say change your life because if he is mine then there's no doubt in my mind that taking on a small boy who has lost his mum, maybe never had a man in his life, isn't going to be easy. Oh, I'll bond with him and love him, that won't be a problem. However, how can I put this on Holly?

Yeah, she has a big heart, huge and she says we'll be in this together, but I feel I'm asking too much of her. She's already took Lucas on as her own and I know she loves him dearly. She shows so much love to my older sons, Izzy and my grandchildren then in less than three months' time she'll be having a child of her own. Our child, the one we created together which I know she will love with all her heart; we both will but she's going to need all her energy to take care of our new-born baby and it worries me that taking on another child that isn't her own will be too much for her.

I love all my sons equally and if he is mine then I will love him the same. I would never want him to think I didn't want him because I do, but at what cost?

"Vlad your phone," Holly's soft, caring voice brings me out of my torment and I relax at the gentle touch of her hand on my arm. As I place it to my ear four pairs of dark blue eyes study me from the dining room table, my sons eager to learn whether they have another brother.

"Yes," I answer, my voice low, and as I listen to the police officer telling me that the test is back and it's ninety-nine-point-nine percent sure that I am his biological father, Holly wraps both her arms around me and lays her head on my chest. "Okay," I say then listen carefully to what PC Grimes tells me. Once she's finished, I place my phone back on the breakfast bar and lower my face into Holly's hair. Inhaling deeply her sweet smell, gaining strength to take on this challenge. Hoping, praying and needing my family to rally together so that this little boy has a loving stable homelife.

Holly's eyes catch mine when I move my face from her hair and she gently puts her hands on the sides of my face, bringing my mouth to hers. She places a soft kiss at the side of my lips, "Everything will be fine love," she reassures me, letting me know that I'm not alone.

"Paps," Sebastian gets my attention as he stands and strides towards me, a look of concern on his face. I don't need to tell him that the three-year-old boy, that I've never seen, whose name I don't know or who is taking care of him, is my son and his younger brother. "Sit down," he says, pulling out a chair from the table that he has led me to. I rub my hands up and down my face, feeling his hand on my shoulder and Holly's warm hand holding mine. She sits at the side of me, threading our fingers together and I bring our entwined hands to my mouth, kissing her knuckles then place them in my lap.

"Well?" Daniel says, wanting to hear me say what they already know. I just nod my head.

"Fucking hell," Nicholas shakes his head, blowing out a breath.

"Dad..." Lucas joins us, standing by Holly's side. "When can we see him and bring him home?" he asks as he pulls out the chair next to her. His innocent face looks up at me as if that's all there is to this.

For me to go wherever he is staying and bring him home here, but I don't think it's as easy as that.

"I don't think it's as easy as that, Lucas," Holly confirms what I thought, knowing a lot more about this type of situation than I do. "I think they might be some paperwork to go through then supervised visitation while he's getting used to all of us. It's going to be a little scary for him coming to a new home, so we need to show him he's loved."

"Well that's easy enough. He's our little brother. Why would we not love him?" he says, looking around the table where his three older brothers nod at him, their smiles wide.

"What did they say?" Nicholas asks.

"That the test proves that I'm his father and that they need to speak with me about a few things. They're coming over in an hour…"

"Are they bringing him with them?" Daniel cuts in with.

"No, they just said that they needed to discuss a few things before we can see him."

"How are you feeling?" Holly places her hand on my thigh and gives it a reassuring rub.

"I'm feeling overwhelmed by it all. I don't even know his name or what his favourite food is. Then there's you lot," I point at my sons. "I don't deserve you…"

"Shut up," Sebastian rolls his eyes and shakes his head at me. "Dad, shit happens, and we deal with it. Men and women have one night stands all the time." He shrugs his shoulders, giving me a tight smile. "Then years later you find out you have a son or daughter you knew nothing about."

"He's right," Holly agrees. "I never knew my biological father and whoever he is, I don't think he is aware he has a daughter out there." My arms wrap around her, she's not upset about it, I think she got over not knowing her real father a long time ago. She's never mentioned him.

"Holly, are you ok with this?" She gives me a look as if to say are you stupid then puts her hand on my chest.

"What? Am I ok that you have another son? Yes. What's one more?" She chuckles when she glances at my sons who are all smiling at her. "More the merrier. Am I ok that the poor little bugger will not have a clue what's going on? No." She shakes her head. "That's why as a family we need to show him he is loved and wanted," she explains, a softness in her voice but it's also an order and I know any trepidation I had about this being too much for her I need to get right out of my head because she'd kick my arse if she knew what I'd been thinking.

"Fucking hell, it's going to be like *the little old woman who lived in a shoe* in here," Nicholas laughs.

"What?" I ask, not having a clue what or who he is waffling on about. Holly laughs a long with him then gives me that smirk that tells me I'm going to bear the brunt of their daft humour.

"Have you not heard about the little old woman who lived in a shoe she had so many children she didn't know what to do?" She bites her lip, holding back her laughter and Nicholas high fives her.

"No, I haven't," I roll my eyes at them. "There's something wrong with you too," I joke. "And I'm no little old woman or little old man."

"We know, love," Holly pats my chest. "Just trying to lighten the mood."

"I know. Thank you. All of you."

An hour later PC Grimes arrives, she's not with Mr Stanton, the guy from child services, she has another police officer with her. He's a huge motherfucker and I wonder whether she's brought him because of my reaction the first night they turned up. They needn't have bothered; I've got my head around it now. He introduces himself as PC Miles and shakes my hand. As I lead them into the sitting room, Daniel offers them a drink. They both want coffee black and take a seat on the opposite settee to Holly and me. I tell them that my sons are joining us as this concerns them too and they both agree.

"Where's Mr Stanton?" Holly asks.

"He's taking care of some necessary paperwork, he will meet with us later," Joanne states. I nod my head, understanding that he has probably got a lot to sort through and god knows how many other cases he has to deal with. As I'm sure these two do as well.

"So, you said you have some things to discuss with me before I meet my son," I say, wanting to hurry them along. Daniel brings in their coffees and as they both take a sip; I see unease on their face, their eyes are troubled.

"What's wrong?" I ask, my voice firm.

"Mr Petrov this case is very delicate," Joanne explains. "Your son, Max, that's his name…" she stops a moment, letting me take it in. Holly squeezes my hand when I say his name out loud. "Max lost his mum six months ago and for that six months he has been living with his older brother Mathew and his dad." I nod, blowing out a long breath because my instincts tell me I'm not going to like what I'm about to hear and from how tight Holly is holding my hand she thinks the same.

"Please get to the point. Don't drag this out whatever it is," I express, rubbing my hand over my two-day old stubble. Both police officers glance at each other as PC Miles sits up straighter, nodding his head.

"Ten days ago, we were called to a house because the tenant had been hearing a dog whimpering and howling on and off for a couple of days and wasn't quite sure where it was coming from. She also told us she thought she could hear the cries of a small boy. We knocked on a few doors and eventually found where the dog was. Unfortunately, that's not all we found."

Holly sniffles, already imagining what the officers found and I hear Sabastian curse. My arms automatically wrap around her as I try to stay focused and calm because now is not the time for my anger to rear its ugly head. "Please continue," I tell them as Daniel takes a seat at the other side of his step mum, handing her a tissue.

"Mathew, the older boy, was laid unconscious in the living room. From our initial findings he'd sustained some head injuries and had lost quite a lot of blood."

"Fuck," I curse, shaking my head as I try not to envisage what the poor boy had gone through. While I try to put out of my head that my boy had endured the same attack, Holly speaks.

"Who did this to him?" her voice quivers as she tightly holds my hand.

"His father," the police officer says and the way he has just spat out the words like they were poison on his lips shows he is as sickened as the rest of us.

"And what about Max?" I ask, still trying to stay calm but I'm getting more agitated by the minute, knowing a grown man has attacked his own son, leaving him hurt and alone. Then there's Max, my son...

"He was in his bedroom with the door shut, we think he'd climbed out of his cot but couldn't reach to open the door," Joanne the policewoman explains. "An ambulance was phoned for both boys because besides Mathews' injuries both of them were showing signs of dehydration."

"Had my son been hurt?" Although I don't want to hear that he was, I need to know the truth.

"They were some old bruising to his wrists and the tops of his arms, as if he'd been grabbed or held too hard, as well as some faint marks on his body but they were no new marks to say that he'd also been assaulted at the same time as his brother."

On the outside, I look composed but on the inside I'm anything but. I'm tying myself in knots with thoughts, hoping these beatings were not regular. Of course, they were. She's just said Max had old bruises on his arms. I take a couple of deep breaths and rub Holly's back who's struggling with the information that we have been given then I blow out a shuddering breath.

"Let me get this straight. Mathew was beaten by his own father and left alone in the house while my son was left in his cot alone." Both police officers look sick to their stomach as they nod their head and I have so much respect for them because I don't know how they cope with the job they do. The things they must see day in day out. It sickens me how people can be so cruel to children.

"How long were they left?" My voice is low and croaky as I try to hold back my emotions.

"A couple of days," PC Miles answers as PC Grimes phone pings. She glances at her message then slips the phone back in her pocket.

"Do you have him in custody?" Nicholas asks, gritting his teeth as he stands between both settees, his arms folded over his broad chest and his dark eyes saying exactly what I am thinking. *I will rip the fucker apart who did this but not before I've watched the colour drain from his face. Not until I see fear run through him so violently, I can hear his cowardly bones shake while his blood runs cold, terror gripping him tightly as he struggles to breath and when he is on his knees begging for forgiveness. When his eyes are bulging from their sockets then I will take great pleasure in letting him know my name and who I am and why I am ending his life.*

"Not yet, but there is a warrant out for his arrest," Joanne interrupts my thoughts as she takes in my sons' reactions. There's a growl that rumbles from Sebastian's chest, Nicholas snarls sarcastically and Daniel curses loudly. The sadness for both boys gripping at their hearts. They have always been brought up to defend and protect one another and even though they haven't met either of the boys yet, they've taken them on as family. Anger towards the man who has hurt Max and Mathew will be tearing away at them. They may have been brought up around violence and crime, but I've always made sure they were never involved and kept them within the law. But this is different.

"Mr Petrov," PC Miles speaks. "We know this is hard for you and your family, but you must focus on Max and leave us to do our job. We will find him," he pronounces the last sentence, letting me know they are not taking this lightly.

Holly lets go of my hand as she stands up, wiping at her eyes wet. "Don't worry," she glares at me, her words firm, and I know whatever I want to do to him won't happen. Holly means everything to me and she's carrying my child, I will not upset her any more than she already is. "No one will be taking the law into their own hands." She stops and turns to my sons, giving them the same look she gave me. They take heed of her words and nod their heads. She may not be their mother, but they listen to her. She may be tiny in size to their huge build but that doesn't scare her in the slightest. She will not stand by and watch them get in any trouble and I love her even more for that. I nod my head at the police officer, agreeing to leave it to them although I'm not comfortable with how I am feeling. I may not want to upset Holly by taking the law into my own hands but if I come face to face with this man, I cannot promise that I won't hurt him.

"Are both boys in the hospital?" Holly asks as she sits back down, taking back my hand in hers.

"Yes. They're sharing a room; Max has the staff eating out of the palm of his hand. He's adorable. The hospital had him on a drip for a few days getting fluids back into his body, he was very shy to start with and cried for his brother…"

"Did they not keep them together when they first brought them in?" Sebastian interrupts Joanne. This will be causing my sons all kinds of pain. No matter what has gone on in their lives they've always been kept together. When Lucas was in and out of hospital, they didn't want to leave his side even now as old as they are, they're hardly ever apart. Working at the clubs, going to the gym, if they're not here they're at Sebastian's and even though Nicholas and Daniel have a small apartment they are rarely there.

"When they were admitted Mathew was still unconscious and not very well so until they had him stable it was best to keep them apart. I'm sure the doctors will fill you in but both boys are now out of bed and Max is a lot happier now he is back with his brother."

Involuntarily my hand taps my knee, agitated with what I'm hearing. Anger trying to rear its ugly head. I'm built to protect. My family will forever be everything to me and knowing this is troubling them, pains me. Knowing that I have another son who's only a toddler that I knew nothing about and only finding out because some cowardly bastard has hurt him, breaks my heart. Then there's his older brother, Mathew, whom I'm sure has been the one to take the brunt of this man's anger on many occasions while protecting his younger sibling. Maybe he has had to do the same for his mum over the years.

"Mr Petrov, there's a meeting this afternoon at the hospital." I nod my head at the policewomen while I try to appease the rage, the upset that keeps building within me. Holly senses my unrest and squeezes my hand. Not giving a fuck who is here, I wrap my arms around her and bury my face in her hair, needing her love and strength to calm all these feelings that are threatening to explode like a ticking time bomb.

Everyone is silent while I gather myself and when I look up, I see

I'm not the only one struggling to keep it together.

"As I said, the doctors and child services are meeting at two today and we hope that you and Mrs Petrov will be present. If you have any more questions about the welfare of Max and Mathew, then I'm sure they will be able to answer them."

"Are we allowed at this meeting?" Sebastian asks, pointing between his brothers and himself. His teeth worry at his bottom lip as he rubs at his forehead. My eldest has always been a fantastic father, putting his children first. Showering them with love and affection. What he has heard today will not just be overwhelming him but will have alarmed him.

"It's not our call, so I don't know. I'm sorry," Joanne answers, getting up from her seat as she gives my son a tight smile. "I will be there, and I will see what I can do. It's obvious that you're all close and equally concerned. I'm not promising anything," she says, sympathy etched on her face.

She hands me a piece of paper, written on it is the department and the floor where we need to be. She then tells me to contact her if there's anything we need. I shake both PC Grimes and PC Miles' hand, thanking them. My family do the same then I see them out of the door. As I make my way into the kitchen I take in a very deep breath and hold it. When I let it slowly out, rubbing at the back of my neck, Holly walks straight into my arms, laying her head on my chest.

"Are you ok?" her soft voice vibrates into my chest as her love wraps around me. Calming me.

"I don't know," I answer as I breath into her hair. "I feel as if I've been put through the washer then hung out to dry in a force-ten hurricane." Her arms come up to wrap around my neck and I lower my head, burying it in the crook of her neck, trying to shake off this fear that keeps coming over me. That taking on a three-year-old boy, my son, may be too much for Holly, he is bound to have some issues. Will she cope? Will I cope?

"Dad, Holly, we need to talk," I rub at my temples as Nicholas calls from the kitchen, grabbing our attention. Making our way through, my four sons look as thick as thieves, their expressions tell me they all have something to say.

I stand behind Holly, my hands stroking our bump, staring at my sons who I love deeply and would do anything to make sure they were safe, struggling with the knowledge that Mathew's father was the one that hurt him and Max. My own father was the vilest of men. Evil. Wicked. A terrible father and I place this man that beat these children, left them alone and hungry up there with him. Sickening.

"Dad, what are we going to do about Mathew?" Sebastian asks, pity for the boy adamant in his eyes.

"What do you mean?" My hand rubs at Holly's belly as our baby who is already a lot like her mother; doesn't like to be kept out of anything, gives a little kick. My wife places her hand on top of mine, aware that our little one is wanting to get in on the conversation. A smile graces my face and I kiss the side of Holly's neck as we both feel our daughter, *fingers crossed*, kicking away.

"Well, let's just say if something had happened to you while we were growing up," Holly flinches at what he has just said and I shake my head not wanting to contemplate the thought, "would you have wanted us separated?" He points around the breakfast bar where they are all stood, their dark blue eyes questioning.

"God, no. Never. Why would you ask that?" Holly moves out of my arms towards the fridge and grabs a bottle of water then returns to me and rubs my back, offering me the first drink. "No thank you," I say, pulling her back to where she was then fix my gaze on my sons.

"When Max is allowed to come home here, have you thought what will happen to Mathew, his older brother, who probably has no one to take care of him?"

"Jesus." I rub the back of my neck. I hadn't given it a thought at all. "Fuck," I shake my head. "No, I haven't," I growl, angry with myself for not considering what he must be going through. If he is aware that they have found me, then he knows his little brother could be taken away from him. A pain shoots straight from my gut to my chest. This just goes from bad to worse. How can I separate two brothers? I can't.

"Well maybe you should because nobody would have taken these away from me without a fight on their hands." I can tell he is serious. I know he is serious. None of them would have let it happen.

"He may have grandparents, other relatives who have already sorted out where he is going to live." I hope. "I can organise visits…"

"And maybe he doesn't or maybe he does, and they are just like his fucking father. Scum," Nicholas grits his teeth, putting in his two pence worth. It's very rare you see him this worked up, so I let go of my wife and make my way to him, putting my hand on his shoulder.

"Don't worry, I'm not going to leave him on his own," I say then pull him in for a fatherly hug. To them what I've just said is a promise because throughout their lives I have never said I'd do something then gone back on my word.

"Let's get ready for the hospital," Holly says, tears welling in her eyes as she sniffles. Lucas moves straight to her side ready to comfort the woman he looks at as his mother. "Thank you," she whispers, placing her arm around his shoulders when he gives her a tissue. She wipes her nose then kisses the top of his head. "I think we should all go. You could all go to the café and if you're allowed in the meeting then I'll come and get you or phone you to let you know where we are," she says. They all agree but she doesn't need to tell them where we will be, they know that part of the hospital like the back of their hands, they spent enough time there with Lucas when we first came to England. Which has me thinking if Dave knows anything, it's the department he works in. "We can ask Mr Stanton if Mathew has any family or if they have a place for him."

"Place, what do you mean?" I query, not fully understanding how the system works.

"If he has grandparents or any other family then if they want him, he will go live with them and probably won't have a say in the matter. You also need to be aware that if they are the biological family of Max then they could fight you for custody."

"Like fuck they will!" I roar. "Where the fuck were they when these boys were been beaten and starved," I shake my head, blowing out a breath as I try to calm down. "At least I have an excuse, I didn't know Max existed until a couple of days ago… "

"I know. I know," Holly complains, standing in front of me, her hand on my chest, her eyes downcast.

"Aw angel, I'm so fucking sorry, I wasn't shouting at you, sweetheart." I take her in my arms, my sons shaking their heads at me for being a twat. I could kick myself. "It's a lot to take in at the moment…"

"I know," she stops me. "I just wanted to prepare you if the worst comes to the worst." I place a soft kiss on her lips and she excepts, letting me know I'm forgiven. I fucking love this woman with all my heart, hurting her again is never going to happen. I need to think before I speak. "However, I'm sure they don't have anyone otherwise I don't think Mathew would have given the piece of paper with your name on to the doctor."

"I don't understand why Max's mum didn't try to find you when she found out she was pregnant?" Daniel questions. "It's not like she didn't know your name." Obviously out of my three eldest he is the naive one and doesn't understand when two consenting adults have a one-night stand then that is all it is supposed to be. Only sometimes this happens, and I wish she would have looked me up.

"Okay," Sebastian rolls his eyes at his younger brother. "I'm going to ring Izzy to keep her up to date then I think instead of speculating about things none of us are sure about we should just wait until you have spoken with the powers that be."

"I agree," Holly says, and I take her in my arms again, placing my lips on hers, still upset with myself for raising my voice at her even if I didn't mean it to come across that way.

"I'm going to give Dave a quick call, just to see if he has heard anything." I shrug my shoulders, taking my phone from my back pocket.

"Couldn't do any harm. I'm sure if he can tell you anything, he will do, but his hands might be tied with red tape."

"Hmmm," I think Sebastian's right. I've known Dave a long time and we've become good friends. I think if he knew anything and was able to tell me then he would have been calling me.

Chapter 7

Holly

Finally, we're led to an office on the third floor of the children's department. We arrived forty minutes ago and came straight to where we needed to be, Vlad knowing the hospital very well due to Lucas spending lots of time here when he was a baby. We were told that the meeting had been put back thirty minutes as the doctor was running late and to take a seat.

Joanne, the police liaison officer, turned up five minutes ago, giving her apologies for our wait then led us straight to the office where we will be meeting with Mr Stanton from the child services and the doctor who's been taking care of both Mathew and Max.

Joanne gives a light tap on the door and pushes it open without being asked to come in. Clearly, they knew we were here. Stopping Vlad before we go in, I take hold of his arm, "Are you ok?" I ask, genuinely concerned for him. This news has hit him hard. It's one thing to be told you might be the father of a three-year-old that you knew nothing about. It's a shock. Then to be told that you definitely are, well you've probably started coming to terms with it from the initial revelation. But to be told that this little boy and his older brother have lost their mum, then been mistreated by someone who was supposed to be one of the boy's father is hard to comprehend without becoming angry and agitated. I understand that Vlad is used to dealing with men like him in a certain way, but I can't let him do that. He needs to focus all that built-up energy into being the father that little boy deserves and reassure Mathew he won't be left on his own. I agree with Vlad and his sons that these boys can't be split up and although Vlad is scared that this is all too much for me, it isn't. How could it be?

God knows where I would be if my adopted parents had not taken me in, giving me a loving caring home. Helping me to get over whatever I'd endured at a very young age. And they did just that, then, when they were taken from me, Jay, Ivy, Jack, Nick, Olivia, and Sarah stepped in without a second thought, giving me yet another loving family. One that I'm so grateful for and love with all my heart. Vlad is a very passionate man with lots of love in that huge heart of his and his sons have inherited that from him. Whether it's love for whomever they claim as they partner or for each other, it's palpable. And I count myself extremely lucky that I am a part of it. Therefore, without a shadow of a doubt I know these boys will be given the love and care they need and flourish amongst it.

"I'm good," he says, lightly squeezing my hand as he sends me a wink and raises his lip, letting me know he's got this. He'd been as nervous as hell while we were sat waiting, now he's calm and ready to get on with this meeting.

Once we step into the office there's no need for introduction as Dave, Lucas' old doctor and good friend of Vlad's, strides quickly towards my husband with his hand out.

"It's good to see you, Vlad," he greets, shaking his hand and slapping him on the back.

"And you, Dave. Didn't think I'd be in here seeing you again," he glances around the small office, familiar with his surroundings. Vlad had spent many long days and nights while his youngest was hospitalized due to his immune system not being able to cope with a simple cold. Of course, this was all due to him being addicted to drugs when he was born but with the help of the doctors in Russia, then Dave and his team here in England, as well as the love of his father and brothers, he got through it.

"No neither did I. I do prefer to see your ugly mug on the golf course or over a beer." Vlad chuckles at his humour as Dave's warm brown eyes switch to me. "Holly you look really well and as beautiful as ever. How was the honeymoon?" he asks, smiling as he directs Vlad and I to sit down while he takes a seat on the opposite side of his desk.

"It was beautiful, thank you," I say, realising that Mathew and Max must have been brought in here the day after our wedding and that Dave will have found out that Max might have been Vlad's son just after we came back from our honeymoon. "Paris is a very romantic city."

"Yes, it is. Been a few times with Marie," he smiles, nodding his head.

Once we are all seated Vlad takes hold of my hand placing it on his knee as he threads our fingers together. Dave shuffles a few sheets of paper around his desk then sets his sights on Vlad. "Right, let's get down to a more serious note," he states, clearing his throat. "First let me apologise... You understand, Vlad, why I wasn't able to ring you directly myself when we found out that you might be Max's father, I am sorry, but my hands were tied." He gives Vlad a sympathetic smile and leans back in his chair, rolling up his sleeves.

Nodding his head, Vlad speaks, "Of course, I understand. This has all happened so fast, I didn't know for sure until this morning that I was definitely his father or that he was here at the hospital... " His voice trails off as he inhales deeply then blows out the air slowly. "I know if things were different you would have done."

"Yes, it has all happened very quickly. The boys had been here a week before Mathew gave us the piece of paper with your name on. However, as I was telling Mr Stanton before you arrived, Max is a lovely little boy and smart for his age," his eyes brighten when he smiles. "He's quite a character, now he has gotten used to all the staff, likes to keep them on their toes with his mischief."

"And how's Mathew doing?" I ask, concerned that he might not be doing as well as his younger brother.

"He's on the mend," sadness passes over his face as he says it. "Vlad, I need to tell you how surprised but relieved I was when Mathew told us how he found your name with Max's birth certificate indicating that you might be his father. As a doctor I see many parents, a lot of them single parents. Some of them cope just fine and some struggle, but you... I've known you a long time and seen how you have cared for a baby who was extremely ill, kept two boisterous teenage boys in order as well as dealing with a nine-year-old who struggled with the change of coming to a new country, losing his mum and starting a new school." Dave has some insight into Vlad's past but nothing that could incriminate him.

"Not once did any of them not have your attention and love while you were back and forth coming here and running a business. You and your boys stuck together and supported each other, and I know that has never changed over the years. Your family have a lot of love to give." He smiles as Vlad nods his head at the truth.

"Thank you. I will always love and take care of my family. There's nothing I wouldn't do for them," his loving eyes turn to me as he lifts my hand to his lips, placing a soft kiss on my knuckles.

"I know. And I also know that you, Holly, and your family will give Max the care and love that he needs," he runs his hand through his greying hair and takes a drink of the glass of water that's on his desk. "But... " His eyes move from Vlad to Mr Stanton who's yet to say anything then he focuses on Vlad again.

"That's a very big but, Dave," Vlad says, addressing him as the man he plays golf with or drinks with. He's known the doctor for a number of years. I'd bet that he was out with Vlad the night Max was conceived.

"Yes, it is. And I'm probably speaking out of turn here but it's not just about Max. His brother Mathew isn't coping well. He wants Max to have the loving home he needs but he doesn't want to lose him, he has no one else..."

"That's not going to happen," I say, firmly butting in.

"No, it is not," Vlad confirms as he gives my hand a gentle squeeze. We're adamant we will do anything to keep them together. Dave smiles, nodding his head. He knows Vlad and his sons well enough to know that they will have discussed this matter at some length, he is also aware of my childhood and that I was adopted. This is what he wanted for us, to take on both boys. "Holly and I will do all we can to make sure that the boys stay together, they don't need any more added stress."

"I'm sure you are more than capable of giving both Max and

Mathew a loving home," Mr Stanton states, giving Dave a sideways glance. "However, that is not how this works as I'm sure you are aware, Dr Young. We cannot just place a child into the care of a family that are not registered with us. There's a process..."

"Mr Stanton," my husband rudely interrupts him, not happy with being told what he can and cannot do, especially when it involves two children who need a loving stable home. "Maybe you're right and there are procedures to follow before we can make this happen but as I have already said we will do whatever it takes to make sure my son and his brother are kept together. So, as soon as we have been able to see Max, I hope I will be able to speak with Mathew and get to know him. I want to reassure the poor boy that I'm not here to take his brother from him, no matter what the outcome." Mr Stanton eyes soften at Vlad's words. We know his job is to protect these boys from anymore unnecessary hurt, taking care of their welfare is paramount.

"As I have said, I'm sure you will do whatever it takes to give Mathew and Max a stable home but we're getting a little ahead of ourselves, there's still a lot of enquiries to be made and we do..."

"We know this, Nile," Dave interrupts, calling Mr Stanton by his first name, obviously it's not the first time the doctor has had dealings with him. He's a decent man, caring, but he is a professional and wants to play this by the book which I'm sure he is legally obliged to do. "But I still think Mathew should be given the choice, he is nearly sixteen and after speaking with him earlier I know that he wants to speak with Vlad before he meets Max. If they meet today..." Mr Stanton raises an eyebrow at Dave's suggestion and interrupts him.

"I will agree to this, but I don't want the boy given any false hopes. I've heard what you have said, however in my job words are not always good enough and children get let down. It's not easy taking on a teenager who is troubled, especially when you will have Max to take care of and a baby on the way. I suggest you let him do the talking which won't be much because at the moment he is still very withdrawn and doesn't trust easily. We're not sure what has happened over the last six months, he is reluctant to tell us everything, so we can only piece things together from the titbits he has told us and the information we have been given from his school.

Do you understand, Mr Petrov?"

"Yes, of course. I'm eager to meet him but I'm not here to cause him anymore pain. And just for the record I have brought up four boys, one of which is still a teenager and as the good doctor here has mentioned, it hasn't always been easy." Mr Stanton nods his head at Vlad's statement, oblivious to Vlad's past. Saying that, I don't think he is talking about their life in Russia. Considering what I know about my husband and his sons since they came to live in England then I would agree that they've had obstacles to overcome when the boys were younger.

"Before I see Mathew is there anything between the last six months and him ending up in here that you can enlighten me on, I don't want to put my foot in it? At least then I'll be able to tread carefully." Dave stands from his chair and walks round to the side of his desk and perches on the edge of it, so he is nearer to Vlad.

"Mathew had been here a couple of days, too poorly to comprehend what had happened to him and his brother, but once he was coherent everything came back to him rather quickly. The poor boy was beside himself thinking that his little brother had come to harm. So, we knew straight away how protective of Max he was. Is." Vlad nods his head, understanding brotherly love. "He soon calmed down when Max was brought into his room. Joanne and I spoke with him about his family and found out there was no one for these boys. Without a thought for himself he gave me your name, knowing his brother would have someone who might care for him..."

"Can you tell us anything about Mathew's parents?" Vlad asks. "What kind of life both boys have had and why their mother never tried to find me when she found out she was pregnant with my child?" Vlad swallows hard, his jaw set firm as his lips form a thin line. He wants answers and I understand why.

"Mr Petrov," the policewoman says as her eyes circumspectly glance at Mr Stanton, him giving a concise nod. "We're still making enquiries into why these two boys ended up with Mathew's father when he hadn't been on the scene for a number of years. All we can tell you at the moment is that Mathew's father was abusive towards Miss Rogers, the boy's mother, for a number of years and it wasn't until Mathew was ten that she left him. From what Mathew told us, one night, while his mum and dad were arguing, he jumped in the way to protect his mum which ended up with him been on the other end of his father's fist. Although Mathew had been subjected to hearing and seeing the violence towards his mother it was the first time he'd been hit."

"Did she not think to call the police and have him arrested?" I query.

"We have no record of any domestic violence been reported. We do know through Mathew that when his father left that evening to go out to the pub, Miss Rogers packed a suitcase and left, taking Mathew with her. As Miss Rogers had no other family, she travelled up here to Yorkshire and stayed with an old friend for a few years until she could afford a place of their own. I'm assuming it was around that time when she met you and fell pregnant with Max." Vlad nods his head, acknowledging the time scale to when he met Mathew's mum.

"So, when she was hit by the car where were the children?" he asks, concerned for their welfare.

"At the time of the accident there was no witnesses and no camera footage in that area, so we believed Miss Rogers had been alone and it was a hit and run..."

"You never mentioned hit and run when you told us that she'd been knocked over and killed."

"Oh, God," my hand covers my mouth as Vlad's body tenses at the side of me. Who would do such a thing?

"Have you not caught the person who did this?" his voice is raised, barely keeping it together.

"No. But we now think that it could have been Mathew's father..."

"Fucking hell! This just gets worse."

"Vlad," I sooth, rubbing his arm trying to calm him down but I do understand why he is getting worked up. We weren't told that it was a hit and run and now from what she's just said it could have been on purpose.

"Mr Petrov this is all speculation at the moment, there's no concrete evidence to place Mathew's father at the scene of the crime. All we have to go on is that when Mathew arrived home from school that evening his dad was at the house taking care of Max. He was told that his mum was shopping. He didn't query as to why his dad had turned up out of the blue, he just assumed when his dad had said that his mother had agreed to talk with him and reconcile their differences, he was speaking the truth. Then about an hour after he had got home from school the police called and told them the tragic news about his mother." Vlad covers his mouth with his hand, shaking his head. He's seen and heard some terrible things in his life, he has done some terrible things, but hurting women and children was one of the things that turned him against his father. It didn't matter that it was indirectly, his father might not have been out on the streets selling the drugs, but it was him supplying them.

"Mathew told us that before the funeral his dad was taking care of them..."

"Did no one question where he had come from or where he had been over the last few years?" Vlad asks, cutting in.

"Not one. But questions should have been asked because he is known to the police and it seems a little strange that he turned up out of the blue on the day of Miss Rogers' death." Her words *known to the police* drag me into another world and I don't hear anything else she says as I think about Vlad's world in Russia. Is he known to the police? How the hell will he be able to foster if he has got any kind of criminal record? I don't even know how he was allowed to stay here, I'm sure there's some law that would have stopped him being able to live in England. It's something we've never talked about.

"Holly, are you ok, sweetheart?" Vlad crouches in front of me, taking my hands in his, a worried look on his face.

"What? Yes." I shake my head and cover my mouth, "I'm sorry it's all a lot to take in, I'm a little overwhelmed." It's not exactly a lie.

Dave passes Vlad a glass of water and he places it to my lips. "Take a sip, Holly," he orders while smoothing my hair back, his loving eyes watching me carefully. "Feeling better?" he asks after a few minutes.

"Yes, thank you." He tilts his head, still gazing into my eyes, studying me. He knows there's something bothering me but now is not the time to be asking him questions, so I stand. "I need the ladies."

"Okay. Would you like me to take you home so you can have a rest?"

"No. Honestly I'm fine. I'll join the boys in the café while you go see Mathew." I place my hand on his chest as he helps me up from my chair.

"You don't want to come with me?" He questions, lowering his eyebrows as his thumb strokes over my knuckles. Well, yes. I would love to go meet them both, but I think Dave and Mr Stanton wanted Vlad to go alone for the first meeting and I can understand that. Don't want the situation to be too overwhelming and I can assure you it would be because as soon as I see them, I will be blubbering like a teenager who's just been dumped by her first crush.

"I think it's better if you go alone on your first visit. There's plenty of time for the boys to meet Holly and your sons," Mr Stanton says, standing from his seat. "Plus, I think your wife could do with a little fresh air. A breather from it all." Dave nods in agreement and moves towards the door, opening it.

"Take Holly to the café, Vlad, then meet me back here." Vlad follows him out of the door, keeping hold of my hand. Once we're out into the corridor he turns to Joanne and Mr Stanton.

"Thank you, for all your help," his voice is low and appreciative.

"You're welcome, Mr Petrov," Mr Stanton says, stepping past me. "I have another meeting to get to, but PC Grimes will be joining you and I will be in contact with her later to see how everything has gone. If all is well then I'll be in touch and we can move forward with the next steps." He doesn't say anymore, satisfied with our meeting he leaves moving on to his next one.

"His hearts in the right place," Dave says, jutting his chin out towards the corner that Mr Stanton just turned, "and it would be in your best interest to follow any advice he gives you because where he cannot tell me how to do my job, I cannot tell him how to do his. I can only keep singing your praise as the father I know you are. You'll always have my support." He smiles and slaps Vlad on the back.

"Thanks Dave," Vlad says, a smile tugging at his lips. I link his arm after saying bye to both Joanne and Dave then we set off to find the ladies.

"Holly what's wrong?" he says once we're out of ear shot, his deep concerned voice warming me to the core. As much as I'm eager to ask the question – does he have a criminal record? – now is not the time to get into such a conversation, so I lie.

"Nothing," I say, tugging on his arm when he comes to a sudden stop and turns me to face him.

"You and the baby ok?" His hands stroke over my swollen stomach.

"Yes, we're good," I smile. I certainly don't want him worrying that there's something wrong with either me or the baby.

"Angel, don't lie to me, if there's a problem you need to tell me," his voice low as he runs his thumb over my chin, hurt in his eyes and a worried frown embedded deep into his forehead. He can see straight through me, I'm no good at lying and Vlad knows this. And now I've added to his stress level.

"It's nothing to worry about," I say, placing my hand on his chest. "We can talk about what it when we get home," I kiss the side of his mouth, hoping that will suffice.

"Ok, but don't lie to me again when it's obvious there is something bothering you." He softly bites my bottom lip then takes my hand, leading us down the corridor towards the ladies.

"Sorry," I murmur, like a scolded child, listening as he lets out a heartfelt sigh.

Chapter 8
Vlad

Seeing Holly drift off into her own little world, her eyes wide and fixed onto Dave's desk while her teeth gnawed at her bottom lip, suggested whatever she was thinking about had worried her. Which undoubtedly worried me. Her telling me it was nothing, a lie that I saw straight through, had me on edge thinking there was something wrong with her or our baby. Once she assured me they were both fine I calmed a little but still wasn't happy that she had lied to me over something that had bothered her during the meeting. What it was? I don't know. But I'm sure it's something that I'm not going to like, otherwise she would have told me then and there instead of wanting to wait until we get home.

"What's bothering you?" Dave questions as we stop outside the door to Mathew and Max's room. "*A fifteen-year-old boy that's scared and hurting, my three-year-old son that I've never met. The fact that they've both been harmed in one way or another, suffering and traumatized. Then there's my wife. Choosing to keep what was troubling her to herself because she didn't want to add anything else to this stressful situation when she should be able to discuss anything with me knowing that I will always take care of it has me feeling like shit.*" I want to say. But I don't.

"I'm good, all things considering," I tell him. "A little nervous but nothing I can't cope with."

"Everything will be fine," he slaps me on the shoulder, smiling as he opens the door and the sound of a small child giggling stops me in my tracks. It's a sound that warmed my heart and filled me with elation, helped me in the dark times of my life, lifted my spirits and pulled me through. My sons. Toddlers. Small boys excited to see me. Chuckling as I spun them around in the air. High pitched, animated screams as we rampaged around the house, chasing, playing, spending quality fun time together. Overwhelmed, my heart swelling, I swallow hard and wipe at my eyes, knowing whatever harm he has come to, he is still happy.

"Sorry Vlad, I thought Max would be in the playroom with the nurse," he says just as a mop of mousy blond hair appears and charges like a bull at Dave's legs.

"Doctor Dave, pway woom, pway woom!" Max squeals as he tugs at Dave's legs, not one bit bothered that he is tugging at mine too. "Pweaseee," he politely says, looking up at Dave with eyes that I've seen many times before. Looking down at Max, if I hadn't been told he was mine then just seeing those huge dark blue eyes, the shape of his nose and mouth, I would have guessed anyway. All my sons have inherited these from me, Max being no exception. His long eyelashes flicker as he waits for a response, a wide toothy smile pulling at his lips. I want to reach down and take him in my arms, breath him in and hug him tightly like I did with my boys when they were his age, even now they all still expect a fatherly hug from me.

"Come on, Max," the nurse says, stopping me from reaching for him which is for the best really because I need to reassure the boy who silently stands, hands in his pockets, his shoulders tense as he stares, unblinking at me, that I'm not the bad guy here. I'm here for him as well as my son.

"I'll take him to play for a little while," she says, taking hold of Max's hand, him squealing with delight as they make their way out of the door past PC Grimes who ruffles his hair as he pulls on the nurse's hand eager to play.

"Hi Mathew," Dave says as the door clicks shut. The sound of Max giggling echoing from outside the room has me rubbing at my face to hide my anguish of getting a short glimpse of him for the first time and not being able to cuddle him. I breath in deeply, shaking off the overwhelming hurt then make my way further into the room.

"Wow, my brother is going to be huge," Mathew states, exaggerating the *huge* as he slumps down onto a soft two-seater sofa, a smile now appearing on his face while his eyes take in my size.

"Probably," I smile, taking one of the chairs and placing it near the settee he's sat on, happy the ice has been broken and he doesn't see me as a big bad ogre that's come to steal his brother from him.

"Mathew, this is Mr Petrov who we talked about," Dave says as he sits on the edge of the settee, his focus on the teenage boy. Putting my hand out to greet him properly, I give him a friendly smile.

"It's good to meet you, please call me Vlad." He sits forward, tilting his head at me and stretches out his hand. His handshake is firm and strong for a young lad who's not much bigger than Lucas. Looking at him you wouldn't think he was just getting over an attack, not until his head turns slightly and I spot the small wound at the side, above his right ear. Apart from that he looks healthy enough but who knows what's hiding under his long-sleeved T shirt and inside his head. Both boys have lived with an animal for six months and although I've been given some insight as to what happened to them just recently, this may not be the first time they've been hurt since their mother died.

"Vlad," he says. "What kind of name is that?" It's a genuine question. To a young English lad my name is unusual.

"It's short for Vladimir…"

"You have an accent," he narrows his eyes at me as he sits up straight. "Where are you from?" Dave chuckles at this confident boy who doesn't seem nervous about questioning a man he's only just met and someone who looks like he could snap a tree in half with his bare hands. But the poor boy knows why I'm here and probably wants to know every detail about the man who is his brother's biological father and for all he knows might take him away from him.

"I'm from Russia," I answer him, watching him nodding his head, his light blue eyes widening.

"Are you planning on going back?" His tone is abrupt as he sits forward, glaring at me.

"No." I shake my head, wanting to set his mind at rest but it's the truth, my home is here. "Everyone I care about and love are here, so

I have no reason to. England is my home."

"Ok," he relaxes back into his seat, happy with my answer.

"Wow you could get a job with the police force with all that interrogation, Mathew," PC Grimes says, smiling as she pushes herself off the wall she'd been leant on while we were talking; I forgot she was even there.

Mathew chuckles at her as she gets comfy on one of the beanbags that's scattered on the floor. "He's fine he can ask me anything he wants." I smile, hoping he'll see that I am sincere.

"Do you have any other children?" I like how he says other, at least he has come to terms with me been Max's father.

"Yes," I smile. "I have four more sons. Sebastian is my eldest, he's married to Izzy and they have three children." His mouth falls open and his light blue eyes widen as I continue to tell him about my family. "Nicholas is next, he's twenty-six, he is the joker of the family and most days has me tearing at my hair," I chuckle, and I'm rewarded with a smile from him. "Then there's Daniel who's a musician. Well, he plays the guitar and sings in a band," I joke.

"Cool," he says, his eyes lighting up.

"Lucas is thirteen and still at school," I don't say my youngest because he's not anymore. "He enjoys sketching and loves anything to do with computer games. And I'm sure you and Max will have lots of fun and get along famously with them." I watch Mathew taking in what I just said to him and as he rests his elbow on his knee and pops his chin in his hand, I carry on. "They are very close, we all are. Then there's Holly, my wife. She cares about everything and everyone and has so much love to give that me and my boys are lucky to have her in our lives."

"She's not their mum?" he asks.

"No, but she treats them as if she is, especially Lucas, and they all love her dearly. We do have a baby on the way. I'm hoping for a girl." I smile.

"I'm sure Holly's hoping for a girl," Dave chuckles. "There's a lot of testosterone around your house." Mathew laughs along with Dave, obviously understanding poor Holly is surrounded by males and if he's picked up at what I mentioned earlier they'll be another two.

"Where are they now? Do they know about Max?" he questions, his voice low.

"Yes, they know about the both of you and they're all downstairs in the café. They're very eager to meet you both."

"Can we go for a walk downstairs so I can see them?" his eyes flick from me to Dave then to the policewoman, not sure whose decision it is. "I was allowed yesterday; Sandra went with Max and me." I tilt my head at Dave, unsure to whose call it is and who the hell Sandra is.

"Sandra is one of the nurses that's taking care of Max," he's read my mind. "And I think it would be wise to ring Mr Stanton, he wants to be kept informed… "

"I'll make a call," Joanne says, getting up and making her way towards the door. "Hopefully he won't be at his meeting yet."

Joanne disappears out of the door and Dave gets up from his seat. "Just going to the gents, be back in two minutes. Oh, I think you should spend a bit of time with Max before we meet with your sons, Vlad, then we'll take him with us." I nod my head at him, smiling on the inside, overjoyed that I'll be able to meet my son properly then take him and Mathew to see my family.

Once the door clicks shut there's a short silence and just as I'm about to ask Mathew a few questions, he speaks first.

"Can I ask you a question?" His voice is quiet and not as confident as it was when Dave was here.

"Of course. Anything." I want him to feel comfortable around me and be able to ask me anything, but I know I need to earn his trust, it's early days yet.

"What happened to your sons' real mum?" And a few month ago, I might not have been able to answer that question without feeling some sort of anger for the way she behaved, but not anymore. Now I have put that hatred to rest. However, I can't tell him the whole truth, so I give him the shortened version.

"She died after giving birth to Lucas," it's not a lie.

"Sorry, I shouldn't have asked," he lowers his head, a sadness passing over his face.

"Hey, don't be. I've told you, ask me anything," I try to lighten his mood by giving him a few tales about my sons and grandchildren, but I can see he's still thinking about his mother. Missing her.

"I hate my dad, it should be him that's dead not my mum," he blurts out suddenly, tears welling in his saddened eyes. He wipes at them quickly, not wanting to seem weak in front of me and my chest hurts for him. I'm a father and a bloody good one and I know what I would be doing if it was one of my sons. I would be taking them in my arms and soothing away their pain, only I can't with him. It's not my place. Not yet anyway. So, I do the only thing I can do.

Getting up from the chair, I move and sit at the side of him and knock him with my shoulder, he needs a friend.

"You know, I had the same thoughts about my father." He wipes at his tears again and turns his head to look at me with questioning eyes.

"You did? Why?" he sniffles. Sitting slightly forward in my seat, I place my elbows on my knees and clasp my hands together.

"Like your father, he wasn't a good man." I give him a sideways glance, his eyes now dry and intrigued.

"Did he hurt you?"

"In so many different ways and I hated him until he died and a long time after. But all that energy I wasted on anger, despising him for years, didn't do any good. I should have let it go a long time ago and you will. What you're feeling is natural. I never spoke about my father to anyone, not really, and it slowly ate away at me. It wasn't until Holly came along. She wouldn't put up with my bullshit. She wanted to hear my secrets no matter how dark they were and not judge me. And I wanted to tell her, needed to tell her. And it felt good. So, I can seriously say whatever you're feeling, and take it from someone who's seen a lot of hurt and pain, let it out. Don't hold it in. Talk to someone, go to the gym and knock ten piles of shit out of a punch bag. Use that energy for something good. Something to make your mum proud of you..."

"I miss her..." he mumbles into his hand that's covering his mouth. "So much. We never got to say goodbye and it hurts." He sniffles again, wiping at his face and I don't speak. I want him to let it all out, the poor boy probably hasn't had the chance to grieve for the loss of his mother.

"My dad was there when I came home from school, playing with Max. Even though he isn't Max's dad, he acted as if he cared about him and he was the same with me. I'd missed him, so when he told me that him and my mum were back together, I was happy because he looked as if he'd changed. More put together." He stops for a moment, reflecting on his life. Memories. I see them pass over his face. A whole bunch of them.

"He used to hit her when he'd had a drink, that's why she left him, well that and the fact that one afternoon I jumped in the way and he hit me."

"There's nothing wrong with wanting to defend your mum, shows the man you'll grow into."

"I don't ever want to be like him. Do you know if the police have found him yet?" he asks.

"No, not yet," I shake my head. "But they will do," I reassure him. I hope for his father's sake the police find him before I do.

"I want him to go to prison for what he did to me and for how mean and nasty he was to Max." This kid's breaking my heart. What they must have gone through living with him for six months when they should have been grieving for their mother, needing love and kindness to help them but instead they got a man who was evil.

"Mathew," he looks up at me. "What happened over the six months after your mum died while you were living with your dad?" In one way I don't want to know, I think I know enough but knowing the full story will help me understand the impact of what both boys have gone through. Plus, I don't think he's told the police everything. It will help him to let it all out.

He stays quiet for a while, just staring at me. I know this is hard for him, I'm a stranger. He doesn't know me but sometimes it's easier to talk to someone who you don't know. Someone who won't judge. I glance at the clock on the wall, wondering where Dave and the policewoman have got to and when Mathew stands and wanders over to the window, I think maybe I've asked a little too much of him.

"When the police came to tell us my mum had died," he surprises me when he speaks, turning to look at me, leaning back against the window frame. "I didn't believe it. I mean I'd just seen her that morning before I'd gone to school. She was telling me that she had a day off work and was going to take Max shopping for some new shoes then they were going to visit the park. Max loves to feed the ducks... " He trails off, biting at his lip, his eyes pointed at the ceiling.

"Mathew, we don't have to do this now if it's too upsetting for you, it will wait." He shakes his head, still chomping on his lip then lowers his wet eyes to me.

"My dad seemed distraught for a couple of days, I'd catch him crying," he lets out a sarcastic laugh. "And Max," he blows out a breath and shakes his head. "he didn't understand. He'd cry, go searching round the house for her, calling out for his mummy. Night-time was worse. He'd wake up crying. Screaming, not knowing that she wasn't coming back... " Tears stream down his face and I wipe at my cheeks to catch the ones that are falling too, then I swallow the lump in my throat and listen attentively as he continues.

"My dad would scream and shout at him to shut up, grab him by his tiny arms and shake him... " his lip trembles and he rubs at his face. "I... I tried to stop him many times but he's a lot bigger than me and would push me out of the way. After the funeral it got worse and I couldn't tell anybody... I was scared we'd be taken into care and separated, so every night I put Max in my bed and if he woke up, I was there for him. By this time anyway my dad was drunk most evenings and wouldn't have woken up if Max cried. Then each morning I'd leave the house and take Max with me. We'd go home when we were hungry, and he'd gone out..."

"What about school? Did no one enquire to where you were?" He shakes his head and lowers his eyes to the floor.

"They did but he told them I was grieving for my mother and some other crap about getting me counselling. He'd arrange the dates and not tell me then when I didn't show he'd lie, telling them that I was too upset when all the time I didn't know." Mathew moves from the window and sits back down on the chair where I'd been sat earlier. He picks at some thread on his tatty jeans and lifts his head, his eyes bloodshot and tired.

"A couple of days before he knocked me out, there was hardly any food in the house, and I didn't have any money. I'd told my dad we needed shopping and he got aggressive... Picking things up and throwing them around. Shouting, how it wasn't his place to take care of Max and me then he walked out and left us. We didn't see him for two days. We ate what bread and cereal was left and some mouldy cheese that wasn't fit for a mouse... there was nothing else. I was starving and I knew Max was, he kept crying and telling me his tummy hurt. So, I tried to keep us hydrated by drinking plenty of water. While he was gone, I searched my mum's bedroom that he'd been stopping in just to see if there was any money lying around but there was nothing. All her jewellery was gone; I presumed he'd sold it for beer money. And that's when I found a letter with your name on it. It was with our birth certificates." Smart woman, I think, when he stops speaking. I'm not on Max's birth certificate but anyone with half a brain would know to look into it if they found a man's name with it.

"The evening he came home it was really late. I heard him use the bathroom then go to bed, he didn't even check to see how we were. Max was asleep when I crept into the bathroom. My dad always left his trousers on the floor in there. I checked his pockets and found fifteen quid, so I took it. Knowing he wouldn't be up until after nine, I had our clothes ready to leave early the following morning. Max thought it was a game when I told him he needed to be quiet while we dressed and snuck out of the house," he gives a little smile and I understand why. Kids love games, creeping around and sneaking out. I offer a smile of my own.

"We ate like kings with that fifteen pounds. The café near the park do a fantastic breakfast and the woman behind the counter has a soft spot for Max, so we ended up getting a cupcake for free and free refills on our drinks. She gave us some bread for Max to feed the ducks and I bought us a sandwich to have for our lunch."

"Wow you did well with the money you had, breakfast and lunch," I chuckle at him, I've paid fifteen pounds and more for one breakfast.

"Ah, wait a minute," he smirks. "She only charged me for two kids breakfast even though I did have a man-size portion, so I had enough money for two kids' meals at McD's for our tea." His eyes light up in triumph, knowing they got to eat out all day on such little money.

"Yeah?"

"Yeah," he sighs and the light that was in his eyes a minute ago goes out. "I didn't want to go home and if it had just been me, I wouldn't. I would have taken my chances on the street." I grimace, not wanting to envisage what could have happened to him. Homeless. Then again look what happened when he went home. "But it was cold and wet, we'd been out all day and Max was tired, he needed a sleep. The house was empty when we got home so I took him straight upstairs, gave him a bath, put on his pyjamas and stayed with him until he'd fallen asleep then I went downstairs. Our dog was in the garden, my dad wouldn't allow him in the house, and I knew he needed feeding. He didn't have much dried food left but I had saved him a couple of sausages from our breakfast. I brought him in to get warm and feed him and just after he'd scranned down his food my dad walked in drunk." Mathew blows out a long breath, rubbing his hands up and down his legs then he stands and makes his way over to the window again.

Tucking his hands in his pockets, light blue eyes well up and he blows out another breath. "Mathew," I say, standing then I walk towards him. He puts his hand up, stopping me, shaking his head.

"No. I need to say this, I need to get it out."

"Have you not told the police or the doctors what happened to you?" He shakes his head answering no. I'm shocked. I know they know it was his father. They told me it was.

"They asked, who'd hurt me? And I told them my dad, but I haven't been able to tell them about that night."

"And you want to now?"

"Yes," he says, nodding his head.

"Are you ok telling me, or would you prefer I get Dave or Joanne?" I need to be certain he's okay with this because God knows what he is going to divulge.

"I'm ok telling you."

"Ok."

"He was drunk and when he's drunk, he becomes angry and nasty. Very nasty. He ripped into me straight away about stealing his money and spending it on that little bastard. I could feel myself shaking when he called Max that. I'd never felt how I felt that night. Every ugly word he spoke about Max, about my mum, calling her a whore and other awful words, I wanted to kill him." I can understand that, anybody would. This man had mistreated them for months. Left them without food and then berated his dead mother as well as poor Max.

"When he wasn't looking, I tried to open the kitchen drawer; I'd already played it around in my head how I would kill him. I wanted to stab him. Only he heard the drawer and before I'd got hold of the knife, he slammed it shut on my hand." I hadn't noticed his slightly swollen knuckles until now. Not until he's just rubbed his fingers over his right hand. Must have been some fucking force because he's been in here nearly two weeks. "When I cried out in pain, he punched me in the face and told me I was weak, just a kid that wouldn't amount to anything. I wobbled and fell backwards, catching hold of a stool to steady myself. And without thinking I raised that stool and wacked him as hard as I could. This time it was him who wobbled but he held onto the work surface to right himself then backhanded me across the face. The dog went for him and he kicked it against the wall that hard that he didn't move. Then he turned on me again. I remember wrestling with him, punch after punch to my ribs." He lifts his T shirt and there are still marked from his father's cowardly attack. I grimace and cover my mouth, wanting revenge on the poor excuse of a man who did this.

"I couldn't breathe, then I remember been thrown and my head hitting the side of the cabinet and I blacked out." He lowers his head into his hands and I'm up out of my seat. As gently as I can I wrap my arms around him, giving him a fatherly hug, a motherly hug, just comfort to let him know he's not alone.

"Mathew," I say when I let go of him, lifting his chin to look at me. "You are not weak. You are a strong young man, one that your mother would be proud of. You were never going to beat a man like him." I wipe a tear from his cheek with my thumb. Knowing his father fights dirty, hitting this young man with words that would hurt him, drawing out an anger that he didn't know how to use but one day when he's older, men like his dad he will beat without a thought. Without having to raise his fist.

"When you're older you will understand how not to let words hurt you and to retaliate without violence." He nods his head at me. "And just so you know, you and Max will not be separated because I will promise to you that I will do all I can to make sure both of you stay together under my roof and you will never have to see your father again." I knock him under the chin playfully, "If that's what you want?" he stares at me for a moment, then nods his head.

"I'd like that."

"Good. But you know we will need to go through the proper channels, and I haven't got the foggiest idea what I'm doing. However, my solicitor and my wife do. Which is good because they're like a dog with a bone when they want something," he chuckles at the comparing of Holly and Zach, my heart swelling that I've been able to make him smile.

"Ok," he nods at me just as the door flies open and Max comes flying through the room crying, closely followed by Dave, Joanne, and Sandra the nurse.

"Spot," he cries, rubbing at his eyes as he heads towards his elder brother who is stood by my side. "Spot!" he cries out again as his little legs bring him closer and my fatherly instinct kicks in. I crouch to his level. He sees me amongst his tears and snot and runs straight into my waiting arms.

With his face buried into my neck and my arms tightly wrapped around him, I shush him as I stroke his soft hair. "Spot?" I mouth at Dave, my eyebrows raised in question.

"He's our dog," Mathew tells me.

"Where is he?" I ask, remembering him telling me that his dad had kicked him against the wall. "Fuck," I curse, getting me a raised eyebrow from the policewoman then I remember her telling Holly and I that the neighbours had called the police when they heard a dog whining. "Sorry," I say, for swearing. "What happened to the dog?" I ask Joanne.

"He was taken to a local vet to be treated. I think they said they would keep him there until we got back to them." She takes her phone from her pocket and scrolls through it. "I'll get their number and give them a call."

"Thank you," I tell her, as I bury my face in Max's hair, breathing in his sent of apples and a clinical smell which I'm sure will go once he gets to leave here.

"Hey little man," I say when he lifts his snotty face from my neck, I don't bother to wipe it from my neck, but I do wipe his face with my sleeve. It's not the first time and I'm sure it won't be my last. I don't always carry tissues around. I will be calling in at the shop. "Spot's at the doggy hospital, getting better just like you and Mathew but he'll be home real soon then you can see him," I say softly and give him my best beaming smile, hoping he'll understand. Dave chuckles, as does Mathew, and I give them both a look. "What?" I question.

"I've never known you hold your breath for so long, anticipating someone's a reaction. You look hilarious." I shake my head at him and turn to Joanne who's smiling too.

"Can you tell them if Spot is well then I will collect him later today and pay his vet bills?" She nods her head then Dave opens his mouth to speak.

"I think it's time we went for a walk. We could all do with a bit of fresh air, so we'll meet you either in the cafe or outside in the garden."

Joanne agrees and makes her way out of the door while my poor boy tugs at my T shirt. "Spot coming home," he murmurs, his bottom lip covering his top.

"Yes," I tell him. "Is it okay if he comes to my home so I can look after him until you can come home?" He studies my question for a moment, probably not understanding and wondering who the fuck I am.

"Max," Mathew says as he strokes his tear-stained face. "This is your daddy and he's going to take care of Spot," he tells him, and my heart burst open again. Just hearing the word daddy I'm a goner and I bite my lip hard to stop the tremble. These kids, along with the four downstairs in the café, will be the death of me and I have another one coming soon. I'm having a fucking vasectomy.

"K." His soft breath blows across my cheek like a warm wind when his quivering voice speaks. And I breath in deeply, placing my hand on his head when he buries his face into my neck again.

"Come on," Dave says, shaking his head. "I need a strong coffee, I can't cope with all this oestrogen," he chuckles, taking the piss. I flip him the finger and Mathew laughs at our interaction.

We make our way down to the café, Max still snuggled in my arms, and when we pass the little gift shop, I make my way inside. This shop has been here years and sells everything one might need if you're a patient or a visitor wanting to buy something for whom you are visiting.

"You soft bastard," Dave mumbles when I wave a small cuddly spotty dog at them then tuck it into Max's arms who is now asleep. A little snore quivers from him as he hugs it tightly then he settles again. I then pass Mathew the bag in my hand and he takes out what's inside, his eyes large, lighting up.

"I didn't know if you had one, but I'd like you to be able to contact me if you need anything while you're in here."

"No, I don't have one anymore, it was broken," he quietly says. "Thank you," he smiles as he opens the box.

"We'll set it up in the café and I'll put my number in." He nods his head while examining his new phone, walking ahead of Dave, me and his brother.

"He opened up to you, didn't he?" I nod my head, not wanting to discuss what he said with him only a couple of feet ahead of us. I know I'll need to speak to Mathew about what he told me and let him know that we will need to inform the police with the details. "I knew he would that's why I left you alone. If you want a change in profession you could always work with the children services," he chuckles. Obviously, it's a joke, I only have patience with my family, Mathew already gaining a place in my heart.

"I'm fine with what I do, thank you."

"I know, but you do have a way about you, and I knew he was getting there, he just needed someone who would listen; someone he could trust." He knocks my shoulder, smirking. "You're a big softy really."

"Yeah," I chuckle, nodding my head. "Don't tell anyone though, I have a reputation to uphold."

Chapter 9
Vlad

Today has been such an emotional day, it's left me exhausted, and I know Holly has felt it too. It's been a long day with us not getting home from the hospital until nearly nine o'clock, all of us reluctant to leave the boys.

Introducing Mathew and Max to my sons couldn't have gone any better, all of them getting along well. According to Dave I'm some kind of child whisperer as he hadn't seen Max cuddle anyone while he'd been in hospital, except his brother, but he ran straight into my arms when he was upset. He didn't stop at me once he woke up, he was happy to be fussed over by my sons, all eager to get to know him. Never once did they leave Mathew out, giving him the same attention. Holly became overwhelmed with it all and burst into tears after she had taken both boys in her arms and cuddled the hell out of them. Seeing her take herself off to the ladies had me following her as I knew it had all become too much for her. I let my wife cry in my arms, her face buried into my chest while mine was nuzzled into her hair. Both of us needing just a moment together. Just the two of us to come to terms with what we had learnt today.

PC Grimes got back to us about Spot, he was safe and well at the vets. She had suggested picking him up tomorrow, knowing we were all at the hospital, which was fine with me. Nicholas and Daniel went shopping to buy a dog bed, toys and food, dropped them off home then came back to the hospital with some new clothes for the boys. Where Max didn't seem interested in what he'd been bought, his brother's eyes nearly popped out of his head. My sons have expensive taste, so when Mathew pulled out jeans, shirts, trainers and underwear from the bag – all designer wear – his face lit up like a full moon. He appreciated their thoughtfulness but then seemed a little embarrassed afterwards. Quietly while they were all chatting, I took him to one side, explaining to him that my sons have very big hearts with the ones they care about and he'd just been added to their list.

When we arrived home from the hospital, we quickly grabbed something to eat and Lucas organised where Spot would sleep before he took himself off to his room, then both Holly and I went for a soak in the bath.

Sprawled out on top of the bed, I turn onto my stomach, then hear the dressing room door click shut, Holly has now finished drying her hair. The mattress dips as she sits down, her warm hands stroking down my tired back. Her touch loosens the tight muscles and ignites a feeling that only she can and when her teeth sink into my arse, I groan as the sensation shoots straight to my dick. Slowly turning over, so I can see her beauty, I gently lift her on to my lap. She straddles my thighs and runs her hands over my bare chest. Seeming more relaxed after her soak in the bath and from the way her eyes are glazed over, she's clearly feeling a little frisky. "I don't think so, lady," her eyes widen in shock as I move her wandering hands and place them on her stomach with mine.

Holly had something on her mind earlier while we were at the hospital and with not having two minutes to ourselves, I haven't been able to find out what had caused it.

"Sweetheart are you going to tell me what was worrying you earlier while we were in Dave's office?" I let go of her hands so that mine can feel our baby if she decides to start moving about and watch as Holly lets out a light sigh.

"Did you get in touch with Zach?" she asks, changing the subject as her hands move to my chest again.

"Don't change the subject, Holly," I playfully nip at her bottom lip with my teeth.

"I'm not, I just want to know what he said."

"I spoke to his dad and he's going to get back to me tomorrow when he's spoken to Henry," I answer her question and she tilts her head, looking confused.

"I thought it was Zach you needed to speak with. His dad is retired, isn't he?"

"Yes, he is but Peter, Zach's dad, knows a lot more about family law than Zach plus Henry, who's the judge, is his brother." Peter was my solicitor before he retired then Zach stepped into his shoes. We got along well, and I learnt that he had practiced family law before he studied cooperative law. I had also met his brother on a couple of occasions when they ate at Dimitri's and he seemed a decent sort. That's why I'm hoping he will be able to pull a few strings and get Mathew placed with us.

"Oh."

"Yes, oh. So, I've given Peter all the information I could. Told him about Max and Mathew and how we want them both to come and live with us. How we think it would be in the best interest for them both to stay together." She nods her head, agreeing with me, and presses her soft lips against mine. I take advantage of her mouth, but I am still aware she hasn't answered my question. "He also told me just to take the paperwork that states I'm Max's biological father along with some identification to the registrar office and they will issue a new birth certificate with my name on it."

"Holly," I say as I reluctantly pull away. "Speak to me," I run my finger down her cheek and onto her lips and she kisses in gently.

"It's nothing really," she shakes her head, blowing out a breath. "Well no that's not exactly true because it could be a big issue if we're planning on fostering Mathew."

"What is it?" Her sapphire eyes study me for a moment, concern written all over a face. And I feel like shit. She shouldn't be getting this amount of stress. We've been married just over two weeks and she's six months pregnant, I'm sure she didn't sign up for this when she said *I do*. Maybe she's having second thoughts.

"Holly I'm sorry," I shift her closer to me, so my chest is touching hers. "I know this is a lot to ask of you, but I can't leave him on his own..."

"What are you talking about, you silly man? I would never ask you to do that. Having those boys here as a family is as much my decision as it is yours," she scalds me.

"I just thought," I shake my head because I'd like to think I know my wife better than that. And I do. She would never have Mathew and Max split up. "Sorry."

"Vlad shut up." She breathes in deeply through her nose, letting it out slowly as she shakes her head, her beautiful eyes closing and when she opens them, she bites her lip. "Have you ever been convicted? You know when you…" and she can't say the rest, but I know what she means.

"No," I answer quickly, wanting to relieve the stress she's been carrying around all day.

"Oh, thank God," her hand moves to her chest. "I thought that maybe there may have been a time when you'd been arrested." I shake my head.

"No. Never." I move her gently from my knee, laying us both down on our side facing each other. "Holly I have a very clever older brother."

"Have you now?" She raises her eyebrows at me. "What do you mean?"

"Sasha had always known I wanted to come to England and while I was a teenager, that wouldn't have been a problem. I would have had a place to stay, a part time job at the restaurant working for Dimitri's parents with plans of doing my business degree here. However, due to things beyond my control, that never happened but I did hope that one day I'd get here. When Natalia died, then my father, I had the chance to do what I always wanted to do. The boys were happy to travel and when Dimitri told me that his parents were selling up, I was only too pleased to purchase the restaurant and this house from them," I wave my hand in the air, smiling because I love the home we have here and the business' that my sons have helped me to build and keep running.

"The thing was, I had the means to pay my way and not depend on anyone for anything but if I'd been asked by the authorities to produce any documents on what I'd been doing for work while I was in Russia, well then I had nothing. No pay slips or bank statements with a regular income that looked legit. My bank balance was bulging, and I had no way to prove that it wasn't through illegal activity. If I'd have been asked what I'd been working as since leaving school, what would I have said... " Holly gives me a tight smile, listening and knowing fine well that I wouldn't have been able to produce any documents to prove I'd worked in any employment that was legal.

"I'd never been in trouble with the police, my father paid serious money so that his business was overlooked, and I was always careful when I..." I don't finish what I was going to say because I know my wife does not want to be reminded of what I had to do.

"However, while I was getting stressed over it all, as well as taking care of four sons, one of which was a poorly baby, my brother was laughing at me. Turns out when I was seventeen, he used our father's money to open an upscale restaurant. He'd put it in both our names and even opened a joint business bank account where he paid the bills from. I had no knowledge of any of this. He'd never once mentioned it. Forging my signature was easy for him so he was able to set us both up with separate bank accounts and have wages paid into them, monthly. He regularly used the accounts paying money in and out just so they were no questions asked."

"Wow. That was clever but highly illegal."

"I know, but he did it out of love." I run a finger over her bottom lip then place my lips on hers, stealing a warm kiss.

"To say I was surprised was an understatement when he turned up with all the paperwork for us to travel, I didn't need to do anything. He had taken care of it all and I couldn't have been more grateful to my brother for how he'd always had my back." Holly smiles, relief in her eyes as she shifts the pillows, getting comfy.

"Why did you want to know?" I ask, sitting further up the bed with her.

"Police checks. If we want Mathew to live here, then we will all need checking out and I just wanted to make sure."

"Holly I have three licensed premises, of course I've been checked out by the police," I cut in with. "Plus, when Sebastian started the adoption process for Joseph, they all lived here, so we all had some forms to fill in. I don't know all the ins and outs of it all. I just went along with everything and signed my name where I needed to." I shrug my shoulders and watch as the stress she'd been harbouring all day lifts and that smile I love so much appears on her beautiful face.

"I didn't know that," she says as her leg slides over my hip. She presses on my shoulder, forcing me onto my back then proceeds to straddle my thighs, laying her hands on my chest.

"Anything else I should know?" she asks, moving a little further up my legs so she's sitting nicely against my groin. *Hello,* my groin twitches. Hardening beneath her and the tiredness I felt not so long ago is suddenly gone.

I manoeuvre us further up the bed so my back rests on the headboard, my hands running up her smooth thighs and taking hold of her hips while my lips move in close to her ear. "You should know I love you with all my heart and count myself very lucky to have you in my life," I kiss down her neck, along her collarbone then touch her lips with mine. "You should also know it feels like forever since I've been inside you." She moans into my mouth as she sinks down on to my hardness while I'm careful that she doesn't take all of me, I gently thrust my hips as she gives a little swivel of hers. I'm in heaven.

We move at a lazy pace, in no hurry to get there, a little gyrate of Holly's hips and tender thrusts from me as our lips fuse together. I appreciate the seductive sounds she makes into my mouth as well as the grip she has on my chest and let out a few moans of my own which Holly swallows up. Wanting to flip her over, needing to sink deep and hard into her, letting her take all of me, I know I won't. I don't like being rough with Holly since she's started showing more, so I'm careful in giving her what she needs without losing control.

When Holly breaks our kiss and nuzzles her face into my neck, her shoulders shaking, I freeze. Is she laughing or crying? "Holly," I say, lifting her head so I can see her face. And there she is sat on top of me chuckling away. "What's so funny?" I ask, chuckling with her because her laugh is contagious.

"I'm sorry," she stutters out, struggling to contain her amusement. "You won't hit the baby on the head if you thrust all the way in, you know." And my dick softens. The mention of our little one while we are fucking is something that bothers me. I know she's there and I try to be gentle and I don't like baby talk while where in the throes of passion.

"Holly if you weren't pregnant, I'd be flipping you over and spanking that fucking arse of yours," I say, biting my lip trying not to smile at her as I watch her eyes light up and she laughs harder.

"I'm sorry," she says as she calms a little. "I just find it funny how gentle you are lately when we make love." She grins, giving a swivel of her hips, making me groan, then she tries to take all of me as I harden fully again. Not happening. I don't need to go deep for us both to enjoy ourselves, we can raise the roof, get hot and sweaty, crying out in ecstasy just as easy when we take it slow and leisurely.

I swiftly turn us both onto our sides and raise her leg higher up my body then ease into her heat, gyrating my hips, still careful not to go in too hard. She lets out a moan, throwing her head back then brings it forward, her lustful eyes locking with mine. "Better?" I ask, wondering if me holding back isn't enough for her. I've never questioned my ability to give a woman what she wants, I know I can have them screaming my name in no time at all. But wanting to take my time, being tender and caring with my angel, might not be enough for her.

"Oh, it's always good. I just find it hilarious how you try to hold back that animal streak of yours."

"Just good," I say, a little cocky as I grit my teeth, loving the feeling of her wrapped around me and yes, trying to hold back the animal in me that wants to lose control. I bring my hand between us, stroking over her warm heat as my mouth lowers to her hard nipples while I twirl my tongue around one then the other.

"Oh God, no," she moans and it's my turn to chuckle. "Mind blowing," she moans again while tugging at my hair and I know it won't be long before she's screaming my name. I move up her body, our foreheads touching as I ease in and out, my hand moving up her thigh, holding her leg in place. "Feels so good," she murmurs against my mouth and I kiss her hard, holding back my release.

"I know," I say when I nip across her jawline and onto her neck, feeling the tell-tale signs of her orgasm pending. A few more gentle thrusts and a swivel of my hips and her teeth sink into my shoulder, stifling her moans as her heat grips me hard, pulling me in and sending me rocketing into space. We stay joined as Holly pulsates around me, her legs straightening, still gripping me hard, the sensation of an aftershock has me shaking and shivering in her arms.

Once our breathing is back to normal, I sweep her hair back from her face, her pupils allowing me to see straight into her soul and I know she sees straight into mine. I kiss her swollen lips gently, "And I know what I'm good at," I say then kiss her again.

"Hmmm, I know," Holly whispers as she snuggles into me, her eyes closing. I close mine too, happy that we've sorted that out and hoping tomorrow we'll be able to sort out what is happening with Max and Mathew.

Chapter 10

Holly

Vlad holds Max against him, settled on his knee, stroking his back as I run my hand through his soft hair while he sobs lightly; the second nightmare of the evening.

It's been two weeks since we met the boys and with the help of Zach and his dad, Dave and Mr Stanton we have been able to bring both boys home. Although we could have brought Max home five days ago, we had promised that we wouldn't separate him from his brother Mathew, so while we were waiting for confirmation from the powers that be on whether Mathew would be able stay with us, they both stayed at the hospital.

Mathew was well enough to leave too, but not wanting him to be put in temporary foster care, Vlad paid for a private hospital room for them where they could stay together without taking a bed from anyone that needed it. It was Dave's idea, one that everyone had agreed to knowing that splitting them up for a few days wouldn't do either of them any good.

Even though this is the first night they have slept here, it's not the first time they've come to visit their new home. We've had many visits where they have come for lunch or tea. Had trips shopping and eaten out. We've all been bowling as a family, my friends coming along too, and we've had many official visits from child services.

Each time having to take them back to the hospital before seven o'clock. Having so many friends holding jobs in high places has played a huge part in getting Mathew's case rushed through and placed in our care. Max wasn't a problem with Vlad being his natural father but as Mr Stanton told us there's a procedure to follow. However, even he could see that Mathew wanted to stay with us and that we meant what we said; we would do anything to keep the boys together. So he jumped on board and got the documents signed to have Mathew placed into our care. A case worker will call regularly, along with Mr Stanton, but we've been told that these will become less frequent once all the police checks come back. We've also been told that it's unusual for them to place a child in a home without all the proper checks but due to Mathew having ties to our family through Max they've been able to go ahead.

So here we are at midnight, comforting a little boy who throughout the day will run riot around the house, play normally and chuckle loudly as he interacts with his new family. But after sleeping only a few hours into the night, the first disturbed sleep began. The heartfelt whimpers then the calling for his mum broke my heart. I sat soothing Max, stroking his hair as his eyes stayed closed, still asleep but the torment and loss he had gone through playing out in his sleep.

"He'll calm down soon," Mathew claimed, sitting down on the other side of the bed while Lucas and Vlad searched for the small spotty dog that he'd slept with every night since Vlad bought him it. "He usually cries a couple of times in his sleep then settles until the morning." And once Lucas tucked the soft toy in his arms he did settle. Snuggled up, taking comfort from the dog, he drifted off into a peaceful sleep. Only to wake up an hour later.

Vlad and Sebastian had organised the bedroom next door to Lucas' for both Mathew and Max, knowing that it might take some time before we can put him in a room of his own. When the second night terror began, Mathew and Lucas were asleep. Not wanting to wake them we brought Max into our room. During his cries and whimpers he wet himself, so we cleaned him up, changed his pyjamas then settled him in with us.

"He seems to be calming down," Vlad whispers as he shifts himself, resting against the headboard. He kisses the top of Max's head, shushing him and the little love snuggles across his chest. Calmed. Loved. Asleep.

"You're good at this," I quietly say as I pull the quilt up, covering our legs.

"I've had plenty of practice," Vlad says, as he lowers himself further into the bed, careful not to wake Max.

"Daniel." I remember him telling me about Daniel's nightmares when they first came to live here in England. He nods his head then turns on his side, laying Max between us. "Were they like this?"

"No. Daniel's were aggressive. He'd be angry and kick out a lot. Shouting and screaming. The only similarity is they're both heart breaking to witness." Looking at Max now sprawled out on his stomach in the middle of the bed, mouth slightly open as his small arm lays across Vlad's chest, you wouldn't think he'd been crying on and off for half an hour. Sobbing as if he'd had something precious stolen from him. And he has. His mum.

Whomever it was that hit their mother with the car then left her there to die, and we're still unsure who it was as the police are still investigating; Mathew's father being the prime suspect and still on the run, well they've robbed them of a mother who cared, loved and did her best to bring these two boys up. I know that we can never replace her, but we will make sure they are cared for, loved and grow up to be fine young men. Sons she would have been proud of.

Vlad's arm wraps around me, his hand placed on my back and I watch his eyes flicker shut. He's shattered. The last two weeks have taken it out of him. Trips back and forth to the hospital, meetings and heated phone calls all concerning the boys. Then work-related issues, even though Sebastian, Nicholas and Daniel had told him not to worry about work as they would deal with anything that was needed. Then the day he saw the small faint bruise and old marks on Max's arms I thought he was going kill someone.

We've spoken in lengths about Mathew's father and every time Vlad and his sons have struggled with their promise to leave him to the police. I know it's hard, I'm not sure how I would behave if I was to come face to face with him. Even Jack, Nick, Olivia and Sarah have threatened to do him harm if they ever meet him. However, for now we need to try and put him behind us because as soon as he is found then poor Mathew may need to testify against him which will be a distressing time, I'm sure.

*

"You've got to be f***ing kidding me!" Sebastian hollers, chuckling, trying hard not to say the F word. "He's pissed on me again," he says, looking down at his jumper as he holds Spot in his outstretched arms.

Spot, the cross Dalmatian, what he's crossed with we don't know because he's no way near as tall as a full pedigree; we do know he's only a year old and is as daft as the two men who he's taken a liking to. As soon as Seb and Nicholas walk in the door he gets overly excited and dribbles a little. You would think that both of them would know by now not to pick him up as he's been doing it since the day we picked him up from the vets and brought him home. He jumps up at their legs and tugs at their socks until they give in and every time they bend down to pick him up, letting him lap at their face, then he pisses on them.

"He got me yesterday," Nicholas laughs as he slaps Sebastian on the back while everyone laughs at him. He puts him back on the floor, moaning as he makes his way down the short hallway towards the bedroom he uses when he stops here. Spot scurries off under the dining room table, turning three times as he gets comfortable where he has made his bed.

"He's done it again," Vlad groans, running his hand through his hair as he stares frustrated at Spot who stares back triumphantly, resting his head on his clumsy looking paws. They do look far too big for his body.

"I don't know why you don't leave him there; he obviously prefers it to laying by the door." Since bringing him home Vlad's tried to get him to lay in the doorway of the kitchen that joins the utility room but the dog's adamant it's not happening. Spot is not very big but that doesn't stop him from gripping his new bed with his teeth, dragging it from the doorway, around the kitchen island and across the room until he's got it safely tucked under the table. My husband moves it back every time and sure enough it's back under the table when he's not looking.

"Little shit," he says, scrunching up his face at the dog who lays there wagging its tail at him, Vlad puts his arm around my shoulder and growls teasingly at Spot then kisses my neck. "Maybe you're right," he mumbles. "But he needs to get out of pissing himself when he gets giddy, otherwise I'll be putting a fucking nappy on him," he chuckles when he directs the words *nappy on him* at Spot and the dog lets out a groaning noise.

"I'm sure he will. He's still young and he's still getting use to his new home and all the attention."

"Have you ever had a dog?"

"No," I say, shaking my head. "Have you?"

"No. Sebastian and Nicholas wanted one when they were kids but with things the way there were, I didn't think it was wise."

"Understandable," I say, giving his arm a gentle squeeze, which is now wrapped around my waist, his hand stroking my stomach while his chin rests on my shoulder as we watch Spot happy in his new surroundings.

"Owee, Owee, wook," Max squeals excitedly as he races through the kitchen from the garage closely followed by an equally excited Rebecca. Lucas, Mathew and Joseph join them tossing a football around and Izzy follows, dashing at some dust on her jeans after rummaging through the boxes of shoes in the garage for the wellies Max has on his feet.

"Wow, you found some," I smile at his cuteness, slowly getting down to his level. "These look great. Are you ready to go stomping in the puddles with daddy?" His big eyes light up, excited as he nods his head.

When everyone called in at lunch time, they decided that if the rain stopped, they would take a trip to the park for a kick about with the ball and Vlad wanted to take Max and Rebecca for a kick about in the puddles. It's something he did a lot with the boys when they were small. Although we've been and collected a lot of Max and Mathew's clothes and personal things as well as bought them new clothes, we did overlook that Max might have needed wellies. Izzy was adamant that there were some old ones of Joseph's in the garage from when he was Max's age so off she went to look, taking Rebecca and the boys with her to search for them.

"Wook," he says again, stamping the heal on the floor, showing that his wellies light up when he stamps his feet. "Bue, yewow and wed," he grins, showing me his milky white teeth, happy with what he is wearing, and I can't help but pull him in for a hug. This kid is adorable. Having trouble to pronounce words with Ls in them, well he sounds so bloody cute, I could listen to him all day. "You coming," he scrunches up his face, throwing his arms around my neck.

"No love," I tell him, kissing the top of his head as Vlad brings him his coat.

Last night when he had settled in the middle of our bed he didn't wake for the rest of the night. Not even when the heavens opened, and torrential rain battered at the windows while the thunder rumbled loudly, and lightning lit up the sky. He never stirred but it did keep Vlad and I awake for a few hours. This morning when Max woke you wouldn't have thought his sleep had been disturbed with nightmares as he rampaged around the house giggling while chasing Spot. As for me I feel drained with the lack of sleep and I have a terrible back ache so I'm hoping to have a rest while they are all out. Izzy is staying home too with Ben as she also had a sleepless night with the little cherub.

Max gets side-tracked and pays me no more attention as Vlad helps him with his coat then they both grab Spot's lead. The dog shoots from under the table, sitting perfectly straight up at Vlad's feet, head in the air, tail wagging. Clipping it to his collar they make their way out of the kitchen while Daniel has a moan. "It looks like its gunna piss it down again." Nicholas tugs on his ponytail, shaking his head, and rolls his eyes at him.

"You're not made of sugar, you won't melt."

"I know. I'm just saying. When we all come back wet through and covered from head to foot in mud, we'll all need to get changed. Well I'm calling first dibs on one of the showers, I have a date later tonight," he grins at Nicholas, knowing that he hasn't been on a date in a long time, too hell bent on waiting for a certain lady to take a chance on him.

"It's like listening to a pair of girls listening to you two," Seb says, slinging his coat on then wraps up Rebecca in hers. She chuckles at her dad's reference to her uncles being like two girls and grabs their hands, dragging them out of the kitchen.

"Come on Aunty Daniella and Aunty Nicola," she giggles, her face lighting up with mischief then she drops their hands and runs towards her granddad, stopping them both from tugging at her plaits. Laughing at her comment, I follow them into the hallway, noticing what a miserable afternoon it is when Vlad opens the door.

"Are you sure you don't want to come with us?" Lucas asks me as he tosses the ball to Mathew.

"No. Holly needs a rest," Vlad says before I have chance to answer. He takes hold of my hand, pulling me into him and nuzzles his nose into my hair. "Make sure you catch up on some sleep, sweetheart, and don't be cooking for everyone, we'll get a takeout when we get back." It almost sounds like an order but it's not. It's him knowing that it's been a hectic few weeks. A stressful time for all of us. Lots of running around, late nights and upset. Vlad constantly reminds me I need to rest more but it's been hard with everything that has been going on. He's also aware that I will think nothing of cooking up a feast for the whole family so his instruction to have a sleep is out of love and worry that I've been doing too much.

"Don't worry, I intend to," I say, pecking at his soft lips, then I lean into him, giving him a cuddle. "Don't get too muddy," I smile, patting his chest, getting me an eye roll when he looks up at the pending rain clouds.

Once they've all gone out of the door, Izzy and I have a cup of tea listening to the quietness. Now that Ben is asleep and everyone's gone out you can hear a pin drop.

"I'm going to have an afternoon nap while I can," she says, yawning. Making her way to the downstairs bedroom where Ben is fast asleep, I get cuddled up on the settee needing fifty winks as well.

I wake a while later, not knowing what time it is or how long I've been asleep. What I do know is I feel well rested. I here Izzy cooing at Ben so I sit up, watching her blowing raspberries on his tummy.

"Hello sleepy head," she smiles, turning her head to me. "You've been dead to the world." She grins, then lowers her head again to Ben's belly and blows another raspberry. He kicks his legs and lets out a little gurgle, chuckling at the sensation.

"I have. What time is it?" I ask, smiling at Ben who is now throwing his arms around.

"It's just after four, you've been asleep for two hours; I thought you were dead for a while. This one," she picks Ben up, snuggling her face it his hair then kisses the top of his head, "screamed blue murder when he wanted feeding and his nappy changing and you never flinched."

"I needed it; I was shattered but I feel a lot better now."

The gate buzzer sounds, and Izzy stands with Ben, passing him to me. "Here, take hold of your grandson, I'll answer it." No sooner is he in my arms, his hand comes out to grab my nose, followed by his mouth trying to chew on it. Laughing at him, I cuddle him into me, shaking my head at the mention of him been my grandson.

It doesn't seem two minutes ago that I was a divorced thirty-seven-year-old, living alone in my small apartment. Now, I'm married to a man who worships me and me him. A step mum to three grown men, two teenagers and a three-year-old. I have a daughter-in-law and three grandchildren then there's our little bump. In two months' time our baby will be here and, like Vlad, I too am hoping for a little girl as this family has become even more top heavy with the male members.

"It's Mr Stanton, I've opened the gates for him to come in," Izzy tells me, as she clears away the soiled nappy and changing mat.

"I wonder what he wants, he hasn't made arrangements to call round." She takes Ben from me as I get up, making my way into the kitchen to switch on the kettle. "I better ring Vlad to let him know, he might want to speak with him and Mathew."

"No need, they're on their way home. Sebastian phoned just before you woke up." I nod my head at her then set out three cups. Mr Stanton usually has a cup of tea when he calls, and I know Izzy never says no.

"I'll go let him in," I say, knowing it won't take him long to drive up from the gates. Just as I'm opening the door, he stands there, hand ready to knock.

"Hi Holly, sorry it's just a quick visit."

"Come in," I tell him before he gets soaked. The heavens have opened again while I was asleep and it's throwing it down.

"Thanks," he says, shrugging off his jacket and hanging it up then follows me into the kitchen.

"Vlad and the boys are out at the park, but they won't be long," I say, watching his eyebrows raise as he places his briefcase on the floor.

"Are they mad? It's pouring down."

"They all went earlier when it had stopped for a kick about with the ball, they'll be home in a few minutes. Would you like a cup of tea?" I ask, lifting one of the cups.

"Just a quick one. I need to get home to my wife before she divorces me," he chuckles to himself as he shakes his head.

"Are you in the doghouse?" I smile at him as I finish making the tea.

"I will be if I'm not home in the next hour. We're going to my brother-in-law's fiftieth birthday party and I've been stuck in an emergency meeting for the last few hours."

"I don't know how you do it," I say, genuinely in awe of how he deals with some of the cases he must come across.

"It has its rewards," he smiles, taking a sip of his tea. "When you meet boys like Max and Mathew and what they have gone through then seeing how happy they are when they are placed with a family like yours... Well it helps."

"I'm sure it does." I sit down on one of the chairs at the table, picking up my tea. When I've had a drink, I wonder what has brought him here.

"So why are you here instead of being on your way home?" I ask, putting my cup down.

"Oh, yes. It was easier for me to call now while I was passing instead of Monday morning due to now having to be in the office by seven thirty and will probably be in meeting after meeting."

"Oh, okay," I nod at him. I didn't even know he was calling in on Monday.

"I just wanted to see how Mathew was settling in and if you or your husband have made arrangements for when he starts back at school."

Bloody hell, they've only been here one night, he's keen.

"Mathew is fine. He's happy," I shrug my shoulders. "He gets on really well with the whole family and our friends. But it's only been one night, so I'm under no illusion that we'll come across some issues with him along the way. However, Vlad is more than capable of dealing with teenage boys." He nods his head at me knowing that he has four sons who too lost their mother even though the circumstances were different. "Vlad spoke with the headteacher at Mathew's school yesterday when we had talked about his education. We have a meeting on Wednesday with hopes Mathew can start back on Thursday."

"Good. He needs some familiarity in his life and what I've learnt from his teachers at school, he was a good student with lots of potential to do well in his grades..."

Commotion and laughter echoes through into the kitchen from the utility room, stopping Mr Stanton from what he was saying. Sebastian appears first with Rebecca perched on his shoulders, both of them giggling and looking like drowned rats as they chant, "Winners, winners." They've discarded their coats and boots, probably in the garage which is a good thing because they're most likely to be as wet as these too. "We are the champions," Rebecca sings as she raises her arms in the air then her dad lowers her to the floor.

"Look at the state of you both," Izzy clucks as she fusses over them with a towel, trying to dry their wet faces and hair.

"Mummy we won," Rebecca's eyes are wide with excitement as she looks up at her mum.

"What did you win, sweetheart?"

"We had a race from the gate and me and daddy were the fastest!" She beams just as two of her uncles come barrelling through the door, shoulder barging one another to get through.

"Get out of the way," Daniel grabs the wood on either side of the door, stopping Nicholas from getting past his large frame.

"Twat," Nicholas curses as Daniel enters the kitchen before him. "Sorry," he says when he sees Mr Stanton sat there, a look of bewilderment on his face. He shakes his head, then his lip rises at one side when Lucas flies through in a fluster, Max slung over his shoulder, Joseph not far behind him. He squeals with delight when Lucas lowers him to the floor and makes a beeline for me.

"Come here," I say, putting my arms out, wrapping him in a towel while I pass one to Lucas who uses it to dry his hair and his face and Izzy throws one to her son who catches it one handed then rubs at his mop of hair with it.

"I'm soaked to the skin," Daniel says, wiping his face on a towel as he strips off his hoodie. Max is still giggling as I rub at his hair then strip him of his jumper, wrapping the towel back around him.

"Where's Mathew and your dad?" I ask but I needn't have bothered as they both come darting through the door, towels in hand as they pursue Spot who wraps himself around their legs, enjoying whatever game he thinks they're playing.

"Come here, you little shit," Vlad says as he tries to cover Spot's body with the towel at the same time as Mathew attempts to cover his head but Spot's having none of it. He's loving this game and scoots past them both, rounding the kitchen island, his claws clipping on the tiles as his wet fur brushes past Izzy's legs, causing her to scream.

"He's all wet," she states the obvious, laughing.

"No shit, Sherlock," Sebastian chuckles, slinging his arm around her shoulders and kissing her cheek when she digs him in the ribs with her elbow for taking the piss. Spot stops still in front of my husband, Mathew now edging away slowly towards the fridge.

"Don't you dare…" Vlad's eyes widen as he puts his hand out to try and stop the inevitable. It doesn't work. The hoots of laughter sound off the walls as Vlad stands looking down at his clothes. Spot shook himself that hard that I'm surprised he has any spots left on his body, leaving my husband covered from head to foot in wet dog spray.

"That was the funniest thing I've seen in a long while," Mr Stanton states as he wipes at his eyes, still laughing at Spot giving Vlad the run around, who is now laid at his feet.

"I didn't know you were calling today," Vlad says as he crouches down then looks up from his position on the floor.

"I was in the area but it's fine," he holds his hand up, standing from the stool he was sat on. "I will call you next week after your meeting at the school." He says bye to everyone, and I walk him out to the door, "It's good to see the boys happy, they fit in well."

"They certainly do. And so, does Spot," I claim, smiling.

"Yes, I can see that. I'll see you next week, Holly," he waves his hand as he makes his way to his car.

"Have a good evening," I tell him then close the door.

"You lot need to shower," I tell them as I walk into the kitchen. Daniel moves quickly towards the stairs in a hurry to get in before anybody else.

"I'll take Rebecca and Max, get them showered and in their pjs," Izzy says, taking hold of Max's hand and heading down the hallway.

"I'll get Max some pyjamas and bring them into you." I make my way into utility room knowing there's a few pairs of new ones that I washed and ironed and left on the worktop in there. Vlad stands in my way, looking like he's been through the ringer. His hair is wet and dishevelled, there's mud covering the knees of his jeans and his socks are soaked too.

"Ok there, big man," I smirk, shaking my head. Seeing him like this always makes me smile. It's a far cry from the man I met months ago in a night club.

Chapter 11
Vlad

If someone had said to me last year that over the next coming year I would be married again, have a baby on the way, find out that I have a three-year-old son that I knew nothing about, foster his teenage brother and take in their dog then I would have told them to fuck off and go book in at a clinic for the mentally insane. Because only in my nightmares would I have seen that coming in my distant future. Just me, my four sons, Izzy my daughter-in-law and my grandchildren were enough. They were all I needed, or so I thought. How wrong was I?

However here am I, smiling like a loon, my heart beating fast as I stare down at the gold band on my finger, loving the feel of it and missing my wife already. This is what she does to me when she's not here. Thinking about her being home in a couple of hours, I shake my head, I'm a lost cause. She's only popped over to Olivia's with my three-year-old son Max to meet Lucas, my teenage son who is growing up too fast. He'd planned with one of Jack and Olivia's sons to go straight from school so that they could swap a few of their video games. Needing Holly out of the house for what I need to do, I suggested she took Max over there so she could spend some time with Olivia who absolutely dotes on him then I would pick the three of them up later. My older sons are all at work and I don't expect any of them here until later this evening. And while I wait for Mathew, my foster son, to arrive home from school, Spot the cross Dalmatian growls and tugs at my sock, drooling and wetting it through as he tries to get my attention. I stop stirring the bolognaise that I'm cooking, lean down and pat his head, remembering he needs feeding. Usually the boys or Holly do it but it's just me and him at home for now until Mathew gets home.

I hear the door open then close as I put Spot's dish on the floor in the utility room. He waits there patiently, sitting up straight, thudding his tail against the freezer, his dark brown eyes smiling at me as he waits to be told he can eat. He's a good dog and very protective of the whole family. It took him a while to get out of his giddiness but now six weeks later he's settled down and we're free from his dribbling when he gets excited.

I give him a nod of my head and he moves like lightning to his dish, tucking in like it's his last meal. I leave it him to it and make my way back into the kitchen to take care of the bolognaise while I contemplate how I am going to approach a problem that's been niggling me all day.

"Hi," Mathew says as he drops his school bag on the floor then gets himself a drink from the fridge. "Where is everyone?" He looks around, noticing it's just me and him.

"They're all out," I tell him, watching how much he has settled into his new home. Max settled in straight away, apart from his nightmares which don't happen as often now, in fact this week he's only had one. The way he's taken to all of us you wouldn't have thought we had missed the first three years of his life. Mathew was a bit shy to start with, called me Mr Petrov a lot and was reluctant to just help himself if he wanted a drink or a snack but after the first week he came round and relaxed, becoming one of the family.

He went back to school a week after moving in. He didn't want to change schools and was happy to go back to his old one that he hadn't been at for six months. He took advice from the careers advisor and opted to re-sit most of his GCSE next year. Some he can sit this year, so most of the time he's just revising.

He's a growing lad and needed new uniforms and clothes as well as footwear but struggled with accepting what we bought him. I gave him money to go out and buy new trainers and anything else he wanted but he came home with the cheapest pair. Now, he accepts money from me for whatever he needs but one thing that worries me is that I give him enough money to buy top of the range gear, but he only ever buys the cheapest. When Lucas wants anything, no matter how expensive or cheap it is, he always brings change home and so did his older brothers when they were teenagers, but Mathew never does. Now I'm not a tight-fisted man. I'm quite generous really with my family. But I would love to know what he is doing with all that spare cash. He can keep it as long as he's spending it sensibly and not on anything he shouldn't be. Then there's the money pot we have. I've always put money it the pot that sits on the work top just in case any one of my sons needed cash. I have done it for twelve years. If I wasn't at home and Seb or Nicholas needed anything they would dip in the pot, leaving me a note in it. Mrs White always used it to pay the window cleaner. Daniel and Lucas have used it too, even Izzy has left me an IOU in it.

Holly loves just dipping in it so she can leave me a love note and we also use it to pay for the takeaway when we order one.

Only this morning when Lucas came to me and told me I was slacking because the pot was empty, just a few coins in there, it got me asking where is the few hundred pounds that was in there just a few weeks ago. Like I said, any of my sons would have left a note and so would Izzy and Holly. Pointing the finger has never been my thing and I'd hate to think that someone was stealing from me when all they need to do is ask. But I have noticed a difference in Mathew over the last couple of weeks. Something's bothering him and I haven't got a clue what it is.

So not wanting to embarrass the poor boy and ask when everyone is here, I've made sure that the whole family was out so that we can have a chat.

I've always been good at being open with my sons and they know that they can discuss anything with me, and I want the same relationship with Mathew.

"It's just you and me for tea, if you want to get changed first you have fifteen minutes while the spaghetti is cooking," I say, giving it a stir as he picks up his bag. He finishes his drink and makes his way up stairs.

When he comes back down, I'm just plating it up. "Just in time, I'm starving," he says, smiling as he sits at the table. "Thanks," he says when I pass him a heaped plate that he tucks into straight way.

"You're welcome," I tell him, taking a seat, tucking into mine too.

"Where's Max and Holly?" he asks, after swallowing a mouthful of spaghetti then takes a drink of his water.

"They're at Olivia's, I'm picking them up at six."

"Is Lucas still at school?" Normally they arrive home within fifteen minutes of each other unless they decided to meet up off the bus. They go to different schools, both taking different buses. I do offer to take them and pick them up or get one of their brothers to do it but they both prefer to make their own way. Lucas used to like getting a lift until he started year nine back in September but stopped when his friends were all getting the bus.

"He went to meet Nathan to exchange some games so I'm picking him up too when I go for Holly and Max."

"Oh, I'd have gone with him if I'd have known." He looks a little put out when his eyes dip down towards his plate as he scoops up another forkful. Mathew gets on really well with Lucas, as he does with Olivia's sons, and now I feel like shit for wanting to speak to him on his own.

"We'll drive over when we've finished eating and cleared the pots away, if you want?" That gives me a bit of time to find out what bothering him and why he needs money. He smiles, nodding his head and continues to eat his meal as I contemplate how to approach the subject.

"So, how's school?" I ask, then kick myself because if this had been one of my sons, I'd have just asked straight out if there was a problem, not pussy foot around and maybe that's the problem. He's not mine. I'm not his father. He has one somewhere out there. Where? Who the fuck knows? The police haven't found him yet, but he can't stay hidden for long. People like him have a habit of turning up when you least expect it. I want Mathew to look at me as a father figure, someone he can respect and go to if there's a problem. If he's in trouble or needs anything. Because I know he'll never be able to go to his own father and I don't think he would want to.

I finish my meal, placing my knife and fork on the plate. "Mathew is everything okay at school? Are you happy here?" He lifts his head to look at me, guilt and something else written all over his face. "Is there a problem you're not telling me about, Mathew... ?"

"I'm happy here," he says, his voice quiet. He takes a drink of water then places the glass back on the table and rubs his hands over his face. "I do want to look for a job. Now I'm sixteen, I want to work part time while I'm still at school."

"Ok, so you want to earn your own money, I can relate to that," I say, getting up to scrape my plate then put it with everything else that needs washing up. "If you want a job then I'm sure I can get you one at the restaurant working in the kitchen or waiting tables. I do know the owner," I smile at him as I sit back down.

"You would do that?" His eyes light up as he sits up, straightening his shoulders.

"Of course. All my sons have worked at Dimitri's, washing up, helping in the kitchen or in the restaurant. Well, all except Lucas but as soon as he's sixteen then if he wants some work experience and to earn his own money then there will be a job for him too. Mathew you are no different to them; if you want, I will ring Maureen now and ask her to get you some shifts at the weekend," I state then watch him wipe at his watery eyes.

"Thank you," he sniffles upset or overwhelmed with the extent of my support.

"Is there anything else bothering you, Mathew?" I want him to come clean about taking the money, I also want to know why he's so eager to work and earn his own money.

"No," he says sheepishly, shaking his head.

"Are you sure?" I lift an eyebrow at him, my eyes not leaving his. "Because if there is then that's what I'm here for. Holly and I want you to be happy here. We're here for you, Mathew." He picks at something that's not there on the table and lowers his eyes to it. I sit there waiting patiently. Giving him time to come clean and tell me the truth.

"You know, don't you?" he says. A mixture of emotions crossing his face. Sadness, embarrassment and anxiety.

"What do I know, Mathew?"

He blows out a shaky breath as he stands and shakes his head. His cheeks flush, "I'm sorry," and I see it in his eyes that he is truly sorry as he walks slowly out of the kitchen then up the stairs. I don't follow him. I want to give him time. He'll come back down. Then I remember the beatings he got from his father after he stole from him. Does he think I'm going to be angry with him, hurt him or send him back to Mr Stanton? Oh, fuck, I don't want him getting all upset, I never thought this through properly. Just as I'm about to get up to tell him it's fine, that I understand, which I don't really because I'm still no wiser as to why he took the money, he comes back downstairs with his school bag and just as I'm about to tell him it's ok, whatever the reason we'll sort it, he sits back down and starts rummaging through it. He takes out a wad of money and places it on the table. "I am sorry," he says, placing his bag on the floor. I look at the notes that are rolled up, there must be about four hundred quid there. This is the money from the pot and any money he's had left from shopping. I know he's sorry, I can see that, but I need to know why.

"Why Mathew?" I ask, calmly. "What do you need it for? If there's something you want, you only have to ask."

"I know... I would have put it back as soon as I got a part time job, but I needed to pay a deposit..." His chin quivers and his eyes well up, stopping him from continuing and I'm out of my seat in a flash. This boy has gone through too much and it breaks my heart to see him upset. I sit on the seat next to him, passing him a tissue to wipe his face.

"Mathew, talk to me. What do you need a deposit for?" He looks up at me, wiping his face on his sleeve rather than the tissue I just gave him then he leans down and takes a brochure out of his bag.

"For this." Oh fuck, the poor boy. I pick up the booklet and read the front cover. Robinsons Headstones. I flick through it, landing on one that's been circled with a black marker. It's white, made of marble and in the shape of a love heart.

"For your mum?" I swallow the lump in my throat, understanding that he is still hurting. The death of his mother and everything he's been through afterwards is going to stay with him for a long time. He might be only sixteen, but he's had to grow up fast to cope with it all and I really do admire him for wanting to make sure his mum's grave gets a headstone. I just wish he had spoken to me about it instead of taking it all on himself.

"Yes," he says, picking up the brochure. "Since going back to school, I've visited her grave a few times on the way home... It makes me sad to see all the beautiful headstones and she only has a wooden cross with a small brass plaque." Mathew uses the tissue this time to wipe his face then takes a drink of his water. "I just want something nice for her... Somewhere I can take Max, so she knows that we still love her."

"She knows," I squeeze his shoulder and his light blue eyes stare unblinking at me. "You'll always love her, Mathew. They'll always be a place in your heart for your mum..."

"And what about Max? He barely remembers her."

"Then we make sure that he never forgets her. We can show him the photos of her and from time to time take him to visit her grave. He might not be able to remember much about her, he's too young to understand, Mathew, but we will make sure he knows that your mum loved him very much," I assure him.

"Thank you for understanding." I stand, and he looks up at me. "I shouldn't have taken that money; I know that, and I am sorry." I nod my head at him and take the brochure from him, having an idea. If I offer to pay for the headstone, which I will, I know he will refuse. He wants to be grown up, be treated as an adult even though there's still so much for him to learn. Knowing he wants to pay for his mum's headstone, which would take him a very long time, I need to get him to compromise.

"Forget about this," I point at the money. "I believe you would have tried to pay it back but I'm not sure how you would have paid the rest of the money." He goes to speak, and I hold my hand up. "Let me finish. Headstones are not cheap, Mathew, and you may have had enough to pay a deposit, but you would have had to get a full-time job to pay the rest. Which isn't going to happen because your education comes first." He blows out a breath, shaking his head at me and I raise an eyebrow at him.

"Mathew your mother would want that and so do we. I will pay for the headstone…"

"I can't let you do that," he shakes his head again.

"You're not letting me do anything that I don't want to do. Your mum brought Max up on her own without coming to me for any child support, so I think I owe her, don't you?"

"No," he pouts.

"Mathew you want me to treat you as an adult then you need to be realistic here. You cannot afford to do this on your own, you need to let me help," I say firmly, not budging on this. He needs to realise he's not on his own anymore and being stubborn is not going to get him anywhere.

"I suggest you let me pay for it. You take on a part-time job and you can pay half of it back to me when you start getting regular pay. Just a small amount every month until it's paid off then you've paid your share and I've paid the other for Max. What do you think?" He plays with his glass of water, biting his lip while he studies me. I'm not giving him the chance to try and go this alone. It's a lot of money for a young lad to pay out, especially one who has no means of paying for it. I know he was desperate to pay the deposit on the headstone and that's why he's been acting differently over the last couple of weeks, worrying.

"Okay," he eventually says, nodding his head. "Thank you. I thought you'd be angry with me for what I have done."

"I'm not angry with you. I'm disappointed with you and with myself because maybe I haven't made it clear enough since you came to live here. We, and I mean all of us, are your family now and you can come to any of us if there's something you need, something troubling you, anything. So as long as you promise nothing like this will happen again then there's no need to worry about it. Ok?"

"Sorry, I promise I won't do it again." I nod my head at him, appreciating the truth I see on his face, so I offer him my hand. He stands to take it and because I want him to feel like one of the family, to me he is one of the family, I pull him into me and hug him as I would with any of my sons. He doesn't pull back. He accepts the fatherly hug I offer, and it feels like a breakthrough. It is a breakthrough. I'm sure he's felt like an outsider under my roof, not that he's been treated as one, but I understand his trepidations.

Now I think addressing this little stumbling block has made him realise he can trust me to put him first. As he pulls away, I still need him to realise that stealing is not the way and remind him of that.

"Make sure you don't, or I won't be as understanding," then I slap him on the back, not hard just as I would with Seb, Nicholas, Daniel and Lucas and I'm sure when Max is older, I'll be doing the same with him.

"Does Holly know?" he asks, taking his plate into the kitchen.

"No. Nobody does and nobody else needs to know about the money." I'm not lying to Holly or any of my sons because they know nothing about it. When I asked them to give me some time alone with Mathew, they assumed I just wanted to chat about how he was getting on.

A few weeks ago, the police and Mr Stanton called round to tell him that they were treating his mother's death as suspicious and that they had found the car that had hit her burnt out. The car belonged to his father who they were still looking for in regard to Mathew's attack and now possibly the murder of his mother. We already knew this, but Mathew hadn't been informed about it. I think they thought they would let him settle here first.

The boy was so distraught that he cried in Holly's arms then wouldn't come out of his room for the rest of the day. We let him grieve and waited until he was ready to come back downstairs and talk. My sons are good at cheering people up, so it wasn't long before he settled down and was back playing on the PS4 with Lucas. But he was still hurting. Holly could see it, we all could. So, knowing it was his sixteenth birthday a few days later we organised a party at Dimitri's for him, inviting as many people as we could to take his mind off things. And he enjoyed it. We didn't go over the top with presents. I bought him an electric razor, knowing he'd been using disposable ones. The odd nick on his chin was a big give away. Holly bought him a bottle of Tom Ford which he loved, and we picked out a few games for the PS4. Everyone else bought him gifts or vouchers. He got a little overwhelmed with it all which I'm sure anybody would. However, I do think it was the information he received that had him going to visit his mum's grave, resulting in him wanting to see that she got a headstone. And rightly so.

"Are we going to Olivia's?" Mathew asks, bringing me out of my musing.

"Yeah, once we've loaded the dishwasher," I tell him as I cover the pan of bolognaise, not sure if Holly, Lucas and Max will have eaten already then, I wipe down the worktops as Mathew sets about filling the dishwasher.

Once we've finished cleaning up, I collect my keys and breathe in a sigh of relief. Now I've got to the bottom of why Mathew had been acting strange and where the money went, I feel happier and in desperate need of seeing my angel. "Come on, let's go," I call to Mathew, not wanting to waste another moment until I can see her.

Chapter 12

Holly

"And he sleeps," I whisper, placing a soft kiss on Max's forehead as Daniel finishes humming the tune to Puff the Magic Dragon, happy that the little man has finally give up the fight and drifted off.

Vlad and Lucas went to collect Mathew from Dimitri's half an hour ago and Max wanted to wait up until they had gotten back. Normally Mathew would only cover one or two short shifts at the weekend, but due to a large party that had been booked in they needed all hands-on deck. So, he went straight from school, arriving at four and finishing at eight. When Vlad mentioned he was setting off to collect him, Max, who was overly tired, refused to go to bed without seeing his big brother first and his dad tucking him in. It's not often he gets upset these days but when he does, we do give into him a little, which meant that we would let him stay up until they got back. Within minutes of them leaving, he'd climbed onto my knee and got himself comfy up against my huge belly, with only having two weeks left until my due date, I can safely say it was a struggle for him. Daniel sat chuckling away at his little brother who although was as snug as a bug in a rug still refused to close his eyes, happy to have his head nestled against my chest while his little hand patted my belly.

As Daniel started singing, Max's eyes began to flicker shut then once he reverted to humming the tune, they stayed closed, a soft snore revealing that he had fallen asleep.

"He's a cute little bugger," Daniel says as he runs his hand over Max's hair, standing up to put his guitar away.

"That he is," I chuckle and kiss his head again. "He's such a lovable little boy, it's hard to believe someone could be so mean and nasty to him."

"I know," Daniel shakes his head, making his way into the kitchen. "But he's safe and loved now," he continues just as the front door opens.

"Hi, how was work?" I ask Mathew as he strolls into the room, looking absolutely shattered.

"Busy," he says, blowing out a breath and flopping down on the opposite settee. He usually works on the washing up and is looked after by Alex, the head chef, who is Maureen's husband.

Tonight was his first night working out front, waiting tables. Maureen had said she would put him with the more experienced staff while he was learning the ropes.

"I got £13 in tips," Mathew pats his pocket, his eyes widening, happy with his stash.

"Did you? That's not bad," I nod at him.

"Yeah, I know. The women I was working with shared what was in the glass before I finished."

"That's nice of them. Were you just helping them out?"

"Yeah, just clearing tables and fetching drinks."

"When did he fall asleep?" Vlad asks, sitting at the side of me, his hand strokes Max's head which lays across my stomach as he places a soft kiss on my lips. Mathew chuckles and shakes his head at my husband's show of affection and Lucas, who's just sat down, rolls his eyes. They're both used to seeing us all loved up, but they still like to act as if it's embarrassing.

"A few minutes before you came in."

"Give him here, I'll take him up to bed," Vlad takes Max from my arms as Daniel steps back into the room. He sits chatting with Lucas for a few minutes then stands ready to leave for his night out.

"Well that's my babysitting duties done for the evening," he chuckles, bending down to kiss me on the head.

"Cheeky get," I slap his arm because he's not talking about babysitting Max. Vlad doesn't want me being left alone just in case I go into labour early. He's scared to death that it might happen when I'm either on my own or when there's just Max and me. So, when he's not here he has one of his sons stay with me, if they're not available then it's Izzy, Olivia, Sarah, or Mary and Tom. I haven't even argued with him about it because it's pointless. He's not going to give in and I'm actually glad that there's someone with me just in case. I'd be petrified if I went into labour when I'm alone. Plus, how can I say no to him when he means well.

"Thanks Daniel, have a good night," I call to him as he makes his way out of the door.

"Have you eaten?" I ask Mathew. We all ate earlier on but Mathew went to the restaurant straight from school so he may not have had the chance.

"Yeah," he nods his head. "Alex made me this spicy chicken sandwich with lettuce, tomato and mayonnaise. It was really good. I had some of those thick salt and peppered chips with it. I'd just finished it when Lucas and Vlad arrived."

"Hmmm, sounds nice. I could eat something spicy," I say, rubbing my belly, thinking about what we have in the fridge that I can whip up quickly. For the last couple of weeks, I've had cravings for anything hot and spicy and even though we had chilli con carne a few hours ago, I could eat something else.

Both boys laugh at me when I stand and make my way into the kitchen, knowing I'm going on a rummage to see what I can find. They both follow me, leaning against the island with their arms folded.

"What are you looking for, Holly?" Lucas smirks at me, tilting his head.

"I don't know really. Anything that's got a kick to it," I answer with my head in the fridge. I've done pretty well throughout my pregnancy; I've ate healthily except for the Danish pastries and this craving for all things hot and spicy.

"We'll leave you to it," he chuckles. "I've got some maths homework to finish then we're going to have a game," he points between himself and Mathew.

"Are we playing down here?" Mathew asks. "I'll set it up while you're getting on with your schoolwork. You don't mind do you, Holly?" I take my head out of the fridge, frowning when nothing in there appeals to me.

"No, I don't mind, go ahead," I tell them, opening the cupboards to check if there's anything in them.

"Ok," they both say then go about whatever they have planned, leaving me rummaging tirelessly.

"Need any help?" Vlad's deep, amused voice stops me in my tracks.

"Why haven't we got anything decent to eat in the house?" I grumble, pulling myself out of the bottom cupboard, which is usually stocked well with goodies. I sit on the floor looking up at my handsome man who grins at me before he crouches on the floor then sits up against the cupboard door and pulls me onto his knee.

"That's because you," he actually points a finger at me which if he does again, I will bite off and wipe that bloody grin off his face. "told Mary a few weeks ago that you would do the shopping. Your words, *'Mary love you do enough with all the baking you do for us. You're not well so I'll do the shopping'.*" Bugger. Yeah, I did. Since I moved in, Mary and Tom have always turned up with bags of shopping on a Wednesday and frozen meals that she's cooked at home. I've always felt guilty with being the woman of the house. Having someone shop and cook meals for us doesn't feel right, it should be Vlad, the boys and me doing it. Which we do but we usually have a well-stocked fridge and cupboards for me to whip something up with. Or the freezer is normally full of home-cooked meals.

However, when I mentioned it to Vlad, he told me Mary wouldn't be happy if I was to take her job from her so not wanting to step on anyone's toes or upset her, I've let her continue to do it. Both Mary and Tom look at Vlad and the boys as family and love making sure they have plenty to eat and since I moved in, they look at me the same and I know Vlad loves them dearly, as do I.

That is why a few weeks ago, when Mary had a virus, I told her to leave the shopping to me, that she did enough with all the meals she cooks and brings over to put in the freezer. Only I haven't done a big shop, just bought in the essentials we needed. With having so much in at the time, not much was needed but now it has all run down.

"Oh," I say as Vlad snuggles his face into my neck and kisses all the way up to my ear.

"What do you need?"

"I thought I'd have some hot chilli tortillas with some salsa dip, but we haven't got any, so it doesn't matter."

"Up," he taps my bottom, helping me off his knee. Vlad stands, taking my hand to help me off the floor. "I'll nip to the petrol station down the road, they'll have some."

"No, it doesn't matter. I can do without." I feel bad now, he's only just gotten back in after picking up Mathew. He's had a busy week. Some of the apartments are ready to let so he's been going through application forms for tenants and all the necessary paperwork. He was going to bring in a letting agency but since Seb told him he wants to sell Aphrodite and come into the property market they decided that they don't need to bring anybody else in. So, he's been handling all the paperwork along with Seb, Zack, and his accountant for the club, ready for the evaluation for when it goes up for sale. He's also had the health and safety officer at the second building checking it out.

"Yes, it does matter," he pecks at my lips. "It will take me five minutes, I'll just go up and turn on the monitor, I forgot while I was up there." We always turn on the monitor in Max's room just in case he has a nightmare. Fingers crossed, he's been doing really well and sleeping through.

"Thanks," I say, throwing my arms around his neck. "I owe you."

"I know," he raises his eyebrows at me. "And I will be claiming what you owe tonight," he murmurs into my lips, stealing a kiss and slapping my arse. When he moves away from me, he throws me a naughty wink and calls out to Lucas and Mathew. "You boys want anything while I'm at the shop?" Then he takes me in his arms again and kisses me hard while the boys real off from the living room what they want, not taking their eyes from the television.

I'm left feeling dizzy when he makes his way upstairs to turn on the monitor and thinking it's a bloody good job I enjoy repaying my debts to him.

Lucas and Mathew join me in the kitchen, waiting for Vlad to come back downstairs, "We've changed our minds," Lucas says. "We'll have the same as you."

"Ok, I'll tell him."

Hearing a creaking noise coming from the garage, we all turn our heads. Sometimes if the door that leads from the garage into the utility room isn't shut properly then it will creak and rattle, it's quite annoying really.

"I'll do it," Lucas says, making his way through the door as I pick up a dishcloth to wipe down the worktops and Mathew takes off towards the downstairs bathroom.

I can hear Vlad moving around upstairs now the monitors are switched on, it causes me to chuckle when I hear him whispering to Max. I know he'll be sat there just stroking the boy's hair while he tells him a tale, it doesn't matter to Vlad that Max is fast asleep. He said that hearing his voice while he's asleep will keep the nightmares away because Max knows that he's safe with Vlad and that he loves him. Cute really and so true.

"Holly," Lucas' strained voice has me turning towards the door of the utility room, his eyes are large and terrified and when he's shoved from the doorway into the kitchen, I drop the dishcloth into the sink, stepping back to get a look at who is stood behind him.

"Ah the pregnant wife, so much better," the man sneers, baring his teeth as he glares at me with crazed eyes. He grips Lucas' neck with one large hand, edging him further into the kitchen with his shoulder.

"Who are you? Let go of him!" My words are hurried as I move forward to grab Lucas' arm but stop suddenly when I notice the gun he has pressed into his back. The scream I want to let out to alert Vlad gets stuck and I become mute. With a pounding heart and shaking hands, I swallow, trying to lubricate my dry mouth.

"Let him ago," my voice but a croak.

"Gladly." In one swift movement, Lucas is pushed to the floor and I'm taken in his place.

"Get off her," Lucas demands, quickly springing to his feet and lunging at the man with the gun. I can see the man raising his arm and call out to Lucas to stop. He does and stumbles backwards when he's caught under the chin.

"Leave him alone," I struggle with the man only to stop when I feel him dig the gun into my ribs.

"Quit it before I hurt one of you," he snarls and I freeze, wanting to protect Lucas and my baby.

I place my hand on my belly and widen my eyes at Lucas, shaking my head in the hopes he doesn't try to be a hero. He gets my drift and stands against the island, tears in his eyes.

"Who are you? What do you want?" I ask, trying to stay strong and calm. Letting him think that I'm not frightened of him when really inside I'm tied in knots.

Vlad will be down any minute and I know things will turn ugly and there's not a thing I can do about it. I've no sooner thought it when I hear his footsteps and I start to shake uncontrollably.

"Holly," Vlad calls from the stairs. I can't answer him. The man's hand covers my mouth and the stale smell of cigarette smoke and dirt invade my senses, making me want to vomit. I swallow it down, trying hard not cough and choke.

"Who the fuck are you? Get your fucking hands off my wife!" Vlad bellows when he sees I'm being held against the man's chest, his arm around mine. He charges like a bull towards us, his nostrils flaring like one too. A look of rage on his face.

"I don't think so," the man grins as he waves the gun around, stopping my husband stock still. His eyes search mine, checking that I'm alright and I quickly nod at him, not wanting him to get shot by this crazed man. Lucas stands against the kitchen island more near his father than me and when Vlad's eyes flit from me to Lucas, he notices the red mark on his chin. Torment and anger mar his handsome face as his chest heaves heavily and I can see his fists clenching tightly.

"Don't get any silly ideas, big man. The gun is loaded, and I won't hesitate to use it."

"Let my wife go and tell me what you want." Gritting his teeth,

Vlad takes a step forward.

"I don't think you're in any position to give demands and ask questions, do you?" He digs the gun in my ribs, making me moan. Vlad grimaces, closing his eyes as he looks towards the ceiling, mumbling. I don't know if he's throwing up a silent prayer or cursing. Maybe both.

"Let Holly sit down and take me in her place," Vlad says as he takes a step forward, his eyes full of concern, flicking from me to the hand which holds the gun.

"Not happening. Move back," he directs at Vlad.

"Who are you?" I ask, I've now found my voice.

"He's my dad," Mathew says, stepping to the side of Vlad who looks down at him then turns towards the man we now know to be Mathew's father.

Mathew comes closer but Vlad stops him, putting his hand on his shoulder. "Stay where you are, Mathew. What do you want?" Vlad asks him again. "And let Holly sit down, you can see she's heavily pregnant." He flicks his chin towards me, suddenly sounding composed. Maybe he thinks he needs to take a different approach. And I agree. This man isn't sane. He's desperate and volatile. He might be calling the shots because he has a gun, but I can feel is body twitching nervously behind me. Which makes him dangerous with or without a gun.

He walks backwards, taking me with him, then pulls out one of the stools, instructing me to sit.

"Now, tell me why you are here in my home and what you want?"

Chapter 13
Vlad

"He's a coward!" Mathew shouts, stepping past me and out of my reach. "You killed my mum and now you're holding a pregnant woman at gunpoint, real brave. I'm ashamed to have you as a dad." He spits out at him. What he's saying is true and Mathews just shown he's a damn sight braver than his father, but I can't allow him to aggravate the situation, not when he's got a gun pointed at my wife and unborn child. I step forward and place my hand on his shoulder.

"Mathew," I say, trying to calm him but his so-called father opens his mouth.

"I did not kill her!" he yells, his breathing heavy. "It was an accident... I never meant to..."

"You hit her with a car and left her there to die! Of course, you meant it." Mathew's eyes are flooded as he confronts his father. And I understand how much he must hate him because if I didn't want to kill him for what he did to Max and Mathew, looking at Holly and Lucas, how scared they are has me wanting to kill him with my bare hands. Which I will do. For what he's done to these boys, taking their mum, hurting them in a way which is inconceivable. I've noticed the red mark on Lucas' chin and for that alone, I will rip him to shreds. Then there's my Holly and my baby which he has a gun trained on. I can see she's petrified which will be causing stress to her and the baby and that I cannot allow, so as soon as I find out what he wants, and I think I have an idea, I will do everyone a favour and kill him with his own gun.

"I'm sorry but it was an accident." His eyes close as he breathes in deeply and just as I see my chance to overpower him, he opens his eyes, stopping me. "Don't even think about it," he shifts closer to Holly, moving the gun from her ribs to her neck and I let out a growl. I feel absolutely useless, if I try to rush at him then I risk the chance of him shooting Holly, killing her and our baby, or the bullet going astray and hitting Lucas or Mathew. Shaking my head, ridding the thoughts that are circling, I gaze at Holly. Our eyes meet and I gather strength from her love. *Don't do anything stupid,* I say to myself. *Find out why he's here and give him what he wants. Anything to get him away from my family.*

My angel sends me a tight smile and nods her head, encouraging me to stay calm. "Why are you here?" I ask with as much serenity in my voice as I can muster up at the moment.

"Why am I here?" he leans against the worktop, "Let's take a minute to think about that," arrogance oozing from him. He's definitely not playing with a full deck of cards. He's shaky and yelling then focused with a calmness to his voice, if I thought I could lose it quickly then he beats me hands down.

His attention turns back to Mathew, completely ignoring me. "When your mother took you away from me, when she left, I was so angry. I didn't understand why. Couldn't comprehend that I'd hurt her and hurt you. So, I went on a binge. Nothing new, I liked a drink," he smiles sarcastically. "I thought she'll come back, I'll give her a week and she'll be back. Only she didn't. When I tried to find you both, I kept hitting a brick wall every fucking time. No one knew where you were, and it drove me insane." He lifts his hand that's holding the gun and taps his head, pulling at his own hair as he grimaces. He's losing it.

"I loved both of you, your mother was everything to me."

"Only because she put up with your shit. If you had loved her you wouldn't have hurt her," Mathew sniffles. From what I've learnt, he manipulated her for years. Made her think she was worthless and that she needed him because nobody would want someone fat and as ugly as her. According to Mathew she had put on a few pounds and was a little self-conscious about it and this poor excuse of a man tapped into it, making her feel insignificant until one day she'd had enough and left him. From what I can remember, she had a beautiful curvy figure. Men love curves. Her eyes were beautiful and when she spoke, she spoke the truth. I was never one for a full-on conversation with women I met in clubs or anywhere really, but I do remember her saying that she didn't normally go for one-night stands. Random bunk up. She also told me that she had a son who her friend was taking care of and needed to be home before he got up. I know I rejected the idea of having another son out there when it was first brought to my attention and I know I said I didn't know her. I had my reasons for that, which I've explained to Holly.

"After a while without you both," he says, dismissing what Mathew had said as he rubs at his forehead. "I couldn't cope. Drinking landed me in prison, doing a stretch for assault. I swore when I got out, I would find you and make amends and hopefully your mum would take me back. But..." he shakes his head, stopping from what he was going to say then he glares at me with as much hatred in his eyes that I'm surprised I haven't turned to stone.

"You." He points the gun at me, gripping at Holly's arm, making her flinch as he leans closer towards me and I just about to lose it. "You did this," the gun waves around in his hand. Holly's eyes widen as she frantically shakes her head. "Can you not sleep with a woman without knocking her up?" He looks down at Holly's stomach.

"What?" I don't understand what his problem is. I slept with Mathew's mum when they weren't together. She'd left him a few years before. Granted I don't think either us thought that she'd fall pregnant after a one-night stand, I know I didn't but it's not like they were getting back together. Ah, now I understand.

"When I found her, she had the little boy with her. We argued. She wouldn't listen to me. Rejected me. Told me I was a fool to come and find her after so many years had passed. And she was right, I didn't want to take on someone else's kid, so I stormed off back to my car."

He lifts his head, staring at the ceiling, breathing deeply. "I sat there for a few minutes trying to control the anger that I was feeling; that she'd been with another man. It took a while, but I thought yeah,

I could give it a go…"

"She didn't want you back," Mathew cuts in with. "Didn't matter whether she had a man in her life or not she didn't want you back."

"Shut up!" he bellows at Mathew, his eyes narrowing on him. I place my hand on Mathew's shoulder, hoping to calm the boy down. This man will turn on his own, no trouble. He doesn't need antagonising. Mathew needs to let him finish without riling him up any more than he is.

"Let him finish," I say calmly, raising my eyebrows at him. Then at least we'll get to know what he wants.

Mathew's father blows out a breath and shakes his head. "When I set off to look for her, she'd gone. I went round to the house and she wasn't there. I'd found the address a few days before, but it had taken me time to build up the courage to speak to her. I was going to wait for her to come home but I got too impatient, so I set off roaming round the streets. I knew she couldn't have gone far; we'd only been a couple of streets away from where she lived when we first argued." He rubs at his head with the gun and I notice his hands shake.

"The streets were quiet. I'm not sure how long I'd been driving around when I saw her at the end of the road, turning the corner. I put my foot down to catch up with her. When I turned the corner, Max was on the pavement and I was going too fast. I couldn't break in time…" His voice turns croaky and a lone tear slips down his cheek, which he wipes away quickly, shaking his head. You almost feel sorry for the man because from what he's just told us, I know what he's about to say next. But I don't feel sorry for him, he's a nasty selfish bastard without one ounce of decency in him. What he's done to his own son and mine, their mother, and now he's in my home threatening my family. No. I feel no pity for him.

"Louise was crouching in the road, picking something up," he says once he's composed himself. "and I went straight into her. It was an accident."

"But you left her there, on her own," Mathew whispers, tears in his eyes. When I look at Holly, she too is wiping her eyes and Lucas bites his lip, trying hard not to let his emotions escape.

There's no more to be said, we'll never know if Louise would have lived if he'd have stayed and phoned an ambulance. And whether it was an accident or not he's still accountable for her death and the abuse he inflicted on Mathew and Max. At least Mathew has some sort of closure. Knowing his dad didn't set out to kill his mum might help the poor boy. But he'll still always wonder, what if?

"So, what brings you here to my home waving that around?" I nod my head at the gun in his hand which is now resting by his side. I know he doesn't think highly of me due to some mistaken idea that if I hadn't have slept with Louise, causing her to fall pregnant, then there might have been a chance for them. I don't think so.

"I think you know." Yeah, I do.

"How much?" He needs to get away. The police have a warrant out for his arrest, and I don't think he's looking at a slap on the wrist. Which means he needs money for a passport...

"Fifty thousand," he says. "And don't tell me you're not good for it because I know you are." Yes, I am, but I don't have that amount at home.

"I only have twenty, here."

"Not enough," he says.

"You're not planning on giving him it, are you?" Mathew looks up at me, a questioning look on his face. Yes, I am. I'd give him whatever he asked for to get him away from my family and out of my house. Once they're out of danger then that's a different matter.

"Mathew take a look around you. He has a gun pointed at Holly. It could switch to you or Lucas and I'm not going to stand by and let any of you get hurt. So yes, he can have the money."

"Good man. You know it makes sense but twenty's not enough." He almost has a smirk on his face when he runs the gun down Holly's arm.

"*I'm going to break your neck and laugh while I do it,*" I curse in Russian.

"Now, now, we'll have none of that. English please." Such a cocky bastard.

I know I have twenty in the safe upstairs. The only other way I could get him the money he wants would be to ring Nicholas at the club to see what's in the safe there. I haven't got a clue if any of my sons have done the banking this week, if they haven't then there will be, but I don't want to involve any more of my family in this mess.

"Like I said, I only have twenty in the house."

"And like I said, it's not enough." He moves the gun quickly, digging it into Holly's ribs, causing her to cry out.

"You hurt her again," I warn, stepping towards them, unable to stand here and do nothing while he causes my wife pain.

"Vlad, I'm fine," she stops me, holding up her hand, a pleading look on her face to retreat and give him what he wants.

"Okay." My hands go up as I step backwards. She's such a strong woman that I'm in awe of how she's keeping it together while been held by a man who is holding a gun to her and could lose it anytime. Me, I'm bordering on losing my mind and praying I can keep it together for the sake of my family.

Chapter 14

Holly

I'm barely holding it together as I watch my husband barter with Mathew's dad. I keep thinking maybe I could knock his arm away or stand on his foot and he'd drop the gun then Vlad would be able to rush at him and... Well do with him whatever he felt fitting. But I daren't. If it went wrong and one of the boys were shot or Vlad, then I wouldn't be able to live with myself.

I know Vlad is barely holding it together too. I keep hearing him curse and growl. I can see the torment on his face. Me and his unborn child been held at gunpoint and him not able to do a damn thing about it will be tearing him up inside. Invading his home and threatening his family will have him wanting to murder him with his bare hands. And as much as this man deserves it, I can't let Vlad do anything stupid that may lead to one of us getting hurt or him killing a man and ending up in trouble with the police. No, he needs to stay focused.

Even though my arm is sore with the tight grip he has on it and my ribs will be bruised with being jabbed by the gun, I can't let Vlad know that I'm hurting and scared. Every time he looks at me, I try to let him know that I'm doing ok but I'm sure he sees through my pretence.

He wants money and I know Vlad has an overly sized bank

account; I didn't know he had twenty thousand pounds in the house though. The safe is hidden in our bedroom, in the dressing room. Tucked away behind his suits. I only know it's there because Vlad has me storing my watch and jewellery in it when I'm not wearing them. I've never noticed wads of money in there, just brown envelopes and jiffy bags.

"I need fifty, so maybe you ring one of your sons and get them looking in the safe at one of your clubs," he demands. I watch him raise an eyebrow at Vlad who shakes his head, then covers his mouth with his hand. "You see, I know you have three older sons who work with you. I know you own a very well-established restaurant. I also know you have two clubs that are filled to the rafters most nights, I've actually been in them just last week. And then there's the apartments you have just started letting out. It's surprising what you can find out about someone without even having to google them. Just plain old conversation with bar staff over a few drinks or flirting with a waitress while I ate a very expensive haddock and chips. Delicious though."

He has a very self-assured attitude about him. I'm sure the staff are going to get a roasting after this. Discussing Vlad's business is a big fat no but I can imagine that Mathew's dad could be easy on the eye once he's cleaned up and I bet he can charm the birds from the trees, which would have had some of the young staff eating out of his hand.

"I'll need to ring my son," Vlad says, sounding defeated. I doubt for one minute he wanted to involve anyone else in this. "Or we all take a trip to my office," he suggests. What's he up to?

"I don't think so. Ring your son but be very careful. You let it slip that I'm here and..."

"Do you think I'm going to let any harm come to my wife? Just ease off her and you'll get your money!" He yells as he gets worked up. The deepness of his voice and the thickness of his accent tells me everything. He's had enough. He's angry and he's tired of this man calling the shots. I'm not sure how long he can keep it together.

I watch Vlad lift his phone from the worktop, press one of the buttons then put it to his ear.

"Nicholas, are you at the club? Go into the office and get me thirty thousand pounds out of the safe and bring it straight here. What? No." Vlad's eyes never leave mine as he speaks to Nicholas and when Mathew's dad indicates with the gun for him to wind the conversation up. He tells Nicholas to hurry up.

"I'm buying a caravan from one of the neighbours and they want cash," he tells his son. He must have asked why he wanted so much money. It's not something he would normally do so I'm sure Nicholas will be suspicious. Really, buying a caravan from a neighbour? I'm sure that's sent some alarm bells because Vlad's never spoken to any of them. The nearest is five hundred yards down the road.

"Oh, and Nicholas you may need to get Frank to add his code if Seb or Daniel aren't there. Yes. Don't be long, they have another buyer coming soon." He ends the call and I need to pee. I know what he's just said must have a meaning behind it because you don't need two codes to get into the safe in his office. I've seen Vlad put just his code in and I've also seen Sebastian and Nicholas and I'm not even sure if Frank, his head of security, has a code. And I really need the ladies. I can't hold it in. Too much presser down there with the baby.

"I need the loo," my small voice sounds pathetic.

"Sweetheart, are you ok?" Vlad's concerned voice warms my core. He probably thinks my waters are ready to break. They're not. Well they could do, who knows, but no, I genuinely need to pee and if I don't go soon then it will be like Niagara Falls in here. Ah, maybe that will cause him to drop his gun if I was to wee on his feet.

I cross my legs. "I need to use the toilet."

"Let her go so she can use the toilet," Vlad demands, getting worked up. I watch the man's eyes circle around the room.

"Where is it?" I point out into the hallway. There's a downstairs bathroom just in the entrance next to the front door. Or there's one in the room down the corridor in Seb and Izzy's room.

"You," he points to Lucas. "Come here." He wants to swap me for Lucas, and I don't feel happy about that. I think I'd rather wet myself.

"No. I'll wait."

"It's ok, Holly," my brave boy says as he walks towards us. Lucas and I have a bond. I don't know how it happened; it just did. He's the son I never had and I'm the mother he needed. From day one of meeting we clicked, and I can't let him do this.

"Sweetheart just go to the loo. I'm here, nothing's going to happen to him," Vlad calms me, sensing my trepidation.

"Don't worry, sweetheart," the monster mocks. "As long as your man here plays nice and these two don't try to be heroes then everything will be just peachy." I want to punch him in the face when he aims the gun at Lucas, letting go of me and dragging him by his arm into my place. "In fact, move along everyone. Lead the way, we're all going," I can't hold back any longer. Turning quickly, I spit in his face, catching him in the eye. I know it's a revolting thing to do but he makes me feel sick. He is sickening. He laughs vociferously, wiping it away then shakes his head. "Move. Now," he commands, pushing my shoulder.

Vlad's whole body stiffens. His eyes darkening to black as he glares at the man who has a gun pointed at his son's head and me in his line of fire as well. I've just provoked him, resulting in him ordering me around and being aggressive. I dread to think what's going on in my husband's head at the moment. He's probably plotting his revenge and getting ready to do something stupid all because I was unable to hold back. I need to calm him before he pounces.

Passing by Vlad, I squeeze his hand and smile at him, letting him know that I'm ok. He nods his head, taking in a deep breath.

Mathew and Vlad are told to follow me, Lucas behind them with the gun pointed on the back of his neck. Reaching the downstairs bathroom, Mathew's dad tells me to leave the door slightly open and not to do anything that will result in him having to use his gun. I wouldn't dream of it; the last thing I want is for any one of them to get hurt.

When I've finished Vlad and Mathew are told to stand by the far wall while he checks that I haven't picked anything up in the bathroom. To be truthful, I did have a look round but there's nothing, not even a razor. This bathroom is used by the kids: Max, Joe, Rebecca and Megan when she comes over so anything that could harm them has been removed. Plus, I'm wearing a pair of leggings and a baggy shirt or would be baggy if I didn't have a large pregnant belly stretching the life out of it.

Once we're back in the kitchen Lucas and I are swapped and I'm back to where I was with a gun in my ribs and my arm held in a vicelike grip. Mathew hasn't spoken since his dad explained what had happened on the day his mother died. Lucas stands to my left just a few feet away, trying to look brave but I can see he's scared; they both are. Vlad has been told to stand at the other side of the island, not too close but so he can be seen clearly.

Undoubtedly everyone is nervous and on tender hooks and when a loud noise comes from the utility room, we all turn towards it.

Nicholas' large frame is first to appear with an even larger one behind him. "Paps what the fuck do you want thirty grand for…" Suddenly the situation comes to light when the gun is waved in the air and Mathew's father steps forward, his grip still heavy around my arm.

"Who the fuck are you?"

"Nicholas, just give me the bag."

"What?" His eyes are flitting between his father and me and the man holding the gun. He passes the bag to his father, his eyes never leaving me then he moves back to stand at the side of Frank when Mathew's dad indicates with his gun to move back.

"Who the fuck is he?" Nicholas snarls, directing his question at his father.

"Mathew's dad," I answer for him as I watch the discreet looks pass between Frank and Vlad. Whatever they are thinking or planning they really need to be careful.

"Fucking hell!" Nicholas bellows, moving closer towards me as if he's on a mission. Swiftly, Frank grabs him by the shoulder and pulls him back. "Get your fucking hands of her, you coward…"

"Nicholas, shut it! Now is not the time," Vlad says, rubbing at his face. I pray to the heavens above that things don't take a turn for the worst but looking at Nicholas I can see he's had a drink which will only fuel his determination to confront the man who attacks women and children. The man who left Mathew and Max's mum to die then physically abused them both, leaving them alone: no food, Mathew unconscious after his beating and Max locked in his room.

Now he's here, in our home. Holding us at gunpoint demanding money and Nicholas wants revenge.

He shrugs Frank's grip from his shoulder, eyes glaring. "Take your fucking hands off her, you poor excuse for a fucking man!" Nicholas voice bellows around the kitchen. "You think you can come in our home demanding money, waving that around," his chin juts out at the gun. "It wouldn't surprise me if it isn't loaded."

"Wanna try it?" The gun points at Nicholas, causing Vlad to move swiftly towards his son. Protecting him.

"Nicholas you need to be quiet, let him take the money and go," he says firmly, not wanting his son to get hurt.

"Back," he waves the gun around then tucks into my ribs again, triggering Vlad to stop in his tracks, cursing through is teeth, his chest heaving. Heavy breathing also hits the back of my neck as I'm pulled closer into the man's chest. Nicholas glares frantically. This is a side I've not seen in him before. He's normally playful and jovial. Fun, loving man. Obviously, he's not his father's son for nothing, wanting to protect his family, but he needs to reign it in and let Vlad give him the money so we can get rid of him. "Slide the bag across the floor carefully," he says to my husband.

"No fucking way! Give him nothing... "

"Nicholas calm down, he can have the money," Vlad stare at Nicholas, pleading to keep quiet and not antagonise this man any further. Nicholas shakes his head, cursing and calling the man again; unhappy that we're giving him what he wants.

"Leave it, Nicholas," Frank's tone is composed and firm. As well as been in the security business for a good number of years, he's ex-army which I'm sure will come in handy. "Let him take the money and leave. No need to make matters worse, is there? I'm sure he'll be on his way once he's got what he came for and everyone will be safe." Frank stares directly at our assailant, nodding his head at him. The man nods back, agreeing with him that he just came for the money then he'll be on his way. Then we can call the police.

However, my stepson wants his pound of flesh and either he's had one too many alcoholic beverages or he's got a death wish. Or both.

"You're sickening!" he growls.

"Shut up!" Mathew's dad shouts, spit flying from his mouth.

"You want to hold someone at gun point then use me instead of a pregnant woman," he stabs his finger hard into his chest, taking a step forward.

"Nicholas, don't!" It's a warning not to be ignored but he's not listening to anyone and takes no notice of his father.

"You want to hit someone then hit me. Instead of women and children, you spineless bastard!"

"Shut up!" Mathew's father bellows.

In a split second, holy hell breaks loose. Angry voices all around. Panicked voices.

"Shut up! Shut up! Shut up!"

An arm. A gun, raised, pointing towards Nicholas. Nicholas goading. Cursing. Moving towards us.

The sound of the gun going off. Deafening.

The sound of my husband's roar, "Noooooo!" Heart breaking.

My legs give way. I fall to my knees, hitting my head on the way down.

My head throbs. I see stars. Darkness all around.

Prising my eyes open, blood, lots of blood. Nicholas in his father's arms. Frank holding a towel to his chest. Then everything goes black.

Chapter 15

Vlad

My hand holds on to Holly's while my forehead rests on the side of the bed, the coolness of the metal frame is welcomed. Lifting my aching head, rubbing at my chest, trying to rid the weight that's pressing down on it, the lump in my throat threatens to choke me as I stare at the white clinical walls. I swallow hard to rid it, but it doesn't budge

I place her small delicate hand on top of her stomach, mine joining it. That's where she'd want it to be.

Tears fill my eyes when I look at the white dressing on the side of her head, she didn't deserve this. She's pure and innocent in this world of evil and shouldn't have been subjected to such torment and hurt. Me. I probably deserve it. Payback for my past life.

Quietly, I stand. Leaning down, my lips gently kiss the wound to her head as I stoke her soft hair.

In the mist of all the commotion last night when Nicholas, my poor boy, decided to provoke the bastard that had invaded our home, Holly collapsed. Hitting her head on the kitchen island and knocking herself out. She wasn't out for long. Awaking to a sight that put her into shock.

My son bleeding to death in my arms. Shot by a man who became so unstable, I saw it happening before he pulled the trigger. As Nicholas hailed abuse at him, calling him out for what he was. A coward. A vile excuse of a human being, he lost it. I could see it in his eyes that he was ready to explode. The menacing voice as he repeatedly told Nicholas to shut up; not liking the truth that was spat out at him. His hand shaking as he pointed the gun at him. I tried to move quickly, knowing he was going to shoot, only I didn't get there fast enough. I was too slow.

Holding Nicholas' lifeless body in my arms, trying to stop the bleeding and watching my heavily pregnant wife collapse onto the floor, my heart broke. Shattered.

Within what seemed like forever, but I'm sure was only minutes, Holly was awake. Dazed but awake. And Nicholas was taken from me by the paramedics so they could work on him.

Mathew had phoned for an ambulance and the police while Lucas, Frank and I attended to both my son and my wife.

I don't remember much about who did what. It all seems like a dream. A nightmare that I've yet to wake up from. What I do remember is having Nicholas prised from my arms... Blood everywhere.

I remember being in the back of the ambulance, holding Holly so tight while we watched the paramedics hook my son up to drips and machines. I remember the noise of the siren as the ambulance proceeded at speed, passing through the red lights. It pulling over and the sound of the heart monitor as my son's heart gave up and the machine flatlined.

I recall Holly's short intake of breath and my own when they sent a shock through him. And I remember the noise of the machine flatlining for a second time... Tears, so many tears as we held each other tightly, not wanting to believe what we were seeing.

No one's ever prepared for what we went through last night, I know I wasn't. Not able to protect my family cut deep and has forced me to come to a decision I never ever thought I'd have to make.

The door opens behind me and a hand gently taps my shoulder. "How is she? How are you, mate?" Jack's hushed voice asks, trying hard not to wake Holly.

"She's sleeping," I stroke my hand over her hair. Cried herself to sleep.

I'd asked Olivia and Jack to come and sit with her. They're her friends, family, and I don't want her left on her own while I attend to a matter of importance at home. When she wakes God only knows what she will be like. Both Olivia and Jack as well as Sarah and Nick were here until the early hours, them too not wanting to leave but I persuaded them to go and get some sleep.

"What have the doctors said?" Olivia asks.

"Concussion but hopefully she'll be able to come home later today. Her blood pressure is fine now." That's the two reasons why they had kept her in on bedrest. "And the baby is doing well, no signs of coming yet though." Thank God. I need to leave Holly for a while and I certainly wouldn't be leaving her if they were any signs that the baby could come anytime.

"You go do what you need and have a shower." Olivia points at my shirt that I'm still wearing from last night, the blood brings the memory flooding back, not that it wasn't at the forefront of my thoughts, and I take in a deep breath, trying to beat down the torment I'm going through.

"Come here," Olivia squeezes me hard as she wraps her arms around me, her head on my chest and I take comfort in her embrace. "This shouldn't have happened... " she mumbles into my chest, wiping under her eyes when she pulls away. I nod my head, agreeing but not able to speak. Fear of my emotions getting the better of me. And no, it shouldn't have happened and now I have something to do.

"I won't be long," I whisper, laying another soft kiss on Holly's forehead while my hand holds onto hers that are laying across her stomach. I struggle to pull myself away from her and our unborn child knowing what I'm about to do will cause her more heartache. Hopefully she'll understand.

Leaving the ward, I take a slow walk out of the hospital and inhale the fresh air. Wanting... Needing to clear my head.

Taking a seat on one of the many benches, I watch people coming and going, wondering what brings them to this place. Do we ever just sit back and ask ourselves why? Why is the man in black trousers and white shirt with his hair cropped short weaving in and out of the people that are in his way? In a hurry to get to where he needs to be. Is he late for work? An appointment? Possibly. Or is he trying to get to a loved one that's been hurt... Who knows? The old couple, shuffling across the road, arms linked together. Heads slightly lowered, stopping the wind from blowing in their faces. Probably been married for fifty years or more and have seen their fair share of what life throws at us. Happiness. Sadness. Love and heartache. Why are they here? Shifting my outstretched legs for a young woman who is passing by with a baby in a pushchair, she can't be any older than twenty. She smiles as she lowers her head to the child cooing and shushing the little one who is making a lot of noise. Opening his lungs; whaling to gain her attention. Happy now that he can see his mother's face. Is she here for him, herself or for some other reason? Who the hell knows?

I've spent so much time over the years coming and going from hospitals. Mainly for Lucas. A few months ago, I didn't think I would be here for anything else other than Holly's scans and to see our baby being born. Happy times. But here I am, tears in my eyes. A lump in my throat and heavy heart. Sighing, I stand and make my way to the other side of the hospital.

Striding down the long corridor, I turn left at the end. The blue doors are closed, and the sign stands out like a beacon, ICU. I'd been here through the night, but everything is in a bit of a haze.

The room is dimly lit, two nurses at their desk and a doctor looking over one of the patient's charts. The noise of the machines brings back memories of when Lucas was born, and I halt, not able to go any further.

"Paps," Sebastian's low voice calls to me, causing me to glance over to him, sitting at the side of his brother's bed. Lucy sits on the other side, holding Nicholas' hand.

While we were in the ambulance on our way to the hospital, the loss of blood that Nicholas had sustained due to the bullet wound in his chest and his lung collapsing caused him to go into cardiac arrest. Holly and I clung to each other, praying they could bring him back. On the second electric shock, I almost threw up when there was nothing, just a tone I never want to hear again. The paramedics stood back, waiting, then went at it again and on the third go they brought him back.

He was rushed straight into surgery when we arrived at the hospital to have the bullet removed from his chest. Holly too was taken from me, her needing medical attention.

Holly was admitted and kept on one of the maternity wards due to a slight concussion, but the main reasons was that her blood pressure was sky high. She didn't want to go on to a ward, not knowing what was happening with Nicholas, but she didn't have a choice. So, between my sons and I and Holly's friends we've taken turns in sitting in a family room waiting on news about Nicholas or sitting with Holly. I sat with Holly most of the night, needing her to keep me sane while I waited on any update.

Nicholas was brought here around five this morning. The bullet had been removed, and he had been given a blood transfusion. We were told it's not uncommon for a lung to collapse with a chest trauma and to go into cardiac arrest, lucky for us he was able to be saved. It will take a few weeks to fully recover and may need longer. For the next couple of days, he will stay in intensive care then hopefully be moved on to a ward.

"How is he?" I ask, moving to the side of the bed. Looking at Nicholas, his skin so pale. A tube in his mouth, a drip attached to his arm and the steady rhythm of the heart monitor piercing the silence of the three-bedded ward.

"Well he hasn't woken up yet, but the nurse said it could be later this afternoon or tonight. Even then he won't be with it. They're gunna remove the breathing tube this afternoon. See how he goes on. It will probably be the middle of the night or early tomorrow morning before he's fully with us."

"And where are your brothers?"

"Gone for something to eat with Izzy. And before you ask the kids are fine with Mary and Tom. She said Max is happy, oh, and they have Spot with them," Shit, poor Spot. Last night before I went to pick up Mathew, I put him outside on the patio to play with his toys and the poor thing was left there all night, forgetting about him when Mathew's dad turned up. Mathew had said not to worry because before they came to live with us, he was left outside a lot of the time anyway. I still felt bad, he's become part of the family.

"Okay," I nod at him, placing my hand on top of Lucy's who

gently holds Nicholas'. "And, how are you?" Her normal emerald green eyes that usually sparkle and shine, so full of life, look desolate and red raw. I know they are close. They've been good friends since they met but something has been going on between them resulting in Nicholas hitting the bottle more than his typical couple of drinks when he's at the club.

Lucy stares up at me, tears in her eyes. "I'm sorry, Vlad," she sobs into her tissue. "This is my fault... We argued and he went out drinking... And maybe if he hadn't have had that much to drink then he might have handled the situation differently." She sniffles.

Another one that blames themselves. I had Mathew crying, blaming himself that it was his fault his dad turned up because he was there.

"Lucy I'll tell you the same as I did Mathew. It is not yours, Mathew's or anybody else's fault that that bastard," I grit my teeth, "did this." My hand moves to my son's head, my thumb stroking over his closed eyes. I swallow hard and close my eyes when I think about how I could have lost him. Nicholas is Nicholas. You never know how he's going to react to a situation. As a rule, he's normally fun-loving, a joker, but under those circumstances it's a different matter. He'd been brought up around guns. Even though mine were always locked away out of sight he'd seen his uncle with them. On the occasions when I would take them to visit their grandmother, my father's men were always around with guns. He'd witnessed the games they would play outside my father's home. Shooting at each other's feet, having to dance or move quickly so they weren't hit by a bullet. And maybe one or two more that he shouldn't have seen.

Having his brothers, Holly, and I held at gun point would have sent him over the edge, especially with the drink down him. He wouldn't have been thinking straight... "It's not your fault," I tell her again, moving my hand as I step back.

I know what I have to do, and I need to do it now. "I need to go," I tell them.

"Where are you going?" Sebastian asks, shifting back in his chair. Pulling at my shirt that's covered in blood and probably Holly's tears and snotty nose from all her crying, I tell him I'm calling home to shower and change. Which I am. It's not a lie. I don't tell him what my other plans are, I don't want him getting involved. Which he would. This is his brother lying here in this hospital bed. Holly, his step mum who he cares for dearly, lying in another hospital bed. Me, his father, going out of his mind.

I take a deep breath, anger rising from the pit of my stomach. An ache in my chest that won't go away and a determination to rid this man once and for all.

"Who's with Holly?" Lucy questions.

"Your mum and dad. She's asleep." She nods her head and I turn to leave. "I won't be long. Make sure you two get something to eat when the rest get back." There are only two visitors to a bed so they've been taking it in turns while I've been with Holly.

They both nod at me and I walk out the door.

*

Arriving home, after nipping down to the canteen in the hospital to borrow Daniel's car keys, I head straight to the shower. The house is quiet, which is what I need at the moment, wanting to clear my mind and rid myself of last night if only for a short time.

I let the steam surround me as the spray of the scalding water hits my skin like pellets. I'm so full of rage, guilt. Call it what you will. Unable to do anything to stop Holly and Nicholas from being hurt last night eats away at me and has me punching at the marble tiles. I sink to the floor, burrowing my head in my hands, yanking at my hair. "Fuck!" I roar, needing to let the anger out but it bounces all around the shower unit coming back at me full force as it hits me in the chest. Tears burst from my eyes and flow like the river Nile and I let them. I need to let it out and focus on what I must do.

In all the commotion last night, Mathew's dad ran out of the house after shooting Nicholas; the rest of us too absorbed with Holly and my son. Like the coward he is he ran, taking the thirty thousand pounds that Frank and Nicholas had brought from the club with him. The police are doing everything to find him but it's not enough. They had a warrant out for his arrest before all of this but couldn't find him. Well I'm not willing to sit back and do nothing while he tries to run from his crimes.

Standing, I step out of the shower and curse. My hand throbbing from hitting the wall. I dry myself and quickly dress in the clean jeans and shirt I had laid out in the bedroom then I head back into my dressing room. Parting my suits, I press in the number and open my safe. Two brown jiffy bags holding what I need. I leave them where they are for now, knowing I will need them very soon. Then I lock up the safe and make my way downstairs to my office.

Once I'm settled in my chair, I take out my phone and dial in the number of the man who I know will be happy to help me find the man I want.

Mathew Simpson. The same name as his son. I didn't know his name until last night. Now, I know his name, date of birth and that he has a tattoo of a dragon on his shoulder. Where he was born and the school he attended. Not that I need all of those details. He will have gone underground now, wanting to get a fake passport to get away. And that is where my brother, Sasha, comes in handy. He might have given up all the old family ways the same time as me, but he still has his fingers in a few pies. And will know who to hire to find him quickly and without being traced.

"Привет," (Hello) my brother's thick abrupt accent startles me. I don't normally phone him, we usually Skype or facetime. Clearly I've caught him at the wrong time.

"Sasha."

"Vladimir, how are you?" He switches to English, knowing it's my preferred language and his tone softens.

"I'm... " I can't tell him I'm good because I'm anything but.

"What is wrong?"

"I need your help."

"Why?" I can hear him moving around and doors closing, I assume he's just gone into his office.

"I need you to find someone for me or hire someone to do it."

"Okay. Are you going to tell me why and what has you sounding miserable? The last time we spoke you were... Happy. All loved up with a baby on the way. What has happened, brother?"

Over the next half hour, I tell him all about how I have another son that I knew nothing about. All about Max and Mathew losing their mother and what they went through because of Mathew's father. I even tell him about Spot our crazy dog. He never interrupts, just listens attentively. Then I tell him about last night.

Again, he doesn't interrupt me. Just curses every now and then, until I finish. He doesn't speak for a while, probably in shock, then when he does, he practically deafens me.

"Fuck! Vladimir, I will find this man myself and slowly torture him until he begs me to end his life." And he would. He'd do anything for my sons and me. But he's done enough for me over the years and this is one thing I will take great pleasure in doing.

"Нет, Sasha." No, I tell him. "I'm not asking you to do that. Just find him for me and I will do what needs to be done."

"If you are sure."

"Yes, I'm sure."

"Okay. I need his name and a photo or a descent description." Shit, I don't have a photo of him. I give him his name and a good enough description, wishing I could get my hands on a picture of him. Sasha will hire only the best for this job which means they will be flying in from Russia as soon as possible and probably meet with whomever they need to in London. I won't be contacted directly, it will be done through my brother who will call or message me when they have him. And where they are holding him.

It's easier to find someone this way. Money talks if you offer enough and I will pay whatever it costs to have this man brought to me. I know the police will be doing their best to catch him, but their hands are tied up to a certain extent. Plus, there's also the fact that they would not hand him over to me.

"It would be easier with a photo of this guy, Vladimir."

"I know but I don't have one... " Wait. The club. He said he went into both clubs. The cameras will have picked him up in the queue outside or in the entrance. "Sasha, I need to phone my head of security, I may be able to get one."

"Okay, send me it as soon as you have it. I'll start the ball rolling from this end."

"Thanks brother."

"No thanks needed. Anything you need, you know that?" Yes, I do.

"Okay. I'll be in touch."

The call ends and I dial Frank's number straight away.

"I was just setting off... "

"Are you at the club?" I know he was coming over here to set up extra security and a panic button. Mathew's dad is still out there. He might have money to get away but I'm not taking a chance that he won't come back for the other twenty grand that he didn't get. I need to protect my family.

"Yes. Why?"

"I need you to check the cameras from last week. He was in the club," he knows who I mean. "Find me a still and send it to my phone.

"Vladimir, what are you up to?"

"Just do it, Frank, no questions." I will apologise later for being short with him. He knows I'm stressed.

"Okay, but you better know what you are doing."

"I know."

"I'll need some time to go through them. Do you know which night he was in?"

"No."

"Shit. Okay. Leave it with me." I hang up and I collect some clean underwear and clothes for Holly then set off, needing to get back to my family.

Before I make it to Holly's room, Frank has sent me the picture and I have forwarded it on to my brother.

Chapter 16

Holly

Sat up in bed, my mind racing with alternative solution to what could have happened last night; what ifs and buts, my head hurts. Olivia and Jack talk through them with me but whatever we come up with, it doesn't matter because the outcome resulted in nearly losing Nicholas.

"Have you been in to see Nicholas, yet?"

"Yeah, just for a few minutes. We told them we were family and Sebastian backed it up otherwise we wouldn't have gotten in," Olivia smiles, trying to lift my mood. I'm desperate to see him. Until the doctors tell me that I'm fine to get out of bed, then I'm stuck here, unable to visit Nicholas. I know he's out of danger now but seeing him last night, lifeless, scared me to death and broke my heart.

"Lucy hasn't left his bedside since they were allowed to go in, apart from to stretch her legs when she went to the loo. So, when Vlad arrives back, we'll have a walk over and take her for something to eat," Jack says, wanting to make sure his only daughter doesn't worry herself sick. I nod my head at him and ask for the thousandth time, "What time did Vlad leave?" He was here when I fell asleep and when I awoke, Olivia and Jack were sat in his place. I love that there are here, but I need Vlad with me.

He's hurting and going through so many emotions at the moment, I fear he will do something stupid. I don't blame him, anybody would. Seeing your family held at gunpoint and not being able to do anything about it, then your son getting shot. Well it takes a very strong person not to react. And at this moment my man has lost control and wants revenge.

Before I fell asleep, I saw how much pain he was in, I could feel it and to be fair, he's going to be. But I also saw something else. Payback. He wants his pound of flesh.

"Did that bump on the head cause you to lose your memory? I've just told you ten minutes ago that he left at…" Just then the door opens, stopping Olivia from finishing what she was going to say and Vlad walks in. He's freshly showered and has on a change of clothes; I also notice his right hand which looks red and swollen around the knuckles and a bag in the other one.

"Come here," I tap the bed, needing his touch. He doesn't hesitate, dropping the bag on the floor he wraps me in his strong arms as soon as he sits on the bed at the side of me. He smells of his familiar woodsy aftershave and I feel warm and safe in his embrace.

"How are you feeling?" he asks when we break apart and his hand lifts to move a piece of hair that has sprung free from my messy bun.

"I'm good," I tell him. "Can't wait to get out of here." He places a chaste kiss on the side of my mouth then sits up.

"I've just seen the doctor; she's coming in to see you in a moment."

"Great. I'm desperate to get out of here so I can see Nicholas." I take his right hand in mine and gently stroke over the knuckles that look sore then narrow my eyes on him. He gives me a tight smile but doesn't enlighten me as to what's happened, and I don't push the matter either. Now is not the time.

"We're going to leave you to it. We need to check on Lucy," Jack says, putting on his jacket.

"Thanks," Vlad tells him, putting out his hand to shake. Jack takes it then pulls him in for a man hug, patting him on his back.

"Anything you need, you call me. Ok?" Jack says, pulling away from him. Vlad nods his head, thanking him again. They've become close over the time we've been together, and I know both Olivia and

Jack think the world of Nicholas. Olivia is next to wrap my man in a hug, causing me to chuckle because she's really good at giving hugs and I know Vlad embarrasses easily when she smothers him and kisses his cheek. Jack leans down and kisses my cheek, telling me to take care and he'll see me soon, then it's Olivia's turn who practically squeezes the baby out of me.

"Sorry," she says with tears in her eyes, "I just…"

"Come on, love," Jack intervenes before she gets too worked up, leading her out of the door. "See you soon," he shouts then the door closes behind them.

Vlad sits back down on the bed and I shuffle up a little so he can lay with me. We both turn on our side, one of his hands on my belly, his thumb stroking over my bump. The other one holds my hand between us. "Did you get any sleep?" I ask, running my fingers under his dark eyes.

"Some." I know he hasn't had much, how could he? He's been back and forth all night long between staying with me and sitting in a waiting room for any news, then in the ICU when they brought Nicholas from theatre.

"Why don't you close your eyes, until the doctor comes?"

"Hmmm," he snuggles in, giving up the fight. "I brought you some clean clothes and toiletries," he murmurs as his hand that was sitting on my stomach moves to my back and I hear a slight snore. I know I want the doctor to come in and give me the all clear to leave, then I can go see Nicholas, but I need my husband to have some rest too. So, the doctor can take her time.

"Sorry it took me so long, had an emergency," the doctor says as she comes dashing through the door, a nurse following her. Vlad stirs in my arms then in one swift movement sits bolt upright, rubbing at his face. He looks bewildered and shocked and so handsome; I love his look when he first wakes up. Cute.

"It's okay," I tell her. "It gave him time to shut his eyes." Vlad slips off the bed and stretches out his back then rubs at his eyes.

"Sorry," he says, uncomfortable with been caught by the doctor asleep on my bed. She chuckles at him and shakes her head, moving closer to me.

"Don't worry," she says, "you must have needed it."

"He did." He's had just over an hour where I just laid at the side of him, watching him sleep and hoping he isn't planning anything stupid.

"Right, Holly, let's just check a few things and see if we can get you home." She checks my blood pressure then my pulse rate and my temperature, telling me everything is good. The nurse attaches the heart monitor to my stomach to check the baby's heart rate which is strong and healthy. I'm asked if I have any aches and pains anywhere or headache. "Just a little throb," I point to where the gauze lays at the side of my head.

"That's to be expected," she says as she looks into my eyes. "Okay Holly, you're free to go on the understanding you rest up at home and come back if there's anything bothering you," she turns to Vlad. "Holly must not be left alone for the next forty-eight hours. Keep a check on her sleeping and if you have any trouble waking her then ring for an ambulance." He nods his head, a worried look on his face as she passes him a letter on head injuries.

"Can I go see Nicholas?" I ask, sounding like a small child.

"Of course, but don't get stressed or stay too long," the doctor tells me then she turns to Vlad. "He's in good hands and he's young, he'll be as good as new in no time," she smiles. The nurse leaves the room, taking the monitor with her and the doctor leaves, giving me time to get changed and telling me the nurse will be back in a moment to change my dressing, then I can go.

Half an hour later, we're taking a slow walk across the hospital towards the ICU, hand in hand. "Do you want to call to the café for something to eat or a cup of tea?" Vlad asks me.

Shaking my head, "No. The nurse brought me a sandwich and a drink before you arrived," I tell him. "Maybe later. What about you, have you eaten?"

"Not yet. I'll grab something later."

"Vlad, you need to eat," I chastise him.

"I will. Let's go see Nicholas then we need to take the boys to Sebastian's and pick Max up from Mary and Tom's."

"Why are we going to Sebastian's?" I stop walking.

"Because the boys have been here since last night and Max has been at Mary's. I don't want you home without me. I will want to call back later, and you need to rest. So, it's best if you all stay with Izzy and the kids and I will pick you up afterwards."

"What if I want to stay?"

"Holly you need to rest." He takes both my hands in his.

"I can rest here, Vlad, I don't want to be without you." I know I sound pathetic but I'm afraid.

"Sweetheart I don't want to leave you either, but you can't stay all day here and Nicholas might not wake up until later tonight or even tomorrow. Plus, we have to leave at eight, they won't let us stay any longer and I'm going to have my hands full trying to prise Sebastian, Daniel and Lucy from his bedside."

"I know. I'm sorry. I'm being selfish."

"No, you're not. I understand you want to be there for Nicholas, and I understand this has been… " His hands rub at his face then he takes mine again. "Terrifying. Heart breaking. But we'll all get through it. I just need you to listen to me, Holly. You don't need any more stress. You need to rest, and I need to keep you and our baby safe. Please…"

I place my finger on his lips, hushing him. He tells me I don't need any more stress but when I look at him, I see it written all over him. In his body language. In his voice and in his face. Sadness and hurt lives there too and I don't want to add to that. We're in this together. I'm an adult. His wife and his sons' step mum. The mother of our unborn baby. I need to help him with this, not add to the problem. I love him with all my heart and when we love someone, we will do anything for them.

"You're right." I pull his head down and kiss the side of his mouth.

"I am?" he looks surprised that I'm agreeing with him.

"Yes," I chuckle. "We'll go see Nicholas then take Lucas and Mathew home so they can shower," he nods his head at me. "If Izzy has her car with her then we can go pick up Joe, Rebecca, Ben and

Max. Oh, and Spot, and we'll stay there until you come for us."

"Thank you," he leans down and kisses me and when he pulls away I see some of the tension and stress leave his body.

We continue on with our slow walk towards the intensive care unit, holding hands. Every now and then Vlad raises our hands to his lips, kissing mine. Which reminds me about his swollen knuckles. "How did you hurt your hand?"

"Huh?"

"Your hand," I point down to it. "Your knuckles are red and swollen." He flexes his hand, looking at it.

"I lost it in the shower and took it out on the tiles." I know he's hurting and upset with everything that has happened, who wouldn't be? But he's also angry and I know he'll want to find Mathew's dad and take out some of that anger on him. Again, who wouldn't? Nevertheless, he doesn't need to be getting himself into any trouble with the authorities. His family need him. I need him.

"Vlad promise me you won't do anything stupid," I look up at him, pleading that he'll listen.

"Define stupid. If you mean hitting the tiles, then I won't be doing that again. It hurt like hell."

"You know what I mean." The look he gives me and how he bites his lip tells me everything.

"I can't promise you that, angel," he throws his head up, staring at the ceiling, cursing, knowing he's just upset me. At least he didn't lie, that would have upset me more.

I grab his hand because now is not the time to talk about this. We need to see Nicholas then sort out the boys. This will wait until later.

"Okay," I tell him. "But this isn't the end of this conversation, Vlad." And it isn't, I just need to try and persuade him not to take the law into his own hands.

When we reach the ward, Sebastian is stood outside, leant up against the wall looking at his phone. "There you are," he says when he sees us approaching. "I was just going to phone you."

"Is Nicholas ok?" Vlad worries as he squeezes my hand.

"Yeah. No change, he's still out of it. How are you, Holly?" He leans down and kisses my cheek then accidently knocking his dad out of the way he embraces me tightly. My arms automatically hug him back just as tight. I've gotten use to the cuddles Vlad's sons give me, the affection they give freely is one that a mother would be shown from her sons which I return with just as much love.

"I'm good thank you," I mumble into his chest. He kisses the top of my head and lets go of me, Vlad takes my hand back in his. "Who's in with Nicholas?"

"Just Lucas. Daniel and Mathew went with Jack, Olivia and Lucy back down to the canteen and Izzy has just gone to the ladies." I nod my head at him and put my hand on the door, ready to go in.

"Is it ok if I go straight in?"

"Of course," Vlad opens the door for me. "I'll swap places with Lucas in a moment, I just need a word with Seb." I acknowledge him by placing a kiss at the side of his mouth then walk straight in.

Lucas looks up when he hears the door open and a nurse turns too. She smiles nicely at me, going about her business and Lucas stands, walking straight into my arms. Once I've hugged the hell out of him, we sit down at the side of Nicholas' bed. Glancing around as I place my hand on top of his. There's the usual tubes and drips when someone has had a serious trauma and had to have an operation resulting in them being taken care of in the ICU.

"Do you think he can hear us?" Lucas asks, his head tilting to look at his older brother. I'm not sure. They say when someone is in a coma then you should talk to them, hoping they can hear you, but Nicholas isn't in a coma. He's still under the influence of the anaesthetic and drugs they have given him, so I don't really know.

"I'm not sure. He might be able to, it wouldn't harm speaking to him."

"Good. I've been telling him what an idiot he is."

"Why?" I don't need to ask why but I do anyway. If he'd have let Mathew's dad take the money, then he wouldn't be laid here now.

"Because he could have gotten himself killed… He didn't need to wind that man up; dad was ready to give him the money so that he'd leave without harming anyone."

"I know, honey, but sometimes it's hard not to say what's on your mind and people deal with things differently. Your dad's a lot older and wiser than your brother, he knew what to do. Nicholas is…" I stroke his hand, looking at him and his eyes flicker. "Have you noticed his eyes flickering like that while you've been sat here?" Lucas shakes his head at the same time as one of Nicholas' fingers move and he lets out a groan from deep inside his chest.

Standing as quick as I can, I turn and call for the nurse. She's by the bed in an instant and we all watch Nicholas' eyes flicker open. He stares unblinking, a pained, panicked look on his face.

"I'll get the doctor," she says.

The doctor arrives in no time and we're hushed out of the way. The nurse closes the curtains as we hear the doctor speaking. "Now then, Nicholas, glad to see you're back with us. Let's make you a bit more comfortable and remove that tube."

Lucas and I make our way out of the ward to let Vlad and Sebastian know what is happening. I find them talking quietly alone, looking as thick as thieves. Seb agreeing with what Vlad is saying to him. As we approach them, they stop what they were discussing and with a look on their faces that tells me they are up to something.

"Nicholas is waking up," Lucas explains a huge smile on his face.

"He is?" They both say in unison. I nod my head, explaining that we need to wait until the doctor and nurses have finished with him before we can go back in.

Over the next hour, the doctor finished his assessment on Nicholas and removed his breathing tube. We are all allowed to go in to see him two at a time and told not to stay long as he needs to rest.

He's doesn't say much when Vlad and I go in, his voice croaky, nothing but a whisper. He slips in and out of sleep and Vlad decides we should all go home and let him rest. Lucy cries when she sees he's awake, happy that he's going to be ok and Seb, Daniel and Vlad decide they will call back for an hour later tonight.

When we arrive home, Frank is still installing some added security. Vlad and he talk idly over a cup of coffee and the boys take a shower and get changed. Once they're done, we leave Frank to it and make our way to pick up the children from Mr and Mrs White. They both fuss over all of us and ask how Nicholas is doing, telling Vlad that they will call at the hospital tomorrow. All the children are excited to see us, Ben puts out his arms for Izzy as he sucks hard on his dummy.

We load the cars up with the kids and Spot, leaving Mary and Tom in peace as we make our way to Sebastian and Izzy's, everyone wanting pizza for tea. The kids are chatty. My stepsons seem happier now that their brother is out of danger as they laugh and argue with Izzy and Mathew about what takeaway to order from. Spot has settled himself under their kitchen table and when I glance at Vlad, he stands quietly, watching everyone, his arms folded across his huge chest while his fingers pull at his bottom lip. Deep in thought. Contemplating. Me, I sat here wondering what he's planning.

Chapter 17
Vlad

Holly sits at the bottom of the stairs as I make my way down from the bedroom. As I'm reaching the bottom, her questioning eyes meet mine. I close mine, unable to look at her, knowing I can't answer the questions she wants without lying. So, bending down I claim her lips, my hands placed at either side of her face. I would love nothing more than to spend time with my wife, some alone time to relieve the pent-up stress that this week has bestowed on us. Unfortunately, that's not going to happen tonight.

Twenty minutes ago, I was sent the message that I've been waiting five days for. An address and what time to be there.

After my family was held at gunpoint, Holly hurt, my son Nicholas shot and Lucas and Mathew exposed to it all, I had no over choice than to seek out the man who did this. When your family is put through such an ordeal and all you can do is stand there, feeling useless, trying not to lose it so nobody gets hurt, giving the man what he wants, hoping he will take it without harming anyone, well let's just say it's harrowing. Then when the unthinkable happens and again you feel useless because no matter what, you couldn't have stopped it, you question your actions or lack of them. Should I have tried to overpower him before Nicholas and Frank got there? Should I have insisted that he swapped me for Holly before I gave him any money?

Who knows? What I do know is that he needs to pay for hurting my family and in an hour's time he will be coming face to face with his worst nightmare.

Letting go of Holly's face, my lips reluctant to leave hers, I make my way over to the front door without looking at her. I feel the daggers in my back from the scowl she's been wearing all week. And it makes me smile. Even with everything that's going on when she tries to throw a mucky look, she's still beautiful and adorable. Let's face it, Holly is an angel. Doesn't have a bad bone in her body. Wouldn't hurt a fly so throwing mucky looks is quite comical and cute.

When the police called to take our statements the day after the incident, they offered a police officer to sit outside in his car just in case. I declined their offer as I had already arranged for four of the security staff from the club to alternate twelve-hour shifts outside my home. Holly flipped her lid with me for not taking up their offer, but I had my reasons. Having the police around would give them insight to my comings and goings and although we had spent most of the time at the hospital, I didn't know when Sasha would be in touch. I wanted to be able to just up and leave at a moment's notice without anyone knowing where I was headed, bar one. Sebastian is aware of my plans and is on his way over to sit with Holly and the boys. Even though he isn't happy that I will be taking the law into my own hands, he understands that it is something I have to do. Holly knows I'm up to something, she just doesn't know what and that is why I need Sebastian here.

Once I leave this house, leaving my wife still questioning what I'm doing and where I am going, she will need someone here to keep her calm and Sebastian is up for the job. I need him to stop her from going out of her mind which she will do because she's been piecing things together all week. Me, agitated, not been able to sit still. Not me. Constantly checking my phone. Again, not me. And that I declined the offer of the police protection. She's been asking what I am up to and not to treat her like a child. She knows I'm planning to do something stupid. Is it stupid? Maybe. Maybe not. I know not knowing his whereabouts, whether he'll come back for more money or whether he'll return to take his son with him, has been driving me insane. Now that I know where he is and that he's no longer a threat to my family, or won't be very soon, I can relax.

I want Mathew to feel part of the family and not worry about his father being the reason why Nicholas is in hospital or worry that he's going to turn up again to try and snatch him. I want Nicholas home fit and well, and he will be. He's on the mend. He's been moved to a ward and is driving the staff potty. So, I reckon they will be kicking him out soon. And I want us as a family to enjoy the birth of our baby.

Holly has less than a week to go unless she goes over her due date and I'm still crossing my fingers that we have a girl. It's a special time for all us, which we should be excited about. We were excited. Couldn't wait for the little one to arrive. But with everything that has happened it's dampened our mood. Put a dark cloud over everything which I need to lift before Holly goes into labour. Because I certainly do not want anything in the way, spoiling the day when our baby is born.

"Vlad tell me where you're going?" Holly demands and I'm sure I hear a little stamp of her foot, frustrated with me. I continue to lace up my boots, forcing myself not to turn and look at her. "Vladimir don't ignore me. I know you're up to something otherwise you wouldn't be going out dressed like a bloody... Ninja." I give myself a once over and she's right, I'm all in black. Black trousers and T shirt. My jacket's black and so are my boots, I didn't realise. All I need is a black bandana and I'm all set.

Feeling her warm hand on my shoulder has me standing and turning round to see her. I wished I hadn't.

The sadness on her face. The hurt in her eyes and as her arms wrap around me her head lying on my chest, I almost buckle. My chest constricts, seeing how much she's struggling with all this which has me struggling too.

My arms hold her tight as I snuggle my face into her neck, ready to throw in the towel. I could always tell the men who are holding Mathew's father to drop him off at the nearest police station or get them to do the dastardly dead for me. It would be no hardship for them, it's what they do.

"Don't do this, Vlad," Holly pleads just has the front door opens and I take a deep breath, shaking myself from her hold, the power my wife has over me. Sebastian is here and as much as I would rather not do this; I know I need to.

"I'm so sorry, Holly," my voice but a whisper as I hold on to her shoulders, watching the tears build in her eyes. Then I turn and walk out of the door.

*

Checking the inside pocket of my jacket, the contents feel heavy and alien. It's a very long time since I felt the cold steel under my fingertips, never thought I would again. Locked away, in the darkness of my safe with the intension of getting rid of it. Now here I am ready to become that man again. *My father would be so fucking proud.*

I hit the accelerator, gaining speed. Leaning into the bends of the narrow country lane, trying to rid the image of my father, his stare and reptile-like snarl as my heart racing faster. "Fuck," I curse, hitting the steering wheel trying to focus on the job in hand. Bright lights glare at me from the other side of the road, blinding me for a second, so I slow the car to a steady speed. Taking deep breaths to slow down the pounding in my chest. Expelling any distractions including him. Remembering this is for my family, to keep them safe.

I keep at the speed limit for a few more miles, turning on the radio to keep my mind from wondering. I'm running late. It doesn't matter, the men holding Mathew's father will have already received half of the money they are being paid. A tidy amount without getting their hands dirty. That's my job.

The old abandoned farm comes into view. Standing alone surrounded by the sprawling fields, a gentle light washes over it as the moon hangs proudly in the clear night sky. The crunching sound under my tyres when I pull up outside the front door causes the tatty curtains to twitch then the door opens.

I'm met by a shaven-headed, suited man who is as broad as the door he's just opened. His ruthless look would scare the average man, but I've never been one to intimidate easily. He nods his bald tattooed head in greeting, stepping to one side so I can walk through. No words are spoken, he knows why I'm here. Nothing to be said.

The lingering stench of decaying vermin mixed with the crawling mould and damp that have occupied this run-down building far longer than when it was a loving home to some family, turns my stomach and has me breathing through the want to be sick. Making my way through the dimly lit kitchen the flickering of the candles cast an eerie shadow across the walls. Not a stick of furniture stands erect. Broken into pieces, lining the rotten wooded floor as pools of dank water shimmer from the glow of the temporary lighting. Brought in from the cavities in the roof.

Hearing sounds of footsteps coming from the room next door, I step over the wrecked furniture and sidestep the puddles, making my way into what would have been the living room.

This room is lighter than the rest of the house. Lit up by various size torches but is still in a state of disrepair.

A nod of a head from the second man who stands large by the window, his meaty arms folded across his broad chest. I expected there would be two of them to get this job done but now they've done what they have been paid for they can leave.

Turning to see the man that I came here for sat on an old wooden chair, arms tied behind his back, I take off my jacket, laying it carefully on top of the stone fireplace. "Untie him then leave," I command, watching Mathew's father lift his head at the sound of my voice. He's been well taken care of. Not a hair on his head has been harmed while he's been in the care of his two captors. My brother will have given strict instruction to handle the package with care. No information to what he's done. It's hard to keep your hands off someone who beats young children and women as well as the other crimes he's committed.

"Sorry, unable to do that," the first man that greeted me at the front door says as he unfastens the rope that binds his wrists to the chair. "We were warned not to leave until the job was finished, so we'll hang about if it's all the same to you." Yeah, I can hear Sasha's voice demanding that they stay to dispose of the body, not wanting anything to come back on me.

I nod my head then direct them into the kitchen. If I want Mathew's father to take me on, then I need them out of the way. I'm not an animal. Unlike him. I will give him the chance to show me he's got a backbone to fight a man one on one. Instead of brandishing a weapon to hold my family while demanding money. Shooting an unarmed man, my son or hurting women and children.

His own son attacked and left unconscious while my three-year-old boy was locked in his room, scared and alone for two days. Their mother knocked over and left to die. Then my Holly...

"Stand up!" I growl, my anger getting the better of me. Thinking about what he's done boils my blood and has me wanting to get on with this. He stands, shaking both arms and rubbing at his wrists. They're probably numb with been tied behind the chair. Arrogantly, he glares at me, not one bit threatened by me which is a bad call on his part but a good one for me. At least I won't feel like I'm taking advantage of him, and neither will I feel any remorse when this is over.

Chapter 18
Vlad

With a curl of his lip, he charges forward. Clearly, he thinks he can overpower me and maybe escape. Not going to happen. I was planning on making this quick. Dive straight in there and end him but he deserves to feel some pain before his lights go out permanently.

His head goes down as if he wants to ram it into my chest. Sidestepping to the right he travels past me. Turning quickly, I reach out and grab the back of his neck, my other hand taking hold of his shoulder. In one swift movement his face smashes into the harsh concrete blocks of the wall and he lets out a moan. Blood drips from his nose as he falls to the floor, but he doesn't stay down for long. Staggering to his feet he sweeps his arm across his face, removing some of the blood, his breath coming fast. Still breathing hard, his steely eyes unblinking, he comes at me again. This time I send a powerful kick into his chest and he tumbles backwards into the stone fireplace, hitting it with a thud. I don't wait for him to get up this time. Storming towards him my foot connects to the side of his head, sending it rocking back and forth as blood sprays from his mouth and just like the films where the bad guy snarls at the good guy, he shows me his bloodstained teeth. Laughing at me.

As I lunge at him, he traps my foot between his legs and

somehow, I end up hitting the floor. True to life because I'm a big man I go down like a ton of bricks, hitting the ground with a heavy thump. The wind taken from me. He sees his chance and throws himself at me, landing on my chest. His fist travels towards me, my face its intended target but my head moves to the side and his fist hits the wooden floor. Throwing him off me, my strength no match, I end up hovering over him staring into his cold eyes and this time my rage intensifies when I think about what he has done.

The faint marks on Max's small body that he caused has me yanking him off the floor and I launch him across the room. He squeals like a pig when the side of his body hits the windowsill, collapsing in a heap. "Get up!" I roar, nowhere near done with him yet when I envision Mathew unconscious on the kitchen floor, ending up in hospital. The bruises he had shown me and how he cried, his mum robbed from him by this man who killed her. I march over to him when he tries to scramble to his feet and grab him by his hair, lifting him up so he's stood on his feet, I let my fist pound heavily into his body then I throw him against the window, listening to him cry out in pain when his shoulder hits the glass with a crack.

Moving away from him, my eyes still focused on his crumpled body; not so fucking tough now, I pick up an old rag and open a bottle of water that's lying on the floor. Pouring it over my throbbing knuckles that are still tender from when I hit the tiles in the bathroom. The water causes them to sting so I give it a shake then dry it on the cloth.

The sound of gurgling coming from his chest and him moaning as he tries to sit up has me lifting my head and I remember the look of terror and the bruise on Lucas' face because of this coward of a man. Blood spilling from Nicholas. Flatlining in the ambulance. I stride across the room and grip his throat tightly. Even now while he's struggling to breath, blood and bruises covering his face, he still looks at me with a callous expression. With hatred for this man pumping through my veins, I stop him from struggling against my hold and let my fists pummel into him, wanting to take that look off his face. I hear his screams and how he howls in pain, but I continue to let my fist rain down on him.

I've lost all control. Not sure I had any to begin with. No sooner did I see this man sitting in the chair, any restraint I had fucked off and left the building. Leaving me with just rage and revenge, hell bent on causing him as much pain as possible.

Scrambling to my feet, adrenaline running through my body like wildfire, I wipe the sweat that's dripping into my eyes as I stare at his silent, motionless body. He's not dead, the slow rise and fall of his chest tells me that.

Bending at the knees, my hands placed on them, I focus on my heavy breathing. trying to combat the pounding in my chest. Holly appears in my mind and I picture my pregnant wife's terrified face, falling to her knees and the split to her head. Purposely, I move towards the fireplace, lifting my jacket off the old stone. I insert my hand into the inside pocket, pulling out its contents, holding them firmly in my hand. When I recall how she cried, holding tightly onto me in the back of the ambulance, scared that Nicholas wouldn't make it, I attach the silencer slowly.

With gun in hand, I make my way back to the man who is now letting out a low moan. I stand over his body, taking aim and time seems to stand still when I think of how many times I have done this and how I swore I'd never do it again. My hand falls to my side and I shake my head, ridding any such thoughts, then I try to focus again. Lifting my hand, I aim the gun again. This time Holly's plea plagues me. *Don't do this.* I hear her voice over and over again. The pain in it. My hand falls to my side for a second time and I take a step back, inhaling deeply through my nose.

"Vladimir." I shake my head, thinking I've gone mad, hearing voices and lift my gun again. "Vladimir," a black-gloved hand sits on my shoulder and I'm in shock. What is he doing here? "You don't need to do this."

I turn to see my brother standing there, he greets me with a smile. He's aged so much since we last stood face to face. Seeing him on Skype or facetime doesn't show the wrinkles around his eyes or how grey he really is. And it doesn't show how much he really looks like our father, only with a softness in his dark blue eyes.

Before I can speak, we're hugging. No words need to be spoken. A brother's love is strong and none stronger than ours. He pats me on the back, and we release each other. Apart from aging he hasn't changed. Still wearing his crisp white shirt, bespoke suits and long cashmere coat. Obviously, he misjudged the weather here in England. Russian spring days can be bitterly cold.

I look down at the man on the floor who is still not moving and tap my gun on my leg. "I have to do this, Sasha."

"No, you don't," he shakes his head, taking a deep breath. "Vladimir, this isn't you." He points down at Mathew's father. "It never was. I tried to keep you from... " He closes his eyes and shakes his head again. I know what he's trying to say. He did try to keep me away from what our father wanted us to do but it was inevitable. "I failed. I won't again."

I shake my head, he didn't fail. He did what he could.

"You don't think he deserves to die for what he has done?"

"Fuck yes. He deserves to go to hell, but it will not be you sending him there." He places his hand on my gun, wanting me to give it to him. "Do not ruin the life you have made for yourself. For your family, Vlad," he waves his other hand around. "You have so much. If you do this, then you could lose it all. You have such a loving family," he smirks at me and lifts an eyebrow. "A very large loving family. And a beautiful wife who adores you." I nod my head. Yes, I have, and I love them so much and worship my wife. I would do anything for them.

"Give me the gun and go home to them. I'm sure Holly is beside herself wondering where you are." Rubbing my hand up and down my face, I know he is right. But letting this man go angers me.

"What about him?"

"Leave him to me. He will be taken care of." His eyes widen then he looks down at our hands. The gun still firmly held in mine. "Do I need to remind you that you have a baby due any day now?" No, he doesn't. I'm well aware. "If you do this and the police find any evidence that it was you then you'll never see your baby girl... Grow up." And I want to punch him in the face. He knows what he is doing and so do I. "You have his son living with you. How do you think you will feel when you get home after killing him? Do you think the guilt won't choke you when you see Mathew? If you kill this man, his dad, your conscience will never be free. It will eat at you every day." I wonder if that is how he feels about killing our father. I know I wanted to do it. Many times. The day Sasha took his life, I would have done it in anger. No remorse for trying to recruit my sons into the life that he so easily brought both his sons into. If I killed this man now for what he has done, I don't think I would feel an ounce of guilt.

However, I can't take that chance. Sasha is right. Looking at Mathew, knowing I'd just killed his dad, no matter what he has done, I'm sure Mathew doesn't want him dead, so yeah, I would feel guilty. If I was to get caught by the police for this crime, which I'm sure I wouldn't, we have a strategic plan in place, but I can't risk it.

I'd go crazy without Holly. Without my boys and grandchildren. Not being there for my baby. Unable to hold her in my arms and watch her grow up, *still rooting for a girl*, it would kill me.

I would rather die than be without them. And I know how much it would hurt them if the unthinkable did happen. I also know what my angel would think about me if I was to do this. She would know as soon as I walk in that door what I had done. It would break me to see that look on her beautiful face. Sasha is right, I have too much to lose.

He takes the gun from my hand, unscrewing the silencer from it then he shoves them in his overcoat pocket. "Come on, there's a bag of clothes to change into," he points towards the doorway. "Then we get out of this place," he turns up his nose, looking around at the derelict farmhouse. He's such a snob.

"I'm sure it once was a loving family home."

"I'm sure it was," he says, rolling his eyes as we step over the puddles and ruined furniture. It must be raining now outside because you can hear the drips coming in from the hole in the ceiling.

Once I've discarded my bloodstained clothes which will be incinerated, not leaving a trace, we make our way outside and over to my car. The two men that Sasha hired are still hanging around in the house. "How long are you staying?" I'd love it if he could come and stay with us for a few days. His nephews love him and it's so long since they've seen him, Lucas not ever meeting him. Holly and Sasha would get along famously, they have a mutual love for the same thing. Me. And it would be wonderful to sit and have a few drinks and a catch up with him.

"Not sure," he shrugs his broad shoulders, turning to look at the blacked-out four-by-four.

Even though I'm unable to see anything inside the car, I know he won't have come alone. There will be a couple of guards sitting in there which will have been told to stay put while he came to talk to me. Although he no longer does anything illegal, well nothing major, he's a little paranoid. Adamant that one day someone from our past will rise from the ashes, intent on revenge. That's why I can see he's itching to get back to Russia, to his wife and daughter and I don't blame him, I'd be the same. He's probably got a private plane waiting on the tarmac ready to whisk him back at a moment's notice.

"Don't worry," I slap him on the back, "I'll message you as soon as the baby's born."

"You do that," he grins. "And maybe think about getting a vasectomy," his eyes widen, laughing at me.

"Fuck you," I laugh back at him. He grabs me once again in a man hug, not knowing when we will see each other again.

"One day," he says, slapping my back. I know what he means. One day, he won't feel so paranoid about things that are not going to happen. He could stay here in England, bring his family for a holiday and stay with us, but he's not ready yet. More therapy needed. He's better than he was. It's only in the last few years that his wife and daughter have been able to go out without him being by their side. He has a lot of issues to work through, I understand that. I'm shocked he left Russia without them even if it is just a flying visit. The life that our father bestowed on us has taken its toll, leaving us both with our demons.

You never know, one day maybe I might return to my place of birth. Visit my mother's grave and take some flowers. But I'm no way ready for that yet.

"Go home, Vladimir. Give my love to your lovely heavily pregnant wife and tell my nephews that I love them. Oh, and tell Nicholas to get his malingering arse up and out of that hospital bed," he jokes as he opens my car door, motioning for me to get in.

"What about him?" My head tilts, pointing to the house where Mathew's dad lays hurt. Still breathing though.

"Leave it with me, I know what to do." I'm sure he does. It wasn't long ago when he would have just put a bullet in his head or burned down the farmhouse with him in it. But not anymore.

We hug again and I wish him a safe flight and send my love to his family then I drive away, knowing I'm going to be in the doghouse and will have some making up to do. It's going to be a struggle to get Holly to look at me, never mind speak to me. God only knows how I'm going to get her to believe that I didn't kill him when it was obvious before I left home that she knew what my intentions were.

Chapter 19
Holly

Knowing what Vlad is capable of doing doesn't lessen the anxiety that's consuming me. I hear his apology over and over in my head, *I'm sorry Holly*. And I picture him walking out of the door nearly three hours ago with only one thing in mind. Revenge. Effortlessly, my tears fall again.

As soon as he left me standing in the entrance of our home, I broke down, not been able to stand the thought of what he was about to do. Sebastian was there in a heartbeat, trying to comfort me. Leading me into the living room and helping me sit down, then he made me a cup of sweet tea, telling me it would make me feel better. What is it with people and sweet tea? It didn't. Daniel came home not long after and with Max fast asleep in bed and Lucas and Mathew upstairs, they both sat there freely speaking about their father.

Daniel was convinced that Vlad went out seeking revenge on Mathew's father. That he had found him and wanted to make him pay for what he had done. His brother Sebastian, on the other hand, lied through his back teeth. Covering up for his hero. Trying to persuade us that he had just gone out to let off a bit of steam, which was bullshit.

I understand that he wants to protect his father and I understand that lying to me would have been hard for him. He doesn't want me knowing what his father's intentions are because he knows what it would do to me. However, it's too late for that, I already know.

Watching Vlad this week, seeing the pain in his face, the anger it produced as that night played over and over in his head, I was under no illusion what he had planned, and I was helpless to stop him. My husband is a smart man. A kind and gentle man that will help anyone out until he is crossed. That's when you see a different side to him, a dark side. Rationality leaves him and where I can usually bring him back, get him to see sense, I'm afraid when it comes to his family – our family – being hurt, then even I don't have the power to stop him.

Unable to sit and listen to Daniel and Sebastian anymore and knowing Lucas and Mathew had now gone to bed, I decided I would do the same. I leave my two stepsons sat downstairs, waiting for their father to come home.

Trying to keep what Vlad was up to from turning over in my head, I set about cleaning the bedroom then took a relaxing bath, it didn't help. Images of what he was doing kept popping in and out of my head, and I couldn't help but let the tears flow as my anxiety levels rose. There was also the fact that taking a bath when you're heavily pregnant and your husband isn't around to help you out of the sunken bath, well it's not a good idea. So, I struggled then cried again.

Once I was dried, I chose one of Vlad's T shirts to sleep in and got settled into bed, still with thoughts of my husband. Upset that he had left me stood in the entrance while I pleaded with him not to do anything stupid, scared that he has. Worried he will be arrested and also afraid that he might not come home. What if he's been hurt?

Eventually I must have dosed then woken when my bladder decided it needed emptying. I sit there in the dark for a moment, tears stream down my face when I notice Vlad is still not home yet.

Wiping at them, I turn on the bedside lamp and quickly sit upright when I hear the shower turn on. Making my way over to the dressing room the door is shut with the light out. When I open the door, the bathroom door is also closed but I can just see a slither of light from under it. It's obvious he didn't want to wake me that's why he's kept the doors closed and the dressing room light off.

I'm glad that he is home safe, but my heart stutters, scared of what he has done. My bladder lets me know why I woke up, so I push open the bathroom door, not able to wait any longer.

The bathroom is filled with steam and there's a pile of clothes that I don't recognise in a heap on the floor. I make my way past them, sitting down on the toilet with thoughts of why he would come home in clothes that do not belong to him. Only one thing comes to mind, he needed to get rid of his own. Before I have a chance to get off the loo, the shower turns off and Vlad steps out. He reaches for a towel and wraps it around his waist, not yet noticing that he's not alone.

When he turns, he looks shocked to see me sat there. The anger that's marred his handsome face all week is absent, leaving a very worried expression in its place.

"Sorry, didn't mean to wake you," he says nervously, his voice low. I stand and flush the toilet.

"You didn't," I sound abrupt as I move to wash my hands. Watching him through the mirror as he dries himself then slips on a pair of black boxers, he catches my eye.

"Holly," he moves to the back of me, and I turn to look at him. Even though it's late and I'm exhausted, I need to know where he has been and what he has done.

"Where have you been?" I ask with as much strength in my voice as I could possibly muster up at a time like this. Not knowing whether the police are going to turn up and cart him off scares me. The thought of giving birth to our child without him there scares me even more. But the fear that has built up throughout the evening, that he just might have killed, absolutely petrifies me. He's capable of it, that I know. However, I'm hoping he's remembered that he has a loving family that need him and went lenient on the man that has caused so much upset and hurt. I know he doesn't deserve any leniency. What Mathew's dad has done; well he deserves everything he has coming to him, but I don't want my husband ending up locked up because of him.

Vlad's eyes lower to the floor and he chews on the inside of his cheek. When he raises his head and his eyes meet mine, I can see he's sorry for what he has done. Not sorry for the man he has hurt but sorry for hurting me.

Folding my arms across my chest, I nod at the clothes on the floor then rub at my forehead. "Vlad I need to know what you have done."

"I know," he says softly. "Can we sit down?" He kicks at the jeans and T shirt that lay on the floor, knocking them out of the way, then puts his hand on the small of my back while he holds the bathroom door open for me.

My heart beats fast as I sit on the side of the bed, Vlad sitting at the side of me and my stomach tightens. There's no pain. Just Braxton Hicks which I've had a few of over the last few weeks. With less than a week to go and no signs of the baby coming, I'm feeling very uncomfortable, wishing the birth over and done with. Having all this hassle I can do without. Vlad takes my hand in his which I let him, noticing that the faded marks which he had on the knuckles of his right hand from hitting the tiles in the shower cubicle are now looking angry.

"Just tell me," I stress as I watch him, his hand rubbing at his face. "Did you kill him?" He doesn't need to tell me where he has been or what he has been doing because I know. But I do need to know how bad things are. He shakes his head, lowering his hand from his mouth.

"Can we just go to bed and talk about this is the morning, you look shattered?" He brushes a strand of hair from my face. He's joking, isn't he? If he thinks we can just forget about this, then he's got another thing coming. He shook his head. Am I supposed to believe him? Do I believe that he didn't kill him? I'm not sure.

"And whose fault is that? You left me for nearly four hours." I stand up, taking my hand from him. "No. I want to know what was so important that you left your heavily pregnant wife upset in the hallway and left your sons to deal with her," I'm more than aware of what it was but I need him to tell me.

"I'm sorry I did that," he shakes his head, closing his eyes. "I needed to go out."

"What for?" I push, not budging from where I am stood in front of him.

"Holly don't," he pleads, taking hold of my hips gently. I step back out of his hold, not allowing him access to any part of me and his dark eyes search mine. He sees I'm not standing for any crap and lifts his eyes to the ceiling. When he looks at me again, I can see he's not happy with discussing this now. Well tough because I'm not happy either.

"You know why I went out, Holly, so let's not pretend you don't."

"Do I? Really? Well how am I supposed to know anything when you've kept everything a secret," I place my hands on my hips. "Scared that the little woman can't take the truth about what you were up to. Well I'm not some little girl that needs protecting. I'm your wife, the soon-to-be mother of your child!" I practically scream out the last bit and realise that I need to calm down. I don't need the stress and I don't need to wake up the boys.

"Holly don't, sweetheart," he reaches for me again and I step away again.

"You need to talk to me, Vlad. You should have told me what you intended to do. Discussed it with me…" Tears well in my eyes and this time he's up off the bed holding me in his arms. I let him hold me while I gather myself together then I step out of his warm comforting arms.

I wipe the wetness from my eyes and take in a deep breath. "Vlad, I want to know the truth, no sugar coating it. I want to know how you found him when the police were unable to and I want to know where he is now?"

He sits back down on the bed and reaches for me. This time I don't stop him when he places his hands on my hips and I don't stop him when he rests his forehead on my tummy. I give him a minute to think about what he has to say.

"He's not dead," his voice is low and when his eyes connect with mine, I can see he's trying to determine whether I believe him or not. I just nod my head. "He's badly hurt but he will live."

"Why did you not kill him?"

"What?"

"You went out of here with one thing on your mind and that was to kill the man who had hurt your family. I'm not stupid, Vlad, I know what you are capable of."

"I wanted to. And I would have done, he deserves nothing less," his tone is laced with disgust and his accent is thick. "What stopped me was… " He breathes in deeply. "Was you, my sons and our baby," he leans in and places a soft kiss on my bump then lifts his head, "and Sasha."

"What's Sasha got to do with this?"

"He turned up before I had the chance to shoot him."

"What? How did he know?" I'm confused, I didn't even know that Sasha was aware of what had happened.

Over the next fifteen minutes I listen to my husband tell me how when he left my hospital bed to come home, he contacted his brother and told him everything. He then asked for his help to find Mathew's father. Sasha hired two men to track him down and when they did, his brother contacted him letting him know where they were holding him. After beating the crap out of him he was then going to shoot him but had second thoughts when he thought about how he had sworn he would never kill again. When he thought about how it would hurt me and what he could lose, he knew he couldn't do it. While he was contemplating all his thoughts, whether to shoot him or not, Sasha turned up and helped reverberate what he was already thinking.

"Wow. I thought Sasha didn't work in that business anymore."

"He doesn't but he knows who to contact when you need someone finding." I nod my head and stand up; I'd sat down on the bed when Vlad was explaining how Sasha had gotten involved.

"So where is he now?"

"Who, Mathew's father or Sasha?"

"Well I meant Mathew's dad but is Sasha still here?" He shakes his head, sadness in his eyes. I'm sure he would have loved to have met up with his brother under different circumstances. They were both very close and he's told me how much he's missed him over the years. However, they both chose the life they have now. Vlad and his family here in England and Sasha and his in Russia.

"Sasha was flying back tonight, and I left Mathew's dad with him and the two men he hired. They were still at the farmhouse when I set off."

"Oh, God," I cover my mouth, thinking the worst. If he was still alive when Vlad left, then I'm sure he won't be now. Two men from the Russian Mafia won't want to leave any evidence that they were here and Sasha well, he'd slit his throat just for upsetting Vlad, so God only knows what he has done to him for almost killing his nephew Nicholas and everything else he had done.

"Vlad what have you done?" My hand goes to my chest. I know Mathew's father deserves whatever they have done to him, but they will have buggered back off to Russia and it will be my man who will be left to face the consequences when they find his body, if they find it.

"Hey," Vlad stands quickly, his hands hold my shoulders while his eyes search my face. "Everything will be fine."

"How do you know that? You said you left him alive but leaving him with those men and Sasha you might as well have killed him yourself... But you knew that anyway," I whisper, moving away from him.

"Holly, they will not have hurt him. Please believe me, angel." I want to believe him but knowing their past and who they have involved in this, I'm struggling. "He will turn up alive and will then face up to the crimes he has committed." He turns me in his arms, placing his hand under my chin, "Holly forget about him, you need to rest. It's late and you need to sleep." What? How can I sleep with all this hanging over us?

"Yes, Vlad I am tired. I'm tired of all this," I wave my hand around. "I just want things to go back to normal."

"So, do I, Holly. And it will."

"You don't know that, Vlad." I rub my hands over my face, staring at my husband and not able to listen to any more of this. I need to be on my own. "Go to bed, Vlad, I'm going downstairs."

"What?" His eyes widen and he reaches for me. "Holly you need to sleep, sweetheart."

"No Vlad, what I need is to be alone at the moment," he looks at me as if I've just asked him for a divorce. "I'm going to get a cup of tea," and to think about how we can get through this. I take his hand and run my thumb over his bruised knuckles. "I need time to come to terms with this." He nods his head at me and sits back down on the bed as I turn and walk out of the door.

Downstairs I make a cup of tea and get myself comfortable on the sofa, the last few weeks play over and over in my head like someone's just pressed the repeat button and not taken their finger off it. Spot wonders over, laying his head on my knee, his paw comes up too. His big dopey eyes stare at me and when I don't react, his nose nudges my arm. "You want a cuddle, Spot," and it's as if he's telling me it's me who needs one when he climbs up on to the settee, curls up and places his paws in my lap with his head on top of them.

For the next ten minutes, I run my finger through the soft fur on his head and sip my tea, relaxing. Who knew stroking a dog could so therapeutic? My eyes start to feel heavy, so I decide it's time to go to bed. I get a groan from Spot when I give him a soft nudge to get down, Vlad would have a coronary if he saw him up on his Italian leather sofa. I dash the few dog hairs off that he's left behind then make my way up to bed.

Chapter 20

Vlad

Watching Spot cock his leg to piss again, I stop in my tracks and shake my head at him. We're both in the doghouse, so I brought him out for a run. We haven't gotten very far due to him wanting to stop at every lamppost, bush or tree to take a piss. If he's not watering the plant life, he's sniffing out anything that's caught his attention and finds exciting.

I tug on his lead and set off running again, only I come to a sudden stop when he buries his nose into someone's garden hedge and refuses to move as he sniffs something that's more appealing than me. I roll my eyes at him and decide to knock the run on the head. Might as well, I'm not even breaking out a sweat.

Running isn't my usual exercise. I can't remember the last time that I wanted to run to clear my head. My preference is the gym. Weights, exercise bike and the odd bout of kickboxing with one of my sons. Over the last week I've used the gym every day, wanting to take my mind of my wife who's being very unreasonable at the moment, but it hasn't worked. She's all I think about.

I sigh as we cross the road and take a left towards the park, contemplating my last thought because who am I kidding she has every reason to be annoyed at me. And at Spot.

Holly is still upset with me. Ignoring her plea and giving Mathew's father a good hiding, my wife scared that I was going to kill him has left her angry with me. I could see how much everything was upsetting her when I returned home from my little drive out to the farmhouse and I knew that I had been the one to cause it. Apologising and trying to reassure her that I hadn't killed him, even though I wanted to, well, I don't think she believed me. For three days I was ignored. When she couldn't ignore me any longer, I was screamed and shouted at and told to fuck off. This isn't how Holly acts or deals with things. She's a rational person, non-judgemental and level-headed, however, my wife hasn't been any of those, so I knew I had to give her a wide birth while she calmed down.

The police called round to inform us that they had found Mathew's father. Although he was in the hospital in intensive care, an eye for an eye and all that, we were told he would live. Apparently, he'd been found outside an hospital in another part of the country and even though he needed hospital treatment, he was able to speak. He'd kept his mouth shut as to who it was that had put him there which I knew anyway. Sasha and the two men who he hired had put the fear of God into him, advising him it was in his best interest to keep his mouth zipped. My brother had already enlightened me as to what they had done and how they had burnt the abandoned farmhouse to the ground to cover our tracks. They had also cleaned him up and changed his clothes in a way that none of my DNA would be traced just in case he didn't comply, due to beating I had given him.

Mathew Simpson had been blindfolded when he was taken to the farm so he wouldn't be able to give any details of where he'd been assaulted and, so far, he was putting the blame on a gang he owed money to. Sasha's plan had worked and now thinking back I'm glad he was there to stop me from killing him although I'm not sure I would have gone through with it; I did have second thoughts while pointing the gun at him.

Once Holly was given this information, she seemed to come round a little, knowing that I hadn't lied to her, but she was still short tempered and cold towards me where everyone else was treated with the same love and kindness that she always shows.

Nicholas came home from the hospital yesterday and was given the red-carpet treatment while he's still healing. I'm sure once he's up to taking a dressing down Holly will lay into him about how foolish he was to provoke a man with a gun, I know he will be getting a few choice words from me.

Our home has been like a knocking shop since yesterday so this morning I asked Holly if she would like a drive out to the coast, just the two of us. She's normally up for it. Nicholas had plenty of family and friends visiting him, his brothers not wanting to leave his side. Lucas and Mathew were still at home as they were not returning back to school until next week. As for Max, he had plenty of people to take care of him while we were out for the day.

However, my wife, my sweet Holly who is an angel in my eyes turned into woman possessed and ripped into me. *"Do I look as if I want to sit in a car for two fucking hours, walk around cobbled streets then sit for another two hours on the drive back?"* She ranted as her eyes glared at me before they switched to her heavily pregnant belly, then with her hands on her hips, she tore into me again. *"For a smart man, Vlad, sometimes, you are stupid,"* then she stomped off into the bathroom, tutting and shaking her head at me before she slammed the door behind her while I stood there speechless.

You see there's the other thing. Holly is now two days over her due date. And with everything that's gone on she's worn out. She was terrified when we were held at gunpoint then she suffered a head injury as well as witnessing Nicholas being shot. Throughout the whole ordeal she stayed strong for my boys and for me when really she should have been taking it easy with no stress.

Where I should have been caring for her, running around fetching and carrying, attending to her needs, rubbing her back and massaging her tired feet, which I normally do, I gave her what I thought she wanted. Space from me. How stupid have I been. Holly loves me. She craves my touch just as much as I do hers. We ache to be together when we're apart. So, giving her what I thought she wanted instead of holding her. Taking her in my arms reassuring her that everything will be okay. Showing her that I'm there for her and our baby, I let her down. How fucking foolish of me. My wife needed me, and I wasn't there for her. I am an idiot.

Izzy told me I needed to show Holly that everything will go back to normal and I refused to listen to her because I thought she needed some time to get over what I had done. Again, Izzy tried to tell me that Holly knew Mathew's father deserved everything he had got and that she understood why I did it. Any father and husband would want to do the same. But I didn't listen, thinking I knew better. Holly was right when she said, for a smart man sometimes I am stupid.

When we love that one person who loves you with all their heart, even with all your faults, when they know what you need when times are rough and when they give their love unconditionally then they should have it returned. And usually I know the woman I love and what she needs without being told. In my eyes she has no faults and I would create holy hell on anyone who disagrees. And my heart is hers unreservedly. I've fucked up and I need to make it right.

Looking down at Spot, I tug on his lead. "Come on, mate, we've got some making up to do," he tilts his head at me and wags his tail. Yeah, he's not getting away with it. This afternoon he chose to poke the bear. Stupid dog. Chewing the toe out of one of Holly's comfy shoes wasn't a smart move. She didn't scream and shout at him when she found it in his bed. He's never chewed anything before apart from his own toys. Holly took it from him, threw it in the bin and gave him a very disconcerting look then went upstairs. I knew it had upset her. No matter what shoes she wears lately her feet ache, they were the only ones that she felt comfortable in. We've gone out shopping and she's tried on countless pairs; we've bought countless pairs but none of them suitable. So, I think with her hormones running riot that was the last straw.

Arriving home, I kick off my trainers then fill up Spot's water bowl, once he's finished lapping it up he strolls off to his bed and I make my way upstairs for a shower.

Twenty minutes later, I'm making my way into the living room ready to tackle my wife. There are no children running around like there was when I went out, Max is asleep in bed and Lucas, Mathew and Joseph are upstairs making far too much noise while playing on a video game. I did tell them to quiet down. I assume Rebecca and Ben are asleep too as they are all stopping over tonight. Sebastian, Izzy and Nicholas are all sat on one settee, Nicholas with his legs thrown over them and his head resting on a cushion. Daniel is sat on the other with Holly. Both at opposite ends.

"Enjoy your run?" Seb asks as I sit down between my son and Holly.

"Didn't get very far," I answer, taking hold of Holly's feet that were resting up on the couch and placing them in my lap. She doesn't stop me when I start to massage the balls of them just eyes me suspiciously, so I throw her a sexy wink and turn to my son. "You can't run when the pooch just wants to stop at anything and everything for a nosey or to take a piss," I explain as I move on to Holly's calves then move back to her feet, appreciating the little moan she lets out.

I half listen to my sons chatting about Spot then they move on to the football match they had watched earlier as I contemplate my next move. I'm not giving Holly the chance to push me away, not that I think she wants to. I've just shifted us both so she is sat comfortably on my knee with one of my hands rubbing the small of her back while the other lays across the bottom of her stomach. When she closes her eyes and lets out an approving sigh, I seize the chance and bury my face in her hair. Once I've inhaled her sweet scent, I kiss her head softly and she snuggles into my chest.

"When are they going to start you off?" Izzy asks a very sleepy Holly. We visited the midwife last week and was told that both mother and baby are healthy and that the baby was not ready to come yet. We were given a date when Holly will be induced if she doesn't go into labour beforehand.

"The tenth," she answers, lifting her head from my chest as she stretches out, yawning.

"Two more weeks and you might have been getting a baby as a birthday present," Sebastian says, nodding his head towards me.

"What?"

"It's your birthday on the twenty-fourth, paps, have you forgot?" He chuckles.

"So much has happened over the last year, I'm surprised I still remember my own name," I shake my head and smile, remembering it was my birthday when I met Holly. "No, I hadn't forgotten, how could I?" I smile big and wide, staring lovingly at the angel in my arms. "It's when I met my wife." Her eyes catch mine and I see the love she holds for me through them. I also see her lip rise at one side as she smirks at me. Again, seizing the chance, I lean in and steal a kiss. It's a just a brush of our lips, one she reciprocates, and my hearts beats fast in the knowledge that I have my Holly back. We don't linger due to our audience although it's never bothered us before.

"Ow, sweet," Izzy says, and my sons roll their eyes. "Have you tried all the old wife's tales?" She asks. Holly nods her head.

"Yeah, I've tried a few. I been having raspberry leaf tea for weeks now and lots of curry."

"What does the raspberry tea do?" Nicholas asks, sitting up as he rubs at his chest. He's fine, he told us that it's just a bit sore around the wound.

"It softens the uterus?" Izzy answers for Holly.

"Errr," he moans, pulling a face and shaking his head. "I had a cup of that a couple of weeks ago..."

"Don't worry, you'll be fine," Holly laughs, and we laugh along with her when Nicholas purses his lips and shudders.

"What else have you tried?" Seb ask this time.

"Hmmm, walking up and down the stairs and standing up a lot. I've tried pineapple..."

"What does that do?" Nicholas tilts his head, intrigued.

"Haven't got the foggiest idea. I heard a woman telling another woman to try it at the clinic."

"Have you been stealing Holly's pineapple out of the fridge?" Daniel asks, chuckling.

"Yeah, this morning," he shakes his head and rolls his eyes.

"Nicholas, people eat pineapple all the time. There's just something in it that can help bring on the labour in pregnant woman."

"I know that. I'm not stupid," he grins. "I'll share a curry with you, Holly, if you want. Might as well," he shrugs his shoulders. "I've tried everything else."

"I have a birthing ball, if you want to give it a go?" Holly offers, smirking.

"Nah, might damage the goods," he cups his balls, grimacing, and his brothers chuckle. Even Holly laughs at him. *Only Nicholas.*

"Do you want me to order a curry?" I ask Holly as my thumb strokes over a stomach.

"No, it's too late. I'm not hungry," she yawns again. "Thanks though," she says as she places her hand at the back of my head and runs her fingers through it. I lean into it.

I love her hands in my hair. The way her fingers massage my scalp is so relaxing and such a turn on. Better get that right out of my head. Not going to chance my luck.

"I think I'll go to bed," Holly announces as she struggles to get up off my knee. I keep her where she is, on my knee, and move to the edge of the seat then I stand with her in my arms.

"Such a gentleman," Nicholas says with sarcastic humour in his voice.

"Fuck off," I mouth as I stand Holly on her feet, happy that he's back with us and feeling his normal self. I did miss him when he was in hospital.

"Come on, I'll come with you," I'm shattered myself. It's been a stressful few weeks with minimal sleep. I could do with a good night's sleep with Holly snuggled into me. I've missed our cuddles. For the last week or so I've been given the cold shoulder in bed, but hopefully tonight normal services will be resumed.

We say our goodnights to my boys and Izzy then check in on Max. He's cuddled up fast asleep with his favourite toy dog, the one I bought him from the hospital. Holly makes her way to our bedroom and I make my way to Lucas' room to tell him, Joseph and Mathew that it's time for bed. I don't get any moaning from them, it's late enough.

When I open the door to our room, Holly is already in bed. I don't bother with turning the light on, just make my way to the bathroom. Once I've finished in there, I slip into bed. Tonight, Holly cuddles into me, laying her head on my chest and her arm across my stomach, letting her fingers play with the short hairs around my belly button. This is what we need. Normality.

She tilts her head and kisses my jaw and I turn my head and take her mouth, kissing her slowly. Pouring all my love for her in that one kiss. "I love you," I whisper against her mouth, breaking our kiss.

"I love you too," she says then kisses me again before she snuggles down to sleep.

*

When I wake the following morning, I realise I've slept the whole night through. It seems such a long time since I've had such a peaceful night's sleep and I have my wife's loving arms to thank for that. My hand seeks her out and comes up empty, her side of the bed cold.

Turning to look at the clock, I'm shocked to see it's almost ten o'clock. In a flash, I'm up out of bed, visit the bathroom then make my way downstairs. Holly is sat at the dining table with Max, reading to him. I switch on the kettle then join them, kissing my son on the top of the head then kiss Holly on her neck and I don't miss how she breathes me in, a cheeky glint in her eye. Wow, my woman likes what she sees, me in my boxers. Haven't seen that look for a while.

"Daddy," Max squeals as he stands on the chair then launches himself at me. I catch him easily and he buries his head into my bare chest. I switch him to my hip then lean down, so my mouth is near Holly's ear.

"Like what you see, sweetheart?" I ask, my voice low and husky.

"What?" she says, all flustered, her cheeks heating up when she slaps her hand on her forehead and closes her eyes. I chuckle, leaving her sat there while I take Max with me to make my coffee.

When I return, I take a seat and pick up the book she was reading to Max. "Room on the Broom," one of his favourites at the moment, along with many others. Betting is she'll have read it three or four times to him since getting up. "Why didn't you wake me?" I ask, taking a sip from my cup while Max flicks through the pages of the book looking at the pictures. She shakes her head at me, smiling.

"You were dead to the world. You looked too cute with your hair all tousled and that little snore you had going on."

"I don't snore."

"Yeah, you do," I don't argue with her because how would I know?

"Where is everyone?" I ask changing the subject and looking around. It's far too quiet.

"Well I thought it was time that Lucas and Mathew got back into some routine, so I suggested that they went back to school this morning instead of next week."

"And they were ok with it?"

"Yes. I woke them early and asked. They wanted to." Impressive. I thought they would have wanted to wait until next week. But she's right, we need to get back to some normality. Well as normal as we can in this house. "Sebastian drove Mathew and was going to call into the school to have a word with his head of year and Daniel and Nicholas took Lucas and was going to do the same plus they were dropping Joseph and Rebecca at school too."

"Where's Izzy and Ben?" Noticing all Ben's baby bumph is put away and Izzy's bag is not hanging around.

"Seb drove them home first."

"Just us three then. Maybe we should take Max out somewhere, I don't like him being stuck inside all day. That's if you're up for it?"

"Well yeah," she chews on the inside of her cheek. "It will be just you and me."

"Why?"

"Olivia is coming over. She wants to take Max out," her eyes stare at me. Questioning if this is ok. It's not that I don't let Holly make decisions for my sons, I do. She can make any decision she wants; I don't mind. But she knows I'm still wary about where they go and who they are with. And I know I shouldn't be. I nod my head, letting her know that I'm ok with this.

"What time is she picking him up?"

"Around twelve. She said she'll keep him for tea. She's picking Megan and Rebecca up from school, so she'll drop him back home after she's dropped Rebecca off." Holly gets up from her seat, holding onto the table for support. I stand and help her up.

"What do you need? Sit back down, I'll get whatever you want."

"It's fine, I just needed to stretch my back." My hand moves quickly to the bottom of her back, rubbing it soothingly.

"Is it sore?" I keep my hand there and feel her mould into my palm.

"Achy," she says then moves away, stretching her legs.

"Any other pains? You look is if you've dropped a bit." I walk over to her and place my hands onto her stomach. It's very prominent today and lower than it was yesterday.

"No," she sighs. My wife is very uncomfortable at the moment and eager to meet our baby which is understandable, I can't wait either.

"How about we just call to Dimitris for a late lunch then take a short walk around the park?" Holly said, standing and walking helps with her backache, just sitting aggravates it. "That's if you can find any footwear that you can walk in," I say, smirking at her.

"It wasn't funny," she slaps my arm playfully then looks under the table where Spot lays peacefully asleep or maybe he's just pretending.

"No but your little tantrum was," I say, earning another slap. Oh, how I love Holly's love taps. I pull her into me, careful not to hurt her, and take her mouth fiercely. Max isn't watching, he's too busy looking at his book. Once we've both had our fill of each other we pull apart breathless.

"Hmmm, needed that," Holly smiles, running her finger over my bottom lip.

"Me too," I rub my nose against hers.

"I have some knee-length boots that might fit. I'll just wear a pair of leggings and a shirt with them."

"Good," I tell her, sitting back down at the side of Max, stroking his hair. "Why has Nicholas gone with Daniel?"

"He wanted to get out. He's going to call into the office for an hour or two then get Daniel to drop him back off home."

"He's supposed to be resting."

"He knows. I think he's bored," Holly puts her arms around Max and tickles him. He giggles loudly, leaning back into her and rests his head on her belly. "And this one will be starting nursery in a couple of weeks," she kisses his head.

"No school... " he gripes, shaking his head. We've had his name down on waiting lists at a couple of nurseries, but we were told maybe to go further afield because they didn't know when there would be a place for him. He's at the age to start and needs some routine. We don't want him too far way, so Holly said to wait until a place comes up. She's been reading a lot with him, getting him to discuss picture books which he enjoys. She's also teaching him numbers zero to ten and is helping him pronounce his sounds, especially Ls. My sons help too, interacting with him through play and so do the girls. He loves having tea parties and even dresses up in their princess dresses. I actually commented on this but was shot down by my wife. She told me all boys do this in nursery, so I let it go.

Max has gotten too used to being around Holly and me through the day and doesn't like the idea of starting nursery. Every time it's mentioned, he shakes his head telling us no. But we've been working on it getting him ready for the big day. I raise an eyebrow at Holly, questioning her comment.

"They phoned this morning. There's a space coming up in a couple of weeks, so they wanted to plan a home visit. I've made it for next Wednesday."

"Good," I nod my head. "What if you're in hospital having the baby?"

"They know that I'm due anytime. We can rearrange it if I am. Anyway, I'm hoping to have had the baby by then and be at home," she puts her hands on her bump and smiles. Turning in my seat, I join her. My hands connect with hers while my lips graze across her ear then seek out their favourite place.

"Me too," I whisper then kiss her softly.

"Daddy read," Max demands, breaking our little moment as he points down at his book. We both break away laughing and sit down either side of him, Holly picking up the book.

Olivia calls round to collect Max at twelve on the dot and after a quick chat with Holly she takes the excited little man to feed the ducks. My wife's friends love Max and think nothing about helping out with him as they do with my grandchildren, which I'm grateful for. I know Holly has taken care of all their children over the years as well as Megan, Lucy's daughter, so I suppose this is their way of paying her back.

Holly and I left not long after, arriving at Dimitris for a late lunch. It was still busy with the dinnertime crowd so once we had eaten and Holly had caught up on a bit of gossip with some of the staff we drove to the park for a short walk around the lake. On any normal day we don't get much alone time and the past few weeks have been no exception.

Since our fall out, we've never really spoken about how upset she was, we've just slipped back into our usual routine, so I haven't been able to explain to Holly just how sorry I am for adding to the strain we had all been under. I'm not sorry for what I did to Mathew's father, but I am ashamed of myself for upsetting my heavily pregnant wife.

Halfway round the lake, I point to a bench asking Holly if she needs to sit down for a while. We're both eager for the baby to come and walking is supposed to help bring it on when you're in the late stages or overdue and with Holly now been three days over, we'll do anything to get it moving. Saying that, I can see she's tired so sitting for a while won't do any harm and maybe I will be able to say my piece without being disturbed.

"Holly," I say, taking hold of her hand that was linked through my arm. "I am sorry," she cocks her head to look at me, her sapphire eyes shimmering in the sunlight.

"I know," she runs her thumb over my knuckles and her eyes lower to the ground.

"I don't think you do," I shake my head then lift her chin, seeking out her eyes. I need her to understand that I would have done anything to stop Holly and my sons being in any danger. "If I'd have known that he was a danger to you. To my family, I would have made sure you were all protected."

"Vlad it's not your fault. None of us knew, even the police didn't know, so don't beat yourself up about it. What's done is done. He's no longer able to get to any of us and we have you and Sasha to thank for that…"

"What?" I'm shocked. "I thought you were angry and upset with me…"

"I was," she shakes her head, biting her lip. "Vlad I was upset that you wouldn't tell me what you were up to. I was terrified you would do something stupid and get arrested. I even thought you might get hurt in the process but that doesn't mean that I don't understand why you had to find him and do what you did to him," her voice goes quiet, not wanting to think about the violence that took place that landed him in hospital. "Anyone would have wanted to do the same, granted not everyone would have had the means to find him like you did... And thinking about it, I'm glad he got what was coming to him... It just scared me. You scared me... "

"Holly I... " I move closer to her, horrified that she would think I could ever hurt her.

"Not in that way. I know you would never hurt me," she stares up at me and runs her finger down my cheek. "When we love, sometimes it hurts. When we can't take away the pain that someone is feeling or help them because they won't let you in, it's frustrating and upsetting."

"I'm sorry. I never thought about it that way. I just wanted to make him pay for what he had done."

"I know. But it's over now and we need to move on. Focus on our family and us," she smiles that smile that melts my heart. I must have done something right in my life to have such a wonderful woman by my side.

Placing my hands on the sides of her face, my thumbs stroke over her cheekbones. My eyes not leaving hers as I take her mouth with mine. In this kiss I apologise for upsetting her and not realising how she must have been feeling. I thank her for being here for me. For loving me and for understanding me. "I love you," I breath into her.

"I love you too."

"Shall we finish our walk and then go home?" she chuckles when we pull apart.

"Yeah," I answer, helping her up and keeping tight hold of her hand as we continue our stroll around the lake.

Chapter 21

Holly

It's good to have everything back to some normality. Vlad and I are back to being deeply in love, not that we were ever anything else it was just me not wanting to talk to him. He'd put a barrier up between us with his secretiveness and antics, so I'd say he deserved to be given the silent treatment for a few days. Especially with how distraught we had all been, I didn't need the added worry of my husband going all Rambo on Mathew's dad. However, what's done is done, we can move on now and leave the police and the justice system to do their job.

When we arrived home from our walk, Nicholas had just been dropped off home. Sebastian had given him a lift then he went back to work. With just the three of us in the house it gave us the time to talk to him alone. Both Vlad and I wanted to make sure he was ok and talked to him about how foolish he had been the night he was shot. He agreed that his behaviour was out of character for him but wouldn't enlighten us as to why. He also agreed that he had been stupid, and it wouldn't happen again. We all understood that he wanted to stand up for his family but in those circumstances, he should have left it to his father. After our chat he took a couple of painkillers that the hospital had prescribed him then went for a lay down as they make him drowsy.

I was tired too and needed an afternoon nap, so I cuddled up with Vlad on the sofa and had an hour. I woke half an hour ago to a message from Olivia letting me know she would be dropping Max home after she has given him his tea. She has the girls too, so they are having a little tea party. Mathew is working the teatime shift at Dimitris; Lucas has an afterschool activity which Daniel is picking him up from and Nicholas has just come back downstairs after his rest and got himself settled in the living room watching the television.

We had decided to make a curry for tea knowing everyone would enjoy it when they all arrive home. There's also the chance that it might quicken up my labour but I'm not holding my breath that it will do the job, I've had quite a few over the last couple of weeks and not had a twinge. I'm thinking it's going to take a stick of dynamite to get things moving.

Making my way into the kitchen, Vlad already on with the cooking, I take a seat and sigh as my hormones run a mock.

My husband has never looked as sexy as he does now. I stare across the kitchen island, taking in his broad shoulders and solid muscular arms. How the muscles in his back expand as he reaches for the utensils he's using to cut the chicken and the vegetables for the curry he's making. He tosses the meat into the pan, cooks it for a few minutes, then he adds the veg. As he continues adding and mixing the stock, spices and curry paste, my eyes travel to his bottom and his thighs. His jeans fit them like they were tailor made for him. Vlad knows how to wear his clothes, whether he's in a suit, jeans and a T shirt or sportswear, he gets noticed and right now he has my full attention.

I sit up straight and let out a little moan as I get a little hot and bothered, which happens often when I look or think of him. I hear a girlish giggle and realise that it came from me, you would think being over nine months pregnant would put you off sex but no not me. It's been a while since we were intimate together, too much going on. I've missed our spontaneous sexual encounters, as I'm sure my husband has. All day I've been hungry for him, needing him like one of my cravings and I know it hasn't gone unnoticed by him.

"I can feel your eyes stripping me naked, Holly," he turns with that cocky grin on his face. Those dark eyes drawing me in, the heat crawling up my neck as I get caught ogling him again. I don't know why I blush, it's not like he doesn't know that I find him irresistible.

He walks towards me with that sexy swagger he has going on which does nothing to quench my thirst for him and when he places those manly hands on my thighs my legs voluntarily fall open. He settles in between them and rest his forehead on mine while his warm hands come up to caress my face. I inhale his scent like a bloody dog in season and he chuckles at me just before his soft lips take mine. He leads us into a kiss that's deep and explosive and with all the will in the world, I try to wiggle my hips, wanting to bring us closer together but fail miserably when my bump gets in the way.

We both know this isn't going anywhere, not with Nicholas in the living room, a pan of curry bubbling away on the stove and Daniel and Lucas due home anytime but we're enjoying it all the same. Right on cue the front door opens, stopping our heavy petting session and Vlad's mouth moves to my ear. "We'll continue with this later, sweetheart," he whispers then moves away, adjusts himself and continues with making our tea. I slide off the stool, feeling hotter than the curry he is cooking and make my way to the fridge, needing something to cool me down. I take out a bottle of water and leave the door open a little longer than necessary, cooling myself whishing it was bedtime.

"Hi, what are you making?" Daniel asks when he steps into the kitchen. "Smells good," he sniffs at the large cast-iron pan.

"Chicken curry," his dad tells him as he dips in a fork and lifts some of the contents out for him to taste.

"Needs to simmer for a while to let the chicken marinate," he says, wafting at his mouth then puts the fork into the sink.

"Yeah, I thought so too," Vlad turns the gas down and covers the pan. He takes out another pan, pouring enough rice into it to feed a third world country then washes it before he adds the water to boil it in. Daniel retrieves the nan bread from the freezer and Lucas makes an appearance.

"Need any help?" he asks, sitting on a stool and sprawling his arms out over the kitchen island.

"No not yet," his father says as he leans against the worktop. "But you can get changed out of your uniform then take Spot for a walk."

He yawns loudly. Stretching his arms over his head before he agrees. "Tired?" I ask, standing at the side of him. Both Lucas and Mathew have had a lot of late nights over the last couple of weeks, including last night, not knowing they would be going to school this morning.

"Yeah," he puts his head on my shoulder.

"Early night for you tonight and Mathew. No playing on that game until the early hours," Vlad warns. It's hard to get teenagers to bed but my husband is right, they do need an early night.

"Come on sleepy head," Daniel ruffles his brother's hair. "I'll come with you."

Lucas goes to get changed out of his uniform while Daniel gets Spot on the lead. Once they are gone, I open the cupboard and reach for the plates.

"I'll set the table," I say, feeling I should be doing something, it was my idea to make a curry.

"I don't think so," Vlad takes the plates from me. "Go sit down, you should be resting."

"I can set a table, I'm not ill."

"I know but it doesn't need doing yet." I grumble at him and get a raised eyebrow. "Go do as you are told," he says playfully then places a soft kiss on my lips. "There's nothing for you to do plus it's not going to be ready for a while yet," he mumbles into them then turns me so I'm facing the living room and gently taps my behind.

I do as I am told and sit with Nicholas who is looking a bit brighter than he did when he got up. The painkillers make him drowsy and he always feels a little dopey even after he's had a nap.

We chat about his upcoming hospital appointment and how he's coping with what happened to him. The doctors discussed that we all might need to speak to a counsellor and gave us the choice to make an appointment. Although Vlad and I are ok, Lucas and Mathew are only young and may need some sort of support, especially Mathew. He's gone through so much in the last few months that being held at gunpoint by his own father, learning the truth about his mother's death, then Nicholas being shot could affect him and leave him scarred. When they were both asked, they shook their heads, telling us that they were fine. We've been keeping an eye on them both and up to now they have been.

Nicholas declined as well, letting us know that he just wants to get back to normal once the hospital gives him the all clear. They checked his breathing before they let him home and made him an appointment with a physio as the lung that collapsed was not working to its full potential. This can happen but with the breathing techniques they gave him plus the physio he should be back to normal soon.

Vlad alternates between the kitchen and living room, joining in with our conversation. He sits on the arm of the settee and rubs my back then when the front door opens, he makes his way back into the kitchen.

Spot does his usual rounds of giddy greetings as if he'd not seen us just half an hour ago and Daniel moans on that he is starving. He's told it won't be long then the gate buzzer sounds, indicating that Olivia is here with Max.

In no time at all she's coming through the door with Max fast asleep in her arms, she's also closely followed by Jack who's holding Megan in one arm and Rebecca in the other, all of them in pyjamas, dressing gown and slippers.

"Here let me take him," Vlad says, reaching for his son. "I'll take him straight up to bed."

"Thanks, he's getting heavy," she blows out a breath. He has put a few pounds on while he's been living with us, he did need to.

"We didn't know you two were coming," I greet the girls with a sloppy kiss after kissing the top of Max's head then Vlad carries him off to bed.

"They wanted to come and see you, Rebecca's stopping over. We would have kept Max, but we weren't sure how he would sleep." They're aware of the nightmares he had when he first came here but they hardly ever happen now.

"He hasn't had one for a while, but thanks anyway."

"Oh, well, next time we'll keep him overnight, he's so adorable and plays lovely with the girls," she smiles.

"Grandpa," Rebecca squeals as Vlad strolls back into the kitchen. Swooping her up, he hugs her tightly then places a kiss on her head. She grabs his cheeks like she usually does then kisses him back on the cheek. He keeps tight hold of her while he stirs the curry, it's been a big adjustment for his granddaughter over the last few months. She hasn't just had to come to terms with not being the youngest anymore, having a baby brother, but also now gaining an uncle who is only three years old. She's always been the centre of her family's attention. The little princess who has them all wrapped around her little finger and she still has. Only now she needs to share them with her baby brother Ben and Max. We're all aware of this so try hard not to let her feel as if she's being pushed out but over the last few weeks it has been a bit difficult.

The added bonus to all this is that she gets to help her mum with Ben and even though Max is a couple of years younger than her they play well together.

Megan, my goddaughter, just takes it all in her stride. She gets to stay over at Sebastian and Izzy's with her best friend Rebecca and her family has grown somewhat since Vlad and I met. All his sons treat her as if she is family.

"Want a taste," Vlad chuckles while holding a spoon out for Rebecca to taste. She screws up her nose at him and pushes his hand away.

"Errr, nooo," she shakes her head. "Granddad, you know I don't like curry," she scalds then pokes him in the cheek again.

"I know, petal, I was only joking," he puts the spoon down and kisses her cheek then lets her down when she asks if she and Megan can play with her dolls for five minutes. "Play with the ones in the downstairs bedroom, I don't want you going upstairs and waking Max," he expresses as Jack puts Megan down, telling her to keep the noise down. Before they have chance to escape out of the kitchen, I stop them both, needing a hug.

"Hey, you two, where's my cuddle?" I pull on the hoods of their dressing gowns.

They both cuddle into my belly and give it a little pat causing me to chuckle. "Will your baby come soon, aunt Holly?" Megan asks, looking up at me with that cute smile on her face.

"I hope so," I say, my fingers running through her thick curls. Her eyes light up with excitement as do Rebecca's and they both run off down the corridor, chuckling on about how they will both have a baby to play with once mine comes.

"How cute are they?" I ask, shaking my head.

"You should have heard the topic of conversation while we were having our tea," Jack laughs.

"It started with Megan asking, 'is my aunt Holly Rebecca's nanna?'"

"I can only imagine how confusing that conversation got them," I say, laughing.

"Yeah," he nods. "They were not the only ones," he chuckles. "We told them both yes, now that you two are married. Then Rebecca said, 'so my granddad is Megan's uncle?' We told her yes which had both of them excited with the information they had just learnt. Next, they wanted to know about the two of us," he points between himself and Olivia. "Which we told them it was just the opposite way round to you two. When they asked about the baby," he nods to my belly. "Rebecca got confused that if it was a girl then it would be her auntie and if it was a boy it would be her uncle. I don't think she understood that a tiny baby could be her aunt or uncle."

"I can see how that would confuse her, she's still getting her head around Max being her uncle," Vlad chuckles.

"That wasn't even the most confusing part of the conversation," he says, shaking his head. "While they were both trying to get their little heads around that they then asked if they were related now. And after ten minutes, I couldn't come up with an answer as to what they were, so I told them they were cousins and left it at that," he raises his eyebrows and moves towards the cooker.

"Where were you when this conversation was going on?" I chuckle at Olivia.

"Oh. I couldn't get my head around it either, so I agreed with Jack."

"You did right because I'm not sure either," Vlad says, and I can see the wheels going round in his head trying to work it out.

"This smell good, Vlad. Did you make it from scratch?"

"Of course. I'm not just a pretty face," he jokes. "Here, have a taste." He passes a fork to Jack to try it. He takes a forkful from the pan and places it in his mouth, passing it from side to side before he chews and swallows.

"Wow," he blows out a breath and then coughs. "It's tasty but fucking lethal, it will blow your socks off."

"Good. We're trying to get the baby moving so hopefully it might help," I chuckle just as Nicholas strolls into the kitchen, his eyes focused on his phone and a grin on his face.

"Hello, you, how are you feeling?" Olivia asks as she links his arm.

"I'm good thanks," he answers, kissing her cheek. He then puts his elbows on the island and leans down, reading his phone.

"Here, Olivia, have a look at this," she mimics him, her elbows on the island and her eyes fixed on her phone. They both laugh loudly then fix their eyes on me.

"Sex," Nicholas says.

"What?" Three of us say all at once, obviously not having a clue what they are both looking at.

"Google says that sex can start a woman off in labour. There's a whole list here," he points at his phone and I hear Vlad and Jack laugh at him. I laugh too because yeah, I'll give it a go. What put it there might help get it out. It wasn't thirty minutes ago when I could have ravished my husband here in the kitchen.

"Well sweetheart, if you're willing then who am I to stand in your way." Vlad chuckles as he puts his arm around me and kisses my cheek. When I look at Olivia and Nicholas, they are both laughing so hard there's tears in their eyes, even Jack has a smirk on his face. I can't believe I said it out loud.

"Oh, my God," I say, embarrassed, covering my face.

"Nipple stimulation is another one," Olivia manages to get out, still in her fit of laughter setting Nicholas off again.

"I don't mind helping out with that one either," my cheeky husband says, placing another kiss on my cheek then wrapping his arms around me.

"What does that do?" I ask because it's common knowledge that sex might help. People say curry, raspberry tea and pineapple can help and I've already tried them, this one is new to me though.

"It causes your uterus to contract and may bring on labour," Nicholas reads from his phone, his eyes wide.

"Well we will try them both, later," my husband whispers into my ear but it's heard by everyone else.

"I might come and stop at your house, Jack," Nicholas shakes his head. "It's all too much for me," he chuckles just as the girls come back in and Daniel and Lucas make their way in from upstairs.

"It must be ready by now, I'm starving here," Daniel says, tapping his stomach.

"Just waiting for the rice," his father tells him, rolling his eyes. "Set the table, it won't be long."

"Come on then, Jack," Olivia says, taking hold of Megan and Rebecca's hand, "Let's get these two home."

"You know, Vlad, I wouldn't normally say this because I look on Holly as my little sister," he puts his hand on Vlad's shoulder.

"Aw," I coo.

"And I don't want to think about you both in that way. But," he raises an eyebrow. "From one man to another, if you plan on going there tonight make it good and make it last because if she goes into labour tonight you ain't going back for six weeks, mate," he pats Vlad on the back and shakes his head. And Vlad's face falls.

"Look at that face," Nicholas howls. "It looks as if it's just been slapped."

Vlad shakes his head, looking shocked, and I can't help but smirk at him.

"I knew that, didn't I?" He looks at me as if I can answer him but to be truthful, I had forgotten that once you've given birth you can't have sex until you've had your postnatal examination and told everything is fine which is usually six weeks after giving birth. That's going to be a struggle because although Vlad and I are married and have a baby ready to make an appearance soon, we haven't been together for a year yet and our sex life is still very full on. Six weeks is a long time to a couple who would struggle to go six days without being together.

I shrug my shoulders at him, smirking, "Why you asking me? You're the one who's had an army of sons, I haven't even given birth to my first yet."

"Oh, look at that face," Nicholas says again, unable to contain himself as he put his arm around my shoulder. "He looks like someone just stole his comfort blanket," he squeezes out through his hysterics. Looking at my husband's face and how he mouths, *"Fuck off,"* to his son, I burst out laughing too. He does look as if he didn't know but I'm sure we had discussed this when I first found out I was pregnant.

"Look what you've started now," Olivia swipes at Jack's head, even though it's amused her immensely.

"I know but it needed to be said," Jack shrugs his shoulders, humour dancing in his eyes as his lip rises at one side. "Your face mate… Priceless," he slaps Vlad on the back and my husband shakes his head and winks at me with that mischievous smirk of his. He knew all along, the twat.

We all say our goodbyes, Olivia informing us before she goes that Lucy said she will be calling over after work then we set about putting tea out.

*

The film Nicholas chose for us all to watch is a pile of shit, so instead of watching some horror movie we've been sat chatting about the usual topic these days: babies. Lucy chuckles at Nicholas when he comments about Vlad being overprotective with his sons and he dreads to think what he will be like if we have a girl. "She'll be twenty-five before she's allowed to the shop on her own never mind date anyone." Vlad rolls his eyes and shakes his head while his thumb strokes over the side of my bump. I do have to agree with Nicholas because he's bad enough with his sons so I can only imagine what he will be like if we do have a daughter, I see lots of teenage tantrums in our future.

"Have you thought of any names yet?" Lucy asks, shifting in her seat so her legs are curled up on the sofa. She arrived just in time to sit and eat tea with us and because her mum and dad are babysitting, she decided to stay and watch the film. She said she'd come to see me, but we all know she's here for Nicholas or maybe both of us. I shake my head, as does Vlad. We're having trouble agreeing on a girl's name. We narrowed it down to three but then decided to wait until the baby is born, as for a boy's name we still have a whole list.

"No. We have a few to choose from but we're struggling to agree," I tap Vlad's thigh, and smile up at him.

"Once she's born…" he raises an eyebrow at me, daring me to say, *"what if it's boy?"* I don't say anything, not wanting to upset him. "Once she's born, we'll choose one," he finishes.

"Yeah, I think that's best. Megan was Emma all the way through my pregnancy then when she was born, I took one look and thought she looks like a Megan."

"Daniel was Cassandra or Cassy," Nicholas sniggers, slapping his brother on the shoulder.

"I don't know what I was thinking wanting to name him that if he'd been a girl," Vlad shakes his head. "Anyway, yours was no better, if you'd been a girl you would have been called Polly."

"Pretty Polly Petrov," Daniel laughs, "Suits him don't you think," he chuckles again, his hand ruffles his brother's hair which earns him a slap around the back of the head.

"Cheeky bastard," Nicholas states but chuckles anyway.

"Do you remember how I went into labour, Holly?"

"Yeah of course I do," I smile, remembering the night little Megan was born. "Nick was telling jokes which half of weren't even funny, but Lucy thought they were hilarious and couldn't stop laughing. The worse his jokes got the more she laughed."

"I laughed that much at him that my sides hurt," she chuckles "I even thought I'd wet myself," she continues as she closes her eyes and shakes her head. "Turned out it was my waters that had broken and within half an hour my mum and dad were whisking me off to the hospital. The contractions came thick and fast in the back of my dad's car and by the time they'd got me into the birthing room, I was nine centimetres dilated."

"Did your mum stay with you, while you were giving birth?" Nicholas asks, knowing Megan's father has never been on the scene, not wanting to have anything to do with Lucy or his baby once he'd gotten what he wanted.

"They both did. My poor dad got the living daylights beaten out of him."

"What?" Vlad laughs.

"Well, when you are in pain and some idiot is in your face telling you not to push, to breathe through the pain then next minute they're saying push Lucy, I'm sorry but even with all their good intentions they're going to get a slap. And unfortunate for my dear old dad he was the one that got it. Which is stupid really because you'd have thought he'd have known to stay out of the way, seeing as he was present for all his children being born and my mother knocked hell fire out of him on each occasion." Vlad throws his head back, chuckling away, as do his sons and I turn and look at my husband, smirking.

"Hey, you," I prod him in his ribs.

"Yes, angel?" He asks, still laughing as he takes hold of my finger and raises my hand to his mouth, kissing it tenderly.

"You've to go through it yet, I might beat the shit out of you," I widen my eyes at him, biting my lip.

"You wouldn't hurt me, you love me too much," his lips land on mine softly. "You can do what you want to me, sweetheart, it will be worth it," he whispers into them then kisses me sweetly.

"Aww," Lucy's hand goes to her chest. "You two," she sighs.

"Don't Lucy, you'll only make them worse, I have to put up with their lovey dove shit every day," Nicholas whines. Vlad kisses me again then smirks at his son.

"Right Holly," Nicholas says. "What do you call a woman with a frog on her head?"

"Oh, here we go," I smile at him. "I don't know, what do you call a woman with a frog on her head?"

"Lilly," he laughs loudly, and we all groan but still laugh along at his lame joke. "Ok, I have another one and you'll like this one. What's the difference between your wife and your job?"

"I don't know what the difference is between your wife and your job," and I start smirking before he tells us the punch line when Vlad groans and shakes his head.

"After five years your job still sucks, ha ha," he laughs at his joke.

"Nicholas," Lucy shrieks as she nips his arm. But I do find him funny and my belly starts to jiggle.

"Ouch, stop with love taps, woman. I'm delicate at the moment. Still healing," he places his hand on his chest and bats his long eyelashes at her. She just shakes her head at his dramatics and ignores him.

"My turn," Daniel says, sitting forward in his seat and rubbing his hands. "Get ready, Holly, this will have your waters breaking," and my belly jiggles again as I laugh out loud, covering my mouth at his comment.

"Ow let me go next otherwise I'll forget the punchline," Lucy says, slapping Daniel on his thigh, she too sitting forward in her seat.

"Go on then but it better be good," he rolls his eyes at her.

"It is," she claps her hands together. "Which of your children will never grow up and move away?" We all shake our head.

"Don't know," I say, grinning.

"Your husband," she laughs loudly, and we all laugh with her, even my husband lets out a chuckle.

"Lucy how the hell can you forget the punchline? It's two words," Daniel shakes his head at her.

"Shut up," she says, still laughing.

"Right let me tell mine."

"Go on then, I'm ready. Bring it on."

"Ok. A Russian man is walking to work one day when he kicks a bottle that's just lying on the ground," Vlad groans and shakes his head but when I look at him, he has a smirk on his face, obviously he's heard it before.

"Suddenly, there's a puff of smoke and a Genie pops out.

Hello, Master I will grant you one wish. Anything you want.' The man is stunned but rubs his chin as he thinks about what he would want.

'Well I really like vodka, so I wish to drink vodka whenever I want. Make me piss vodka.'" I start laughing even though he hasn't finished, and Vlad puts his hand on my belly as it starts to shake.

"The Genie grants the wish and the Russian man goes on his way. When he arrives home, he takes out a glass from the cupboard and pisses in it.

'It looks like Vodka.'

'He says to himself then he smells it.

'It smells like Vodka.'

'Then he takes a sip and it's the best vodka he's ever tasted so he calls for his wife, pouring her a glass when she comes running. She reluctant at first but gives it a try and it's the best vodka she's ever tasted. They both party all night. Then the next night when he arrives home from work, he pisses in two glasses again, handing one to his wife and the result is the same. It's the best vodka that they have ever tasted and they party until the sun comes up. Finally, Friday night comes and when he gets home, he tells his wife to fetch one glass. She does and then asks;

'Why just one glass?'

'The Russian man holds up his glass and says;

'Because tonight, my love you drink from the bottle.'"

"Oh. My. God!" Lucy yells, snorting out of her nose as she covers her mouth. My belly starts doing the Irish jig as I erupt into a fit of giggles. Nicholas and Vlad laugh out loud even though I'm sure it's not the first time they have heard it.

"That was funny, Daniel," I say once I've got myself in order. "But my waters are still intact," I shake my head at him.

"Oh, well that's all you're getting from me," he says, standing up. "I'm off to meet a few mates," Vlad looks at his watch.

"Don't be drinking, you're on the hospital run if Holly goes into labour."

"What?" Nicholas asks, sounding put out. "I can run you there."

"Not if you've been on those painkillers you can't," Vlad tells him.

"Shit, I forgot about them. Well I'll come for the ride then," he shrugs his shoulders.

"Where are you going anyway, it's already ten o'clock?"

"Just over to the club for a couple of hours, I won't drink," he shakes his head at Vlad then says bye to everyone, dropping a kiss on the top of my head while he ruffles his father's hair.

"Make sure you don't," Vlad warns. He doesn't order that they never drink when they go out, but he wants to be able to sit with me in the back of the car rather than him driving and to be truthful I want him with me too.

"Ready for bed," Vlad asks, leaning in so he can whisper in my ear, "We'll try the other two on your list," his husky tone has me standing, with his help, ready and willing.

"What time are you staying till?" I ask Lucy, knowing that she'll be driving herself home tonight which I don't really like her doing.

"I don't have a curfew tonight," she smiles. "Mum and dad are on babysitting duties, so Nicholas is going to watch a marathon run of the first series of Vampire Diaries with me," she looks at him and he picks up the remote to turn the TV onto Netflix.

"I'll get the popcorn," he says once he switched it on. "Want anything to drink?" he asks Lucy.

"Diet coke, please."

We say goodnight and make our way to the staircase; just as we set off walking Nicholas calls me.

"Holly one more for you before you go to bed," Vlad rolls his eyes but stands with me at the bottom of the stairs, his arms around me while he rests his chin on my shoulder.

"Go on then."

"A woman complains to her husband that he's spending too much time in the pub so one night he takes her with him.

'What would you like?' he asks her.

'Oh, I don't know, the same as you I suppose,' she replies.

'So, he orders two Jack Daniels and hands her one. He drinks his off in one and she takes a sip of hers.

'Eww, that's terrible,' she says and spits it out. *'I don't know how you*

drink that stuff,' she moans.

'Well there you go,' cries the husband, *'And you think I'm out enjoying myself every night.'"*

"What a pile of shit," Vlad says as he leads me upstairs. Me, I'm chuckling away, finding it very funny. Turning to my husband as we reach the landing, he shakes his head and chuckles. "I don't know how you find them so funny."

"Because they are."

Chapter 22

Holly

We enter our bedroom, still chuckling at Nicholas' really bad jokes, and in one swift movement, Vlad has his loving arms around me. My back is pressed to his front and I can feel his hardness already digging into me. I wiggle my hips against him, and I'm treated to a manly groan. The noises he makes alone can undo me and at the moment it wouldn't take much as I've been desperate for him all day.

"Careful sweetheart," he breathes seductively into my neck, moving my hand that I've just slid behind me to stroke his manhood. "Six weeks is a long time," he kisses the curve of my neck that joins my shoulder while wrapping my hair around his hand. "I want to take my time… " With one hand he slides my shirt off my shoulder and places a kiss there, then his lips trail back up my neck until they reach my ear. "Nice and slowly until I've devoured every part of your sexy body," I shudder at his words and the bottom of my stomach tightens with anticipation.

My head leans back against his shoulder and I let out a moan of my own when his gifted fingers sensually stroke around my heavy breast then pinch my hardened nipple. Both hands then make their way down my body until he reaches the waistband of my leggings. He crouches behind me, removing them, then leaves a gentle kiss on my bottom.

I turn around to face him as he stands, and his eyes are aflame. Lust and love burning through them and when he runs the tip of his tongue over his bottom lip, wetting it, I attack his mouth fiercely. I have one hand around his neck, my fingers running through his soft hair and stroking the nape of his neck while my other feels its way across his broad chest. It's hard to get as close as I want with my pregnant belly and when I wrap one leg around him, he places a hand under my bottom, gives it a squeeze then lifts me up. Even with my extra weight, he carries me easily.

He moves us towards the bed, our tongues still duelling, his hands tugging at my shirt. Eager. Hungry with need to see me.

Tonight, I have no inhibitions. No feelings of self-doubt and no reason not to believe that Vlad still sees me has the woman he first met.

Even though I know my husband finds me sexually attractive and gets harder than a sledgehammer every time I'm near him, it hasn't stopped me from becoming a little self-conscious of my pregnancy weight gain and the few tiny stretch marks that I have developed along the way. There's not many, two or three but when your man is built like a Viking warrior with not an ounce of fat and wears his clothes as if he's just stepped off the front cover of a magazine then one can become ill at ease with one's self. My husband is loving and takes no shit from me when I try to keep my shirt on or lower the lights when we have sex, he reassures me. Sees me as he has always done but we haven't been together for over two weeks. Not since the kidnapping and the shooting and I've gained a few more pounds since then. I don't understand why it doesn't bother me when he sees me naked in the shower or when I'm getting dressed but in the throes of passion, I get a little nervous that he won't see me as he normally does. Like I said though, tonight I have no hang ups with baring all. I'm a wanton woman. Desperate for him. So, my hands help him fumble with the few buttons to rid what's covering me and we make it in record time to free my boobs.

"Needy tonight, angel," he says with an edge of seductiveness in his tone, that cheeky smirk appearing on his beautiful face, and he's not wrong. I watch his greedy eyes rake up and down my body and I'm sure the bulge that's restricted behind his trousers grows even bigger. He's a big man on the best of days but tonight he's out doing himself.

I swallow hard, my mouth watering as the flutters in my stomach, somersault vigorously. "You have no idea," my voice takes on a whole new husky tone and I quickly change places with him so he is standing with his legs against the bed. I push at his shoulders and smile when he drops backwards on to the bed. He bounces up and down and chuckles then slowly backs up towards the headboard.

"Come to me, Holly," his tone is low and sexy and as he catches me in his gaze, I crawl onto the bed. As seductively as one can when you're heavily pregnant, I continue to crawl towards the man whose darks blue eyes have me hypnotised.

Without taking my eyes off him, I straddle his thighs, moving from side to side. Needing friction to take the edge off then I lean forward and remove his shirt.

Smoothing my hands over the hard muscles of his stomach, I lean forward to place a kiss on his lips. He takes advantage of my position and cups the cheeks of my behind, squeezing them before he slips his hand between my legs. Holding onto his shoulders while my lips devour his, I move against his fingers and moan into his mouth.

Vlad swallows up the sounds I am making and chuckles against my lips when they get louder. What I feel for him goes beyond anything I can comprehend. Loving him is my life and now I need him like my life depends on it.

My hips take on a life of their own as I move, gyrating and moving faster against his hand. My pulse rate soars as the sensation builds within and in no time at all I explode around his fingers, clenching his hand between my thighs as my mouth grips his shoulder.

Vlad holds me against his chest while I calm myself down and when my head lifts, he places his hands on either side of my face, kissing me passionately. When we pull apart, I'm ready to go again and move down his legs so I have access to the zip on his jeans. I undo the button quickly and pull down the fastener then he lifts his hips so I can remove them.

I free him in no time, his boxers and jeans only making it as far as his knees before I take his hardness in my hand. I squeeze and stroke, appreciating the moans that emit from him. And when he throws his head back and his eyes roll back, I see my chance to drive him wild.

Perched above him, I sink slowly down his length and he hisses between his teeth.

"Steady, Holly," he says, not wanting me to take all of him on the fear he may hurt me or the baby. He sits up and takes a hold of my hips, helping me move up and down. The width of him brushes against my inner walls and hits the parts needed to start the quivers in my lower stomach again.

Vlad's moans become more frantic and he bends forward, taking one of my hardened nipples in his mouth while cupping the other one. His teasing tongue laps around the hard bud and the sensation runs straight to my core, causing me to buck harder. I grip him tight and arch my back as I hover in euphoria.

As I wiggle, grind and move up and down, Vlad's hands tighten onto my hips as he bucks harder underneath me. And as I scream is name, my breathing fast, our arms wrap around each other. Holding tight. My face sinks into Vlad's shoulder and I latch on to his skin to cover the noise. "Fuck, Holly!" He roars as he comes hard, shaking in my arms, his face burrowing into my neck.

We stay wrapped to together, our breathing hard, our skin damp and in our world of sheer bliss.

"I needed that," I muse out loud as I move so my back sinks into my husband's front as I sit between his legs. He chuckles, sitting back against the headboard and kisses my shoulder.

"So much," his voice is husky as he kisses my neck. "Love you," he tells me while his hands lay across my bump, drawing lazy circles.

"Hmmm, love you too," I tell him as my hands join his.

"Well if that doesn't bring you on, I'm not sure what will," he chuckles into my hair and I tilt my head up to kiss his jaw.

"Neither do I, I've tried everything else," I chuckle with him.

We lay like that for a short while then Vlad helps me up when I need the bathroom. He comes with me and when we've finished, we snuggle up together in bed.

"Tired?" he asks while brushing the hair from my face and rubbing his nose with mine. And I should be. It's late. I've just had two almighty orgasms while riding my man but funny enough I'm still wide awake.

"No," I answer, lifting one leg over him as I play with the short hair that runs from his belly button down to his groin.

"Want to go again?" he winks at me and I shiver with desire for only him.

"Why not?" I take him in my hand, feeling that he's solid as a rock again. He brings my leg further up so it's wrapped around his hips and with one gentle nudge we're in ecstasy once more.

*

"Vlad," I call as I watch the water run down the plughole, wishing I'd woken him before I decided to get in.

Waking a while ago, needing to use the loo, I thought nothing about the twinge and how my stomach seemed to tighten like it was making a fist as I made my way into the bathroom. No sooner had I finished then the contraction began. It wasn't too painful and didn't last long. On the scale of one to ten, I gave it about five which lasted about thirty seconds. Certain this was the start of my labour; I ran a bath. While it was running, I checked my bag just to make sure we hadn't forgotten to put anything in, laid out a clean nightshirt and dressing gown. No point going in clothes when I'd only need to change. Once I was happy, I climbed into the bath. I'd only been in five minutes when another contraction began, this time stronger and more painful. It lasted about sixty seconds and I knew I needed to get out and call for my husband. It's a struggle to climb out and Vlad would have a coronary if I tried to get out without his help.

With no sound of him moving I yell his name this time, "Vlad!"

I hear movement. The sound of him getting out of bed, his feet hitting the bedroom floor. A stumble and a curse, "Shit!" I look up towards the bathroom door and he appears looking dishevelled.

"Holly, what the... " He stops, his hand runs through his hair then over his tired face. "Why are you in an empty bath?" He crouches down looking bemused and places a soft towel around my shoulders.

"Because I thought it would be fun," I roll my eyes at him. "Will you help me out, please?"

"Of course," he lifts me out of the bath as delicately as possible, wrapping another towel around me. Vlad stands in front of me bending down, so his mouth is near my ear, "Don't be smart, Holly," he nips my lobe.

"Vlad I'm in labour... " and just as I say the words another contraction starts, and I grip hold of his chest tightly.

"You're in labour and you didn't think to wake me?" His voice is panicked as I breathe through the pain and when I look at him again, he's mimicking me. "Deep breaths, Holly. In and out."

"I am," I say, gritting my teeth then bury my head into his neck. The pain subsides after about sixty seconds and Vlad holds me against his chest and kisses my hair.

"You ok?" I nod my head. "What time did they start?" He looks down at me, rubbing his chest where my fingernails have dug in.

"Sorry," I tell him then kiss the mark tenderly.

"Don't be silly, it's fine," he scolds then lifts my chin so I can see his dark blue eyes clearly. They dance with delight. The happiness sparkling, making them light up and the smile on his face is wide. "I love you, Holly," he lips graze across mine.

"I love you too." My fingers come up and stroke his face. He's so excited to see his child being born and so am I that I can't wait to watch his reaction when it comes.

"You didn't answer me, when did they start?" He takes my hand and leads me into the bedroom, the towel still wrapped around me.

"Mmmm, about forty-five minutes ago." He raises an eyebrow and shakes his head.

"You should have woken me," he shakes his head again. "How often are the contractions?"

"Every fifteen minutes."

"We better get dressed and get to the hospital. I'll ring them before we set off."

Vlad helps me get dressed than dresses himself, quickly. He's showing no signs of being anxious whereas I'm a nervous wreck.

"Come here," he takes me into his arms, snuggling me into his chest, giving us just a moment before we make our way downstairs and the chaos begins.

Lucy and Nicholas are fast asleep on the sofa when Vlad leads me into the living room, the television has gone into sleep mode. I sit down opposite them as Vlad makes a coughing sound then runs upstairs to wake Daniel and retrieve my hospital bag.

"Huh," Lucy opens her eyes and swiftly moves into a sitting position when she sees me as Nicholas' arm comes around her and tries to get her to lay back down. She slaps his arm away and rubs at her face. "Sorry, Holly, we fell asleep watching TV… " she breaks off when my face contorts, and I place one hand on my stomach as the other grips the cushion.

"You're in labour," she squeals and jumps up from her seat as Nicholas sits up, his hair ruffled, and a confused look on his face.

"What? Where's? Where's dad?" he manages to get out as he listens to me moan and pant, Lucy going through the motions with me.

"Holly," Vlad comes into view and Lucy moves out of the way. "That was less then fifteen minutes since you had the last one." He takes my hands. "Did it last longer?" I nod my head.

"And they're stronger now," I pant out just as it subsides.

"We need to get going." He turns to Daniel who has just made his way into the living room, wearing a pair of joggers and shrugging on his T shirt. His eyes are wide and his face pale. A woman in labour clearly scares him to death. "Here take my keys, you're driving," his dad states, helping me up from my seat.

"I'll drive," Lucy says as she watches Daniel rub at his face.

"I'm coming," Nicholas says, picking up his shirt from the back of the settee. "He can watch the kids."

Daniel's colour comes back a little and he nods his head in agreement. I think it's for the best. I'm not sure if he'd be able to cope if something happened before we got to the hospital.

"I don't care who fucking drives, but we need to leave now," Vlad states. Lucy squeal again when she catches the car keys he's just tossed to her. I'm not sure if she's excited about the baby or because she gets to drive Vlad's new Jaguar E-pace.

We arrive at the hospital in record time and just in time to see my waters break in the lift as we were making our way up to the labour room. Vlad has been so attentive to my needs, not once letting go of my hand, even when I gripped it like a vice in the back of the car when another contraction hit me hard. Nicholas has surprised me. During me moaning and panting in the back of the car, he leant over from the front seat and took my other hand that was gripping the head rest, holding it in his, he too going through the breathing techniques with me.

Now here we are in the delivery room. The midwife, Julie, and her colleague, Trisha, have just examined me for the third time. Everything is well and hopefully our baby will be delivered normally within the hour. I'm eight centimetres dilated and was told just to breathe through the pain, easy for them to say when all I want to do is push. I need to dilate another two before I can. I've had no pain relief except for a quick inhale of the gas and air and Vlad has been damping my forehead and my cheeks with a cold wet towel.

He brushes my damp hair away from my eyes and kisses my cheek again, all well intended caring gesture from my loving husband. But I'm not myself at the moment and he's grating on my last nerve. If he tells me to breath one more time and doesn't take his face away from mine soon, I won't be responsible for my actions. My pain threshold has just flown out of the window, leaving me like a snivelling kid. I don't know how some women cope with being in labour for hours on end, I only started a couple of hours ago and I've had enough already. I need this to be over with now.

Lucy and Nicholas pop back into the room as Trisha steps out. They tell us they're allowed a couple of minutes and inform us that they have messaged Olivia, Sarah, and Sebastian.

Lucy's mum and aunty haven't gotten back to them yet but Seb has. He's told them he's on his way. Sebastian will be excited about the baby and will want to be here for both his father and me. There's nothing they can do, it's a waiting game but they won't mind hanging about the corridors.

The hospital has been great since we arrived. The two midwives are brilliant, Julie is in her early thirties with a very caring nature about her. Trisha is a rounded middle-aged lady who is very jovial, her raucous laughter has you laughing along with her and putting you at ease. They've allowed Nicholas and Lucy to stay in the room with us and only asked them to leave when they were examining me. They asked me if I wanted them to stay in when the baby comes, and I did think about it but declined. This is my first baby and God only knows what I'm going to be like when I start pushing and even though Vlad has many sons, it is the first he will be there for the birth. It's a special time. A magical time just for the two of us and our baby.

Just as Trisha opens the door to come back in, I'm hit with the biggest contraction yet. They haven't really stopped since my waters broke but this one has me letting out the biggest moan yet. Vlad's arm wraps around me, trying to comfort me but I'm hot and sweaty and need air, not smothering. "Breathe Holly, we can do this," the voice that I normally love to hear and find soothing says.

"We?" I snap while one of my hands shoots out fast, gripping my husband's chest like a lion grips its prey and I watch his eyes widen and water.

Chapter 23

Vlad

"Urrrrrrr," my angel moans behind gritted teeth as another contraction hits her hard. Her brow is damp with perspiration, so I lean over with a cold towel to wipe it away. Watching her in pain kills me. Knowing she's going through this for us, for our little one, overwhelms me and if I could take the pain away, go through it for her, I would but I can't. So, I sit here watching, coaxing and soothing the best way I can trying to help. Whoever said that the male species were stronger than the female and superior to them was wrong. I actually think that they'd never watched what I'm seeing now or known anyone like my wife. Because she's much stronger than me or any man I have known. Not in the brute strength sense but definitely emotionally and mentally. How she's coped over the last few months, I'll never know and now this, I'm in awe of the woman I love.

She lets out another almighty moan, just as the other midwife strolls back into the room and I lean down, wrapping her in my arms, "Breath Holly, we can do this." I watch my wife's eyes narrow on me as she moves back from my arms.

"We?" she growls and I hear Nicholas chuckle from behind me, feeling a sharp pain hit my chest. My eyes have never left Holly's face and at the moment she looks nothing like the angel she normally does. Possessed is the only word I can think of. Holly's glare is enough to pierce holes through me and the look on her face tells me she wants to kill me.

As I was watching her face change from my loving angel into someone who could strangle me with her bare hands for putting her through this, and I don't blame her, I missed her hand which moved as swift as a Peregrine Falcon as it stoops down and lunges at its prey in mid-flight. But my son saw it and he finds it amusing. The power in that one movement knocked the fucking wind from my lungs and with that menacing look my wife is giving me, I'm surprised her hand didn't go straight through me. In fact, I'm sure that's what has got Nicholas howling behind.

"I'm so sorry," he finally gets out as he wipes the tears from his eyes, slapping me on the shoulder. "Wooh, I thought Holly's hand was gunna come out of your back then and with that look she's giving you," he breaks out again in a fit of laughter, "I half expected to see your beating heart in her hand." He bends at the knees, unable to contain himself while Lucy rubs his back, trying hard to hide her amusement.

The midwives stare at him, both biting their lip and when I glance at Holly the look she had just a minute ago has softened and tears have built in her sapphire eyes.

"Out," I demand, standing and turning to my son. I can see the funny side of this but now is not time. He watches far too many vampire programmes. Nicholas side steps pass me and bends down, giving Holly a kiss on her forehead and patting her hand.

"Sorry," he tells her. "Good luck and don't be too hard on him," he tilts his head towards me. "We'll be out there," he finishes, giving her a little wave. Lucy waves too and blows Holly a kiss as Nicholas slaps me on the back then they both leave as I take my place at my wife's side.

"I'm sorry," Holly says as I take her hand while the midwife examines her uterus. She's an emotional mess at the moment and I'm not sure what to expect next from my angel but whatever it is I will take with a pinch of salt.

"Hey, it's fine," I kiss her lips then rub at my chest, knowing there will be one hell of a bruise there but it's nothing compared to the pain my wife is going through.

Gripping my hand firmly, Holly buries her face into the crook of my neck and lets out a mumbled moan. I wrap one arm around her, rubbing her back as she sits forward, her legs bent at the knees. Her face is flushed, her hair damp.

"Okay, Holly, breathe through it," Julie advices, lifting her head to talk to my wife. "Not long now, sweetie, you're doing really well. The heart rate is absolutely fantastic, strong and healthy."

"Can I turn on my side?" Holly asks, blowing out a breath.

"Of course. Whatever makes you more comfortable." I help my wife shift onto her side where she feels more relaxed. I'm practically sat on the bed with her as she leans into me. I keep one arm around her and rub her thigh with the other, not really knowing if I'm helping or if I'm just in the way but when she raises her head from my chest, her eyes sparkle and her love for me comes flooding out and I breathe a sigh of relief. At the moment I have my own little Jekyll and Hyde in my arms with Dr Jekyll present for the time being. I know the other one will raise her head before the baby comes but I'll take whatever gets thrown at me.

"Do you know what sex the baby is?" Trisha asks, fiddling with the baby monitor.

"No," both Holly and I say together as Holly takes a relaxing break from the contractions.

"Do you have a preference or are you not bothered?" She smiles, moving closer to the bed.

"A girl would be lovely," I answer, still rubbing Holly's back and holding her hand. I kiss her head and smile. "We have six boys," I tell them.

"Wow, that's a lot of testosterone in one household. A girl would be just perfect," she chuckles. "So, you're a dab hand at this dad thing then," she nods her head towards Holly's stomach and then raises her head to look at me. I nod my head not saying anything. Getting into a conversation with the midwife about how I never got to see one of my sons being born because they're mother didn't want me there isn't something I want to discuss with her.

"So, what will you do if it's another boy?" Julie, the younger midwife asks, widening her eyes at me. "You can't send it back," she chuckles this time.

Without thinking I smile at Holly, "We'll try again," I say, gazing at her and regret my statement straight away. Mrs Hyde as just entered the room and she isn't happy.

"Don't think you're coming anywhere near me again," she pants out, gripping my thigh tightly while she glowers at me. I rub her back and kiss her forehead, ignoring the daggers she's throwing and her last comment because I know she doesn't mean it.

"If you say so, sweetheart," I smile, leaning down to kiss her forehead again but notice her eyes narrow on me, "*Don't you fucking dare!*" they say, well maybe not the *fucking* word but she definitely isn't in the mood for my cockiness.

Holly grabs my hand and squeezes it as she lets out a sob followed by a louder cry and her face goes scarlet. "You try pushing out an orange from the end of your penis than we'll see if you want to try again," she grits her teeth at me. I raise my eyebrows and look at the midwives who just lower their heads at me. Obviously, they hear worse, so they just ignore her comment.

"I can see that it would hurt a bit… " I grimace and don't get to apologise for my lack of tack.

"Okay, Holly breath. We can see the head so when I say push, push into your bottom," Trisha tells her as she moves her hand from my wife's knee, who nods her head, panting. "You want to help, dad? Hold Holly's knee."

My wife is laid on her side with one leg bent laying on the bed and the other one bent propped up, her foot resting flat on the mattress. I'll do anything to make her more comfortable, so I keep one hand in hers and lean forward to hold her leg. That's when I'm overcome with such emotion that I'm struggling to explain it. Seeing the crown of our baby's head fills me with pride, love and so much more and when I turn to look at my wife and the way she focused, getting ready to push out our little one, tears flood my eyes.

"Okay, Holly. Push now," Holly squeezes her eyes shut and I can hear the strain as the head comes flying out. "Breath now, Holly, the head's out. One last big push when I say…"

I zone out from what the midwife is saying because I need to show my wife just how much I love her. Keeping hold of her leg I lean in and kiss her smack on her lips. "I love you, sweetheart," I murmur into them then take my position so I can see clearly our baby being born.

"Now Holly, push into your bottom for me…" She doesn't get to finish and say anything else when Holly grits her teeth, groaning, squeezing her eyes shut and pushes.

My hand covers my mouth, not wanting to show my chin quiver, the sight of my child flying out into the world has me bubbling like a little girl and I turn to my wife, wrapping my arms around her. "You did it," I breath into her damp hair then place my hands on her cheeks as I grace her soft lips with a kiss.

"Girl or boy?" she asks as the little cherub lets out a whimpering cry.

"I'm not sure," I turn to look at the midwife who is wrapping the little one in a sheet. "I think we have a girl…"

"Here you are," Trisha breaks me off. "Meet your little baby girl," she greets, laying her across Holly's chest. "You now have a daughter." And there they are. A group of words that I longed to hear so many years ago, then after Lucas was born, gave up on ever having one. I wasn't planning on having any more children, not that any of my children were planned, but I've loved them with all my heart anyway. Then my little minx came along and here we are, proud parents of a beautiful baby girl. And she is beautiful, covered in all sorts of goo and a little red faced but beautiful nonetheless.

"Hey there, little one," my finger brushes across her tiny little face as her eyes flutter open then close quickly. Holly coos at her, nuzzling the top of her head, a tuft of fair hair shimmering in the light. Her eyes open again, showing the colour blue, lighter than mine and maybe just maybe she'll have her mother's eyes. Soft, caring and full of love.

"Do you want to hold her?" Holly's gentle voice asks as she tries to sit up. I adjust her pillows then use the control to higher the top of the bed just enough that she's not sat up straight but enough that she's comfortable if she needs to sleep. She looks exhausted so I'm sure it won't be long before she drifts off.

"I would love to," I smile wide as I take my daughter into my arms. She's so tiny and delicate compared to what her three eldest brothers were when they were born. Lucas was different, he came very early and wasn't well. As for Max, I haven't got a clue what he weighed when he was born. "She's so tiny," I whisper, not wanting to wake her.

"I know," Holly leans in and strokes her head. "I'm glad though," she lets out a chuckle. "I don't think I could have managed a ten pounder," she smiles, kissing her head.

"Thank you," I say, a little choked up as I tenderly kiss my wife.

"What are you thanking me for?" She strokes her thumb under one of my eyes, wiping away the wetness.

"For our daughter."

"I think you'll find we both had a hand in it."

"Yeah," I look down at my daughter as she starts to whimper, her bottom lip quivering. "Here we go," I chuckle as she opens her eyes and her lungs at the same time.

"I think she may need feeding," Julie the midwife says as she come and stands at my side. "Are you breast feeding, Holly?"

"I want to try."

"Let's see if we can get her to latch on then, shall we?" I pass her over to Holly and she tries to have a go on her own. She struggles for a while but eventually without any help she gets our daughter to suckle. I watch mesmerised, unable to take my eyes away from the mother and daughter bonding. It's so natural and so intimate. This is their thing. It's something I could never do for her. I sigh as I watch, happy that even though they don't need me for this part, I still get to be here, holding Holly's hand and stroking my baby's back with my thumb.

"You're doing great there, sweetheart," I sigh again. "Do some women struggle with breast feeding?" I ask, interested.

"Yeah, they can do. Some babies don't always take to the nipple."

"Well she's doing well, must take after her dad," I wink at Holly, smiling because my wife will see the funny side. She shakes her head at me and gently strokes the baby's head.

"You can't help yourself, can you?" Her mouth twitches.

"No," I say as I lean in and kiss her neck.

"You're a little shit, you know that?"

"Not so little, according to my wife," I raise my eyebrows at her then turn crimson when Trisha the older midwife comes to stand at the other side of the bed, chuckling at me. Where the fuck did she come from? I thought they had both left the room.

"Ignore him," my wife rolls her eyes at me.

"Oh, I don't know, he's quite entertaining," she chuckles again, shaking her head. "Don't worry, love, we see and hear a lot worse. You and Holly are quite the loving couple, it's cute," I close my eyes and lower my head, rubbing my hand over my chin.

"How much did she weigh?" I ask, changing the subject.

"Seven pounds two ounces," Julie answers from across the room. I glance over at her, not realising she was there either.

They both fuss around Holly, removing things from the bottom of the bed, then move as they fill in notes and tap into the computer. Once Holly stops feeding our daughter, they both step out of the room. "Here let me take her. Shut your eyes, you look shattered."

"I am," she murmurs, her eyes closing. "You know we need to pick a name," she opens one eye then closes it again.

"I know. We have plenty of time before we have to register her, I'm sure we'll come up with something special... " I stop talking when I hear a soft snore coming from Holly. Sitting back in the chair, I lay my daughter across my chest and gently caress her back with my thumb, trying to come up with a fitting name. The poor girl will have it for the rest of her life, so I don't want to choose something that she won't like. I chuckle when I think about the names I was going to bestow on my sons if they had been girls. No, I better leave it to Holly.

I sit for about ten minutes just spellbound by the little bundle in my arms, her cute button nose and Holly's shaped mouth. My finger gently strokes her hand and her tiny fingers move, opening then closing around mine. Her eyes flicker as if she is dreaming and her rosy lips twitch. I could sit and study her forever. I place a soft kiss on her forehead and then look at my wife who has both her hands together tucked under the side of her face as she sleeps peacefully.

Realising how blessed I am, a lone tear slips down my cheek. I'm sure I will have shed a few when my sons were born but having a daughter, my baby girl in my arms, watching my beautiful loving wife give birth to her has left me an emotional wreck.

I wipe it away just in time to see the door open and Trisha make an appearance. "Your son and his girlfriend plus another one of your sons are outside wanting to know if they can come in," Shit I forgot about them. I don't correct the girlfriend comment just nod my head. "I've told them they can have ten minutes if it's ok with you and Holly, but they won't be able to stay any longer. They'll have to come back at visiting time."

"Yes, let them in. Thank you," I say, glancing at the clock on the wall. It's six fifteen and we've been here just over three hours. The boys will be getting up any minute, not knowing they now have a baby sister.

"Hi," Lucy whispers, the first one to enter the room closely followed by Sebastian then Nicholas.

"Oh, look at her, she's beautiful," Lucy coos as she moves the blanket from my daughter's chin.

"Did they tell you we had a girl?" I ask, thinking the midwives would have left it to us.

"No, silly. She's wrapped in a pink blanket." She rolls her eyes at me.

"Oh, yeah." I chuckle.

"Tired, paps?" Sebastian chuckles, leaning in to have a look at his sister. "Oh, she's so cute, give her here." He takes her from me, laying her across his forearm, close to his body. I stand to stretch my legs, listening to my eldest talk to my daughter. "You know you're going to break dad's heart, little girl, when you grow up. I know because I have a daughter who will do the same to me," he chuckles and shakes his head. And she probably will. I know she's going to challenge any rules I set in place and hate me when I'm still dropping her and picking her up from high school.

"She has Holly's mouth," Lucy comments, "and her shape nose."

"Yeah, she does," Nicholas agrees, taking her from Seb. "Hey there, little one. Your gunna have us all wrapped around your finger, aren't you? And fighting off the boys when you're older," he chuckles.

"For fuck's sake," I moan, rubbing at my face which causes the three of them to laugh. She's definitely going to hate me when I lock her in her room and tell her boyfriends to fuck off out of my house and stay away from my daughter. I've always been protective of my sons and I know I will be a lot worse with my daughter. I'll end up wringing their fucking necks.

"You'll need to have a chat with my dad, Vlad. I'm sure he'll give you a bit of advice on how to cope with a teenage daughter," she kisses my cheek, feeling sorry for me. However, we have a good few years to go yet and I'm lucky that I have a strong, caring wife who will help me along the way and put me right where I go wrong as well as keeping our daughter in check.

"I can't believe you gave your dad a hard time," Nicholas says, looking lovingly at Lucy.

"Huh, are you joking?" She raises her eyebrows. "I'm my mother's daughter. Believe me I was no angel growing up, why do you think he's bald?" She takes the baby from him, sniffing at her hair and kissing her head, not one bit bothered that she's still covered in dried blood and any other fluid that came out with her.

Holly's eyes open and she tries to sit up, giving out a groan, I'm by her side in a split second helping her. "Hi, you lot," she greets, her voice croaky. "Have you been in here long? You should have woken me."

"No," Lucy says, sitting on the side of the bed as she leans in and kisses Holly's cheek. "You need your rest. Congratulations mummy, you did well."

"Thank you," Holly says, taking hold of Lucy's hand. These two are very close, Lucy being Holly's goddaughter.

"Congratulations," both my sons say then take it turns to kiss her cheek. "She's the double of you," my eldest comments.

"Aw, thanks, but I'm sure it won't last long. Your dad has very dominant genes, just look at you lot. So, I'm under no illusion that she'll change over the next few days and be the spit of her brothers," she smiles at them both.

"I'm sure she'll have the best of both," I tell my wife, leaning down so I can steal a kiss.

"I need to pee and have a shower," Holly says just as Julie opens the door and walks in with one eyebrow raised.

"Aw, we have to leave," Lucy scrunches up her nose.

"Can they stay a little longer?" My wife asks, a pleading look on her face. "Just until I've showered so they can stay with the baby."

She shakes her head, "You'll get me shot. You've got twenty minutes until Trisha comes back from her break. I know she's a happy soul, but she's let you in when she shouldn't have so please make sure you're gone before she gets back."

"Thank you," I tell her, reminding myself to order flowers and chocolates for them both. She nods her head and takes hold of Holly's notes.

"What do you want for breakfast, Holly?" she asks as I help my wife off the bed, leaving my two sons and Lucy fussing over our daughter.

"Hmmm, cereal and fruit if you have it or toast and a cup of tea would be great, thanks."

"I'll bring all three, I'm sure dad must be hungry too," she nods her head towards me, "Tea or coffee?"

"Tea would be lovely, thanks," Definitely getting flowers and chocs.

"Okay, I'll get it ready while you're showering and make sure you use the toilet," she nods. "We can't let you home until you and this little lady have been."

"When will I get to go home?"

"Well, your little one is healthy so once she's been checked over again and has had a motion then she should be fine. Then you need to eat, pee and be checked over but you both seem to be doing well so later today sometime. I can't see any reason why we would have to keep you until tomorrow."

"Good. I feel fine, just hungry and tired and she fed okay." The midwife nods her head at Holly.

"You not thought of a name yet?"

"No, not yet."

"When we get home, we'll look through the name book," I say, rubbing Holly's back.

"You don't want to call her Polly then, dad?" Nicholas widens his eyes at me.

"No."

"I like Polly," Lucy says, reprimanding him with a light tap on his arm.

"Yeah, I wouldn't rule it out," Holly agrees. "It's cute."

"Come on, I'll help you in the shower while they babysit," I chuckle, leading Holly towards the bathroom.

Within the hour, Holly has used the ladies and had a shower, got changed into a comfy pair of pyjamas, my sons and Lucy have gone off home and we've cleaned our daughter down, putting her in one of the all-in-one sleepsuits that we brought with us. Holly's bed has been changed, we've shared the breakfast that Julie brought in and had a second cup of tea and now our little baby girl is having her second helping of breakfast.

"You're going to be a demanding little diva, aren't you," Holly nuzzles her hair and strokes her back, our daughter just happy to suckle away.

"Just like her mother," I chuckle, moving swiftly before I get one of Holly's love taps.

"Cheeky get," she smirks, "I am not a diva." She prods my side. I catch her hand and lace our fingers together.

"I know sweetheart," I kiss her hand. "A little demanding, yes," I wink at her, she gets my meaning.

Chapter 24

Holly

"One down, one to go," my husband says as he carefully lays down on the bed at the side of me. He's just gotten Max to bed while I was feeding our daughter. "We'll go through all the gifts tomorrow and put them away," he props another pillow behind my back as he watches our baby suckle then leaves a gentle kiss on my cheek.

We arrived home from the hospital just after five to a welcoming party. Our home had been transformed into any little girl's dream home as white and pink flowers took residence on every surface around the kitchen and living room. Bright pink and silver, 'It's a Girl' balloons floated around the ceiling like Chinese lanterns in the night sky on Chinese New Year and 'Congratulation Mummy and Daddy' banners lined the walls. The house was full of family and friends who were all eager to celebrate the birth of our daughter. Sparkling champagne was passed around with fizzy water given to me. This was all put together by Izzy, Olivia and Sarah who had also arranged enough food to feed an army. Gifts for the baby were given out and to say I was overwhelmed was an understatement. My hormones are all over the place and with every present, I cried. Olivia stated that we didn't get the chance to have a baby shower with so much going on in our lives since we came home from our honeymoon so her and her partners in crime thought it would be a good idea to get it out of the way now then we can get back in to some routine.

It's after ten and we've only just been able to get Max to bed, too excited with the new baby and having everyone visiting at once. Our living room is filled to the rafters with gifts and cards and I'm absolutely shattered. "I haven't got the energy to do anything," I tell him as I shift our little one from my breast to over my shoulder so I can wind her.

"Give her here," Vlad says, taking her from me and holding her against him while he gently pats her back. She lets out an almighty burp and we both chuckle. "You, my darling wife, will not be doing anything but resting until I say otherwise," he leans in and kisses my lips just as there's a small rumble in her nappy. "Oh," he smiles against them, "Apart from feeding and maybe changing her stinky arse," he moves back and lifts her to sniff her nappy. "I can't believe such a dainty little thing could smell so bad." He kisses the top of her head as he continues to gently rub her back. She looks so tiny. She is tiny but against my husband she looks smaller than the average baby at one day old.

Gazing at my husband, his face is awash with contentment. He kisses the top of her head then inhales her scent while still rubbing her back. He lifts his head from hers and glances my way, "I have no words to how I'm feeling at the moment," he shifts up the bed so he's sat against the headboard, our daughter still sprawled across his chest. I don't think he's going to put her down anytime soon. Bless him. Then he puts his other arm around me, pulling me into him and kisses my head. "I feel as if my heart is about to burst," I take his hand in mine when his eyes water. "Watching you in pain while you pushed her out is... I can't explain how I felt, what I'm feeling now. Seeing our daughter come out into the world... It felt like a dream, as if I was having an out-of-body experience and now... now we have her home... Here in my arms, I can't put her down. I can't stop looking at her. I don't ever want to not have her with me. Is that normal?"

"I think so. I feel the same. Earlier when she was being passed about, I wanted her back with me. If I couldn't see her in my line of sight, then I moved so I could."

"Yeah, I noticed. I did the same," he chuckles, leaning in to kiss my lips and lets out a heartfelt sigh. He lifts my hand when he leans back and kisses my wrist. "You know we men have it easy," he gives me a sideways glance, smirking. "All we do is have a night of pleasure or a quick bunk up against a wall or wherever. Then you carry her for nine months or in your case just over, giving her a home. Keeping her safe until she's ready to pop out and greet us. You go through all that pain. Backpain, weight gain and sensitive boobs..."

"It's a very surreal experience giving birth," I break him off. "You have all this pain and emotions but at the end of it, the pain is one of relief or it was for me anyway and you're left with a feeling that's too overwhelming to explain really. I'd say joy and a love that's too big to comprehend. Like you it's as if your heart is going to burst. Too much happiness. Do you understand?"

"Hmmm, yeah," he sighs again and closes his eyes.

"You know she can't sleep on your chest all night," I turn into him and stroke her back then place a kiss on her cheek.

"I know, two more minutes then I'm all yours to snuggle with," he opens one eye and gives me that sexy smirk.

"Oh, second best in the snuggle category, am I know?" I tease, poking him in his ribs.

"Never," he sits up straight and edges off the bed to place our daughter in her crib then bounces down at the side of me once he's kissed her head. She's going to be ruined.

"Come here," he wraps me in his strong arms, facing him and takes my lips passionately and my stomach flutters with its power. They'll be none of that, not for a while anyway. "Love you," he whispers against my lips.

"Love you too."

"We better get some sleep, sweetheart."

"She needs her bottom changing," I move out of his embrace, missing his strong arms already.

"Yeah, I'll let you do this one and I'll do the next," he sits up with his hands behind his head, staring at me with loving eyes while I attend to our daughter. Once finished I slide into bed and into my husband's awaiting arms where we both hope to get a few hours' sleep before our daughter needs us.

*

On any normal day Max is a happy little soul, one that plays happily, chuckles all day long and loves to have cuddle time. Any nightmares are a thing of the past and he is a little darling to have and loves helping out with his baby sister. But today our little man is not a happy chappie and is dragging his feet, kicking up a storm as Vlad and myself walk at either side of him, holding his chubby little hands.

Yesterday, Mrs Richardson and Miss Styles from the nursery that Max will be attending called round for their home visit. Max was inquisitive as to who they were and seemed happy enough to have them in the house. When they spoke to him and asked what his favourite story was, he eagerly toddled off to fetch them his story books which he then gave to Miss Styles as he climbed on to the sofa to listen to her read. Mrs Richardson fell in love with him and informed us that taking him for an hour and staying with him the following morning would ease him in gently, then Friday, the day after, maybe he would be able to stop a bit longer. His official start date isn't until next Monday so with him going the two mornings for a short time, it would ease him in, and we would probably be able to leave him the full three hours the day he starts. Which would be fantastic for him to interact with children his own age and good for me. Emily wakes two or three times through the night then again around eight. Once she's fed and had her nappy changed, she will drift off and not wake until around lunchtime. This means that I can have a rest, maybe grab a nap myself as well as get a few things done around the house while Emily is still asleep.

We'd struggled to choose a name for our daughter and for three days after she was born threw lots of names around, old ones and some I' never even heard of but was still unable to pick one to suit her. On the third day Max had been running around singing at the top of his voice, 'Emily, Emily'. Apparently, there had been an old song on the radio, and he'd picked it up from there. I loved it, so did Vlad, and Max was excited that he had got to name his little sister.

Max stops again, dragging our arms back, adamant he's not moving. Vlad bends down so he's at his level and zips up his coat properly. "Max, mate, it's only for an hour and we'll be staying with you," he speaks softly to his son as he picks him and attaches him to his hip.

We set off walking again, Vlad carrying Max in one arm while I link his other. "But I want to stay with Emiy," he sobs into his dad's shoulder and my heart squeezes in my chest for him. He loves helping and is so gentle and sweet with her.

"Max, love. She wants her big brother too," I stroke his hair, "but she's sleeping at the moment, love. When we get back home, she might be just waking up." Olivia eagerly offered to take care of Emily for us while we visited the nursery and told us anytime we need her she'll gladly take care of her.

He wipes at his eyes as we approach the school and Vlad kisses his head, placing him back on his feet. I take his other hand as we walk through the school gates and head for the nursery entrance.

Mrs Richardson stands at the door greeting the children and parents and when she spots Max, she gives us a reassuring smile. I think we'll need it too.

She invites us in, and Vlad helps Max to take his coat off, hanging it on one of the pegs. "Hello Max, would you like to come and have a look around?" Her voice is gentle, and when she puts her hand out for Max to take, watching him, I'm not shocked when he snakes his arm around his father's leg as he hides underneath them. Vlad looks down, amused at his son, and slides him out from between them. "Come on, Max," he holds his hand out, "I want to have a look."

Tightly holding his dad's hand, Max follows but the frown and pursed lips tells me he's not one bit happy about it.

We are led outside first and shown the garden where the children get to plant vegetables and have flowerbeds. It's bright and colourful with lots of butterflies and flowers attached to the fence, numbered one to ten. There's an area for small bikes and go-carts as well as an area with wooden building blocks. Lots of heavy-duty tables with crayons and pencils and a small tray with water toys. We talk to Max about them, but he shows no interest at all where at home he loves to play out in the gardens.

Once we're back inside, we make our way over to the ICT area, set up with microphones, recorders and a touchscreen computer. Like outside there's a water tray with a sand pit at the side of it. A role play area is set up at the far side and a large reading corner occupies the other side of the room. Miss Styles approaches with a book in her hand and a smiling little girl with adorable pigtails holds her other hand.

"Hi Max," she greets, bending down in front of him. "We're having story time, would you like to join us?" Her smile is wide and genuine, showing she really cares about the children in her care but that doesn't matter to Max because he's still not impressed. With a stubborn stamp of his foot, he tells her no and gets a raised eyebrow from Vlad.

The little girl steps forward offering him a truck she has held in her hand, kindness in her smile as she shows her milky white teeth. Her smile soon fades, and she's left opened mouthed when Max knocks it clean out of her hand then tugs on one her cute little pigtails while wailing, "Go away."

There's a "Wooh," from Vlad as his eyes widen on his son.

Miss Styles lets out an "Oh," in shock as she covers her mouth and the little girl with the cute pigtails that I can't wait to put in Emily's hair when it starts to grow, screams "Ouch," and Max bursts into tears.

"Well maybe that's enough for today," Mrs Richardson states as she takes hold of the little girl's hand asking her if she is okay. She nods her head while Vlad bends down to speak to Max.

"Max what is wrong with you?" he asks, wiping the tears from under his son's eyes. "That's not nice. Now I will take you home but not until you pick up the truck and say sorry to that little girl who was trying to be kind to you." Vlad's voice is low and firm which Max isn't used to. He sees Vlad as a happy playful man, one that never tells him off, so this has Max lowering his head as he twiddles with his fingers in front of him. He knows he's upset his dad.

With Vlad knelt down on his knees, Max steps forward and picks up the little toy. He hands it to the little girl and with his head still low he whispers sorry. He sounds so cute but so sad that I almost cry for him.

We need to remember he has gone through so much over the last few months and since he came to live with us, he has been wrapped in cotton wool. He's loved and cared for and gets away with a lot of things due to losing his mum, what Mathew's dad did to him and

Vlad missing out on the first three years of his life. His older brothers treat him like a baby but then again, he is their baby brother and to be fair we all do.

"Small steps," Mrs Richardson smiles as Vlad takes his hand. "Bring him back tomorrow and we'll see how he goes."

We thank her and say our goodbyes then make our way home, Vlad still in shock with what Max did.

The following morning we take the same walk to the school with Max still kicking his heels. Vlad spoke to him about how he behaved at the nursery, telling him that it's wrong to be mean to girls and that if he gave nursery a try, he might enjoy it and have lots of new friends that he could invite to his birthday party in a few months.

Mrs Richardson greets us at the door and asks Max if he wants to hang up his coat. He's reluctant at first but when his dad takes his off and hangs it on an empty peg Max copies him and takes his hand then searches for mine. I give his hand a gentle squeeze and kiss him on his head. This is progress because yesterday Vlad had to help him take it off.

Miss Styles calls story time and the children all gather around her, sitting on the carpet, she too sitting crossed leg on the carpet. There's a picture of The Gruffalo on the wall and she takes the book from the table. This is a favourite of Max's so maybe he might want to listen to her.

"Well I think I'll join in story time," Vlad says, lifting an eyebrow at Max who tilts his head at his father as he walks off towards the carpet area and sits down crossing his legs at the back. I let out a chuckle, my husband looks so out of place, but this bit of kidology might just work.

Max takes off after his dad, settling himself down on Vlad's lap with his head on his shoulder. Mrs Richardson raises her eyebrows and smiles at me then we make our way over to them. She passes me a tiny chair which I sit on while she stands and watches her class as they listen enthusiastically to the story. The little girl from yesterday sits at the front, crossed legged with her elbows on her knees as she gazes up at the teacher. There's a little fair-haired boy sat on his knees who keeps leaning over to get a better view of the pictures while another little girl with a mop of ginger curls gets up and sits at the side of the teacher, leaning against her arm. I watch Max, comfortable on his dad's knee, playing with the short hairs on his arms. Mrs Richardson looks intrigued with my husband's tattoos as she tilts her head to get a better look.

After talking them through the front cover and asking questions about the deep dark wood, Miss Styles then takes on the voice of the Fox. *"Where are you going to, little brown mouse? Come and have lunch in my underground house,"* Max chuckles and wraps his little arms around his daddy's neck. She then makes a squeaky voice as she pretends to be the mouse and I watch Vlad whisper in Max's ear. *"It's terribly kind of you, Fox, but no…"* Max giggles loud as he listens to her and I know his father has just put on a whiny voice and said the exact same thing in his ear. He reads this story often and has Max chuckling away at the many voices he puts on.

The other children giggle as their teacher continues and without being told Max stands up and takes a seat on the floor at the side of the boy who was on his knees and leans in to look at the pictures. This is definitely progress.

Vlad and I stand back out of the way but in eye shot of Max just in case he turns around looking for us. Mrs Richardson smiles at us as she walks past and sets up a table with paints. When the story ends, Miss Styles looks up smiling and nods her head and we hold our breath anticipating what Max will do. To our surprise, he follows the girl with the pigtails whose name we now know as Abbie and the little boy Sam with the fair hair. They make their way over to the paint table where they all roll up their sleeves and put on an apron. Max stands with his new friends and Mrs Richardson, painting while the other children scatter around interacting at various areas of the room. Every now and then he lifts his head, his dark blue eyes searching for us, once he sees we are still there he continues with a smile on his face.

After twenty minutes and three paintings later, he's had enough. "We go home now, Owee," Max tugs on my hand after drying his on a paper towel. Although he's been doing really well saying words with Ls in them, he still struggles now and again especially when he says my name. I dampen another one and wipe the red paint from his cheek then bend down to wipe the blue off his shoes.

"I'll make you a deal, Max, love," his little face snuggles into my chest while he listens. "All the children are just about to have milk and fruit, if you join them then as soon as you've finished we'll go home," he looks over at another member of staff that we've yet to be told her name as she sets the milk out and chops up pieces of apples then he turns to look at Vlad who's leant back against the wall. He smiles at his son and nods his head, agreeing with me.

Kissing my cheek, he sets off high fiving Vlad's hand that he had held out. He runs off to where all the children are sitting in a circle as the staff offer milk or water and slices of apple to all of them.

"He's done really well this morning, considering where we were yesterday," Mrs Richardson comments while we stand back watching him. She's aware of what he's gone through and that he's only been with us a few months.

"Yeah, I think so too," I say, taking hold of my husband's hand.

"I think Monday you could try and leave him and if there's a problem we'll ring you." I nod my head, agreeing we could give it ago, but my husband doesn't look convinced.

Monday morning came around quickly with the weekend being one of shopping for Max, getting him a backpack and some suitable trainers for nursery, lots of studying for Lucas and Mathew as they both have tests coming up and Emily treating us to a little sleep in on Sunday morning which was short lived when Max burst into the bedroom at six thirty asking if he could take one of his books to nursery the next time he goes.

Surprised with his sudden turn around, Vlad told him he could take whatever he wanted as long as he went back to bed for an hour. He did, choosing to snuggle in the middle of his dad and me.

In the afternoon the whole family was home and Vlad and all his sons cooked a huge roast dinner while Izzy and I relaxed, well relaxed as much as you can when the men in the house act more like kids than the children do.

Lots of brotherly squabbles on who was making the gravy and mashing the potatoes which caused a wet towel fight to start up and end when Vlad threatened to send them all to their rooms if they didn't get out of his way. It was all in fun and the dinner turned out lovely.

"Love your new trainers," Olivia says to Max as she softly strokes his hair. She's just turned up to watch Emily while we drop him at nursery. We were going to risk taking Emily in the pram with us but not knowing how long we will need to stay, Olivia said she would take care of her while we were gone.

"Daddy bought them for me," he looks down at them as he picks up the book, he wants to take with him.

"Room on The Broom, aren't you fed up of that yet?" Vlad asks while tucking it in his new Spiderman backpack then helps him put his arms through the straps. Max shakes his head, screwing up his face. I run the brush through his hair then kiss his head.

"It's your favourite, isn't it, Max?" I glance at my husband, giving him a look as if to say, 'you should know this'.

"Yes," he nods his head at me and takes my hand.

"Give Emily a kiss before we go," I tell him, and he runs over to her Moses basket, leaning in and kissing her cheek.

"Are you going to paint me a picture so I can hang it in my kitchen with Megan's?" Olivia asks him. He studies her for a moment then nods his head.

"Yeah, and one for mummy and daddy," he takes my hand again, smiling up at me and I bite my lip to stop myself from bursting into tears. Since having Emily, he alternates between calling me Holly and mummy. We don't correct him or make a fuss and even Mathew is fine with him calling me it. I think because he hears Vlad and his brothers say, 'Here, go to mummy' when they're passing Emily to me that he's picked it up from there. It doesn't bother me he can call me mum; I am his step mum and we will tell him about his mum when he's old enough to understand.

"Oh, I'm sure they will love that, Max." Olivia tells him as she runs her hand over his head.

"Yes, we will," I lean down and give him a motherly hug, kissing the top of his head, then Vlad put his arm around me and kisses mine.

"Come on let's get going before we are late," he instructs, leading us out of the door.

Arriving at the nursery a little quicker this morning, as we don't need to keep stopping for Max, he hangs his coat on his peg then takes out the book from his backpack. He leaves it with Vlad and skips off towards Miss Styles, handing her the book while we watch from the cloakroom.

"Wow, Max, I love this story, can we read it this morning?" she asks, all smiles that really do meet her eyes. He nods enthusiastically, grinning at her. He's joined by Abbie who seems interested in the book too. The teacher calls the children to the reading corner once they've all hung up their coats and the parents have left. They settle and once again they all listen, absorbed in another world where stories take them.

"I think it's safe for you to leave him, Mr and Mrs Petrov."

"Oh, are you sure?" I say to Mrs Richardson, placing my hand on my chest and biting my lip again, choked up that he's no longer interested with whether we are here or not. It was only a few days ago he wouldn't leave our side and cried that he didn't want to be here and now she just wants us to go without saying bye or giving him a kiss. Well I can't do that. "Can I go tell him we are going? Say bye to him."

"Max," she calls, and he turns his head to look over. "Give him a wave." We both wave, and he waves back, that cute smile of his lighting up his face then he settles in to listen to the story. "He'll be just fine. If there's anything we will call you," she says as she ushers us out of the door.

"You have our numbers?" my husband asks, chewing on the inside of his lip.

"Yes, both of them and half a dozen emergency contact numbers," she laughs, shaking her head. "Go, he's settled and we're quite capable of seeing to his needs. We know it's hard, but it will get easier."

"Okay," Vlad says, taking hold of my hand. "See you later," he tells her, and I say bye as we make our way out.

"He'll be fine, Holly," he says, trying to reassure me, but I know he's having his own internal struggle with leaving him.

Three hours later we're back, and Max is standing ready with his coat on and his backpack slung over his shoulder, a frown on his little angelic face "You left me," he states as he runs into dad's legs and this time he pronounces the L. Vlad scoops him up into his arms, taking his bag from him.

"I know we did but we'll always come back for you," he looks around at the other parents who are picking up their sons and daughters, all happy to skip off out of the door. "Look," he points to the other kids. "All the other children's mummies and daddies left but they came back just like us. You're a big boy now, Max."

He stares at Vlad for a moment, "Okay," he says then wiggles out of his arms. "I painted a picture for you." He takes it from Miss Styles who is holding it out for him.

"Bye Max," she ruffles his hair, smiling.

"Bye," he gives her a little wave then hands me the painting. "Wook," he points at the picture.

"Wow, Max, this is lovely," I tell him as I look at the painting he's done.

"Emwi, you and daddy," he says, pointing at what look like little spiders.

"Ow that's sweet."

"And me, Mat, Cas and Becka," he pops his lips when he finishes. He calls Mathew Mat, Lucas Cas and Rebecca Becka. He's only three and is still trying hard to pronounce all their names.

"You have a big family," Mrs Richardson says, joining us. He nods his head, his eyes huge with excitement.

"This is Dan," he points to another splattered spider. "Nicky, Seb, Izzy, Joe and Ben."

"Wow you're a really good painter. Did you do this all by yourself?" Vlad asks him, proudly.

"Yes. I did anover one but it's still wet, so I have to get it tomowow."

"Is that for auntie Olivia?" Vlad eyes widening as he looks at me, impressed that Max has settled in. He nods his head then grabs our hands.

Dragging us along as he skips, Max leads us out of the door eager to be done with nursery for today but happy to be going back tomorrow.

Chapter 25
Vlad

"Daddy," hearing Max's soft cry wakes me suddenly and I sit up as he makes his way into the bedroom rubbing his eyes. "I hot," he moans. Throwing back the covers, he climbs in at the side of me and I can feel his body heat straight away.

"You are." I feel his forehead as I look at the clock. It's just after one and I've only been asleep an hour. Emily had a late feed. Over the last week we have gotten into a routine where she is fed, has her nappy changed, and asleep by ten o'clock and that is where she stays until about four but tonight, she wouldn't settle, and it was twelve before she went off to sleep.

Max scratches at his chest then his back and moans again. "Daddy I itchy," he wiggles his back and Holly stirs.

"Shush," I tell him, putting my finger on my lip then climb out of bed, lifting him in my arms. I don't want to wake up Holly or Emily, so I take Max into the bathroom, switching on the light and closing the door behind us.

"Let's have a look at you," his sleepy eye lids flicker and he scratches at his neck, lifting up his Spiderman top and sticks out his tummy to show me.

"Spots," he point to them and I glance down to have a look.

There are four spots on his belly and when I turn him around to have a look at his back, he has at least ten and a couple on his neck.

"Spots," he copies me as he looks at himself in the mirror just as the bathroom door opens.

"Hey, what's wrong?"

"I got spots," Max tells Holly, scratching like he's got fleas. "And I hot," he moans, walking into her arms when she crouches down to have a look at him.

"Ow poor baby, you are warm." She feels his head. "Looks like chickenpox," she says, turning to me, smoothing down his mop of stuck up mousy hair.

"You're going to look like Spot," I tap him under the chin, trying to cheer him up but it's not working. He turns his head away from me and snuggles into Holly chest. Lucky bugger. It's four weeks since our daughter was born and four weeks since my wife and I had any alone time. However, I am aware we only have a few weeks to go. I'm not counting.

"We need some calamine lotion and Calpol," Holly breaks me out of my musing.

"We have Calpol in the fridge but I'm not sure about the other." I take Max from her, lifting him into my arms and kissing his head. "Let's take him downstairs before we wake Emily."

Holly gives him the medicine for his temperature while I search through the cupboards for the lotion. Mrs White and Izzy store anything and everything in these so you never know.

"Calamine cream," I call out walking back into the kitchen from the utility room.

"That will do. It does the same with less mess," Holly says, taking it from me as Max continues to scratch and moan. Once she's blathered the areas in the cream, we make our way back upstairs.

"Can I sleep in your bed, daddy?" Our sleepy little man asks as we make our way onto the landing.

"Yeah, go get your teddy," I let him down and he scoots towards his room then rushes past me in no time at all, settling himself on my side of the bed. I climb into the middle while Holly checks on our little girl then she turns off the lamp and climbs in at the other side of me.

"Have you had chickenpox?"

"Yeah, when I was five. You?"

"Can't remember," and I can't. I know my sons have all had them, so has Joe and Rebecca... "Will Emily catch them?" I ask, sitting up.

"She shouldn't. She should be protected by my immunity especially since I'm breast feeding but I'll ring the doctors just to make sure in the morning."

"Good."

Max has drifted back off to sleep and Holly has snuggled into her pillow, her back to my front. I wrap my arm around her, laying my hand on her boob while her bottom nestles nicely against my crotch.

"You can get rid of that," her muffled chuckle has me grinding my hardness against her arse.

"It's not my fault, it has a mind of its own," I squeeze her boob playfully and she chuckles again.

"Yeah well, tell it to get its mind on other things."

"It's hard to do, sweetheart, when you keep wiggling your bottom against it," I slap her arse, this time for getting me worked up.

"Ouch," she moans, straightening her legs so her bottom moves away from me. I pull her back into me and give my man a talking to.

"Wow that was quick," she laughs.

"Yeah, baby sick, shitty nappies and chickenpox will do that."

"Aw you poor thing," she chuckles again, her voice still muffled by her pillow.

"Oh, don't worry about me," I kiss her shoulder, smiling into it. "It is you who should be worried, woman."

"Why is that?" she questions, lifting her head up, a smirk on her face.

"Because in a few weeks' time, my sexy little wife will be getting well acquainted with her favourite part of my anatomy."

"Well," she turns over to face me and I turn onto my back so she can get comfy across my chest. "I might just make you wait a few months," she kisses my chest then lays her head down.

"Don't be silly, you can't resist me. You be climbing me like a tree in no time, sweetheart."

"You're very cock sure of yourself, aren't you?" She jabs me in the ribs.

"No, just stating the obvious," I lay my hands at the back of my head, well aware that my wife can no more resist me than I can her.

"Go to sleep, Vlad, Emily will be up soon." I close my eyes, knowing our little daughter could wake up anytime and that will be another hour or so of no sleep.

Before I drift off, I hear a soft snore from my wife and then I'm subjected to Max's hand slapping me across the forehead.

*

"He has twenty-five," Lucas says as he helps Max back on with his T shirt. Holly's just smothered him in cream again and Lucas and Mathew decided to count how many spots he has.

"Twenty-seven," Mathew counters. "There's two on his leg," he says as he continues to eat his breakfast.

"No nursery for you, young man. I'll give them a ring and let them know." Holly ruffles his hair then takes a seat at the side of him. "Have you had chickenpox, Mathew?" She picks up her cup of tea, taking a sip.

"Yeah. I can't remember exactly how old I was, but I remember mum putting the cream on me and I have a scar on my knee where I picked at one." She nods at him, picking up her toast as I scroll through my phone checking my emails.

I haven't had time to check them since yesterday afternoon, always too much going on around the house. I come across one that's for Mathew.

"I have a message about your mum's headstone," I look up at him.

"You do? I wondered when it would be ready."

"It will be next Monday," I pass him my phone so he can read it himself.

"Cool. I'll visit after school. Thank you," he passes me the phone back.

"What's this?" Holly asks, tilting her head.

"The headstone we ordered for their mum," I point to Mathew and Max. "It will be ready Monday." She nods her head, gazing at Mathew.

"And you're going to go alone on Monday?" He nods his head and shrugs his shoulders as if it's no big deal. To him it isn't, he goes often on his own. But I can see my wife has other plans.

"Would you mind if we come, so we can take Max? I know he doesn't understand but we could get some flowers... "

"No, I don't mind," he smiles, breaking her off. "That would be nice. Thanks."

"Can we all come? I'm sure Nicholas, Daniel and Seb would want to come with you. You would too, Lucas, wouldn't you?"

"Yeah," he answers, nodding his head, "I don't mind."

"If they want to come that would be nice."

"Good, I'll mention it to them, and we can sort out a time and get some flowers." And just like that my wife has shown again just how caring she is and how much she loves these boys.

*

I haven't been out of my office for three hours or looked up from the laptop except for when Holly brought me a cup of coffee an hour ago. It seems ages since I did anything work related, not since Mathew's father turned up and with everything that followed after that, I haven't stepped foot into the office outside my home. Then Holly giving birth to our beautiful baby girl, I haven't wanted to leave them and go into work. Now Max has chickenpox and even though Holly has told me if there's anything I need to do then just go and she will be fine, I don't really want to.

I can leave most things to Sebastian and Daniel. And now Nicholas is feeling much better and desperate to get back to work, it means I get to stay home with my wife and children a little longer. Anything I need to do I can do from home so this afternoon, while our baby was sleeping, and Holly and Max were cuddled up on the settee watching kids TV, I came in here to check on a few things.

Three hours later, and a hell of a lot of emails sent as well as time sheets signed off, I close my laptop.

"Vlad," Mathew gets my attention as he knocks on the office door and walks in with Emily in his arms.

"Yeah," I stand from my chair. "Is everything ok? Where's Holly?" I panic.

"Yeah, she's upstairs sorting out Max. I said I would watch Emily, but the police are here."

"They are?" I take Emily from him when she starts fussing. "What for?" I ask, making my way to the office door

"I don't know. It's Joanne and PC Miles, I left them in the kitchen."

"Ok," I say, making my way down the corridor.

"Sorry to disturb you, Mr Petrov," Joanne says as I shake her hand and PC Miles. I like these two, I got to know them reasonably well when Max and Mathew were in hospital.

"No, it's fine. What can I do for you?" I ask, switching Emily to my other shoulder when she dribbles down my neck. Joanne laughs when I pick up a towel to wipe it.

"Could we have a quiet word with you?" I see uneasiness in their body language, so I lead them to my office thinking whatever they have to say maybe Mathew doesn't want to hear.

"You don't need me, do you?" he asks, having them turning towards him.

"No, Mathew," Joanne smiles at him.

"Good. I'm going to do my homework."

If they are here about his father, then he won't want to hear anything they have to say. He's already told us he doesn't want to know anything about him or hear his name mentioned again and that's fine by me.

"Please take a seat," I point to the chairs on the other side of my desk. They both sit down, Joanne cooing at Emily, who is wide awake at the moment but settled in my arms. "What can I do for you?"

"She's adorable. I bet you have your hands full with her and Max," Joanne comments as she takes a seat.

"You're not kidding. Max has chickenpox. He's upstairs with Holly at the moment, I'm sure he'll be down before you go, telling you all about them," I shake my head, knowing he will do just that.

Now as a rule, I wouldn't normally speak about my family to anyone, I'm not one to make polite conversation but these two are different. They both spent time with Max and Mathew while they were in hospital and it was PC Miles who first found the boys at their home when Mathew's dad had attacked him. They've always been straight with me and I have the up most respect for them and the job they do.

"Mathew's dad has made an allegation against you," PC Miles is the first to speak. Of course, I knew this could happen but was hoping it wouldn't, that he would stick to what he told them when he was first dropped off at the hospital.

"What do you mean against me?" I fake a shocked face, placing my daughter over my shoulder.

"What he claimed had happened to him when he was first interviewed at the hospital, he is now saying he was threatened with his life to say that," Joanne states, rolling her eyes. Maybe she doesn't believe him or doesn't give a shit that he was beaten and ended up in intensive care.

"So, what was the allegation?" I ask, picking up a pen from my desk and tapping it on my chin.

"Apparently, he was kidnapped by two very large men with Russian accents. Blindfolded and driven to an unknown location where he was tied to a chair until you got there."

"Me?" my eyes widen at them.

"Yeah, then you beat the shit out of him until he couldn't stand then you knocked him unconscious." I nod my head at them because it sounds about right.

"Good enough for him," I smile and shrug my shoulders.

"Mr Petrov this isn't funny and I'd ask you to edge on the side of caution because while he's going away for a very long time for what he has done, he's after taking you with him," PC Miles states, moving forward in his seat. "Do you have an alibi, someone who can vouch for your whereabouts that night?"

"Yes, he does," my wife says as she storms through the door and stands by my side, taking our daughter from me.

"Holly," I warn. I don't want her getting involved. She places her hand on my arm, giving it a squeeze.

"My husband was at home with me," she says without blinking and she's just fucking lied to the police.

"Holly, we didn't say what day it was so how would you know?" Oh shit this is where she folds and gives in. She can't lie for shit and I don't want her to. I'd rather admit to what I did than have her lie for me. Just as I'm about to speak she stands straight, one of her hands on her hip and our daughter cradled in her other arm.

"I think if you remember we were told about Mathew's father the day he was admitted to hospital and if you remember that was the week Nicholas was in hospital. So, I think you'll find that Vlad was visiting the hospital every day that week and, in the evening, he was at home with me, his heavily pregnant wife. Or was at the time."

"Sorry we didn't mean that you were lying, Holly," Joanne says, lifting her eyes to my wife. "But you need to make sure you have your dates right because the officer that is dealing with this is ruthless."

"Do you believe him?" I ask, sitting up straight in my chair and crossing my arms across my chest, directing my question at PC Miles.

"I believe you are capable of it, yes, but then I think any father would be if their family had come to harm." I nod my head at him. "I don't care who beat him. I'm a dad myself and... " He shakes his head. "I saw first-hand what he had done to Mathew... And I know everything else that he's done. Let's just say he got what he deserved."

"Are you trying to get me to admit to his claim?" I let out a sarcastic laugh. Because that won't be happening. Not now that Holly has just involved herself and given me a false alibi, which I'm not happy about.

"No," his eyes widen at me. "I might be a police officer but I'm also a husband and a parent to two beautiful children and I don't know what I'd do if someone ever hurt them." PC Grimes listens to him carefully, her head tilted to one side while Holly stands rubbing Emily's back. "We have to look into his claim and we're just here to warn you that you will probably be getting a visit from a DC Evans at some point tomorrow wanting a statement as to where you were on the evening in question. He knows we were calling in to see you so maybe it would be in your best interest to inform your solicitor and have him meet you at the station in the morning rather than him calling here."

The officer seems genuine enough and I do believe that he thinks I did it which means if he thinks I did it then this DC Evans will too.

"Okay, I'll get onto my solicitor straight away, but I have nothing to hide," I lie again.

"Good," Joanne says as they both stand, ready to leave.

"You still have him in custody?" I ask, lifting one eyebrow at them as I stand to walk them out of my office.

"Yes. He won't be going anywhere for a long time," Joanne tells me. She also mentions what prison he is remanded in until he goes to court for his sentencing.

Which is all I need to know to make this situation go away once and for all.

"What do you think you are doing?" I ask Holly as I make my way into the living room after seeing the two police officers out.

"What do you mean?" she queries, laying Emily down in her Moses basket.

"You don't ever lie for me, Holly, especially not to the police," I take her in my arms when I see her eyes fill up and kiss her head. I didn't mean to upset her any more than she already is, but I'm annoyed at her for what she's done.

"What am I supposed to do? Let them cart you off, I don't think so," she mumbles into my chest.

"Holly," I lift her chin so I can see her face. "I'm a big boy, I can take care of myself. Have been doing for a long time now. I don't want you involved in this." This time I speak softly, trying to appease her and cradle her in my arms again.

"Too late for that, I'm already involved," she moves out of my arms, wiping under her eyes.

"For fuck's sake," I murmur, shaking my head as I raise my eyes to the ceiling. This woman will be the death of me.

"Holly," I place my hands on her shoulders. "When the police ask you anything, and they will, you tell them you got it wrong and can no longer remember. Tell them it was your hormones or something… Anything. I don't want you getting in any trouble for this. Do you understand me?"

She nods her head as I take her in my arms but I'm not sure she does understand that she wouldn't cope if she was questioned by the police. I wouldn't cope if they dragged her in for questioning. She's also as stubborn as a mule and will just ignore what I have said.

"I need to make a couple of calls," I kiss her soft lips.

"Okay."

"Are you ok?" I kiss her again and when we pull apart, she lays her head on my chest.

"Yes. You go do what you need to do," she pats my chest, raising her chin to look at me. She's trying to look unaffected by this, but I see straight through her bravado.

*

"Please take a seat, Mr Petrov, you've saved me a job from coming to visit you." I do as he says, as if I had a choice, and sit at the side of Zach, my solicitor.

"I'm DC Steven Evans and this is my colleague DC Chris Williams," I nod at them both in an acknowledgement as they both smile at me and then I sit back in my chair, observing them and the room I am in.

Considering what my life was like back in Russia this is the first time that I've been interviewed in a police station and it's nothing like I expected.

The room is smaller than I would have thought or maybe I've watched too many police dramas over the years with my sons and the two police officers both seem decent men, cheerful and respectful. No good cop bad cop thing going on. They're both of smart appearance, wearing a shirt and tie, one around my age and the other a little younger.

"Right, Mr Petrov, you know why you are here," he nods his head at me, pushing his black rimmed glasses further up his nose then sweeps his hand over his greying hair, setting a loose strand back in place.

"With respect, Detective Constable Evans, my client hasn't been told much so maybe you could enlighten us to why he is here," Zach my solicitor intervenes before I have chance to speak while he writes something down on his note pad.

Zach is one of those men who is good to have around as a friend as well as your solicitor. He doesn't mince his words and is very good at his job. Before he came to take over his dad's business when he retired, he had worked as a defence lawyer for a number of years and like I said was very good at it.

After speaking with him last night he set my mind at ease reassuring me that Holly's alibi might not be used by the police due to her being my wife, they would expect her to be biased anyway. He went through all the law and technical jargon about credible witnesses, but I think I tuned out for a while. He also reminded me that I haven't been arrested, just asked to come in for questioning, and they have no evidence, just the ramblings of a man who is in a lot of trouble.

"Okay down to business then," DC Evans gives me a tight smile and shuffles some papers on the table in front of him. "Mr Petrov I know you're aware that Mr Simpson was found outside St Mary's Hospital with serious injuries to his head and body," I nod my head as he goes on to tell me what time and date he was found and that he was admitted to the intensive care unit there. I let out a yawn and stretch my legs out under the table which causes both police officers to raise their eyebrows at me. I'm not being cocky or ignorant, I just don't give a shit about the man they are waffling on about. Did he care about Max and Mathew when he ran down their mother and left her there to die? Did he care about both boys when he was beating them and leaving them to starve? Did he care about my pregnant wife when he held her at gun point or my son when he shot him in the chest? No, he fucking well didn't.

"Mr Petrov this is a very serious allegation that he has made against you, one that we have no other choice but to follow up."

"Do I look one bit interested in that man? I couldn't care less if he had turned up dead in a gutter to be truthful," I need to calm myself down before I say something I will regret.

"I understand what you and your family have gone through and we do sympathise with you..."

"Then you'll forgive me for not caring in the slightest and I don't think you could possibly understand what my family have gone through in the last few months because of him," I cut in, agitated with this man already.

"Maybe not but like I said we still need to investigate the accusation. Your wife told our colleagues that after you came home from visiting your son in hospital that you didn't go back out," I nod my head, not wanting to verbally agree.

"While your wife is an upstanding citizen is there anybody else that can verify your whereabouts, Mr Petrov?"

"Yes." This is what I didn't want to happen. Having other people brought into this mess. If my Holly hadn't already put herself forward as an alibi then I would have probably held my hands up to it, I'm sure a judge would have taken into consideration what this man had put us through and showed a bit of compassion but who knows. However, my wife has spoken up and I've had to bring in others who can vouch that I was at home. Lucky for me on the night in question I hadn't used my own car to drive to the farm. Borrowing Glen's car, one of the security guards that was working at my home that night, was a strategic move. One that will help with this predicament as any camera footage will show my car went from the hospital straight to my home and didn't move for the rest of the evening if it's picked up on the main roads.

"Can we have their names?"

"Roger Mann and Glen Wilson. They're the two security guards who were patrolling the grounds of my home when I arrived back from the hospital." DC Williams writes down their names then lifts his head.

"You declined a police officer that was offered to sit outside your home, why was that, Mr Petrov?" He narrows his eyes on me, tapping the pen on his slip.

"As I said at the time, I have many security staff that are capable of doing the same job, which left the police to do theirs with no cost to you."

"So, they were already on your payroll?" he asks, tilting hid head.

"Yes, they work at the clubs that I own."

"How convenient," he states, giving his colleague a sideways glance then he jots something else down while DC Evans sits there quietly.

"What are you insinuating... ?" I put my hand up to stop Zach from going on.

"Yes, it was. I have an excellent security team at the club so when my head of security suggested the idea, I didn't hesitate to have them at my home around the clock until Mathew's dad was found. I also had extra security installed inside my home, panic buttons, that sort of thing. You do remember that man had gotten into my home, held us at gunpoint then shot my son?" My tone irked.

"Yes, Mr Petrov, we do," he says while placing a piece of paper in front of me.

"The day after Nicholas was shot you made a call to Russia. Can you tell us who you were calling?"

"My brother," Zach fidgets in his seat. I hadn't told him that I'd been in contact with Sasha but then it's no big deal that I would call my brother to inform him that his nephew had been shot. Well that wasn't the only reason, but they are not to know that. "Sasha is my only family besides my sons, he likes to know how they all are. I called him to tell him about what had happened," I shrug my shoulders. "I've called him a few times since to keep him updated. Just last night I telephoned him to tell him about how his four-week-old niece was doing and that Max, his three-year-old nephew, has chickenpox, isn't that what families do?" Again, that wasn't my only motive for ringing him.

"Do you have anything else to go on?" Zach sits forward in his seat. "Because Mr Petrov speaking to his brother and the lies of a man who originally alleged that he had been attacked by a gang he owed money to then changed it after what four weeks, does not put my client anywhere near him. You have no crime scene or any witnesses to back up Mr Simpson's accusation, so I'd say you're wasting your time and ours pursuing this claim, don't you?"

"We won't keep you much longer, Mr Petrov," his eyes shift from Zach to me, annoyance in them that he's got nothing to go on.

"Good because while I don't mind helping you out with your investigation, I'm needed at home. New baby and a three-year-old with chickenpox, my wife hasn't had much sleep. We both haven't and I also have a business that I've been neglecting over the last few months," I'm not lying, since coming home from our honeymoon it's just been one thing after another to deal with.

"Do you have any Russian friends here in England?"

"No."

"Okay that's all we need for now. Thank you for coming in, Mr Petrov. If we need you for anything else, we will be in touch." He stands, closing a file with a few sheets of paper and puts his hand out for me to shake.

"Please do," I say as I shake his hand. I don't mean it, just playing the game. This will be all over soon enough.

Chapter 26

Holly

Tapping my fingers on the soft leather arm of the settee, I wait for Vlad to answer me.

It's been three days since he went to the police station to help them out with their enquiries and while I'm on edge waiting for them to come knocking at the door, my husband prefers to ignore that they could come and arrest him.

I pick up one of Emily's bibs and throw it at him. Like a feather it barely picks up any momentum, just managing to waft passed his ear and landing at the side of our daughter who is happy now she's had a nappy changed. Jesus that girl can scream.

Our daughter has each and every one of us wrapped around her tiny little finger, which we knew would happen. She only needs to whimper and one of us comes running. We've tried to leave her a little while before we pick her up but find it impossible. Once you hear the cute little whimper which is the first tell-tale sign that she's hungry, her nappy might need changing, or she just doesn't want leaving out then in zero to sixty seconds that whimpering will become a full-on heart-wrenching cry that none of us can bare. Her father's the worst which we did expect although I'm not far behind. We just can't do it like some people can, leave her to self sooth for a little while and to be truthful we don't want to.

Vlad chuckles as he picks Emily up off the changing mat and snuggles her against his bare chest then slings her *daddy's girl* bib back at me. "Your mother is becoming a pain in the rear end," he says, kissing the side of her head as he sits down next to me, moving Emily so she's resting her head on his shoulder. Now she's fed and changed she's content to just lay across her father until she falls asleep.

"Well answer me will you," I poke him in the ribs and lean over to kiss our daughter on the head.

"What's wrong, sweetheart?" he asks, slinging an arm around my shoulder.

"Did you not hear what I was saying?"

"No," he shakes his head. "It's a fiddly job changing a nappy then trying to get her back into that all in one suit, I need to concentrate. Can't listen to you and attend to my daughter at the same time," he smirks at me. He's a liar. My husband has this father thing down to a T, and why shouldn't he? He's been doing it for years.

"I said, what are we going to do?"

"About what?"

"The police. Mathew's dad," I roll my eyes at him, exasperated with the whole ordeal.

With a sigh, Vlad moves his arm from around me then takes my hand in his, kissing my palm. "We do nothing." He stretches his long legs out, leaning back, then links our fingers together as he keeps his other hand on Emily's back, his thumb stroking her soothingly.

"We can't just sit about and do nothing," I turn my body, lifting my legs off the floor and crossing them.

"Holly they have no evidence that I was anywhere near that man. If they had they would have been back by now. So, we don't worry, and we certainly don't sit about doing nothing. We focus on this little one and that little one," he nods towards Max as he snores lightly with his cuddly dog tucked under his chin, spark out on the other end of the settee. Although he's still covered in chickenpox his temperature has come down now but he's still waking up itching in the night so about an hour ago he had a spoonful of Calpol and was blathered in calamine lotion and now he's having a little nap. "We focus on us and our family, Holly, and not worry one iota about anything else. Ok?" His lips skim mine and I know he's right but where he can go about his daily routine as nothing has happened, I do struggle. But he's right, I need to stop worrying about something that may never happen.

"Ok," I whisper against his mouth. I need to try.

"What time are we meeting the boys?"

"Four o'clock." Mathew has re-joined the football team at school, and they are playing against another high school in a Sunday league match. Lucas, Daniel and Nicholas went with him for support and Sebastian and Joseph were meeting them there. Then afterwards we have arranged to meet at a new chicken and rib restaurant that has opened in the city centre. They're all eager to try it out so Sebastian booked a table for this afternoon. Apparently, it has a play area for the kids which will entertain Rebecca and Max if he's feeling up to it.

*

"Can I get you anything else?" the waitress asks when she comes back to collect the rest of our empty plates and the bones from the stack of ribs we've all eaten. The bones are stripped bare, a dog couldn't have done a better job.

"No thanks, love," Sebastian answers her, blowing out a long breath. "Unless you have a bed for me to lie down on, I'm about to slip into a food-induced coma," he smiles wide at her.

"We get a lot of that but sorry no," she chuckles, nodding as she stacks the plates on one arm.

"Just the bill then," he says as Izzy passes a very tired Ben to him. The poor little thing is teething and he's not happy. Izzy pops her finger into his mouth, rubbing some gel on his gums which stops his moaning and has him smacking his lips together, enjoying the taste.

"We're going to shoot straight off home once I've paid the bill, paps. Get this one to bed," he jiggles him on his knee trying to keep him calm.

"Ok. Leave the bill, I'll get it then we'll be off home as well," Vlad turns to me to verify that we will be going home. I nod my head knowing it's already after six and where Emily is snuggled fast asleep in her pram at the side of me, it won't be long before she'll be wanting her feed.

"Is there anything you need us to do for tomorrow?" Sebastian nods his head towards Mathew who is busy on his phone.

"No," I answer. Mathew and Max's mum's headstone is being put in place tomorrow morning, so we've arranged for all of us to go and pay our respects with Mathew after lunch. "I've ordered flowers to be delivered to the house in the morning. Olivia and Sarah are going to meet us there then afterwards we'll go to Dimitris for something to eat."

"Sounds good," he nods his head as he passes Ben back to Izzy then instructs Rebecca and Joe to get their coats on.

"Thanks," Mathew says, lifting his head, catching my eye. "For the flowers."

"You're more than welcome, I hope they're ok. I ordered red roses and white carnations," Mathew had told me his mum loved a mixture of them but didn't get them often enough so I thought it would be nice to have her favourites so the boys could put them on her grave. I also ordered enough single roses for the rest of us to put on.

"They will be," he smiles, nervously. It's kind of a big day for him tomorrow. When his mum got buried it was a very rushed affair with them not able to grieve properly for their loss. We want to show Mathew that we are all they for him and we understand the hurt he went through. This is us showing our love and support for him as a family. And if his mum is watching from somewhere, she will know that he is safe, loved and cared for just like Max. Even though Max doesn't understand now, we will explain things to him as he gets older and make sure he knows just how much his mum loved him. Which is why I've made it into a big deal for them and invited the whole family and friends.

"Are you ready?" Vlad asks, lifting my bag off of the floor and passing it to me.

"Yes."

"Come on then before she wakes. We might just make it home in time before she wants feeding," he looks in at Emily, moving the blanket from her face and stroking her cheek.

"Stop, you'll wake her," I glare as I elbow him in his side. Sebastian chuckles just as Ben gets cranky again.

"You've got this to come yet," he says, smirking as he snuggles his son into his chest.

"I'm not an amateur, you know?" Vlad says as he strokes Ben's hair. "I have nursed you and your brothers many a time through the night when you were teething and if he's anything like you he's going to keep you up all night." This time Vlad smirks, wrapping his arm round Seb's shoulder. "Your cheeks were always read raw and you had a high temperature. They were the same," he nods his head towards Nicholas, Lucas and Daniel. Nicholas lifts his bottle of beer to his mouth, grinning at his dad. "I was lucky to get an hour's sleep most nights."

"You did a fine job with all of us," Sebastian commends, slapping his father on his back. And he has. It doesn't matter what he has done over the years or the reasons behind it, you can't take away from him that he is a fantastic father and granddad. Even though three of them are grown men they still come to him for fatherly advice and he wouldn't have it any other way. Then there's two teenagers that he will lead into fine young men that will respect others and work hard, showing love for their family and friends even if one of them isn't his own flesh and blood. And then he gets to do it all again with Max and Emily. I have no doubt that he will be there to care and nurture them every step of the way through their childhood, guiding them through their teenage years as they blossom into young adults and give sound advice when needed as adults.

When we arrive home, Lucas goes upstairs to finish his English homework and Mathew puts his football kit in the washer while I attend to Emily. While I'm feeding her, Max stays close to me and Vlad and Nicholas take themselves into the office to go over some paperwork to do with the apartments. I suggested to Vlad that maybe it's time he went back to work as I can manage fine with Max and Emily, but he insists he will wait until Max gets over the chickenpox and is allowed back to nursery.

Once she's had her fill she kicks about on her mat for a while before she has her bubble bath. Vlad breaks off from his work to help out, not wanting to miss the faces she pulls when he blows bubbles at her. He then puts her in her sleepsuit and snuggles her close to him until she falls asleep. We both put her to bed and then do it all again with Max. No sooner does his head touch the pillow then he's out, sound asleep with his cuddly dog tucked under his chin.

Vlad goes back downstairs to finish going over some paperwork with Nicholas and I opt to have a nice relaxing bubble bath of my own.

Before I start to wrinkle like an old prune, I get out, dry myself and apply my night cream. Then I dress in my favourite PJs, one of Vlad's T shirts and a pair of old leggings. Not the sexiest of outfits but so comfortable. After I'm dressed, I check on Emily and Max then poke my head into Lucas's room. Both Mathew and Lucas are playing on one of their games, so I leave them to it and make my way downstairs.

The sound of a voice I don't recognise draws me straight into the living room and that's when I see that Nicholas and Vlad are not alone.

"Is everything ok?" I ask, sitting down on the arm of the settee next to my husband, my eyes not leaving Joanne's, the police liaison officer, and the man who is sat at the side of her. It's becoming a regular occurrence, Joanne turning up with a different man in tow. Normally it's PC Miles or Mr Stanton, I'm not sure who this guy is.

Vlad takes my hand and shakes his head.

"Hi Holly, sorry to intrude on your evening, this is DC Evans," she introduces her colleague. He stands, leaning forward to shake my hand. That's when I remember his name. This is the policeman that Vlad went to see the other day. My legs turn to jelly and I'm sure my face pales so before my legs give way, I sit back down, my heart punching its way out of my chest thinking they're here for my husband.

"What's wrong?" I manage to get out, my eyes widen on Vlad.

"Holly, Mathew's dad is dead," Vlad tells me and where I'm sure he is not one bit bothered he does show some empathy as his eyes close and he breathes in deeply through his nose. I'm sure he can understand more than some, how someone you are supposed to love and them you, turns out to be the person who causes you more heartache resulting in wishing they were dead.

"What? How?" My words coming out in a whisper.

"Turns out he can't help but upset people," Joanne says, shrugging her shoulders. "We've come to let Mathew know and yourselves."

"Oh, God. He's... " I cover my mouth, not able to get out what I was going to say because I don't know how he's going to feel or react to this news.

"I'll go get him," Nicholas says, striding through the room.

He's back in no time at all, Mathew and Lucas closely following.

"Hi Mathew, how you doing?" Joanne asks, shifting to the end of her seat.

"I'm good thanks," he tells her, standing next to Lucas at the back of the settee.

"Come and sit down, Mathew," Vlad stands, motioning with his hand for him to sit. "Joanne has something to tell you."

Mathew does as he is told and sits down at the side of Nicholas, Lucas moves to his brother's other side, I stay where I am, and Vlad stands at the side of me. I turn to look up at him as he takes hold of my hand and I widen my eyes at him. Does he have something to do with this? I know it sounds farfetched but if Sasha can hire men to find Mathew's dad then I'm sure he knows people who know other people that can reach him in prison.

Vlad shakes his head, putting my mind at rest, he understands my unease.

"Mathew there's no easy way to say this," PC Grimes starts with, placing her hands together in her lap. "But your father is dead." She stops and waits for a reaction; we all do but it doesn't come. Mathew sits there still, sort of staring at her but not. "Mathew?" She goes to stand, and he breaks his stare. "Are you alright?" He turns to look at Vlad and I then shifts his focus back to Joanne.

"I'm fine," he shakes his head, rubbing his hands up and down his face. "How did it happen?" he asks as Nicholas gets up and Vlad sits in the vacant seat next to Mathew.

"We're not sure of all the details yet, we'll know more when the investigation is finished but from what we do know it seems your father had gotten involved with trying to deal drugs. Someone on the outside was supposed to deliver during visiting. Well let's just say it didn't go down well with some of the inmates when the drugs didn't appear, and your father had already collected the money from them." I sit there listening, taking in what he is saying but not understanding how this can happen in a prison.

"How does this happen? I mean, it's a prison, how do they get money to pay for drugs in the first place and how does someone bring drugs in past the security?"

"It happens," DC Evan says. "It shouldn't but it does, and you would be surprised what gets smuggled in undetected. The prisons do what they can but sometimes it's just not enough." I nod at him, trying to get my head around it.

"Here drink this," Nicholas comes back with a glass of water or it could be vodka, knowing Nicholas.

"Is there anything you want to ask us, Mathew?" Joanne asks, indicating between herself and the detective.

"Nope," he says, shaking his head and we all look at him again.

"What?" he stands, shaking his head. "Did you expect me to be upset about it? Break down and cry?" he yells, turning to look at DC Evans.

"Mathew," Vlad stands, putting his hand on his shoulder. "I think they are just doing their job and want you to know if there's anything you need to know then you can ask," he places his other hand on his shoulder. "Ok?" Mathew nods at him and turns to the police officer.

"How did he die?"

"He was stabbed. We don't think whoever did it meant to kill him, we think it was supposed to be a warning that went wrong."

"Good," he moves past Vlad then turns towards the police officers. "It's saved me from doing it in fifteen to twenty years when he got out."

"Mathew," Joanne calls when he makes his way out of the living room, through the kitchen and up the stairs.

"Leave him. I will speak with him when he's had time to calm himself and come to terms with what you have told him," my husband tells them, which he will. He's had enough experience with hating people and wishing them dead to last a lifetime, I'm sure he'll be able to get through to Mathew. If he can't then I don't know who can.

"Ok," DC Evans says. "We'll leave you to it but if you need to know anything then just call us, you have our number." Vlad thanks them for coming to let us know then sees them to the door. "Oh, we won't be pursuing Mr Simpson's claim but thank you for coming in to see us. At least now you can all get on with your lives," he tells my husband before he and Joanne walk out of the door.

Chapter 27

Vlad

Last night's news that Mathew's father had been killed didn't come as a surprise to me, I'd been notified a few hours before.

When we'd been informed by the police a few days ago that he was now divulging the truth as to how he'd ended up with serious injuries and giving the police my name, I telephoned my brother Sasha. Knowing people in the underworld, it wouldn't be difficult for him to get word into the prison where the arsehole was being held and have a hit put on him. Sasha was only too willing to set this up and told me he would get back to me when it was done. However, before the police turned up yesterday evening, I'd received word that he'd already been attacked by someone who had nothing to do with my brother and been rushed to the hospital due to the amount of blood he had lost. Not long after word must have gotten out inside the prison that he hadn't made it because I received another message to say he was dead.

Mathew's reaction to his dad's death was understandable, he hates him and rightly so. He hurt him in ways that are inconceivable. Taking the most precious thing from him and Max, their mother, will stay with Mathew for a very long time. How he treated them both over the months afterwards exposed a man that was disgraceful, disgusting and someone that only cared about himself. Seeing this first-hand, Mathew had already come to terms that his father would no longer play a part in his life and he didn't care, he wished he was dead. Even when he told him that he didn't mean to kill his mum, that it was an accident, Mathew could not forgive him for leaving her there to die on her own. Then there was Holly, how the coward held her at gunpoint while she was heavily pregnant as well as Lucas. And then shooting Nicholas. Mathew has become very close to my wife and sons so seeing his father hurt them made him sick to his stomach.

It will take him a long time to get over what has happened in less than a year, but he will get there. We've spoken about any anger he is feeling at the moment then the different stages of grief he might experience, and I've asked that he comes to speak to me, Holly or any other adult that will help him with what he is going through. He has promised me that he will and that's all we can hope for at the moment. As for Max, apart from his chickenpox he's doing well. Any hurt he had experienced at the hands of that man hasn't left any lasting damage. He's young and loved enough to get through it and with time will probably never remember it.

In a way I'm glad that it was someone else that killed him because even though I don't think Mathew would have been bothered, I'm sure my angel would have been.

Once the police left, Holly was on a mission to obtain information as to whether I had anything to do with his death. I didn't lie to her, she deserved the truth that yes, I had collaborated with my brother to get rid of this man from our lives, but someone had gotten to him first.

She wasn't shocked at all as to what I was up to, but I could see she wasn't happy about it either. After showing her the messages from Sasha she relaxed and was relieved that it was over with, just today to get through.

My wife will be an emotional wreck today. Watching Mathew grieve for his mum and Max not really having a clue as to what is happening will play at her heartstrings and I'm sure bring back memories from when she was sixteen and lost the two people who had cared and loved her dearly. However, one thing about Holly she has two strong loving arms and a big heart which she will use to soothe their pain. Then when she needs me to step in, I'll be there to comfort all of them.

"Can you help me with this?" Mathew asks, breaking me from my thoughts and causing me to smile when he tugs at the black and grey stripped tie that's hanging from his neck. "I've nearly choked myself with it three times," he says all flustered.

"Give it here." Taking out the knot, I straighten it out then lay it on the kitchen island and unfasten my tie. "Watch and learn, young man."

I show him with mine first then take his and slowly repeat the process, talking him through it, then undo it again to let him have a go. He gets it wrong a few times but perseveres and does a pretty decent job on the third attempt.

"Thanks. I've never needed to fasten one before, my school tie is a clip on," he shrugs his shoulders then runs his hand down it, pleased with himself. It's the little things that they pick up from you, like something as simple as fastening a tie, that melts your heart.

"Lucas is the same, he'll be down it a minute needing a hand to get it right, but a man should always know how to fasten his own tie. He'll get there eventually with practise," he chuckles as he grabs a bottle of pop from the fridge.

"Do you want me to put the flowers in the car?" Nicholas asks as he strides into the kitchen, fastening up his suit jacket. "Daniel is ready and will be down in a minute. I've fastened Lucas' tie," he shakes his head, glancing at Mathew. "I see you've managed to tie yours correctly."

"Na," he smirks. "Your dad helped me," he nods his head towards me, taking a drink from the bottle. "But I did learn to tie my own shoelaces and fasten my own belt." He sticks out a foot and flashes his belt with a smile on his face. "I'm sure I'll master the art of tying a tie before I'm an old man." Nicholas chuckles at him and slaps him on the back.

"I'm sure you will."

Both Nicholas and Sebastian were taught at a very young age how to fix a tie and their shoelaces. Daniel was a lot older and I think it was Nicholas who persevered with him when he kept getting the lengths wrong and which piece crossed over first. And Lucas, well he's still trying to tackle the tie.

"Holly said she'll be down in a minute if you want to get Max and Emily in the car. Mathew and Lucas can ride with me and Daniel."

"Ok," I nod my head. "You get the flowers and I'll get the kids."

*

Pulling up at the cemetery, there's four cars there already with quite a few family and friends waiting. "Wow, I didn't know everyone was coming," Mathew eyes widen at the amount of people Holly has invited. It's not a lot really but when you consider that it was only him, his mum and Max for so long then he's not used to having so many care for him.

"You don't mind, do you?" she asks him as she helps Max out of the car while I lift Emily out in her car seat. It's easier to carry her than push her in the pram with all the humps and bumps in the ground.

"No, I don't mind, just shocked that's all."

"Good. They all wanted to pay their respects and be here for you," she tells him as we make our way towards the gates to join Sebastian, Izzy and my grandchildren who are stood with Lucy and Megan. Olivia, Jack, Nick, and Sarah are already here along with Jack's mum and dad and Mary and Tom. It is good of them to come; I know it will help Mathew knowing they're all here for him and Max.

We greet one another then take a slow walk through the grounds, Mathew leading. It's the first time any of us have been to visit his mum's grave but I'm sure it won't be our last. We have promised to bring Max as regularly as we can until he's old enough to make his own decisions.

"The flowers are gorgeous, Mathew," Olivia mentions as she walks alongside of him. All the women agree whereas the men either say nothing or nod their head.

"Yeah, they are. Holly chose them."

"Well she did a good job," she says, patting his arm as we arrive at his mother's graveside.

Mathew chose well with the headstone. Originally, he wanted a white headstone but went against it and chose a black marble love heart, not too big or over the top. One that can be well maintained over the years. It bears her name, date of birth, the day she died and loving mother of Mathew and Max. Although Mathew had just wanted a headstone, we did go on to choose matching edging and two rose bowls, one for either side, and a third one in the middle.

Everyone stands back, letting Mathew have a moment as he kneels down, running a finger over her name that is written in gold lettering. When his shoulders start to shake and he wipes at his face with the sleeve of his jacket, Holly moves to his side, kneeling down with him. She wraps her arm around him, and he lays his head on her shoulder, taking the tissue she passes to him.

She speaks quietly to him and I'm sure she'll be saying a small prayer.

"Why is Mathew crying?" Rebecca asks Izzy as she tugs on her sleeve, inquisitive eyes looking up at her mum. When Izzy crouches down to speak to her daughter her eyes are flooded too. "Mummy are you crying?"

"Yes, love, I am," she says, wiping at the tears as she puts her arm around Rebecca.

"Why?" Her voice is quiet.

"I'm a little sad for Mathew and Max."

"Why mummy?" she asks as Megan and Lucy come to stand alongside them, Megan taking hold of Rebecca's hand.

"Because their mummy is no longer here for them, sweetheart." She moves a loose curl out of her eye and stands, keeping hold of her daughter's other hand.

"What happened?" Megan asks this time and I can't believe that we have never really explained to these two what had happened.

"She had to go to heaven," Lucy answers for Izzy who is barely holding it together.

"Are the angels looking after her?" she asks, twiddling her fingers.

"Yes, love, they are, and we have to look after Mathew and Max, ok?"

"Ok," both girls say together, nodding their heads.

Holly helps Mathew place a bunch of the flowers in the holes of the bowl then they turn to me, standing, Holly linking Mathew's arm. He holds his hand out for his little brother to join him, so I move forward to take the little mite to them.

Mathew stands behind Max, holding on to his shoulders then passes him a red rose. "Put it in one of the holes, Max," he sniffles while crouching down on his knees. placing one in himself to show him what to do. Max does the same, kneeling alongside his older brother and does as he is told then sits down on Mathew's knee, wrapping his arm around his shoulder, a look of innocence on his face. We'd spoken the other night that we wouldn't mention that it was his mum whose grave we were visiting. There's no way he could comprehend that his mum had died and is lying in the ground, so we agreed we would leave it for the time being, not wanting to confuse him. He thinks she's in heaven.

"Would you like to put another one in, Max?" he asks, picking out a white carnation this time. Taking it from him, Max moves forward, placing the flower alongside the rose he had put in.

"Two," he says, holding two fingers up. "Two flowers, red and white," he says, chuckling, happy with himself.

"Yes, two flowers, Max," Mathew says, cuddling his brother into him and ruffling his hair. He stands with him, stepping back from the graveside. His eyes are teary as he stares at the new headstone then he kisses Max's head. One by one we all step forward to pay our respects and lay a rose. Once Rebecca and Megan have laid theirs, they move to the side of Mathew, taking hold of his free hand. He looks down at them then crouches to accept their hugs. With Max still cuddled into him, his arms wrapped around his neck, they all snuggle together.

Izzy moves first to unwrap Rebecca from him, followed by Lucy who collects her daughter and Holly takes hold of Max. My sons wrap him in a man hug, quiet words exchanged between them. Olivia and Sarah do the same and Jack and Nick shake his hand as they say a few words.

When everyone has finished consoling him, I step up and pull him into a fatherly hug. We stand there for a moment while everyone else makes their way back to the cars. "You ok?" I ask when I let go of him.

"Yeah," he says, sighing. His eyes red and still watery.

"Are you ready to leave or do you need a bit longer?"

"I'm ready," he answers, turning to face his mum's headstone. He kisses two fingers and places them on her name then turns, ready to leave.

Back at Dimitris, Maureen has cornered off an area for everyone. As soon as she sees Mathew, she gives him a cuddle then moves in on Max. Both boys are hugged by the staff that know them and know what they have gone through. Their attention then focuses on Lucas and the girls as it normally does when we all eat here together.

Emily fusses, ready for her feed, so I accompany Holly and my daughter to the back office so Holly can feed her in peace. When Emily has finished and had her nappy changed, I take her from my wife, holding her against my shoulder then I take Holly in my other arm and hold her close, breathing them both in. The last couple of hours has been solemn time and I just need this moment with my angel to calm my emotions.

Once we are both content, we take our daughter back into the restaurant, the staff just delivering our meal. Alex our chef makes an appearance, giving me a nod of his head before he makes his way over to Mathew. He chats quietly to him for a few minutes then tells us all to enjoy our meal as he retreats back to the kitchen where he's at his happiest. Alex isn't one to be at the front of house, he leaves that to his wife Maureen.

It's good to see that Mathew is well liked by all the staff here and is fitting in well. He enjoys working the small amount of hours while he's still in education and I think it's helped to keep him occupied while he's been dealing with the hurt and anguish his father brought to his life.

As the afternoon progresses and we finish our meal, the atmosphere changes, courtesy of my sons, Jack and Nick. Laughter erupts around the table none of them wanting to stay downhearted for long. Mathew joins in on their conversation and jokes and just like that the world of pain he was in lifts.

I take great pleasure and pride in watching my family and friends envelope both Max and Mathew in their love and warmth and I'm truly happy that I brought my sons up the way I did.

From day one they have shown me what good men they are. Caring for the brother they didn't know they had and taking on one that isn't blood related. They could have easily gone the other way and not been one bit interested.

My grandchildren and Megan, Lucy's daughter, involving Max in their games. Interacting with him as he learns and showing him love and kindness when he's feeling lost and confused with his new life.

Holly's friends, the ones she calls family, now my family just like they did with my sons and me embraced us with open arms and as a family we bonded together and now they've taken on Max and Mathew.

Then there's my wife, Holly. My angel. Everything she does makes me love her more. Her heart is one of a kind. The love she shows to everyone she gives effortlessly, especially for me and our family.

Even though she was heavily pregnant with Emily when both boys came into our lives and that she'd already taken on a ready-made family, she still accepted them with open arms. Showing them love and kindness throughout the ordeal they were going through as she battled with her own emotions.

Holly has given me something that I will cherish forever. A love so deep and strong, it's hard to put it into words. A type of love that I didn't know existed beyond my own sons and grandchildren until she came along. And now because of this beautiful woman that stands alongside me through thick and thin, I'm capable of showing the same type of love to others.

Between our six sons, our daughter, grandchildren and Izzy, Holly's friends and mine, we love hard.

When we love, it is a love that is rare, pure and everlasting.

Epilogue

Vlad and Holly

"Come on, Holly, are you nearly ready?" I call out as I wonder into our walk-in wardrobe where she's hiding out. She's been in and out of the bedroom and bathroom for the last thirty minutes.

"Do I look ready?" she asks with a bit of sass in her tone, standing there with her hands on her hips, her black lacy underwear grabs my attention and has my manhood twitching in no time at all. It doesn't take much these days, it's been that long since we've been together. Making love has become a thing of the past so has a quick bunk up whenever we can.

It's been three months since our beautiful daughter Emily was born and three months since I've been anywhere near my wife. I'm not counting, honestly.

When Emily was taken for her six-week check-up, Holly had her post-natal check at the same time; both were healthy and doing well.

So, like any normal married couple with a strong sex drive we couldn't wait to be together. However, our little ones and some of the older ones had other plans.

For the last six weeks, Emily has gotten herself into a different routine and decides she wants attention every time Holly and I try to get it on.

Max has taken up residency in our bed between the hours of midnight until it's time to get up. You can set your clock by him. He'll push open the door at twelve, toddle in all sleepy eyed with his toy dog and climb up onto the bed, settling himself in the middle of Holly and me. If you try to take him out, then he wakes and cries which then wakes Emily. I've tried laying with him in his own bed to see if he'd go off and so has Holly, but he wasn't having any of it.

We did take him out last week to buy him a new bed. We let him pick it, telling him he was a big boy now and needed to sleep on his own. The bed came within two days and, so far, we've only had him in ours two nights this week.

Besides the two youngest, both Lucas and Mathew have had what Holly calls man flu. Mathew started with it first then passed it onto Lucas. Luckily, nobody else came down with it but it did mean we were playing nurse maid to them both for a few days.

Then there was Nicholas. A few weeks ago, he developed an infection in the wound where he was shot. Prior to that he was doing really well until he started with a high temperature and the area around where he'd been stitched became red and angry looking. He was admitted back into hospital and put on an intravenous drip of antibiotics for a few days. Once they had kicked in, he was sent home with a course to take for seven days. He's now fit and well and back to his annoying self.

Then there's my eldest who wanted some alone time with his wife, Izzy. They too, like us, have had a lot on over this last year and he wanted to take her away for a few days. And because we love them dearly, said yes when they asked us to take care of the children.

I've been back at work for the last few weeks, not that I hadn't been working from home anyway. I had. But now there's a lot going on with sorting Aphrodite out before we put it up for sale, as well as the second building I had purchased, now nearly ready for the apartments to let. I was needed back at work.

It's been full on with not a minute just for the two of us and I knew I needed to do something about it.

With everyone back to normal, I rounded up the troops so Holly and I can have a special evening out. Well she thinks it's just an evening, but I've added a few little extras.

"Oh, I don't know," I slap her arse then wrap my arms around her waist, lowering my head to kiss her neck. "For what I have in mind you'll do just fine, sweetheart," I run my lips down her neck and onto her shoulder while my fingers stroke up her inner thigh. She moves my hand from her warm heat then turns in my arms, placing her hands on my shoulders.

"I don't think so. I need to get dressed, I've been looking forward to this night out all week," she pecks at my lips then moves away to pick out something to wear.

"I hope that's not all you're looking forward to, Holly." I kiss the back of her neck then lean forward, reaching for the present I had bought for her.

"What have you done?" she asks when I pick out the dress that I had hung earlier amongst her clothes. She takes the short, silky, backless dress with silver sequins around the neckline from me and quickly shimmies into it. She looks gorgeous as usual and I fucking love that I'm the one who will be peeling it off her later.

"I love it, thank you," she says, giving me a twirl then steps forward to kiss me.

"I love you," I tell her then kiss her hard enough to have her moaning in my arms and her nipples hardening.

"Wooh," she flushes when I let her go. "My man can seriously kiss," she muses out loud then fans herself with her hand as she tries to cool herself down. Oh, I intend to keep her hot all night. Sizzling away until we are ready to devour each other. "Can't wait for later," she chuckles as she searches through the many pairs of shoes that she has accumulated since we've been together. I reach around her and pick up the box that I'd hidden away when I hung her dress.

She stares at the box and covers her mouth in shock. "You haven't?" she asks, her eyes widening with surprise. I nod at her and my heart delights in the fact that as much as she loves presents and I love buying them for her, she doesn't expect them. I would give her the world if I could.

I take the black, toeless Louboutin's from the box and place them on the floor, lifting her foot to put one of them on then I lift the other and do the same. She stands a good few inches taller than usual, sex appeal radiating from her.

"Oh my God, Vlad, these are beautiful!" Her voice becomes high pitched. "Thank you but you shouldn't have," she kisses me and snakes her arms around my waist.

"Why not? You deserve whatever you want and I did see you looking at them in a magazine the other week, so I thought I'd surprise you," I look down into those sapphire eyes that I love so much and my dick hardens again, anticipating the look that will be in those beautiful blues when I'm buried deep inside her.

"I know, but that didn't mean you had to buy me them," she looks down at her feet and wiggles her toes, smiling. "I don't think I dare go out in them, I'm afraid I might snap the heel," she chuckles.

"Shut up, Holly," I place my lips on hers. "Finish getting ready and I'll meet you downstairs." I wink at her and quickly head out of the door. If I stay any longer in such close proximity of her, I'm afraid that we won't get out.

*

Vlad keeps tight hold of my hand as we make our way towards the far end of the lounge in Eruption. I smile wide when I see Sebastian and Izzy, Daniel, and Nicholas standing there along with Olivia, Sarah, Jack, Nick, and Lucy. This is going to be a fun-packed night, one that is greatly needed.

It's been so long since we've been out where we can have a drink, dance and let go so when Vlad told me he'd organised for Mary and Tom to take care of Emily and Max I was all in. They're more than capable and they won't be alone because Lucas and Mathew are at home too. They don't need taking care of, but they can help out with their brother and sister.

"Where have you been?" Olivia yells over the music. "We expected you an hour ago," she taps her watch.

"Sorry, I didn't know we were meeting up with all of you. We've just come from that Italian restaurant around the corner," I tell her, nudging my husband for keeping from me that we were meeting up with our friends and family.

"Yes, well Vlad was supposed to have you here an hour ago so we could do some serious dancing." I slap my husband's arm for not telling me although we were enjoying ourselves in the restaurant, so I understand why he was in no rush to get here. Just the two of us having a romantic night out. It's one of the first restaurants that we went to on a date, the food is gorgeous, and the wine is lethal and if I remember rightly Vlad had to look after me and put me to bed because I'd drunk too much that night, although I don't think drinking a Long Island Iced Tea straight off helped after we danced for an hour in here.

"Sorry," he says to everyone, kissing my hand as he winks at me. "My wife wanted to try tonight's new menu then flirt across the table with me and who am I to stop her," he kisses my hand again then leans down to whisper in my ear. "You need to stop with the flirting, sweetheart, or I'll be dragging you into the nearest cubicle and fucking you senseless then I'll do it all again just because I know you like it." My eyes widen at his threat then I burst out laughing because come on, I'm as desperate as him. I wouldn't be stopping him if he did try, it's been far too long since we were together. But I've had a few glasses of wine and I'm feeling a little mischievous, so I'll keep on with torturing him like he does me.

Sebastian passes us both a glass of champagne as Vlad takes off his jacket, displaying those strong muscular arms and broad shoulders under his white shirt that I love so much. Taking a sip of my fizzy drink, listening but not to what Nick is telling everyone, I run my finger across Vlad's bicep then continue until I reach the nape of his neck and slowly stroke the area that gets him going. He gives me a sideways glance and I watch his lip rise at one side then I feel his fingertips dance across my bare back. Up and down they caress my hot skin, causing me to shiver and when he moves his hand to my hip, stroking his thumb over the cheek of my behind, I know I'm playing with fire.

My husband wouldn't think twice about throwing me over his shoulder and storming off with me to one of the offices or a toilet cubicle to have his way and, while I'm on the same page as him, we need to remember that we are not spring chickens out for a quick bunk up. We are married with a family with some of them here with us as well as our friends. Stepping forward to place my glass on the table I move out of his reach to where I am safe. We can wait until we get home.

We have a free pass tonight. Mary and Tom are staying over and sleeping in Seb and Izzy's room. They told us to set up Emily's travel cot in there and a bed for Max, that way if they waken in the night, they can see to them. Last week Emily went onto formula milk due to her not getting enough from me and she's doing fine. I did want to try and breast feed her for six months but that was one of the reasons she wasn't sleeping very long because she wasn't getting enough. Now she's happy.

"Where did you get those shoes?" Izzy screeches over the music, pointing down at my feet. Everyone follows her and I lift one foot for them to see. With a wobble I grab Vlad's arm to steady myself, causing everybody to chuckle.

"I may break my neck before the evening's out," I say, placing my foot back on the floor. Vlad rolls his eyes at me and shakes his head as he grabs my hand, lacing our fingers together.

"There's some serious money there," she says, bending down to get a closer look. "They're gorgeous. Are those the ones you were looking at the other week?" she asks, beaming. I'm not really a shoe person and as I've said before I'm not one for gifts, but I did see these the other week in a magazine and gushed over them and clearly my husband picked up on it and decided to buy me them. Who am I to say no?

"I don't know about serious money, but they look seriously lethal. You could have someone's eye out with those heels," Sebastian nods his head at them.

"Why would Holly have her feet near anybody's face?" she asks him, innocently.

"Oh, I don't know," he smirks, wiggling his eyebrows at his wife. She picks up on his innuendo and smacks him across his arm.

"Dirty bastard," she chuckles then whispers in his ear, gaining a passionate kiss from her husband.

"For fucks sake, will you two leave it alone," Daniel moans at them. "We've come out for a drink not to watch you two at it like teenagers. We get enough of that at home with them two," he nods his head towards his father and me then takes a sip from his bottle. Vlad sees his chance to wind up his son. Placing his arm around my waist he pulls me into him and ravishes my mouth. The kiss is deep and sends electricity flowing to parts that haven't been touched since before Emily was born. When he lets go of me, I'm lightheaded and need to hold onto him so I don't wobble over.

"Now that's how you kiss a woman," Nicholas chuckles as he nudges Daniel. "Leave them dizzy, wide eyed and wanting more."

"Watch and learn," Vlad says to him. "And you just might find yourself a woman as beautiful as Holly," I nip his arse for winding him up and join Olivia and Sarah who are laughing at the chuckle brothers and their father.

"Ready to dance?" Olivia asks, smirking at my shoes. "They are gorgeous and so is this dress, is it new?"

"Yeah, Vlad bought me it along with these babies," I wiggle my foot.

"Well don't be doing your normal and taking them off while you're dancing or someone else might be walking home in them tonight," Sarah laughs, linking my arm as we walk towards the dance floor.

*

Holding on to Holly's hips, I kiss her shoulder then move my hips in time with hers. Her head rests back against my shoulder as her back brushes with my chest.

I'd been watching her dance with the girls for the last hour, not able to take my eyes off how she moves so seductively. I've seen how other men look at her with want in their eyes and where once upon a time I might have struggled with that, now I don't. Oh, I still have a little jealousy running through my veins. I'm a man and will kill anyone who dares to touch my wife. However, if they want to look then so be it because that's all they're going to get. She is mine and I'm hers and nothing or anyone will ever break us.

Even though we'd come out for a night together, I don't mind sharing her time with our friends, so not wanting to step in and steal her away from them on the dance floor, I watched from afar. Only when I noticed Jack and Seb dance up alongside their wives, I saw my chance to swoop in on her.

My hands run up and down her body as she raises her hands in the air then when she turns in my arms, my lips brush against hers. "I love you," I say against them and I'm rewarded with her teeth nibbling at my bottom lip before she steals one of her own.

"I love you too," she says then lets out a little yawn. I understand how she feels, we're both short of a decent night's sleep, not having one since well before Emily came along.

"Tired?" I ask and she nods at me, laying her sleepy head on my shoulder.

Maybe I didn't think tonight through properly. Our car is booked to pick us back up in half an hour and it won't be taking us home, not that Holly is aware of that. Thinking a night away would do us the world of good, just the two of us, I booked us a room at our favourite hotel so we wouldn't be interrupted. We're good parents, our children want for nothing and are not short of love and attention from both of us, so we deserve a night away. Now I'm thinking I should have booked two.

Holly's head lifts from my shoulder when the next song comes on, her smile lighting up the room and when she turns her back to me, I know what she wants. This is what we do best.

Dancing with Holly, especially to the song that changed our lives forever, comes easily and takes us to a world where there is only Holly and me.

One of my hands takes hold of hers as they rise above our heads while my other runs seamlessly down the curves of her body. Her hips sway in time to the rhythm of the music, as do mine, feeling the firm swell of her behind grind into my groin has me wishing we were already at the hotel.

With one hand I twirl her round and pull her into me, laying my hand on the small of her back. She smoothes her hands up my chest and over my shoulders then joins them at the back of my neck where she proceeds to torture me as she gently strokes the nape. The little minx smiles that smile that would normally have her naked beneath me, but I give myself a pep talk and manage to tame the beast within. As the song continues, I twirl her around, we gyrate our hips together and my hands feel their way around her sexy body as my lips caress the soft skin of her neck. When it ends, I fuse our mouths together and don't let her up until we are both panting.

"Ready to leave?" I ask once we have our breath back and I can't let her move away from my front until my manhood calms himself down.

"I think it's for the best," she chuckles against my chest, running her hand over the bulge in my trousers. It's a good job it's fucking dark in here.

"Give it a minute before you move away," I tell her trying to think of something to take it down.

"Baby sick, shitty nappies and sleepless nights," she helps me out.

"Yeah," I chuckle. "That'll do it. Thanks," I bite her lip then lead us off the dance floor so we can say bye to everyone.

"Do you think we should offer a lift if anyone's ready to go home?" she asks, unaware to where we are going. "That car you hired to bring us here would fit another six people in."

"No," I shake my head at her as we arrive back at the table. Everyone here is aware that I've booked a room at the hotel so wouldn't dream of accepting a lift. Plus, we will be going in the opposite direction to them anyway.

"Vlad," she gives me one of her love taps, digging me in the ribs with her elbow. "Don't be mean," she narrows her sapphire eyes at me.

"Would anyone like a lift home?" she asks, going against me anyway.

"Noooo," they all say together, shaking their heads. It's quite funny really.

"Oh," she says, shrugging her shoulders, "Just us then."

We say goodnight to everyone, and I have a quiet word with Seb just in case we can arrange another night at the hotel. I'm sure they'll fit us in but I'm not sure Holly will want to leave Emily and the boys for two nights. I'm not sure I can.

*

"This car is so roomy," I say, stretching out across the back seat. "I can't believe Olivia and Sarah wanted to stay longer and Jack and Nick. I can understand the rest wanting to stay on, they're a lot younger. Maybe it's just us feeling the strain of the last few months..."

"Holly shut up and come here," my husband commands, stopping my rambling.

"Pardon me. Did you just tell me to shut u...?" The last word gets swallowed up when I'm lifted quickly so I'm straddling his knee and his mouth is covering mine.

His kiss is deep, powerful and controlling as he holds one hand at the back of my neck, keeping me in place and the other strokes up my thigh.

"You drive me fucking crazy," he says against my lips then moves them down my neck, sucking and nipping, then moves back to my mouth. I grind against his crotch as my stomach does a cartwheel and tightens when he pinches one of my hard nipples. He's driving me fucking crazy.

I jerk off his knee when the car comes to a sudden stop, remembering we are not alone.

"We're just at the lights, Holly, nothing to worry about," Vlad says as he lifts me back on his knee.

"What about the driver and people in other cars? They'll be able to see through the windows." I run my fingers through my hair trying to tame it down and take a glance out of the window. "Where are we?" I ask confused.

"Firstly, the driver can't see in the back, there's a divider and I've closed it," he opens it and shuts it again just to show me. "Secondly, the windows are tinted. We can see out, but nobody can see in and thirdly, where we are going is a surprise," he taps my nose then brushes his lips against mine. "And we'll be there very soon."

I turn my head to stare out of the window again, sliding off of Vlad's knee. We've past the built-up area and are now travelling on a darkened country lane. Passing a sign for Watson's Riding School, I turn to my husband and smile. I know exactly where we are going.

"You haven't?" I ask, putting my hand on his arm. He nods his head at me and takes hold of my hand.

"I thought a night away, just you and me, no distractions or interruptions, would do us the world of good," he kisses my hand. "What do you think?"

"I think it's a brilliant idea but what about the kids?" I worry, biting the inside of my cheek. It's one thing going clubbing while Mary and Tom babysit Emily and Max, having a sleepover in their room, we'd be at home just upstairs if they needed us. Staying out all night well that's a different matter. Emily could wake at any time in the night or be up early in the morning and we won't be there for her and Max loves his early morning snuggles even if he has just gotten use to sleeping back in his own bed. He still loves to sneak in when he wakes at around six, he always falls back off to sleep for a little while.

"Holly, sweetheart, don't worry. Emily and Max are being well taken care of and Lucas and Mathew practically take care of themselves. Mary and Tom were looking after Lucas from being a baby as well as a nine-year-old and two teenagers, I trust them," I nod at him, knowing he's right, they treat them like they would their own grandchildren. "Plus, Nicholas is staying at home tonight and I've arranged for Sebastian and Izzy to call over in the morning." He stares at me, waiting for me to say something just as we pull up outside the Lion's Head Hotel.

I love this hotel; it holds a place in my heart. This is where I truly came to know Vlad, what he had gone through and what he would do for the love of his family. I love my husband; he's organised a romantic meal out at a restaurant where we shared our first proper date. He's arranged with our friends and family to have a few drinks, somewhere we could dance and let our hair down. It's also the place where Vlad and I met. And with family and friends, he's planned for them to take care of our children while we have a night away just the two of us.

I watch his loving eyes call for me to say yes and how can I not when he shows how much he loves me and how much thought he has put into the things he does for me and our family.

"Ok," I nod my head, knowing that Emily, Max, Lucas, and Mathew will be having a ball while we are away and it's only for one night.

"Come on," Vlad takes my hand, eager to help me out of the car. No sooner did I say "Ok", he was out of the car faster than a greyhound out of its trap, rounding to my side and yanking the door open.

"Don't rush me," I drag his arm back. "I'll break my bloody neck," I look down at my feet. The shoes he bought me are at least an inch and a half higher than I'm used to.

Slowing down our speed, we make our way through the reception area, it's quiet with just a young man at the desk and a porter ready to take our luggage.

"Vlad, we didn't bring any clothes or toiletries for tomorrow," I stop him as I watch the porter turn from the desk where he had been speaking to the young man.

"It's all taken care of. What do you think I was doing this morning when I went out?" He winks at me and gives the two men at the desk a nod of his head as he leads us towards the lift.

Kissing, nibbling and sucking on my neck, instantly Vlad's lips create a heat so intense that I melt into him and the lift door has only just closed.

"I can't wait to strip you naked and kiss every inch of your silky-smooth skin while I watch you spiral out of control with just my mouth," his husky voice penetrates deep and has me moaning with anticipation. "Then I'm going to do it all again with these," he strokes my thighs lightly, running his talented fingers around to my bottom where he gives it a gentle squeeze. I moan again when he lifts me, my legs instinctively wrap around his waist. The lift bell dings and Vlad strides out with me clinging to him. We make our way along the corridor and up the few steps to the same suite he brought us to last year all the while our mouths are moulded together. Our tongues relishing in the dance they're in.

We make it through the door in a panting mess, ripping at each other's clothes. Stripped down to our underwear, my husband stares at me as if I'm his next meal and my heart beats wild in my chest as my stomach tightens. What he does to me when he gives me that look is nobody's business and I can't help but run my hands down his muscular bare chest, leaving tiny kisses then twirl my tongue around his nipples. He growls low in his chest, lifting me in his arms then throws me onto the four-poster bed, hovering over me as he rests on his solid arms.

I'm so hot and aroused at the moment that it wouldn't take him long to have me pulling at his hair and riving at the sheets. And as much as I want this, I do need him to be quick, because all that champagne has my head swimming and I need to pee. I'm also absolutely shattered. And this bed is so bloody comfy, if I close my eyes, I may just fall asleep under him.

"I need to pee," I say quickly, causing Vlad to lift his head from my breasts where he was happily sucking away. His eyes are darker than usual and the look on his face says *I can't fucking believe it.*

"You do?" I nod my head at him, and he rolls off me, throwing his arm over his eyes. "Quick, woman, I'll keep it warm for you," he chuckles, slapping my arse as I scoot off the bed.

Swilling my face to try and wake myself up, I then use the loo. Once finished, I wash my hands then swill my face again, hoping it does the trick.

I know we are both feeling it. Since coming back from our honeymoon nine months ago, it's been full on. It was a big shock to find out that Vlad had another son and that he and his older brother had been left without a mother due to Mathew's father. What they had gone through caused a lot of upset and stress to the boys and our whole family.

Then when he held us at gunpoint and went on to shoot Nicholas, it was our worst nightmare. Seeing him in the ambulance fighting for his life is something none of us ever want to witness again. Due to this Vlad went on a mission to find the man who had hurt his family and no matter who he had to involve he was going to make him pay for it. And he did. Throughout all this we stayed a united family, showing Mathew and Max what family love is all about.

Putting all that aside, we've had the joyous occasion of our daughter Emily being born which we are truly and utterly grateful for. She is our little angel who we all dote on and we consider ourselves blessed to have her as well as all the boys.

But like any normal family, when you have a new baby in the house, a three-year-old as well as a couple of teenagers, then life is busy. Hectic. Add this to all we've gone through then there's no wonder that I'm shattered and to be truthful it hasn't gone unnoticed that Vlad is feeling it too.

I pat my face and hands dry on the soft white cotton towel, check myself in the mirror and make my way back into the bedroom.

Vlad is laid out, both arms by his sides and his eyes closed. If he was keeping it warm for me then he's not doing a very good job because even though he's wearing boxers, I can see he's as limp as a biscuit that's just been dunked into a cup of hot tea. I chuckle to myself as I climb on to the bed, laying on my side facing him. I knew he was fighting it the same as me.

"Are you asleep?" I whisper, not wanting to wake him if he is.

"No, just resting my eyes," he says, lifting one of them to look at me when I run my finger over his bottom lip.

"Liar," I smile at him then lay my head on his chest. His arm comes up to wrap around me and I place my leg over his while I play with the hairs on his stomach.

"If you're tired, we can just go to sleep," I say, lifting my head to look up at him. I know he won't give in until I do. If he thinks he's letting me down, then he'll keep up with the pretence that he's fine and has the stamina of ten men. "You know?" I place my lips on his chin and leave a tender kiss. "I'm tired so all those things you want to do to me could wait for a couple of hours while we get a couple of hours sleep."

Turning on his side, keeping me tucked into him, our arms and legs entwined, he opens his heavy eyes. "You won't think any less of me, if we sleep first?"

"No," I shake my head. "It would be a shame not to get a good few hours' sleep in this bed, it's really comfy," I say, watching his eyelids drop. "And it's so bloody quiet in here."

"Thank fuck because I don't have the energy to raise a smile never mind enough energy to keep you satisfied for the next few hours," I chuckle and kiss his lips. "I fucking love you," he says against them with his eyes closed.

"I love you too," I tell him, before we drift off into a peaceful night's sleep.

About the Author

I work full-time as a learning support assistant. I live in Leeds, West Yorkshire, England, which is where I was born. I come from an extremely large family which has two sets of twins, me being the eldest of one of the sets. I am kept exceptionally busy with my job and family commitments where I take care of my elderly mother. I enjoy spending quality time with my partner of thirty years, stepdaughter, two grandchildren, my twin sister and her family. Any spare time I have, I can be found reading a good romance novel, contemporary, erotic or thriller. If not reading I will be using my newly found creative side, writing. When I have the chance to take a holiday, you will find me in the breathtaking province of Alberta, Canada, where I get to take in the scenery, sample all they have to offer and spend time with my older brother and beautiful nieces. This is my third book in the *Ain't Nobody Series*.

Also available on Amazon in the *Ain't Nobody Series*:

WHEN WE DANCE

WHEN WE HURT